My Manufactured Soul

Jeffry Dwight

MY MANUFACTURED SOUL
A science-fantasy novel by
Jeffry Dwight
The Sundering Saga, Book One

My Manufactured Soul

Copyright © 2022 by Jeffry Dwight

All Rights Reserved.

Cover Design by Lost Souls Studio

Cover Imagery Designed by DepositPhotos and Brusheezy

Copy editing by Roby James.

Trade Paperback

ISBN: 978-0-9669698-6-3

February 22, 2022

Published by SFF Net *Select*.

Publisher contact: books@sff.net

For Kevin O'Donnell, Jr., who trusted me; for Robin Todd, who believed without evidence; for Catherine Jefferson, who started the conversation; for Vera Nazarian, who offered good advice at the right time; for Danny Lee Shoop II, who tolerated my working habits; and for Ken Geoffrion, who waited the longest.

I hope it was worth it.

MY MANUFACTURED SOUL

A science-fantasy novel by
Jeffry Dwight

The Sundering Saga, Book 1

THE BOOK OF THE SHIP
(RESTRICTED SECTION)

SUNDERING HAS NO NATURAL MOONS, but it has an orbital buoy. Captain Leonais launched it shortly after we established the Second Colony and divined the true nature of the horrors. The satellite's sole function is a continuous quarantine broadcast: *Unknown mutagenic agent. Do not approach. Do not communicate.*

1. BRAWLEY

THE GOD-WINDS URGED me east across the high desert, blowing relentlessly at my back when I stumbled or fell. I carried nothing, not even clothing. The days burned my skin and the nights chilled my bones, with thirst my only companion. I found scant water, mostly seepage in arroyos and old riverbeds, just enough to keep me alive. I had neither past nor future. As far as I knew, I had been born walking the high desert and I would die there. Each day I walked until I could go no farther, then curled on the dust to shiver through the darkness, only to resume my journey at first light. The pattern continued until the day came where I did not rise again.

Brawley found me lying on the ground, near where the cliffs crumble and fall toward the rich farmlands and pastures of the valleys below. I heard his wagon coming long before he arrived, but I didn't lift my head or even open my eyes.

The stamp of hooves raised dust by my face. I coughed weakly. Brawley's wagon creaked to a halt, picks and pans clattering, the smell of overheated mule acrid in the dry air. Brawley's boots kicked up more dust. He stood over me, blocking the sun, and toed me gently. I roused enough to open my eyes and see his bulk looming, grateful for the shadow he cast. He helped me sit up, and then gave me a canteen of water and a rough homespun blanket pungent with mule sweat. I used the blanket as a makeshift poncho to protect me from the sun, and I started gulping the water.

"Just sip," he told me. It was good advice; after so long without fluids, too much water all at once would nauseate me. I reluctantly stoppered the canteen and watched as he cleared space in the back of his wagon.

"I'm Brawley," he said. "Can you get up?"

My throat was still too dry for speech, so I just shook my head.

He hauled me up by my arms and half-carried me to the wagon, where he settled me in the back. I tried to thank him, but no words actually emerged. I surrendered consciousness again before he got the wagon moving. Every half-hour or so, I roused just enough to sip some water, but otherwise slept.

I came fully awake as the wagon jolted down a tiny mud lane toward his farmhouse. I clambered over the wagon bed and sat beside him on the rough wooden plank that served as the driver's seat. I handed him the now-empty canteen. He grunted, hooked the canteen to his belt, and reined the mule to a halt.

I looked around while he unhitched the mule and led it to a barn. A hand pump squeaked, followed by the splashing of water. I assumed he was caring for the mule, but I could only wonder longingly if he would refill the canteen for me. His house was humble, but well tended. I noted recently patched spots on the roof, a sturdy porch, flowers in ceramic vases to either side of the door, and curtains at the windows. Smoke wandered upward from a chimney, bringing the unmistakable odor of meat roasting over a wood fire.

At length, Brawley came back and stood beside the wagon, the canteen gurgling at his belt. He wasn't a particularly large man, but he was burly and had the firm muscles of someone who has spent his life working outdoors. His hair and beard were brown, like his eyes, only a few shades darker than his skin. I guessed him to be in his mid-forties. His plain, honest face showed empathy, but also caution.

He handed me the canteen and waited patiently until I'd taken a long drink. Then he took a deep breath and squared his shoulders.

"Name?" he asked.

I tapped the side of my head and shrugged.

"Talk?" he asked, much more sharply.

I cleared my throat, coughed, and drank more water before answering. "Yes, but I don't remember my name, or anything about my own life." My voice was ragged from long thirst, but not just from that. A hot shock of shame flared through me. Something about not having a name was worse than almost dying, but I didn't understand why. "I don't remember anything before the desert."

"How did you get there?"

"I don't know."

"Where are your clothes?"

"I don't know."

He pursed his lips and gave this a long bit of thought. He seemed more curious than worried, as if I were a child's puzzle box that had to have the corners pressed in exactly the right sequence to open. Finally, he shrugged and asked, "Know where you are?"

I didn't know, but I had a good idea. This was Leonais, the southern continent, and I'd been on the high desert plateau on the shoulders of the Abuttal Mountains. That didn't leave many choices. "Sallas or Wyland," I guessed. "Or one of the smaller valleys."

He nodded. "Wyland. Ever been north?"

"I don't know."

"I mean *north*," he said. "Across the sea."

He was asking about Avermorn, the northern continent. As far as I knew, no one had dared those shores in living memory, although myths told that northerners occasionally wandered secretly among us. Did that mean I hadn't been to Avermorn myself? I had no way to know, so I shrugged helplessly. "I don't remember."

"Age?"

"I don't know."

His questions started to bother me, not because he was asking, but because I didn't know the answers. I had no trouble recalling facts about Leonais and its culture, but about myself, I knew almost nothing.

He moved on. "Where are you from?"

"I don't know."

"Secret?"

I blinked a bit before I understood his question. "No, I would tell you if I knew."

"Stupid?"

"I don't think so. Just amnesia."

"Hurt?"

"Just hungry and tired. Mostly thirsty. I think you saved my life."

He neither smiled nor frowned; he just accepted it. The interrogation wasn't over. "Shave?" he asked.

I didn't need to feel my chin. "No."

"*Ever?*"

"I don't think so," I said slowly. Then, to forestall his next question, I added, "I think I've always been this way."

He paused again, thinking. I could tell he was struggling, and I suddenly understood he was uncomfortable, trying to figure out a way to ask his next question. Finally, he looked down as his feet and muttered something.

Thinking he had spied something on the ground, I leaned over to look, and my hair fell around my shoulders and over my eyes. I brushed it back, saw nothing of interest in the dirt, and looked back at Brawley.

He was looking directly at me now. "Muria?" he asked, and from his tone, I knew this was the question he'd been avoiding, the word he had muttered while examining his boots.

"No," I answered, for once being sure of myself. Despite my lack of personal history, I knew I was not one of the faerie beings from children's stories.

He paused, gesturing vaguely at me, as if to indicate my overall appearance. "Fair skin, blue eyes. Too tall for normal folk. And the hair."

"I know it's blond. I don't know why. But I'm human, not muria. Humans can have blond hair, too."

"Not blond. White," he insisted. "Under all that dirt, it's white."

I found myself trying to explain genetics to him, without recognizing the arrogance of my attempt. Leonais didn't have many towheads, but light hair did crop up occasionally, as recessives will. So did pale skin, and, very rarely, blue or green eyes. Most people on Leonais were olive-skinned and dark-eyed, but even among them, their children were often born with golden-brown hair that only darkened near puberty. The royalty, direct descendants of the captain of the Second Colony, often had auburn or bronze hair; it was considered a mark of legitimacy. In addition, on the east coast, in some of the first settlements, variation was far more common than here in Wyland. But the legends of white-haired muria—half claiming they were elves or pixies, half saying they were remnants of the First Colony—were just folklore as far as I knew then. Even if descendants of the First Colony survived on Avermorn, I wasn't one of them.

He let me ramble, seeming to ignore everything until I denied being from Avermorn, then cut me off with a wave of his hand. If my lecture offended him, he didn't show it.

"Family?"

"Not that I remember."

"Age?" he asked again.

I shook my head. "I really don't know. I've lost my memory."

His face furrowed. I had changed from puzzle to problem. Finally, he held up an arm to help me down from the wagon. As he led me into his house, he said, "You're thirty, from a cothold in the hills, but you fell and hit your head. Don't talk."

Brawley's wife, Lyne, didn't want me in the house. She looked me over skeptically. I was a man, but I had no beard, and my hair wasn't brown. She only knew one category for me, and didn't like it. "He's muria," she said with distaste and told Brawley to take me back to the high desert where he had found me.

"Needs help," said Brawley. After another of his longish pauses, he added, "So do we."

"Then put him in with the goats and make him work," she said.

I told her I was happy with that. I knew how to care for animals, and how to operate farm equipment. But it nagged at me. How could I understand language, know how machinery worked, know animal husbandry, even know the history and political structure of Leonais, all without having any past of my own? I must have had a childhood, an adolescence, a youth—a wealth of experiences from which I gleaned my knowledge. Bare facts about the world, I knew; it was facts about myself that were missing. I didn't care that I was homeless, that I had amnesia, that I was half-starved, or that I was naked under the blanket. Namelessness was the only thing for which I felt shame. Without a name to anchor oneself, to individuate oneself from all others, a man is nothing.

I told Lyne I wasn't muria, that I knew the old stories, and I wasn't part of them. I tangled up my words, thinking more about my lack of a name than what I was saying. I told her about the desert, about being thirsty, about Brawley's kindness and my gratitude. At this she softened and might have relented, but then I told her I didn't know why I had light-colored hair, why I wasn't tanned or burned from the desert sun, or why I didn't need to shave. Her will slammed down like the bar across their home's threshold.

"Harmless," Brawley put in, trying to help.

"Barn or road," she replied, mimicking his spare style of speech, and Brawley acquiesced. He led me to the barn. "Told you not to talk," he said, but with the first touch of humor I'd seen him display: A faint smile quirked the corners of his lips. He took the blanket back apologetically, but let me keep the canteen. "Wait. Rest. Drink," he said, and then left me alone with the goats.

He came back shortly with a tan muslin sheet to replace the mule blanket. I wrapped the sheet around myself.

"Lyne," he called over his shoulder. "Safe now."

Lyne, who must have been waiting nearby for Brawley's call, entered the barn, carrying a basket of simples and bandages. "Sit down and let me check you for injuries," she said. I found a low stool and settled myself. She examined my head carefully, looking for bruises or bumps that might explain my amnesia. Then she manipulated my neck, arms, and legs, checking that all my joints worked. She counted my ribs, clucking to herself at my emaciation.

She looked at Brawley. "Nothing but dirt," she said. "No broken bones, no cuts to bandage. He's nearly starved and went too long without water. I don't have any medicine for that. He's as weak as a baby. He needs food, sleep, and water." She turned back to me. "If we leave you alone, what will you do?"

"Sleep," I answered. "Eat, if there is food. I'm already in your debt."

"Told you," Brawley said to his wife. "Harmless."

"That," she said tartly, "remains to be seen. But he's too weak to be any kind of threat."

"Keep?" asked Brawley.

She dusted off her hands and grunted. "If you must. You'll have to tell Claude, but not today. Get him cleaned up. He stinks."

She picked up her basket and left without a backward glance.

Brawley smiled gently at me. "Patience," he said. "Food soon." Then he followed his wife out of the barn, leaving me to wonder what "soon" might mean. Now that Lyne had mentioned food, my stomach growled. I found a comfortable spot in the straw to wait.

Later that afternoon, Brawley and Lyne's children came to look at the stranger staying in their barn. It was a measure of Brawley's confidence in his own judgment that he left them with me after brief introductions.

Under the sheet, I was still covered in a thick layer of sweat-baked grime from the desert. Sylva was the older of the two children, perhaps fifteen, and wary of me, like her mother. She brought me drinking water, clothing, some food, and more water for washing, but didn't come near. She set the supplies down by the door, and never took her eyes away from me.

The boy, Drust, only seven or eight, found me fascinating and couldn't resist touching me shyly, poking me with a forefinger as if checking to see if I was real. He was shocked and delighted by the paleness of my skin after I started washing my arms; he had never seen anyone who wasn't nut-brown like his family and neighbors. "It's a grey man," he said, and laughed. Even after I finished washing, with enthusiastic but unwelcome help from Drust, and it became obvious my skin was porcelain white rather than grey, he still called me the grey man. Soon the others picked it up. I had no name to offer, but they had to call me something. The name stuck, eventually shortened to just "Grey." It wasn't something we ever talked about.

Brawley let me rest for a few days, but put me to work as soon as I could stand steadily. At first, I was hard-pressed to do even simple chores; exhaustion would overwhelm me after an hour or two. But gradually I built up strength until I could milk the cows, tend the goats, sweep out the barn, slop the pigs, clear rocks from the fields, weed, and hoe. In return, they fed me well, gave me a place to sleep, and, after a time, a place in their hearts.

In the beginning, despite my denial, Lyne assumed I was muria rather than human, and was either lying from shame, or really had lost my memory. She said as much almost every time she saw me. Although I knew she was wrong, I did not correct her. I could cite no parents, no kin, no home village, no friends, no connections to prove I was human. I suspected I knew more about the history of Sundering than she did, but my knowledge had no provenance, so I held my peace.

Brawley and his family relied on old myths, superstition, and prejudice for their worldview, having never seen the elegant descendants of the First Colony that children and fools called "elves" in the ancient stories. I didn't fault them for this—folklore always blooms amidst the weeds of ignorance.

I had a superficial resemblance to muria, but I knew I was no more elf than Lyne. The muria themselves, before they withdrew into Avermorn, showed they were nothing like the old Earth tales of elves. Muria did not mix with humans, and so Lyne feared and loved the north in equal measure, knowing only the rumors and enchantments. Like all humans, she knew nothing of elves. I tried explaining this to Drust once, and he nodded earnestly and continued to believe I was an elf; to a little boy, having an elf around was exciting. I think Lyne and also Sylva believed I was muria, but to them, it was a source of worry.

Brawley took to referring to me as "hauflin," or half-elf,

because he saw that I bled when cut, groaned and ached with exertion like any mortal, and got hungry, tired, cross, or stupid from fatigue. I had no supernatural powers, not even the small magics that educated people grudgingly allowed had existed in the distant past. "Forgotten or forbidden," as the saying went—the same phrase they used for colonial technology. Despite the implausibility of human-muria interbreeding, rumors of hauflin persisted in folklore, and it was easier for Brawley to believe I was hauflin than that I had no past at all. I suppose any Second Colonist of my coloration could have been fodder for the original stories. Although I knew I was not muria, I couldn't say for sure that I wasn't hauflin. It was improbable, yes, but as far as I knew, not impossible. The First Colonists, the terraformers who transformed Sundering into a lush habitat millennia ago, were from Earth as much as the Second Colonists were. Even after six thousand years, interbreeding would be possible. Fortunately, no one asked me if I was half-elf, so I never had to evade the question or lie directly. I didn't know if I was hauflin any more than I knew my name.

The first time I went into town with the family, I wore a hood to hide my hair. But nothing could hide my height, pale skin, or blue eyes. At the market, townsfolk edged away, murmuring. Then someone hit me with a cudgel, and the next thing I knew stones were flying from all directions. I ran all the way back to the farm and hid in the barn.

When Brawley and Lyne arrived a few hours later, Brawley bound my wounds and shook his head sadly. "Too soon," he said at last.

Lyne was less forgiving. "Now you know your place," she said, but slipped me a sweetmeat she had bought at the market, and double-checked Brawley's doctoring. I thanked her sincerely, and she replied with a shy smile. I had yet to prove to her I was harmless, but that simple exchange of courtesies was the first step toward acceptance.

"Only frightened," I told her.

She looked at me oddly. "What's that?"

"The townspeople. I don't blame them. They were frightened." At the look on her face, I hastily added, "And no, I gave them no reason."

"I wasn't thinking about *them*," she said, and we let the matter drop.

Afterward, Brawley took me to meet Claude, the closest thing Wyland had to a mayor or judge. I don't know if Brawley felt he needed permission to keep me or just wanted another opinion. Claude neither approved nor disapproved of me. He seemed more interested in talking about his farm, but he did suggest that Brawley should have me examined by the Monks of Landing. Brawley agreed, but seemed in no hurry about it.

"Sometime," he said. "Now the goats are waiting."

And so we returned home without any real change in my status. Drust was outraged that the villagers had harmed me and clung to my arm during dinner that night, as if to protect me. "I don't care that you're an elf," he said.

"I'm not," I replied. "I don't know anything more than that."

Sylva and Lyne snorted in unison, and Lyne said, "You know too much."

"What do you mean?" I asked, gently removing Drust's hands from my forearm so I could continue eating.

Lyne said, "You answer questions before they're asked."

"What?"

"Yesterday, before it rained, I thought we should bring in the laundry. I went to find you, to ask for help, but you were already taking things off the clothesline and folding them."

"I could smell the rain, too," I replied. "Didn't you want my help?"

"Of course, but you did it before I asked."

I shrugged, suddenly uncomfortable. I had felt the rain coming, but I was busy tending the crops at the time. Lyne was implying that I'd somehow heard her wordless desire for help and responded before she could ask. Was that possible, even for a hauflin? I didn't think so, but I had no good answer. I passed the salt to Sylva and said, "We both knew the clothes needed to come inside. You didn't have to ask."

Lyne pointed at Sylva, who sat motionless, holding the saltshaker in her upraised hand. "You did it again," accused Lyne.

I turned to Drust and said, "Later, at bedtime," then asked Lyne, "What did I do again?"

"Sylva didn't ask for the salt."

Brawley interrupted. "Thoughtful. Observant. Not magic. Eat."

Lyne subsided, and Sylva resumed eating, but Lyne's brow remained furrowed. A small silence enveloped us as the tension eased. Then Sylva, in a very quiet voice, asked, "What did Drust want?"

"Stories from the old days!" Drust answered. I nodded. Regaling him with stories was established routine by now, and his thirst for legends was never slaked. I had only shared what any villager might know—nothing about Avermorn, and only the history of Leonais as taught by the monks.

"He didn't ask," said Sylva, "not aloud."

"He's an elf," said Drust. "He always knows what I want."

"I'm not," I insisted and looked to Brawley for help.

"Habit," he said. "Everyone knows what Drust wants. Never changes."

This didn't really resolve any questions, but it ended the discussion. Internally, I began reviewing all of my interactions with Brawley's family. Had I ever answered an unasked question? Did I know things I shouldn't know? The questions multiplied in my mind, sending me into an introspective spiral that kept me silent through the rest of the meal, through evening chores, and until I put Drust to bed.

That night's story was about the city of Landing, and how the colonists built the first settlements and roads on Leonais, plagued by hallucinations, while the monks preserved the Book of the Ship against the panic of the early days.

"Why did people panic?" Drust asked.

"All the early stories—the ones you like me to tell—are about pixies, unicorns, gryphons, goblins, gnomes, trolls, giants, strange lights in the sky, ghosts, haunted places, and even dragons. They started soon after the Second Colonists landed. Everyone saw visions or had nightmares. That's where all the faerie stories began."

"Unicorns wouldn't be scary," said Drust, propping himself up on one elbow.

A faint stirring of god-winds filled the room, either warning or encouragement—I couldn't tell. "The Second Colonists were technicians and engineers. They expected the world to be logical, not magical. They panicked. Many went mad. And then, suddenly, all the hallucinations stopped."

"What changed? I'd like to see a unicorn or a dragon."

"The First Colonists showed up."

Drust sat straight up in bed. "From Avermorn?"

"I think they were everywhere back then. No one knows for sure. This was thousands of years ago—long enough for real history to get tangled up with myth and fantasy. Lie back down, and I'll tell the rest."

I waited until he had obeyed. "The people at Landing called the muria 'elves,' because the muria didn't seem quite human, and elves fit in with all the other faerie creatures. The muria said they could help with the hallucinations, but by then Captain Leonais had gone mad himself. His lieutenants became the first monks, dedicating themselves to preserving the Book of the Ship."

"What happened to all the goblins and dragons?"

"They disappeared when the muria did."

"So the faerie creatures went to Avermorn?"

"No one knows, because no one ever goes there."

"*You* know, Grey," he said happily, "because you're an elf."

I sighed, refusing the bait. "Your mother will be upset if I spend all night telling you stories, and she will blame me if you have nightmares. So enough about elves and goblins. Let me tell you about the starships."

Drust fell asleep while I was describing the sealed starships that still stood after three thousand years, their secrets locked inside. I patted his shoulder and pulled up his coverlet, then went to my straw bed in the barn. So much technology had been forgotten, even by the monks themselves. The saying "forgotten or forbidden" came to mind again—but for the first time, I wondered exactly who did the forbidding.

My sleep was fitful, and I was unwontedly quiet for the next few days. The answers to my most important questions were inaccessible, as though they had been excised the way a skillful surgeon could cut away necrotic tissue without harming the healthy organs surrounding it. I felt as if I should know more, with the same conviction that told me I should know my own name. Had I forgotten, or was it forbidden knowledge, even for me? I had no resolution, and eventually stopped flagellating my brain over it. Answers, if they existed at all, would not be found by brooding.

I kept finding ways to meet townsfolk and neighbors, so they could see I posed no danger. The market tavern was neutral ground. They never warmed up to me, but I wasn't attacked again. I didn't care what they thought of me. They had something Brawley's family couldn't offer: news and gossip from the rest of

Leonais, and, after much beer, when the tavern's fire died down, legends from the early days of settlement.

I listened to all the stories eagerly, hoping for information about myself, some hint about my past, some clue that would lead to my name. Most thought the muria were the remnants of the First Colony—mutated perhaps, changed by life on Sundering over the millennia—but still basically human. But no one in the tavern had ever seen an elf, so their stories were mostly speculation admixed with a generous helping of folklore. They rehashed the old tales, perhaps goaded by my silent presence in the back of the tavern's great room, but didn't provide confirmation of anything I didn't already know.

Twice, Monks of Landing stayed at the tavern on their way to Sallas, and the locals trotted me out for inspection by experts. Both times, the monks examined me carefully, turning my limbs this way and that, peeling back my eyelids, thumping my chest as would a doctor. They found my hair and eyes especially interesting, but they had no information about muria other than the official story: The First Colonists were still alive at the time the Second Colony landed, but withdrew to Avermorn shortly thereafter. The way they told the story, chanting with their eyes half-closed, the cadence like a memorized children's rhyme, made me think they were reciting legend rather than history. I wondered if they were intentionally duplicitous or just ignorant. They wouldn't—or couldn't—answer the most basic questions about muria, or explain why the Second Colonists suffered nightmarish hallucinations. Of me in particular, they offered no opinion, but they must have reported my presence, for eventually another monk, this one wearing the elaborately embroidered robes and gold filigree chains of a hierophant, came to Brawley's farm to investigate. Drust came running to find me, full of excitement. But when we got back to the farmhouse, I saw immediately that Brawley's mood was tense, defensive.

The hierophant turned at my approach, eyed me carefully, then said, "I will speak with him alone."

"Gently, Holy One," pleaded Brawley.

The hierophant didn't reply or even turn his head. Brawley's muscles bunched under his shirt, but then he seemed to collapse in helpless surrender. Wordlessly, he took Drust into the house. I glimpsed Lyne and Sylva through the doorway before he closed it. I bristled inwardly at the way the hierophant had dismissed Brawley, but kept my face impassive.

He gestured with one hand, inviting me to walk, and I followed him down the road until we were out of earshot from the house. He stopped, threw back his hood, and stared at me for a long time. His brown eyes were flecked with gold, his face was wrinkled from age, and his short, jutting beard had gone grey. Aside from that and his expensive clothing, he seemed ordinary enough. He wore sandals, and his feet were muddy from travel.

"Brawley says your name is Grey," he said.

"That's what they call me," I answered evasively. Unlike the monks I had met in the tavern, the hierophant seemed extremely keen-witted and focused. I didn't know his purpose and decided to give as little information as possible. I didn't trust this man. To deflect further questions about my name, I said, "Brawley called you 'holy.' How are you different from other monks?"

"How do you differ from the farmers in Wyland Valley?"

"My differences are obvious," I said, an answer vague enough that he could take my reply in multiple ways.

"You are not muria," he said.

I shrugged, forcing him to continue without help from me.

His eyes remained sharp, locked onto mine. "Do you truly suffer from amnesia?"

"Only about myself. You didn't say what makes you holy."

"I am a hierophant, not a novice, acolyte, or docent. I am an initiate of the oldest records and deepest mysteries. By right of age and attainment, I am empowered to act as judge. I am also trained to detect falsehoods."

"And trained to conceal truth?"

He folded his arms across his chest. "I am bound to the secrets of my order, but within those strictures, I do not lie."

Enough sparring, I decided. I was either outmatched, or he had no desire to trade barbs. "Then tell me what I am."

"If I knew, I would say. You are not in any of the records, either public or restricted. We have no evidence of half-elves. If you are hauflin, you are the first to walk among us. I came to ascertain what threat you pose."

"And?"

"You are arrogant and insolent, and you choose to withhold your thoughts from me. You do not accord me the honor due my station, age, or long study. I suspect you hold no reverence for our entire order or for the knowledge we preserve. Nevertheless, I perceive no threat in you."

"Knowledge?" I repeated incredulously. "Can you make the starships fly again?" I let my anger show in my face and voice. "On Sundering, humans have lost their heritage. Mathematics, chemistry, physics, engineering, biology, genetics, history—nearly all science is gone. Do you preserve *that* knowledge? Can you restore it?"

"You do not merit answers to those questions—and should not even ask them. Even the names are forbidden."

"By whom?"

He remained unruffled. "Of that, also, I may not speak."

"Then tell me of Avermorn."

"No," he said without hesitation. "The monks know nothing of the northern continent. It would be bootless, even foolhardy, to share mere speculation. Our vows require us to alleviate misinformation, not reinforce it. Where I cannot answer with certitude, I do not answer at all. There is no shame in saying, 'I don't know.' Some consider it wisdom."

"That attitude is scientific, not religious."

His eyes narrowed the tiniest fraction. "Religion is not our devoir, and you have no right to judge us."

I took a step backward and broke his gaze for the first time since we had begun talking. I disliked his casual assumption of superiority and was disinclined to continue the debate. Perhaps that did make me arrogant, but I thought of it as reasonable caution. He had nothing of value to offer me, and I risked much by confirming my own ignorance. As with the lesser monks, he either wouldn't or couldn't provide any information about my past.

"Then we have nothing left to discuss," I said.

He pulled up his hood and then tucked his hands into the folds of his cloak. "I see that. But before you go back to weeding, or tending goats—"

"Yes?"

"Know this: The monks are not a militant order, yet if you should prove false, we will work against you. My word can close every door across Leonais. I can make you unwelcome at every hearth, a nameless outcast fit only to be chased away by dogs. And if you break faith, I can have you imprisoned."

"Or killed?"

"That's rarely necessary. Why? Do you intend harm after all?"

"No, but thanks for finally explaining what 'holy' means. I think it's something I can do without."

"You," he said severely, "will never understand holiness until you discover something to hold sacred. I hope that day comes."

Perhaps he had a point, but I would not yield. I inclined my head a fraction, backed another step. Then, when he did not object, I turned and walked rapidly away.

He stayed at the tavern that night and held to his vows. He

told everyone that he had no information to share about me. The following morning he left town. I never learned his name, nor saw him again, but thereafter ordinary monks came through Wyland slightly more often than before. They avoided interacting directly with me, but I knew they were spying for the hierophant. I carefully gave them no cause for concern.

Things got both better and worse for me after that. Some of the locals took the hierophant's lack of verdict to mean I must be hauflin; the rest gave me grudging acceptance as a harmless oddity. It didn't matter to me at all if I were hauflin, except as a means to finding my name. And after they came to know me better, it didn't matter to Brawley's family, either.

When I had been with them nearly three months, I overheard Lyne and Sylva defending me to a quarrelsome old woman at the market—Ella by name, Claude's wife—and I knew they had forgiven me the strange way I had entered their lives, forgiven me my lack of personal history, and forgiven me my lack of name. Defending me in public was the same as claiming me as one of their own. I was glad of that, but not as easily satisfied for myself. Ella suffered from some wasting disease and was on her last legs, so pity prevented me from responding to her wild accusations or bitter complaints. But Lyne and Sylva were passionate enough to argue with a dying town elder, which touched my heart deeply.

I ate with Brawley's family at their table, although I still slept with the goats. The house was small, and I didn't begrudge them the space. It was their home, and they had already been generous with me. Of rare afternoons, when my chores were finished early, I swam with Drust in the river, or helped Sylva churn butter, or walked by myself in the fields. Summer passed in an idyll, as if my namelessness didn't matter and nothing would ever change. Yet something inside me regarded the quietude with distrust. *Not for you*, I told myself. *Never for you*. I knew it couldn't last. Still, those quiet conversations with the women in the bright kitchen, and the hours spent frolicking carefree in the sun with the boy, stood not as highlights, but as the very essence of my time with them. I was a visitor, privileged to observe and perhaps share their lives, but they were not my true family for all they made me part of theirs.

Brawley remained taciturn, and I found it suited me. We often worked side by side, sometimes passing a whole day with only a few words between us, usually at mealtimes. It was an amiable partnership, and I saw no reason to burden him with my doubts, my private grief, or questions he couldn't answer. He seemed content to have my silent company, and although I caught him several times looking sideways at me, questions in his eyes, he kept those misgivings to himself. He was glad enough for my help on the farm, Drust being too young, and too flighty, to be trusted with anything more serious than getting into trouble. The boy had chores, but light ones, and he did them quickly, leaving most of the day for play. Lyne and Sylva were almost always together in the house, or in the herb garden, or at the market, only coming to the fields at reaping time, when all hands were needed. Brawley never said, but I suspected he had been lonely for many years, working the farm by himself. I'd like to think I was his friend as much as he was mine, but with a man like Brawley, it was hard to know. He knew I wasn't a farmer at heart. I think he would have understood had I told him Wyland was insufficient for me, and he wouldn't have asked why.

For all that I had nowhere to go, I was nonetheless restless, as if recognizing, perhaps unwillingly, that I had something to do in the larger world. My body grew hard and strong from the exercise and plentiful good food, and I came to love the gentle farmers of the valley, but I fretted, knowing I could not stay with them forever—although I couldn't say how I knew.

News from outside reached us from occasional travelers—news which increased my disquiet, but made me hungry to listen anyway. The city of Jappa was overrun. Ashe and Gaheris, brothers, battled over the empty throne. Most recently, Gaheris was the victor, styling himself Archon rather than King, and Ashe had fled north across the Justian Bridge, up the east coast, to regroup and establish his base at Halmar-by-the-Sea. After years of division and bitter fighting, both armies remained strong, but Gaheris seemed poised to win. His ascendance troubled me, mostly because his tactics and ruthlessness made me worry for my family.

Despite the reports of the Archon's cruelty, his branding of his own men, his murder of whole communities, the Wylanders didn't find it unsettling that his soldiers were even now cutting a swath of terror through the lowlands, heading in this direction. They worried a bit, yes, but the Archon and his men were still far off, and the business of kings had never troubled them. They grew food, raised livestock, and sold to anyone who would pay. For this, they expected to be left neutral. But I feared that this time, for this conflict, they would have to choose sides, and the choosing would be at sword point.

Of a certain night in early autumn, as I lay dozing beside the goats, I dreamed of the Archon. He was standing alone on a parapet, pacing back and forth. I didn't recognize the overlook, but I knew it was Jappa. I could have drawn a map to the exact spot. He was dressed in leathers, as if he'd recently been riding, and his dark hair was damp with sweat. At first I didn't know of whom I dreamed. He paced, and I watched in the manner of a dreamer, as if suspended in the air behind him, a ghost detached from emotion and from reality. Then he turned, and with a shock like the unexpected sting of a hornet, I recognized him: his face, his mannerisms, his walk, his name. He was Gaheris, the Archon, and somehow I was connected to him.

I gasped aloud in my dream and moaned, trying to wake myself up. Yet the dream—the vision—persisted. As if he had heard my gasp, his eyes narrowed, searching. Then he saw me, or seemed to, and he turned away contemptuously, but not before I glimpsed a corresponding recognition in his eyes.

He knew me.

I woke to the sound of the god-winds singing like a chorus around me, seeming to vibrate the wooden barn walls, rattle the rafters, shake the very ground. It was so loud I was sure it would wake the household, until I saw the cat, languidly stretching its legs in the starlight, unconcerned, oblivious. Then I knew it was a sound that only I could hear, but I spared no wonder on it, for I had finally discovered someone who recognized me. Another person might surmise that my own hunger for a name had led me to imagine the meeting, that dreams were just my subconscious at work . . . but I never once doubted it had been a true vision. Against all reason, I was convinced that the Archon and I had seen each other across the miles, both seen each other and recognized each other.

My dissatisfaction suddenly had a focus, my life a purpose. If the Archon held my name, I would wrest it from him. I was as twitchy as a battle horse smelling blood, but I forced myself to wait for dawn. I couldn't leave without supplies and a plan, nor without bidding farewell to Brawley and his family.

I spent the remaining nighttime hours hunched over a lantern, drawing a map, relying on my imprecise memory for places, names, and relationships.

For a man on horseback, traveling openly at a pace to spare the beast, the city of Jappa was four weeks or more away on a direct route. I had neither horse nor willingness to travel that path, for the lowlands were seething with the Archon's soldiers. The closer I got to the capital city, the more dangerous it would become. I would have to forego the direct and easy southeast path to the coast and cross the high desert plateau instead, working my way north and around the feet of the Abuttal Mountains. From there,

I could go east toward Landing, skirting Halmar-by-the-Sea before finally heading south along the coast to reach Jappa.

The only other path was straight south into Amrhyn, then east along the southern coast. The Amrhyns were a strange and dangerous people. They occupied the wide grasslands of the southwest, where they raised horses and practiced a dark religion with even darker rites. I would not willingly venture into Amrhyn, despite perhaps being able to get a horse there. Unlike the muria powers, hotly debated and only half-believed by the townsfolk, Amrhyn sorcery was universally accepted, so not even the Monks of Landing visited there. Rumor said the Archon had come to an agreement with them; their horses in exchange for some unholy payment no one knew. Yet eye witnesses said the blue-cowled sorcerers now moved freely in Jappa, selecting people from the street and sacrificing them within the stone circles that dotted the entire southern continent. I neither believed nor disbelieved in Amrhyn magic, but I also didn't want to test it at the point of a stone knife. That left either the straight path or the northern circuit.

I feared Ashe's men less than the Archon's, for by all reports, Ashe was a true prince, given to civility and honor in all matters except the war with his brother. Still, even in war, he restrained his men from pillage and rapine. He didn't burn the crops, kill the villagers, or salt the earth behind him when he was forced to retreat. His goal was to have Leonais whole after the war, with the people grateful to accept his rule. He meant to be their savior and king, not just the despot who deposed the Archon. I could respect that, and hope that even if his soldiers caught me, they would treat me fairly.

Though I would have to journey between Ashe and Gaheris eventually, I hoped to hide within the shadow of Ashe's army all the way to Jappa, or at least pass through their ranks unmolested.

And I must get there first. Gaheris could not die before yielding up my name; after that, I cared not.

My journey would therefore take me months, unless I had the fortune to acquire a horse or find passage on a merchant ship. It would be a grueling, dangerous trip, afoot or not, yet I was eager to start right away.

At dawn, I gathered the family to tell them of my vision, of my belief that my name was somehow, inexplicably, known outside Wyland Valley, and that I must therefore leave.

Thoughtless, or rather so wrapped up in my own thoughts that I heeded no one else's, I was surprised by their reaction to my announcement. Drust burst into tears and clung to me. I hadn't considered how quickly a boy can come to love a man who treats him kindly. I didn't know what to say, and my awkward patting of his head only made things worse. Sylva pried him loose, and, with an unforgiving look at me, led him from the room.

Brawley was quiet, looking at his shoes or picking at his thumbnail, not inclined to speak yet. But Lyne just nodded to herself, as if confirming something she had long suspected. "Avermorn? Will you go back whence you came?" she asked.

I had never considered trying to get to the northern continent. She well knew no ship would take me there. Perhaps she thought I would sprout wings, or levitate across the ocean. I answered her other question instead: "I'm not an elf, Lyne."

"Hauflin, then, as Brawley says?"

I shrugged, uncomfortably aware that Drust was still sobbing in the other room, although Sylva had rejoined us. "I don't think so," I told Lyne. "I feel human. The hierophant didn't think I was hauflin."

"Then where will you go?"

"Jappa, eventually, but the long way around. I've no love for armies."

They were surprised, and nothing would do but that I explain my vision again, my sureness that the Archon held my name. I couldn't explain to them how important that was to me, but they could read it in my face.

Sylva was confused. At her age, a name was just a word, a sound that people called to get your attention, or to tell you to do chores. Why should I care what word was used, as long as I answered to it? Lyne understood a bit more, for she tried to tell me that I had earned a name and place with them, even if it was not the name I had before.

I stared at her evenly, letting the silence speak. My pain surfaced, gave lie to her assurances. There was no "before" for me. My name was my past, and my past was myself, and I had lost both of them. There could be no meaning in either "now" or "later" without the foundation of the past to inform them, to give reason to my choices. She withered under my stare, and I softened it, but did not concede. Perhaps, too, she felt a faint touch, a whisper, of the god-winds that impelled me. She shrank back and offered no further demur.

Brawley looked up from his thumbnail, fixed me with a level look. "Can you trust a dream, Grey?" he asked in his slow, kind voice.

"This one, yes. It was more a vision than a dream."

He considered my earnestness for a long moment, giving no hint of his own thoughts. Finally, he sighed. "It would be a kindness to the boy if you delayed a bit."

I knew what he was asking, and Drust had nothing to do with it. Brawley grew sweet corn, which commanded a high price at the market, and it was almost ready for harvesting. We'd brought the spring wheat in a month ago, but now the corn was heavy on the stalk, the ears almost filled out. In a week or so, the tassels would start to dry, and it would be a mad rush to get the corn in at its peak.

I smiled at the gentleness of his question, the way he'd given me the means to yield graciously while keeping him from having to ask directly for my help. Brawley was a proud man. Delay chafed, but I recognized the honesty of his need. "What if I stay until the corn is in?" I offered. "Would that do for the boy?"

Brawley nodded, and the conversation was over. Drust was overjoyed to learn that I wouldn't be leaving immediately, but his mother gave him chores all morning, and Sylva took him to the market in the afternoon, and we all knew they were keeping him busy so he wouldn't be thinking of me. I did my work and slept that night, hoping for more dreams, but if I had them, they were the ordinary kind, and I didn't recall them in the morning.

After breakfast, Brawley slopped the pigs while I let the goats out and smacked the mule so it would move aside to let me sweep. Brawley rejoined me, and together we completed the remaining morning chores. As usual, he didn't talk, but I broached the silence to ask if he could spare a day to take me prospecting while we waited for the corn.

It was a transparent excuse to show him my map and get his advice, and I didn't fool him. He allowed that he hadn't been up on the plateau since late spring, and that trip had been cut short by finding me. There was always a market for metals, he said, and the ridge lines offered an easy way to find outcroppings rich with minerals. Brawley was no miner, but Wyland boasted both an ironmonger and a coppersmith who would pay for a new showing, and, since the upper plateau was an ancient seabed, there was always the chance of finding an uncontaminated salt crust. Pure salt was as good as money.

The following morning, I hitched the mule to the cart, and we set off, supplies clanking and banging. We followed the miners' road northwest, climbing steadily, until we came to a sizeable stream. Then we followed the water due west into the rift it had carved, the walls of the canyon rising sheer around us. Brawley had found me farther north, where the plateau was almost flat, like a tabletop a hundred miles wide. Here the land cracked and crumbled into a thousand twisting ravines and fissures, and we were sheltered from the winds that whipped unchecked across the highlands. I recalled that the farmers of Wyland called this area "the broken lands," and I found it an apt description. What they hadn't mentioned was the beauty. Brawley named the rocks for me. Shale and limestone and quartz I already knew, but chert, gypsum, and chalcedony were new to me. The strata were clear: basalt and granite at the bottom, the sediments of the former seabed layered above. The colors amazed me, ranging mostly from grey to deep red, but with streaks of orange, yellow, amber, tan—a hundred shades of brown—and even green. The top of the plateau, the only part I remembered having seen before, was an almost uniform dull reddish brown. The colors, like the water, hid below in these recesses.

Beside an abandoned mine entrance, the rock shelved up in easy steps, some of them natural, some showing the marks of tools. We left the cart and mule and climbed past the adit to the top in less than an hour. From here, we could see the tabletop spreading north and west, with the ravines, gorges, arroyos, and ridges of the broken lands running along its east edge. Brawley pointed out the paths that gave the easiest access to the valleys, including the broad one that became the rich Wyland Valley. Too far off to see, the next valley north was Sallas. I could find water and provisions there, he told me. I marked everything on my map. The best travel was along the edge, but not too close. Behind us, to the south and east, across the massive Leonais River that drained half the continent, lay the green lowlands, the fertile farmlands and forests that stretched two hundred and fifty miles to the East Ocean. Mist and distance hid even the river, and I could see nothing beyond. If I dared, I would go that way, finding roads and inns, with habitation thick about me the whole way—but also soldiers, refugees, and war. I turned back north, gazing at the bare plateau that stretched as far as I could see. I shivered, even though the midday sun was warm. I wondered if my plan was a good one, or if my estimate of the time was realistic. But what did it matter? I meant to find the Archon no matter how long it took, and if I had to take the long way, skirting civilization, so be it. My name was the only thing that mattered.

Brawley watched me as I studied the landscape. He was looking, I think, to see if I had the determination I would need. Health and stamina I had, thanks to him, but my resolve was untested, and I had no money.

"A horse would be nice," I said at last, and he chuckled. On the scale of farmers scratching out a living, he was wealthy enough, but even Brawley didn't own a horse. Donkeys could be had, and mules, but only the nobility and their fighting men had horses. Horses were more valuable than gold to the military, and scant few were available for farmers or travelers.

"Let's get to work," he said, and we passed several hours prospecting. The high desert was as dusty and hot as I remembered it, but having canteens and company made it bearable. We found nothing, of course, for this area had long been explored and worked out. Brawley had been well to the north last time for a reason, but this area had the best vantage. By bringing me this way, Brawley tacitly acknowledged the trip was just a token exploration, an excuse to show me the lay of the land. Still, our methodical investigation turned up one oddity—hoofprints in the grit. The wind blew constantly enough that surface marks would not last long; someone had been this way only recently.

I thought perhaps it was a donkey, for the tracks looked too small for a horse. Brawley said no, the marks showed no sign of shoes, and neither horse nor donkey went unshod or walked so lightly. A mule, then? No, the size and shape were wrong. It was a puzzle we couldn't decode.

He stroked his beard. "Unicorn?" he suggested, a small grin

crinkling the corner of his mouth, paying me back for my jest about having a horse.

"All right, all right," I said, laughing. "I won't tell Drust any more stories about faerie. He told you?"

"Won't stop telling." He shrugged and smiled, the fondness for his children lighting up his features.

I smiled back, and as we climbed down the escarpment, I said no more of it, but my blood had run cold at his suggestion, for I knew something he did not.

Maddeningly, the earliest records were incomplete or missing, some say purposely destroyed, and only legend persisted. Those legends were half-nonsense—but only half. Settlers bring their myths along with their other chattel, and misapply old names to new things, as humans are apt. It is natural to shape the unfamiliar in terms of the known, no matter how poor the fit. Later we realize our error, make new names, discard the mistakes, laugh at our naïveté, and call it progress.

But sometimes our first impulse is the correct one.

"Faerie" was a poor name, but *something* had caused the hallucinations suffered by the Second Colony. Whatever their source had been, it was not gone, only hidden. I felt a name hovering just out of reach, perhaps part of my missing memories. The god-winds thrummed and vibrated in confirmation, exulting like a gleeful shout from a thousand throats at once.

Brawley seemed unaware of the jubilation, but it overwhelmed me. The echoes from the canyon walls made my ears ring and my sight blur. For me, the meaning was unambiguous: I now had two mysteries to solve.

2. NINA

MEMORY IS A CHEAT AND A LIAR. We interweave our dreams, imaginings, and expectations into our experiences, and this texture we accept as truth. But then we review, analyze, reinterpret, or glean new insights, and in the process, without meaning to, we revise, the new memory now supplanting the old. As we reweave a story, we embroider the edges, repair the holes, use dye to transform the colors, and finally wave the new cloth proudly, believing it to be unchanged. We make events and motivations what we should like them to have been, rather than what they were.

Who can trust that a good intention was not added afterward, to excuse a misdeed? Or that a remembered slight, multiplied over the years into a gaping wound, was not imagined in the first place? Who, as either victim or perpetrator, has not seen a lie told often enough that the liar no longer knows the truth? Rationalization bests rationality, whether looking forward or back.

The more that something means to us, the more often we examine it, and since the act of examination alters the original, our least reliable memories are therefore the ones we hold most dear.

Ask me what I ate last supper, and I can get minor details wrong while still telling the truth. No matter if it was potatoes, not turnips, with the meat.

Ask me how I met Nina, and all that happened that night, and I can recite each detail perfectly while never approaching the truth. The events are seared into my mind with the sharpness of a bas-relief, but I do not trust any of it happened the way I remember.

After Brawley and I returned to his house, I could not sleep. I was exhausted from the long day, and from doing all the neglected chores afterward, but every rustle of the goats, every owl's hoot, every moan of the wind would wake me. It didn't help that Drust had panicked at my absence, and nothing would settle him but sleeping in the barn beside me. His worship was cloying but endearing; his snores and fitful tossing were intolerable.

At length, I stopped trying to sleep. It was warm enough, and the stars were bright in a clear sky, so I walked, carrying neither cloak nor lantern, to see if my restlessness could be alleviated by motion. I had no destination in mind. I cut through the corner of the wheat field, went to the end of the lane, and started down the road. I went south only because my feet wandered that way.

As a rule, farmers go to bed early and get up early, following the sun's rhythm. It is only townsfolk who have the luxury of turning their days into nights, their nights into days. I wasn't expecting to find anyone awake anywhere near Brawley's place, and indeed all was quiet. I crossed the main road and continued on country lanes, content to be alone in the autumn tranquility. I found it very peaceful under the stars, easy to collect my thoughts, easy to become lost in them. I walked slowly, inattentive to my surroundings, only watching my feet to guard from misstep. Dawn was not far off; the eastern sky already showed faint rose. I had been walking all night.

I encountered a loop of the main road again, much farther

south than I had expected. The road was no straighter than the lanes or wildlife trails, dignified only by being wider, deeply rutted from wagons and carts, and by virtue of connecting towns rather than fields. I followed it until it crossed a small bridge, my feet thudding on the wooden planks, the stream chuckling to itself underneath, then struck off on a lane that continued into a lightly wooded area. The lane narrowed and twisted, reduced to little more than a path, branches meeting overhead and blocking most of the starlight. The air, sweet with cedar, maple, and birch, made me breathe deeply while walking.

I noticed abruptly that everything had become utterly still and hushed, as if all the crickets and small animals had been frightened into silence. The temperature had also dropped a bit, enough to make me wish I'd brought the cloak. I paused and scanned the trees left and right, wondering why this spot had such a sudden eldritch feel. I saw nothing out of place. Then, one by one at first, finally all in a rush, the hairs on my arms and neck stood up. I froze, only my eyes moving as I focused again on the path before me.

At first, I thought a stag stood motionless on the trail. Then I was sure it was only a tree branch misleading me. I blinked furiously, trying to see through the dim starlight. The branch became a discarded wagon wheel, cocked at an odd angle, half buried in the path. I took a few paces forward, and the wheel's spokes dissolved into legs. Another step revealed the torso of a giant, its head far above the treetops. I rubbed my face roughly. Phosphenes exploded within my eyeballs, sending swirling dots of light scattering in all directions. After the spots subsided, I took another step forward, and *willed* myself to see clearly. I suddenly froze in place again, holding my breath.

A woman stood watching me, still as sculpture, seeming to have coalesced from the shadows under the trees. Perhaps she had been standing there all along, and I had simply not noticed;

certainly I had heard no steps. We were miles from any dwelling, not even near any worked land. She was alone and didn't seem threatening, yet my skin crawled.

Her long black hair fell straight, like a sheer curtain, almost to her knees. Her skin was as ebony as her hair—a coloring as rare on Sundering as my own—and she met my eyes directly, almost arrogantly. She stirred, holding up a hand, and I realized with sudden interest that her hair was her only clothing. Black on black in the shadows, her body was almost invisible except for the eyes that caught and reflected the stars. *How could I have overlooked her, or mistaken her for something else?*

I was no stranger to nudity; after all, I had been naked when Brawley had found me, and I had bathed and swum with his family. No one found it awkward or even remarkable. Unlike in the bigger cities, where modesty was the rule and fashion counted as sophistication, the villagers and farmers of Wyland were pragmatic, almost indifferent to clothing. Coverings were for protection, hygiene, and comfort, not for either concealing or enhancing the body's image. On hot days, women and men alike stripped off their tops to work outside, and very small children wore nothing at all unless it suited them or their parents managed to catch them. So it was not exceptional to see a naked woman in Wyland, but the context was wrong. This was not a hot day in the fields, nor a washstand in the barn, nor a summer swimming hole. Yet there she stood, naked under the stars, with eyes as commanding as any general's and tresses that would make most women weep from envy. Could that cloud of jet-black hair possibly be as soft as it looked? For all I suddenly longed to touch it, I didn't move.

"Hello," I said, my voice surprisingly normal.

"You must leave now," she replied. "Don't go back, not for any reason."

I had been bemused before; now I was bewildered. "Who are you? What do you mean?"

"Names don't matter. Call me Nina."

"I'm Grey."

"No," she said with a peculiar intensity, "you're not." She looked past me, down the path at my back, as if seeing something in the distance. I turned to look, too, but saw nothing other than trees and the dim outline of the lane. Behind me, she said, "It's already too late."

I swung back, intending to demand explanations for her odd behavior and even odder words, but I was alone on the path. Trees rustled beside the road on my right, branches gently slapping. "Wait!" I called, and was about to thrust my way into the undergrowth after her, when I heard horses in the distance. Nothing quite makes the same sound as a troop of horses thundering together in a disciplined group. They weren't close, but even the jingle of harness and tack carried through the unnaturally still air. I had come quite a distance from the main road. At least a dozen horses, I estimated, ridden hard, with no concern for stealth. Soldiers, then— but whose, and why here, and why just before dawn?

Sudden apprehension, overwhelming, convinced me the soldiers sought me personally. Rational thought said I was being foolish. Distance and time separated me from the rest of the world, as if Wyland were another country. It would take weeks for a message from Jappa to reach local troops. Even if this were somehow connected to my vision, and the Archon had divined my location, he could not strike so quickly. And I had no good reason to think the soldiers were coming for me.

In this, I suppose, I fell prey to my own unbelief. Willing to leave Brawley's farm and undertake a journey across the continent on the strength of a dream, I never doubted that my vision had been real. At the same time, I didn't consider reality a shared construct. If I believed that I had seen the Archon and he had seen me, that the recognition was mutual, why would he not be goaded to action as I was? If I really didn't believe I was the goal of the soldiers, I should not really believe I had seen Gaheris on his parapet. But in that moment, even as the sound of the soldiers died away in the distance, I finally believed both. It couldn't be true for me and not true for him.

More urgently, if my dream could reach him two hundred and fifty miles away, why should I think that the Archon's dreams couldn't reach his captains the same way? The soldiers might have been set in motion the very night Gaheris and I saw each other.

Was it foreknowledge or logic that caused me to discard philosophy and begin running? I hoped it was all my imagination, just the paranoid fantasies of a self-important fool. Though my head was confused, my heart and feet were sure. Nina's warning didn't dissuade me; it made me want to run faster.

By the time I found my way back to the farm, breathless, panicked, the soldiers were already gone. The dirt was packed and scuffed from hooves, and boot marks tracked to and from the broken front door. They hadn't bothered to knock. Brawley had had time to spring from bed and brace them in the main room, but Lyne and Sylva had been spitted where they lay. Lyne, I felt sure, had been awake, for she was half out of bed, and her hands and arms were cut and torn with defensive wounds. Sylva had likely been asleep. Of Drust, I found no sign. The stench of blood and spilled intestine in the house was unbearable. Nausea overpowered me, and for a long time all I could do was vomit, leaning heavily on a doorframe, grieving for my family.

The barn! I suddenly remembered that Drust had slept in the barn. That was why I hadn't found him in the house. I sprinted around back, heart in my throat. The goats and the chickens put up a tremendous fuss, and the pigs squealed and grunted in their pen. With all this noise, perhaps Drust had heard the soldiers and managed to hide from the swords. But before I even entered the barn, I knew.

The mule lay dead in the doorway, its throat cut. Goats wandered free, trampling the mule's blood into the straw, bleating their fear and confusion. I pushed past them, slapping when they wouldn't move quickly enough, and went inside. I found a lantern and lit it with shaky hands.

The cart was overturned, pans and tools scattered, one wheel broken off completely. The hay from the loft had been forked and dumped. Beer and flour barrels, their lids smashed, had been rolled so the contents spilled out. The soldiers had been thorough, making sure no one was hiding in the recesses of the barn.

They had found Drust right off. He lay face-down in a pool of blood not far from the straw bed. They had stabbed him ineptly, and he had crawled several feet before dying, evidenced by the smears leading back to the bed. I was glad I didn't have to see his face. The nausea faded, replaced by a leaden heaviness in my limbs. I forced myself to carry him back to the house, and laid him beside his father. They were all of them still warm, pliable; except for the blood and stillness, I might have thought them only asleep.

I sat on the doorstep, weeping, trying to understand. If the soldiers were searching for me, why had they slain Brawley? Why the children? I supposed they had not been told whom, specifically, to kill. Gaheris was known for this sort of work, killing whole communities to catch a single man, heedless of the slaughter and pointless pain, perhaps thinking ruthlessness served him better than precision. The fear spread by the very rumor of his displeasure could dissuade the most hardened rebel. Those to whom life is cheap spend it recklessly.

Obviously, the Archon had known to send his men to Wyland. So he knew where I was. Did the soldiers think me dead? Had they gone back to their garrison, or was this deliberate cruelty a feint, meant to draw me out? They could be waiting in ambush along the road. They could be in the trees now, watching, laughing amongst themselves.

No breath from the god-winds came to inform my despair. Drust's blood dried on my hands and clothes as I sat there, and nothing changed. They were still dead, I was still impotent, and the soldiers did not come back. The sky was lightening toward a cloudless sunrise. *It should be raining*, I thought. My grief was wide enough to encompass the sky.

Gradually, I recovered my ability to think clearly. The heartache was not lessened, but I was able to consider things beyond my own loss, beyond my own fear. What if the soldiers had not withdrawn, were not in hiding, but instead were going house to house through the valley? I dashed the tears from my eyes with sudden alarm.

I ran to the nearest neighbor, only a mile down the road. The farmhouse was quiet, but I saw a light in the kitchen. Through the open window, I smelled bread baking. I banged on the door, frightening the woman. She had been friends with Lyne and had sat in our kitchen more than once. I dredged my memory for her name, but nothing came.

"Soldiers," I gasped. "Brawley, Lyne—"

She recognized me, and my tone convinced her something was seriously amiss. With a startled squawk, she ran to wake the house. I didn't wait, but went to the next farm, two miles down. At this one I banged and bawled out, "Soldiers! Murder! Defend yourselves!" the moment I arrived, waiting only to be sure they were awake before going on.

The next farmhouse, five miles further toward the market, belonged to Claude, whose wife, Ella, had just died last month—the same woman who had bad-mouthed me to Lyne and Sylva. I found Claude and his four large sons already out and working. He was well-respected in the community, reputed to be fair-minded and honest, and was the closest thing these simple farmers had to a sheriff. He could help me raise the defenses, if any were to be had.

I was so out of breath that I couldn't give my warning at first. I gasped, chest heaving, a stitch in my side. I leaned over with my hands braced on my knees, breath roaring in and out of my lungs. "Easy, Grey," he said, and had one of his sons bring me water.

As soon as I could talk, I gasped out, "Brawley's dead. The whole family. Archon's soldiers. Ten or twelve of them, mounted. Swords. Murder."

Claude snapped his fingers, and his sons sprang to get weapons—rakes, hoes, iron bars, knives, hunting bows—and stood quivering at the ready.

But Claude was a leader precisely because he knew to pause and gather information before acting. Before he set his boys loose, he questioned me. "How do you know they were soldiers? Did you see them?"

"I heard the horses, chased them— Too late— Couldn't help."

"Then how do you know how many?"

"They are all *dead*, dead and lying in their blood. Brawley and Lyne and Sylva and Drust. I didn't stop to count the hoofprints in the dirt."

"But why? Why them?"

I didn't want to say that the soldiers had been looking for me. I had no way to prove it, not even a theory that would make sense. I was sure of it, but there was no profit in confusing things for him now by trying to explain a dream. And it didn't matter. My family was dead, and others were at risk. "How should I know?" I said, peppery in my anger and frustration. "Maybe Brawley was just the first."

He nodded, having heard enough for now. He turned to his sons, issued rapid-fire orders. The young men whirled and ran, each a different direction. Claude took me inside, made me sit, and quizzed me for the rest of the details, making me say everything two, three, or even four times. After, he told me he needed to go to Brawley's to see for himself. I made to follow him, but he said no, I must not. Then I volunteered to go warn other farmers, but he said no again, and by then the big market bell was tolling, and we heard the boom of a cannon which echoed off the surrounding hills. "Stay," he bade me, more of a command than a request, and he mounted his donkey, kicking the spirited beast into something resembling a trot. I waited outside, wondering what I was supposed to do.

One of his sons returned shortly with a handful of other men raised from the surrounding farms. They were all armed, all angry, spoiling for violence. In a few minutes, another son showed up, likewise accompanied. While we waited for Claude and his other two sons, the men spoke heatedly amongst themselves, but did not talk to me at all, even though I was the only one with any information.

I don't know what poison Ella had spewed about me at home —her comments in the market were vile enough, calling me "unnatural" and "soulless" among other things—but it was clear that her sons had absorbed her lessons. They glared at me with distrust, if not outright suspicion, and the other men, looking for an outlet, followed their lead. I paid them no mind; Brawley had been their friend, too, and it was natural they should be upset. I only wanted to make sure no one else got murdered that day, that the soldiers were either avoided or pursued as the farmers deemed best. It wasn't until Claude returned, looking grim, that I suspected I was in danger from them.

Other than the violence at Brawley's, no one had seen any evidence of the Archon's men. As the reports came in and the last stragglers returned, it became clear the soldiers were long gone, but no one knew where.

About fifteen farmers stayed at Claude's, making it a

temporary fort; the rest were sent in groups to secure the market, check the remaining farms. The cannon boomed again and again, at regular intervals. I thought it likely that everyone in the Wyland Valley had been roused to the danger. Claude told me to step aside, and he spoke with the remaining men quietly for several minutes. The men shot me surprised glances while listening, their faces hard, resolute.

When Claude finished talking, they formed a loose circle around me. Most of them had their weapons down, but I nervously eyed the one with leveled bow. Claude paced toward me, careful to keep the bowman's shot clear.

"Brawley told us you were leaving," said Claude slowly, carefully.

"Yes, after the corn. What—?"

"Were you angry he was sending you away?"

"He wasn't. He didn't," I said.

"Tell us," he said. "They're dead, and you're covered in blood."

I repeated my story, then gave him an abbreviated version of my discussion with Brawley and Lyne, leaving out the dream and her assumption I was muria. I was grateful for the help Brawley had given me, but it was time for me to move on, to try to find my past. Surely anyone could understand that? There was no animus between us.

"Your past," he said, musing over the word. "That's the thing, isn't it? We don't know—"

I risked interrupting him. "So what? That has nothing to do with the soldiers. How are we going to find them, protect ourselves?"

"Soldiers," he said, still speaking slowly, but giving significant glances to the others. "That's another thing. No one has seen any soldiers."

It was clear, then. He thought I had murdered Brawley. I

credited him for trying to be fair about it, for questioning me in front of witnesses instead of just stringing me up, but it was a token gesture on his part. His mind was already made up. Still, both logic and evidence were on my side. I bottled my anger as best I could, and replied evenly, "You went to the farmhouse. You saw the hoofprints. You saw the wounds. Who but soldiers could have done that? Who else has horses and swords?"

"Is that true, Claude?" called one of the men. "Were horses there?"

Without turning his stare from me, Claude answered: "Hoofprints, yes. Heavy ones, almost certainly horses. I couldn't tell if they were armored. Nor how many. Nor how long ago."

"Just before dawn," I said promptly.

"So you say, so you say."

He hadn't yet accused me, so there was still a chance he would back down if I gave him an opportunity. I kept my voice as calm and reasonable as I could. "Claude, I loved them. They saved my life. They gave me work, food, a place to live. I would have fought for them."

"Pity you didn't. Why weren't you there, in the middle of the night?"

"I was sleepless. Out walking."

"Did anyone see you?" he asked quickly.

I hesitated. Should I mention the strange long-haired woman? Whoever Nina was, she wasn't from around here, and wasn't available to vouch for me. I wondered briefly if any Wylanders had ever seen a person with black skin. They had been all too happy to remind me that *my* coloration was unique, as if it were something I had done deliberately to affront them. Ella had blamed me for every pot of spoiled milk in the valley, every baby's cough, every bit of badly timed rain. I hadn't been sorry to hear she'd died, but it was awkward to be answering to her widower now. Had he swallowed Ella's poison, too? Would he think I was making Nina up, an alibi that couldn't be checked? And, too, I hesitated because of Nina's strange warning. How had she known what was about to happen? If she was working with the Archon's men, why warn me? And where was she now? My head began to ache. I hadn't slept, my family was murdered, and I didn't want to deal with this suspicious farmer.

Claude was waiting for an answer, and he didn't like my hesitation. His eyes narrowed. "Come," he said. "Either you were alone or you were not. Which?"

"I was alone."

He stepped back, gave me a little space in the circle. Sweeping the men with his eyes, he gathered their votes, nodding. "Here is what I think," he said at last, using his judicial voice, the one that settled arguments. "I think you knew the soldiers were coming because you called them yourself."

"But—"

He didn't let me speak. "You called them, and then left the house that night so they could do their evil. Then you came back to find Brawley dead, and you cried murder, beat your breast, and pretended grief."

The men of the circle murmured agreement. This was a difficult matter, but Claude had seen to the heart of it.

"Why would I do that? Brawley was my friend, my only friend. They were my *family*." Only the urgency of the village's danger kept me from breaking down and weeping again.

"With them gone, and you there, already knowing how to work the farm, why, it would be natural for you to take over."

I wanted to run away screaming. Brawley was dead, and they thought I wanted his *farm*? I wanted to lie down in the dust and cry. I wanted to seize one of the axes and fight them all. Instead, I lifted my chin, stared him straight in the eye, and renounced all interest in Brawley's land, chattel, and possessions. "There is nothing for me here, not now. My plan was to leave after the corn was in, but I can leave right now if you insist."

"Aye," he said, nodding slowly. "Cut your losses, you mean. But we need to know by what witchery you called the Archon's men. Was it the blood rite, or the dream sending? Or something darker? You are muria, or at least hauflin, as my Ella always said before the strange sickness took her. As she lay dying, she only spoke of you. She was no prophet, my Ella, but she saw deeply. She told us two things while she suffered. She said you were an infection we must draw out, an affliction sent from Avermorn to destroy Wyland. Brawley and Lyne wouldn't listen, probably because you already had them under your spell."

"I'm sorry for your wife—" I began.

"That was the second thing. She said it was you making the pain in her belly, killing her from afar."

"It was not," I said firmly. "No, sir, it was not. Even if I wanted to do something so terrible, I wouldn't know how. I'm sorry for your wife, as I said, but she was wrong about me. I have harmed no one during my time here, not your wife, certainly not my friends." My anger was clear in my voice now, and even though I knew my best hope was in calm words, calm reasoning, I found it impossible to control myself. "If I had the powers you think I have, I could kill you now and walk away free."

It sounded like a threat, and I half-meant it that way, but he laughed. "Oh, I don't think you have *that* kind of power," he said easily. "Some small magics, worked over a fire in the night, taking weeks to make an old woman die—those are the kind of powers you have. And to divide a community with your clever-sounding words."

"If that's what you truly believe," I said, "then be rid of me. Let me go. I will never trouble Wyland again."

"You'll be going nowhere," he said sharply. "My boys and the other men will continue looking for these soldiers, your accomplices. If we find them, you'll have company while you swing tonight. But you'll swing, even if you're alone, unless we can verify your story."

And that was my trial. My version of events was borne out by all the evidence, but evidence didn't count. An outrage—the senseless deaths of a whole family—had been committed, and they had someone to blame. I suspected Claude wasn't completely convinced of my guilt. Something in his slow, measured sentences gave me pause, an inkling that he was just using this situation as an excuse to do what he wanted to do anyway. Maybe he believed I had killed Ella with magic from afar, or maybe he just believed the Wylanders needed the release, the satisfaction that came of catching and punishing someone.

As they hustled me off to the market and shoved me into the stable—the easiest place to confine me—I wasn't consumed by the unfairness of the trial. It was only later that my anger raged. I was no longer worried about the soldiers: I had done my duty by warning the Wylanders, and if they chose to ignore the danger, or treat it as less than it was, that was on them. And although I was still convinced the soldiers had been looking for me, I didn't fear they would come back. Not now, not in daylight with people boiling like bees in their anger. Perhaps tonight . . . but I would be dead by then. As I sat in the musty stable, two husky farmhands standing guard at the door, I was too wrapped up in my grief to care.

One shouldn't expect great virtue from others. That the farmers and townsfolk could seize their loss, using it as an opportunity to rid themselves of me, was understandable. No lauds came with it, no empathy, no pardon. It was very human of them. I was a stranger, and I was different, and that was enough. What was remarkable about my time in Wyland was not how venial and superstitious the ordinary folk were, but how exceptional Brawley had been. He had never once shown any distrust of me. Lyne, after her initial rejection, had overcome her prejudice, making me feel welcome and valued. She and Sylva, despite their ongoing doubts about my origin and differences, had treated me both fairly and warmly. And little Drust had simply loved me, for no good reason at all. That was the sign of Brawley's family, that they were able to accept, even embrace, something new, despite having to overturn prior beliefs.

How many of these others, waiting to hang me tonight, would be defending me, if only I had lived with them instead of Brawley? And how many would be ashamed come tomorrow?

I waited in the stable, hardly caring about the two farmhands posted to guard me. By that point, the adrenaline had faded, and I only had room in my heart and mind for my family. I kept reliving the morning's events, and I could not stop crying until after midday. Exhaustion made numbness overtake my grief, and I sat in the straw staring at nothing.

Claude came to see me in late afternoon. His expression was unreadable, his face stony. He brought two of his sons with him, stationing them by the door and dismissing the former guards. Then he came into the stable alone, a poniard naked in his hand. Enough light came through the doorway and windows to make the slender blade glitter, drawing my full attention.

I thought he had come to kill me, and wondered why. Was he so angry he couldn't wait for tonight? Then I realized he could use the poniard without killing me. Designed for thrusting, the blade was not edged or sharpened, and I thought a flaying knife would suit his purpose better, but he could still wreak damage with it. I pushed myself up on one knee in the straw, and when he didn't advance further, gathered myself to my feet.

I had no skill in fighting, but I resolved to learn very quickly. I might kick the knife from his hand, or pin his arm against the wall. Surely the scuffle would bring in his sons, so even if I managed to disarm Claude, I would have to deal with them, too. I took a cautious step sideways to look past Claude through the door. His sons, tall, strong from working the ground their whole lives, were facing away, more intent on granting their father privacy than preventing my escape. I saw no weapons, although they had packs at their feet.

Claude stepped toward me, and I braced to fight, but he threw the poniard in the dirt. "We found this," he said heavily, "in the trees outside Brawley's, while tracking the horses."

He didn't sound threatening, so I stooped to pick up the blade. Curious, I turned it in my hand, examining the workmanship. Then I saw the insignia worked into the hilt below the cross guard, a stylized letter *A* superimposed on a tree, and I almost dropped the knife.

"Yes," he said. "The Archon's sigil. The same that's branded on every soldier's arm. This is a soldier's knife. At least part of your story is true."

I tried to gauge his expression, but he was still blank. "So you believe me now?" I ventured.

"I don't know yet. The tracks show a troop of horses riding up from the south along the main road. They stopped at three farmhouses, but did nothing. Then they stopped at Brawley's. You know what happened there."

"You mean they were looking for Brawley's place in particular, had some sort of description."

He shrugged. The obvious needs no affirmation. "After, they didn't go back. They went on, around the market, north toward the next valley. We lost the tracks in the hills."

"How do you read things now? I swear I had nothing to do with it."

He sighed. "I think they were under orders to kill everyone there. Else why the boy and the girl? I think they didn't know how many to expect . . . or what kind of being."

This paralleled my own thinking, and it chilled me to hear him say it, because the only logical conclusion was that they'd missed one person, very probably the one they were sent to make sure of. It was unthinkable that Brawley could have come to some captain's attention on his own; a more inoffensive man never lived. The only thing that marked Brawley's house different from all the others in the valley was me, that I had been living there. And although it seemed obvious I was the real target, it seemed equally clear the soldiers hadn't known it. If they'd been sent to kill muria or hauflin, they would have torn the valley apart after not finding me at Brawley's. Perhaps the captain who sent them didn't trust them with that detail.

"It was your good fortune," he went on, "that sleep eluded you last night. But not ours."

Ah, yes. With only a few words, he had laid out the real problem. He didn't mean just Brawley. Although the soldiers didn't go directly back to their garrison, at some point they'd report on last night's work. And that report would eventually reach someone who *did* know the true mission, and that person would realize, from the descriptions of the dead, that I had been overlooked. So the soldiers would be back, subtlety be damned, this time to raze the entire valley if they thought I was hiding there.

"*Are* they after you?" Claude asked bluntly.

"I don't know."

"Why do they want you?" he persisted.

"I don't know."

"I'm not your enemy, Grey."

I suggested, with a rude gesture, that many men in jail, awaiting execution, had been told this thing, and none of them had believed it. To my mind, trying to kill someone was pretty much the definition of being an enemy.

He glared, exasperated. His options were few. He could hang me and send my body to the garrison. He could send me to them in irons. Or he could simply hold me until someone came to fetch me. But any of these actions admitted that he knew their true target, and how would *that* play? Would the garrison commander praise him for his quick thinking, or slaughter the town to eliminate witnesses? I could almost see his thoughts. Claude wanted to keep Wyland off their map, out of their thoughts, the way it had been before my arrival. He wanted me *gone*.

"If you turn me in, even dead, they will not thank you," I said.

He was quiet a long time, and then said, in a slightly strangled voice, "I know that. Why haven't you escaped? I gave you every chance. Why are you forcing this decision on me? I don't want your death, but the townsfolk. . . ."

"You promised to hang me tonight. You put me in prison. You accused me of killing your wife, and of summoning the Archon's soldiers, both by magic. I did neither, as I suspect you know very well."

"Of course I do," he said, exasperation making his voice harsh. "Prejudice doesn't blind me. I never believed my poor Ella; her mind went long before her body. You've given no offence during your time in Wyland, but everyone has heard Ella accuse you at one time or another. I faced a choice this morning—either let the mob kill you right then, or get you out of the way while we investigated. I couldn't let you go then, and I can't do it now. You are still keeping secrets, still here, still forcing me to order your death. If you had escaped, the question would have become moot. Why didn't you leave?"

"The door was guarded," I said, puzzled. I hadn't even considered trying to get by the farmhands.

"The windows never were." He waved abruptly, angrily. "Are you stupid? The window on the left opens to the alley behind the market stalls. No one would have seen you. You were supposed to have run away."

Was the trial all an act, put on for the sake of the witnesses, to gain time? Had he really been expecting me to escape? It would certainly make things easier for him if I disappeared.

"I didn't think of it," I admitted.

"Damn you, tell the truth."

I shrugged. The conflict was beyond me. He was fighting himself, and I knew the stakes, but not the terms of the struggle. "I haven't lied to you."

"You haven't told me everything, either. You think us superstitious fools, but we are honest people, and want honest answers. Why are you here? Where were you before? Are you hauflin? What do you want of us?"

He meant, *Give me a reason to let you live.* I couldn't think of anything, but if I stayed silent, my fate was sealed. I suspected Claude believed himself honest, but this situation was beyond him. Honesty is useless without wisdom and experience. Good is defined by what we make ourselves do; evil is what we indulge. How could I help him see a path through the tangle of events?

"I met a woman last night," I said suddenly. "A stranger, with black skin and black hair. She told me not to go back. I didn't know what she meant, not then. I thought she meant Brawley's, but she meant the whole valley."

"Nina," he said, and when I started violently, he added, "it's how I knew you were omitting things. She told me you were with her when the soldiers rode through. A tryst, I suppose. Good enough reason to be away from home. But you left that out of your story. How was I supposed to trust you?"

"I didn't think it mattered. I only met her last night. Who is she?"

"I don't know. A stranger. I found her at Brawley's. She said she was looking for you, and I told her you were alive. She was naked. When I tried to question her, she ran away." He didn't quite smile, but his expression softened. "I thought you were the oddest thing in Wyland, until I saw her."

"You'll see odder soon," I said softly. "Things are moving, Claude. I don't know what or why, any more than you do, but I can see the signs. Wylanders are no longer safe. Brawley was just the start. You are going to have to choose sides."

"I don't even know what the sides are. The people in Jappa have nothing to do with us." He didn't sound angry any more, just unutterably exhausted, as though he had already given up.

"You need to stop looking to the past. Gaheris means to rule all of Leonais, not just the coasts. Wyland has been safe before only because it was overlooked."

He looked away from me, and when he spoke, I had to strain to hear him. "*Do* you have any hauflin powers? Can you help us?"

"No," I said, as kindly as I could.

When he didn't reply, I gently set the poniard at his feet, and walked past him. His sons looked the other way as I picked up the two packs they had brought for me. Whether they had overheard our discussion or not, it seemed clear now the plan had always been to let me go. It was why the farmhands had been dismissed. Claude's sons would tell everyone I had escaped, and, whether they meant me well or not, I thought it best to do that thing.

One of the packs contained a black, hooded cloak, and although it was too warm for such a garment, I put it on anyway. At first, I was surprised there were so few people around, but then I realized it was almost harvest time. Farmers needed to work during the day. They would gather tonight, only to find me long gone. No hue and cry arose in my wake; only one person looked at me twice. I swiftly reached the edge of the market and left it and Wyland behind forever.

That night, I camped on the plateau. I had left the map in the barn, but I remembered it well enough. My camp wasn't far from where Brawley had found me. In the loneliness and isolation of the high desert, I finally had time to remember my family, not just with grief, but with fondness. In a thousand little ways, they had loved me.

During the day, in the valley, it had been too hot for the cloak. Up here, at night, it was barely enough to keep out the wind. My fire flared and guttered wildly, for all that I had built it between stones. I looked through the packs and found Claude had supplied me well. Food packaged for traveling—salted meat, dried fruit, hardtack, even some carrots, onions, and potatoes. A cooking pan, a knife, a thimble of salt, a lump of soap, a blanket. Clothing, but all too big for me—one of Claude's sons, no doubt, had raided his own closet. Leather strips for tying things, a rope for climbing, snares for hunting, kindling for fires, and an assortment of small tools for making camp and surviving in the wilderness. Even a handful of coins. Of water, I had two canteens, one still full.

For a man who had seemed willing to kill me, he had been remarkably generous. I wondered if I would ever understand him.

I banked the fire and lay under the blanket, one of the packs propping up my head. It was strange to be here again, as if my time in Wyland had never happened. But that was nonsense; I was far richer than the last time. Richer in possessions, richer in health, and, more importantly, richer in memories. That I was alone, on a mission that seemed impossible, didn't matter.

I ate, and eventually I slept.

In my dreams, I ran toward Brawley's farm over and over, horses neighing and thundering always just out of sight, arriving always too late. Behind me, Nina called out, "It's too late! It's too late!"

Dreams need not reflect reality—it signified nothing that, had I reached the farm in time, I would have accomplished little except adding my own death to the total. In the dream, the race counted, but nothing else. The neighing and pounding of hooves echoed my heartbeat, matching my dream pace until I woke.

I lay under the stars, my heart still pounding, the wild

neighing still echoing. The fire had burned down, so I added more wood, and only then realized I could still hear hooves. They clipped slowly, lightly, a single horse at a walk.

My first thought was that the Archon had sent scouts, and one of them had found me. It was too late to smother the fire; stamping would only send sparks from the embers flying into the sky like a beacon. I dug through the packs and pulled out the little cooking knife, a pathetic defense against an armed man on horseback, but it was all I had. I crouched, staring wildly, expecting at any moment to hear a sword drawn, the horse kicked to a gallop.

Nothing happened. The hooves went past, the sound dwindling away into the desert night.

A traveler, then, who didn't care to stop. But mounted. I knew so little of horses that I couldn't recognize the sounds with certainty, but I had heard donkeys and mules, and these steps sounded like neither. The poor beasts I knew plodded or shambled, never pranced. This step seemed too light for a working animal, but perhaps the hard-packed dust and gravel fooled my ears.

I settled back down, hunched against the fire and wrapped in both cloak and blanket. For a long time I waited for the horse to come back, but only the crackle of the wood interrupted the night. At length, I slept again.

At dawn, I broke camp and started walking, north by northeast. I found tracks in the dust, but the wind had ruined them, and I probably wouldn't have been able to read them anyway. I kept a steady pace and spared the water as much as I could, but still was exhausted and thirsty by nightfall. There were no trees, but plenty of scrub brush. Scrub burns, but requires constant tending, and the fuel seems to disappear as soon as it takes flame.

The food, which had seemed so generous only the day before,

was already half gone. My mental map, supplemented by Brawley's instructions, told me I would find a traveler's well and a path back down off the plateau in two days.

That night, I heard the horse, but again saw nothing. Except for the hoof sounds, I would have believed myself alone on the plateau. The next day, I continued on. The sun was a good enough guide, as long as I took care to keep my bearings midday. I hoped the water would last until I reached the well.

I saw a hawk that afternoon, and wondered what its prey might be. Mice and lizards, certainly, but the thought of rabbits kept me fantasizing long into the night as I nibbled the hardtack and sipped the smallest amount of water I dared. Even the lizards sounded good. The damned horse haunted me. Like the ones in my dreams, it was always just out of sight. Why it hadn't left me long behind was a mystery. Whoever rode it must be traveling very slowly, perhaps resting by day and passing me by night, over and over again.

I reached the well and used the bucket to fill my canteens. Then I drank my fill, and poured another bucket over my head. There were clear signs of visitors here, but nothing recent. I was near the edge of the plateau, and the trail forked here, east into Sallas, west toward the Abuttals. As far as I knew, there were no cities west of here, but there were mines, and the trail showed ruts deep enough for heavy carts or wagons. The people of Sallas would be no threat, even if some of them were foolish enough to climb the escarpment in the dark. I determined to make my camp right there, beside the water supply.

The scrub was more plentiful here, and other small plants grew between the rocks. I found enough old, tough scrub to make a good fire, the first one of any size on this trip. I wished Claude had provided more kindling. The area around the well was far from being an oasis, but I laid out my snares in hopes an incautious rabbit would wander by. I was adjusting to the journey finally, and in a better mood. Walking the desert is a different kind of exercise than working the fields. Both require strength, but they use different muscles. The broad back that served me so well wrestling the mule and plow was just extra weight for my aching thighs to carry.

Before sleeping, I removed my shirt and used another bucket of water and some of the precious soap to wash the dust and sweat from my neck and upper body. The wind wasn't as violent tonight, but it was still bitterly cold, especially as the water evaporated from my arms and chest. I wondered, not for the first time, if my planned route was the best one. Sallas wasn't as broad a valley as Wyland, but it had more water. The river at its heart ran northeast out of the hills. I didn't know if it was navigable the whole way, but I suspected there would be portages regardless, because Sallas needed some way to get its ores down to the sea. Halmar-by-the-Sea was my next destination, and it lay directly northeast. Taking the coast meant possibly finding a merchant ship, but if I turned right here and went on land, I could be among civilization the next day, and continually replenish my supplies while traveling. The only risk, of course, was the Archon's soldiers. This was technically Ashe's land, and I didn't know if Gaheris had invaded yet. There was a good chance the people I'd find would be peaceful.

I had just rolled over to go to sleep when I heard the hooves again. I didn't bother getting up to chase ghosts in the dark. If the traveler wanted to stop, he would. I no longer cared.

But the hoofbeats startled a rabbit, and the rabbit ran right into one of my snares, and suddenly I had food. I could hear it flopping around, one leg caught in the snare. It only took me a moment to locate the snare and use my little knife to silence the rabbit. It wasn't the plump and juicy game I'd hoped for, but even a stringy old buck would be a treat. It was a black-tailed jack, technically a hare, quite thin. I hoped to get a full pound of meat from it after discarding the fur and bones.

I hauled out the pan. I finally had a good use for the carrots, onions, and potatoes I'd carried all this way. With the vegetables steaming gently over the fire, I skinned the hare, quickly divided it, and put the strips of meat in the pan. Soon, the scent of succulent, simmering stew filled the air, and I leaned over the pan, fanning it with my hand.

I had been aware, in the back of my mind, that the horse had stopped nearby instead of dashing off into the desert as usual. Maybe the rider would join me for supper tonight. Without turning, I called out loudly, "There's plenty."

A soft whicker and warm breath tickled my ear. I almost leaped across the fire. How had the rider gotten the horse to walk so quietly all of a sudden? I controlled my reaction, and turned to meet him. But there was no rider, and it wasn't exactly a horse.

Midnight black, the hide; midnight black, the long, flowing mane. Lighter on its feet and smaller than any horse I'd seen, but bigger than a mule or a donkey. It had a small white star on its forehead, but otherwise was unrelieved black. I glanced down to see if it was shod—it wasn't—and realized while looking that it was a mare, not a stallion. I looked back up and met her eyes. They were warm and brown and intelligent. She stood still while I looked her over, but shied away when I tried to touch.

"Easy, girl," I said, thinking perhaps this was the best way to talk to horses. "You're a beauty, aren't you? Are you the one who's been following me? How did you survive up here?"

I reached to pat her silky mane, and this time she reared, a fore hoof flashing. I quickly backed away, and she returned to standing still, not a muscle quivering. The star on her forehead caught my attention. I leaned forward, hands carefully behind my back, to look closer. It wasn't just a marking, it had depth. Suddenly, I leaped back, heart pounding. For just a moment, I could have sworn it had turned into a single, neatly spiraled horn.

"So," I said softly, "legends walk the night."

Shadows from nowhere raced to cover her, wrap her in silky arms. When they cleared, Nina stood before me. "You should talk," she said distinctly. Then the shadows came again, and the mare waited patiently for my next move.

"Have you been guarding me, or hunting me?" I asked. She whickered softly, which I took to mean the former.

"Do you need food? I have enough to share." She gave me only silence, which I took to mean no.

"Can you talk when you're a unicorn?"

She reared violently, black against the sky, and let out a shrill neigh. A moment later, she had galloped off into the desert, which I took to mean she was unhappy about something.

I shrugged to myself. I knew even less about unicorns than I did about horses. No one knew about unicorns. They were a myth. Yet this one, with a horn that appeared and disappeared, and a body that could change from mare to woman, seemed real enough. I recalled the stories about the hallucinations that drove many of the Second Colonists mad. If Nina were nothing but my imagination, I was already lost to reason. Pragmatically, I decided it made more sense to assume that I was sane and she was real, even if those words no longer had the same meaning as yesterday.

I had finished eating when she returned. I looked up expectantly from beside the fire, but said nothing. The shadows writhed around her, and the woman, naked as ever save for the hair down to her knees, said, "Don't call me—that word."

"Should I call you a horse?"

"No. Call me Nina."

And then she was gone again. I rolled up in my blanket and went to sleep.

In the morning, she stood placidly by the fire, as if she had a perfect right to be there, as if she had always been part of my life. I greeted her, and she tossed her head.

During the night, I had somehow made up my mind to risk Sallas rather than continue the length of the plateau. I tried to discuss it with her, but she didn't seem interested in talking. I packed up and took the trail to the right, down into the valley. Nina trotted beside me for a few minutes, then kicked up her heels and scouted ahead. For the rest of the day, as I twisted my way along the cutbacks, I would find her waiting beside the trail at intervals. There was enough water in rivulets that I kept my canteens full, but I saw no game. In the evening, she met me with a brace of rabbits at her feet. I had no idea how she had caught them, and I didn't feel like asking. Clambering over the rills and rifts, with the constant ups and downs, unexpected holes, spraying gravel, and ever-increasing vegetation, was far more exhausting than trudging across the level plateau. I was tired and more than a little cross. At least there were trees here, with deadfall for a proper fire. I collected enough for the night and prepared dinner. I had no grain to offer her. Maybe she was living on scrub, or pine needles. It struck me that I had never seen her eat or drink. Maybe she didn't.

"I've decided I don't believe in you," I told her after I finished the first rabbit and stood to wash up.

For the first time that day, she shifted to human form. I expected a clever retort and hoped for actual information, but got neither. She tossed her hair, came very close, and said, "Belief is overrated."

Without meaning to, I reached to touch that impossibly silky hair. She flinched, and shadows interposed themselves, swirling, seething, then subsiding. My fingers found her mane. She stood still, flanks shivering slightly, ears erect, and let me stroke her for a moment. Then her legs jerked, and her hooves danced as she shied away. I couldn't tell if my touch was agony or ecstasy for her, or something else entirely. Perhaps it was something simpler, like shyness or timidity. I dropped my hand, and she quieted.

I don't know if she slept that night, but I did, deeply, without dreaming of Brawley for the first time. In the morning she stood a little way off, waiting.

After that, we traveled together for the most part. She would still sprint off from time to time to investigate the trail ahead, but she came back quickly and trotted or walked beside me. She didn't seem spooked by anything except the prospect of being too close.

Nothing like an actual conversation was possible. She ignored questions she didn't like, and, when she bothered to answer at all, her comments were either cryptic or unrelated—perhaps the second merely being a more subtle case of the first. But little by little, by a word here or there, I gathered the parts of her story she was willing to tell.

Her reluctance to hold human shape wasn't perversity or insouciance; it took extraordinary effort for her to hold her woman shape for more than a few breaths. She could switch as often as she wanted, but reverted quickly. It gave our discussions an episodic quality that would have been disconcerting under normal circumstances, but seemed to fit my mood our first few days together.

She schooled me on protocol. It was rude and inaccurate to call her a unicorn. I must never call her a horse, either. Just Nina, as if she needed no other name. This wasn't all that different from my own situation, for I fit none of the categories of human, muria, or hauflin. We were each aberrant, but whereas she seemed self-sufficient, comfortable with her uniqueness, I found my own condition unsettling.

It was awkward finding circumlocutions to refer to us. I once asked, trying for humor, whether "people like me" ever rode "people like her." She lashed out with a hind hoof and nearly stove in my ribs. I didn't try joking with her again.

If, as I suspected, she was an autochthon, indigenous to Sundering, I wouldn't find out from her. Speculative questions, or philosophical musings, brought no response. She seemed to exist in a perpetual now, as if living were its own justification. I envied her the equanimity, but couldn't share it.

I knew we were fully down into the valley when we began to see cottages and farms every few miles. It was much warmer at this elevation, sheltered from the incessant drafts above. I thought it safer to travel mostly in the darkness. Between my black cloak and her midnight hide, we were all but invisible, slipping silently down country lanes, crossing fields like whispers of wind. Sallas-proper was a walled city, but the name applied to the entire district of industry, housing, and shipping that had spread over the centuries to include most of the river basin. I decided to skirt the built-up areas. Supplies could be had, for a coin or two, from farmers or innkeepers, so there was no need to risk crowds the few times I purchased things. The people of Sallas, like the Wylanders, were mostly of medium height, all colored a rich brown that reminded me of nothing more than roasted almonds, and I would stick out among them. Though the innkeepers here were used to travelers from the east, where coloration was not so uniform, I still kept my hood up. I doubted anyone here had seen hair or skin like mine, and I wanted to leave no gossip or questions behind.

We followed the river for a while, paralleling it as best we could to avoid the main roads, but had to abandon the valley when we found armed garrisons even on the lanes and byways. Soldiers—I thought them mercenaries, for they were undisciplined and unruly, although they bore Ashe's standard—stopped all travelers, inspecting wains and asking questions. Preparations for war are seldom one-sided, and the search for enemy spies turns both parties paranoid.

Nina suggested I carry on, that she would meet me on the far side, but I demurred. Although Ashe's men had no reason to detain me, unarmed and unthreatening as I was, I did not want to face them. More than any others, soldiers are superstitious, and anything out of the ordinary unnerves them. Better to avoid them entirely. We struck due east, toward Landing, across the downs.

The ground rose again after we left the city behind, and although we didn't regain the plateau, the winds found us, blasting across the hilltops. We went back to traveling by day.

Frost covered the short, tough grass at night, often lingering until mid-morning. Game was plentiful, mostly gophers, rabbits, and squirrels. We saw a few deer, but had no way to hunt them, nor any way to use that much meat. We camped in hollows, both to escape the wind and to hide our fire. For several days, we saw nothing more threatening than children herding sheep, none of them close enough to hail, although one waved from a neighboring hillside.

Nina no longer shied from me, and the long nights became more companionable. I still had to watch my words, for she could fly into a fury at the slightest provocation, but she seemed content to listen to me talk. I found talking aloud helped me understand my thoughts. This led me to wonder if I actually *had* the thoughts before speaking of them. An unformed thought wasn't something undiscovered; it was something not yet born. But how could I speak of a thought before thinking it? My musings turned into a tail-swallowing epistemological argument with myself that broke her patience.

"Are you never still?" she asked.

I shrugged. I was never so voluble as when my dialogue went unanswered. A lack of response made me think I hadn't been understood, so I would repeat, rephrase, reiterate, and redo unto death, waiting for the token nod or murmured assent. I must have been slowly driving her mad. I tried explaining this, which only compounded my error.

"You talk and think, think and talk," she said, cutting me off.

"But you never say or understand anything, and you never ask useful questions. Why all these words, and never one about the Archon?"

It was the longest speech from her I could recall, so I sat up, poked the fire, and gave her my full attention. "Because I don't know what to think of him," I said. "Gaheris is just—"

"He holds your name," she said firmly.

Yes. At least I assumed so. As my dream of the Archon faded further into the past, it seemed less real. I could even make a plausible argument for why the soldiers in Wyland were a coincidence, that I had been running from nothing. But I didn't believe it. In my heart, I knew the Archon held the key to my past —or at least had recognized me during the dream.

"Thus do I pursue him," I said, somewhat tartly.

She snorted. "You flee what you love and chase what you fear."

Back to riddles. I sighed. "You can be very annoying."

"How can you be annoyed by someone you don't believe in?"

"Easily enough," I snapped.

She grew quiet. "You never ask about me."

And that was the end. Shadows covered her, and she stood on all fours looking at me. I would have sworn the look of amused condescension persisted through the transformation, though I would be hard pressed to explain how a unicorn's face could be disdainful or patronizing. She whinnied, stamped a hoof in exasperation, and whirled away to run off her anger against the hills.

It was true I didn't ask much about her, but only because she had made it plain questions were unwelcome. But I didn't think she meant asking about unicorns. She meant asking about *her*— who she was, not what she was.

Most humans, I think, would find it strange to be traveling through the wilderness accompanied by a mythical creature who could change shape, who neither ate nor drank. I had just accepted it, not as my due—for I didn't think myself anything special—but as a thing of nature, like the wind or the sun, that a man experiences whether he will or no. Fault me for lack of incredulity, and I admit the blame, but my true error lay in being incurious about her motives. It was fine for a man to accept a unicorn as a companion, but why should the unicorn accept the man?

She did not come back that night, nor the next morning, and the god-winds were silent. I wondered if, by failing to consider her, I had lost her.

3. TAD

BY NOON, it was clear Nina wouldn't come back anytime soon. Sighing, I stamped out the fire, shouldered the packs, and continued. If she wanted to find me, I had no doubt she would.

I tried to keep due east. From the tops of the highest downs, I could see the land sloping away to the left—a huge, rumpled, green and brown blanket made of oat grass, bunch grass, and heather, covering the rocky ribs of land and making the downs look soft, inviting. Somewhere at the edge of the blanket, far beyond sight from here, lay the sea. But my path led east, not north. I trudged on.

Ahead, the land rose sharply, but my mental map said that after the ridge it dropped sharply into the wide, flat bowl of Colonial Plain.

I gained the ridgeline by late afternoon. The sun was behind me, and therefore much of the plain below was already shadowed, but I could see the long lines of roads, cut straight as rulers by the original settlers using machines that would seem like magic today. Justian himself, the great architect engineer of the Second Colony, had crafted some of those roads. One could tell his work at a glance, because his roads were made from ship's metal, incorruptible, unbroken, twinkling gently in the slanted afternoon sunlight.

Trees, both deciduous and evergreen, had grown into mature forests over the centuries, but this land had once been all prairie, from the ridge to the ocean. It was easy to see why Landing, on the far side of Colonial Plain, had been chosen for the first site. It was flat, sheltered, broad enough for settlements, rich with water and good soil, and gave easy access by road or ship to the rest of Leonais. The roads were still in use—by military, I judged, for land had been cleared dozens, sometimes hundreds of feet on all sides, making the lines stand out, from my vantage, like white scars on the face of the forest.

I mentally tagged the locations of the major towns, wondering how I could cut through those thick stands of trees without using the roads. I hoped Ashe still controlled the plain.

The ridge was more of a cliff, a drop-off too sheer in most places for me to scale. I located a trail on the plain below that seemed to head in the right direction, and followed it with my eyes until it disappeared into the gloom at the foot of the cliff to my right. I angled toward that direction, keeping to the ridgeline, figuring to find a break sooner or later. The wind from behind me was fierce and unrelenting. I imagined that, with very little effort, I could let it push me over the edge and send me flying like a hawk over Colonial Plain.

Dusk found me still searching for a way down, so I set up camp, sheltering behind a pair of large black stones that thrust up from the ridge to shoulder height, like a giant's broken teeth. A few flakes of snow blew sideways into my face, but nothing collected on the ground. Even with the standing stones to block the wind and hot-burning gorse for fuel, it was hard to get the fire to hold. Eventually, I had a steady blaze, abating the chill somewhat. I laid out snares, but wasn't hopeful. Wildlife preferred the tender grasses blanketing the downs; the furze clutching to the bare rocks of the ridge was too tough for little teeth. Horses could eat it, and when crushed or bruised by humans, it made good cattle fodder, but it was not food for either rabbits or me. Still, I had water, carrots and a handful of beans left over from Sallas, and most of a squirrel from yesterday's catch. I put everything into the pan and left it to simmer while I watched the sunset turn the downs into flaming orange lumps of land, dwindling to an unrelieved grey, and eventually black. High cloud cover blocked the starlight.

The eyes of the body were useless in the dark, so I closed them and imagined I could travel with my mind, become a disembodied spirit fluttering over the downs. I touched a shepherd, an old man living by himself in a cothold I must have walked right past that afternoon. He ate gruel by candlelight. In his heart, I saw grief, still strong twenty years after his wife had died. As I swept through his tiny home, he looked up suddenly, as if sensing someone nearby.

I opened my eyes, shivering, suddenly frightened for and of myself. I told myself severely that it was just imagination—but at another level, I knew it was not. How had I unbound myself from my body? Was it the privation and the loneliness of my journey, or a hauflin heritage I had finally learned to tap? Was it possible I could always have done this, but had just never tried? Was this the same thing I had done in my dream of the Archon, long ago?

Whatever the cause, once the window in my mind opened, it stayed open. I could dip easily into it, travel any direction at will. I waited until I was calm, then set about exploring my new-found ability.

My range seemed limited. I could not reach Wyland, not even Sallas. A few miles was all, perhaps a dozen. I found and touched a rabbit, nibbling nervously in the dark, and nudged it with invisible fingers. It startled and leaped away. I left it alone and glided over the grasses and rocks, until I found another small cothold. In this one, a girl read quietly by the fireplace while her mother prepared dinner. A word came unbidden to mind, and I spoke it aloud. For a brief time, I saw through her eyes, commanded her limbs. I walked her over to her mother, had her stick out her tongue and flap her hands. Then I fled, leaving both of us confused.

It was both heady and frightening, this power. I wondered what else I could force someone to do. Were there limits? Surely there must be. Now that I thought of it, I wasn't sure if I had controlled the girl or merely planted a suggestion. It had felt like control.

Even though I had been unaware of this until just now, I suspected the Archon had known all along. Was it to eliminate a rival he had sent those soldiers? Did Gaheris have this power, too? Was this how he had convinced the lords and nobles to follow him instead of Ashe, touching their thoughts and encouraging the beliefs he wanted? Could one man stir another's mind like soup, adding a pinch of belief here, a hint of an idea there, until the whole was satisfactory?

I reached out again, felt the minds of hawks and squirrels, cotholders and sheep, the small minds of flying insects, grubs, and spiders. I ignored them. My mind swung like a lighthouse lamp across the downs, looking ever for the one soul hidden from me. Where in all this land was Nina? I changed my probing into a call, my eyes closed, dinner forgotten, putting forth all my strength.

At length, defeated, exhausted, I hunched over, panting, and came back into myself like a bird flapping wearily home to its nest. And I became aware I was not alone. Slowly, I raised my head.

There before me, as silent and still as ever, stood Nina, in her woman form. Without meaning to, I reached out with my mind, but she shook her head and something like a slap knocked my mental fingers away.

"Still rude," she said, "but starting to wake up. I should leave you alone more often."

"Do you know—?" I stopped, confused, for I was suddenly certain she was not here because I had called for her. Whatever power I had did not include commanding her, or even moving her with suggestion. She was invulnerable to that kind of suasion. But she understood it; of that I was fully sure. "What did I do?" I asked, hoping for an explanation that wouldn't make me crumble. "Can you do it?"

"No," she said, and it was the meekest tone I had yet heard from her. "It's not as you think, between us."

She started to blur, to gather shadows, but I called out, "Wait!" and she hesitated.

"Are we both hauflin?" I asked, fearing an honest answer.

She ground her teeth, seeming to keep her anger in check only with great difficulty. "I am not," she said finally, "and as you love life, Grey, do not suggest it again."

Seeing my incomprehension, she went on, though shadows tore at her edges, fraying her into the wind. "We are not . . . friendly with elves."

I nodded, and asked the question she had avoided, the one whose answer I dreaded. "And I? Am I hauflin?"

"I have no name for you yet. You have only touched the beginnings of power."

She bled away into the night, damned cryptic beast that she was, and swished her tail at me. I noticed her horn, usually invisible, pulsed into sight a few times, like laughter. I pushed myself up, aching from sitting still so long, and tended the fire. It had burned low, so I added more gorse until it blazed. I rather thought she had gotten her last comment backward: It wasn't that no name fit me, but that I didn't yet fit any names. I was changing, "waking up," as she put it. However, I still felt like myself from the inside—the expansive second sight on the desert wasn't all that different from my dream of Gaheris, or the ability I had shown to answer unspoken questions from Brawley's family. Seeing beneath the surface, or beyond the reach of my eyes, was just the periphery of the power I now tapped. I could not enter Nina's mind, but I felt no human could forbid me. The implications that came with that realization opened doors I had not known existed.

She joined me behind the rocks and stood silently while I stirred the stew. "I'm glad you came back," I said eventually, but she made no reply other than a shiver of her flanks, which could mean anything. I tasted the stew and then set it aside. I had lost my appetite, and I curled up, fast asleep within minutes.

It didn't cross my mind that my campfire was sheltered only from the west side. On the east, it must have shone like a beacon atop the ridge.

The young man came to me out of the night, a god-gift, a wisp, a blown leaf. He came silently, like an animal, but his scent preceded him. Nina snorted at his approach, else I would have continued sleeping until the crunch of his boot on gravel was right beside me.

I peeked around the standing stones, judged his size, his gait. Pulling back, I laid my hand on Nina's flank to quiet her. "Just a boy," I whispered. "Likely wants food."

She whinnied very softly and stamped a foreleg in protest. I patted her again, and waited while he came around the rocks into the weak glare of the remaining firelight.

I held up my hand, and he yelped, dancing backward. In the darkness, with Nina's midnight hide and my long black cloak, behind the lip of the rocks, we must have been almost invisible to him until I moved. After two steps back, he froze, studying us.

There was wariness and fear in his face, but none of the guilt I had expected, nor malice. Not a soldier, then. He was dressed only in rags against the cold of the perpetual winds. I saw no blade, but he could easily have a knife hidden in his rags. I could see him shiver.

"A horse," he said, looking at Nina with wonder. A sort of

hunger surfaced in his eyes as he said the word, a hunger that wasn't entirely of the belly. His voice was rough. I revised my estimate of his age up several years; he was no less than eighteen, perhaps as old as twenty. He was very thin, making it hard to guess.

Nina tossed her head and snorted in offense. "Easy," I told her. The firelight caught the star on her forehead and, just for a moment, something that was not present glittered, then was gone.

The young man saw and drew a quick breath. His eyes asked a question his voice could not shape.

"She's a friend," I told him, which explained nothing, and was as much as he deserved. I gestured toward the fire. "Are you hungry? I'll share what I have." I moved forward and he skipped quickly away, putting the fire between us. Fear and hunger warred visibly in his eyes. I squatted down by the fire and used a rag to grasp the handle of my pan, ignoring his agitation and trying to make my voice sound friendly, nonthreatening. "There's not much, but you're welcome to it," I said without looking up. "Just carrots, beans, and a bit of squirrel. No salt." I could feel his eyes on me, watching for the first sign of betrayal. I set the pan on a flat rock and backed off to stand by Nina.

He leaned forward and snatched the pan. He hissed in pain as he tried to balance the hot pan on his knees and sucked on a burned finger. He ate greedily, quickly, as though afraid that it would be taken away. He ate with only one hand, and when he turned toward the fire, I saw why.

Nina must have seen it too, or caught the whiff of old blood, for she suddenly reared, forelegs and hooves flashing, and drove him off. With a thin squeal of terror, he dashed away, the pan clattering to the ground, spilling the remains of his meal. I called after him, but it was no use; the night swallowed him up as if he had never been there.

I turned back to Nina, angry. "He only wanted food."

She just looked at me. We both knew I was lying. We stood there glaring at each other for a few moments, then I cursed and began searching for the young man. Nina snorted and followed me. Once out from behind the rocks, fat white snowflakes swirled, blown sideways, and hit our faces like sleet. I wanted to lean one arm on her neck to brace against the wind, but I didn't dare.

Away from the fire, the ridge was dark and treacherous. Clouds hid the stars. His trail was easy for Nina to follow, though I by myself would have had little hope of finding him. She led me to where he lay sprawled face-down in the sleet. He was unconscious, and I guessed from the gash in his forehead that he had tripped while running. "We'll take him back," I said, and bent to pick him up. I staggered a few dozen paces before Nina's warm breath whistled in my ear and she knelt before me in clear invitation.

I was astonished, and more than a little jealous. "Making an exception?" I demanded. "For *this*?" But the young man was a limp weight across my arms, too heavy to carry much farther. I draped him over her back, where no man had ever been, and acknowledged her sacrifice with a nod. She surged up, and faltered once, but it was not the physical weight of the man which bent her neck. She trotted lightly enough, as always. At the campfire, she shrugged him off to the ground and shivered.

"Aye," I murmured, rubbing her nose, "I won't ask that from you again."

I set a pan of water to boil on the embers, got medical supplies from my bags, then examined him. He lay crumpled where Nina had dropped him, still unconscious, bleeding slowly from his right temple, just above the eye. I approached the task of treating him with reluctance. He had smeared his body with grease before wrapping rags around himself. The grease would provide insulation at night and help prevent dehydration during the day, but it had gone rancid with age, and he was infested with lice.

I stitched his scalp as best I could. Soap and hot water removed the worst of the grime. The rags I tossed directly into the fire. He stirred while I tended him and started to wake, but a hand on his forehead and a murmured word moved him to rest again. Finally, I had him clean and the minor wounds tended. His skin was taut and brittle across his bones. He was pitifully thin and small, half-starved.

The deformity of his left arm was more obvious now that he was clean. The bones had been crushed and left to heal haphazardly. The skin showed scars where raw splinters of bone had torn through. The scars were pinched and puckered now, but discolored permanently from old rot and infection. His hand showed signs of crude surgery. The meat had been cut away from the heel of his palm and thumb, probably to prevent the spread of gangrene, leaving only crooked bones and shapeless, useless skin. The hand hung shrunken and black from his wrist like a claw. My own arms shivered in sympathy.

Then I turned the arm to the firelight and saw the pattern below the scars for the first time: the sigil of the Archon. I rocked back on my heels, my breath suddenly panicked and quick. No accident, then, this injury; it was deliberate. I forced myself to be calm. Whatever he had done to earn his disfigurement, the sigil had been in place before the arm was crushed, and therefore he was dangerous. I feared not so much what he himself could do to us—he was little more than a boy, after all, and hardly in any shape to offer injury—but that, if I let him live, he might lead others here. Was he, after all, a soldier? Or one of those who followed along? No matter his story, those bearing the sigil could not be trusted. Even if he was no danger himself, he had a voice and could report us. If the Archon's men found me now, unprepared, defenseless, they wouldn't even know to capture me. They would spike me to the side of the road without blinking and go on about their business.

While my mind reeled through dozens of possibilities, my body continued its work uninterrupted, and I found two other hands helping me as I wrestled him into a pair of my own good leather trousers. I glanced across him at Nina and nodded my thanks. She tossed her long black hair aside and stayed my hand as I started to dress him in one of my shirts.

Her hand slid away from mine and touched the young man's left shoulder. She traced the scars from his biceps to his crushed and useless hand, then rested her palm on his chest. "This," she said softly, "is what must be healed. Else you should not let him wake again."

I couldn't tell if she meant his arm or his heart, and it was too late to ask. The shadows above his body danced, gathered thickly, then melted, and Nina stood on all fours to regard me.

"I intend to go through with it," I told her, as the young man stirred again and moaned. This time I let him wake, but gradually, so he would not be startled. Nina moved angrily away to the other side of the camp. Suddenly he opened his eyes and stiffened.

"Be quiet," I said, putting a hand to his forehead and gently easing him back. "Rest now. You fell."

His eyes slid past me and searched the night wildly. "That black horse, its forehead. . . ."

There was an indignant whinny from beyond the fire, which I ignored. "Shh. Don't call her a horse. Nina will not harm you while I'm here. She probably saved your life tonight. Can you sit up?"

He did so, but too suddenly; he fell back, his face white with strain.

"You hit your head," I told him. "It will hurt for a while. Give me your name."

It was a measure of his confusion and hurt that he gave it without hesitation. "Thaddeus, called Tad." He struggled to rise on his good elbow, and looked across the fire at Nina. "I saw, earlier . . . I *thought* I saw. . . . Not a horse, then."

I sighed. "Not precisely." Was there any way to explain to this young man the complexity of Nina? Why she was offended by the term "horse" and yet would not acknowledge any other designation? I didn't even understand it myself.

"Is she a—"

I interrupted quickly: "Don't call her *that*, either." There was a clear note of warning in my voice and a quick bray of agreement from Nina.

He was confused; I couldn't blame him. "What, then?" he asked at last.

"Best just to call her Nina. I do. It's . . . safer."

"And you? What is your name?"

"I have none." I said it simply and without emotion, but a hint of my pain must have shown in my eyes, for he swallowed and looked away. I did not hate him for it; I imagine far stronger men than he would not have been able to face me in that moment.

"I have mended your hurts," I said after an awkward pause. "You are safe for now, and among friends. But your arm," I said gently, "is beyond the simple medicines I carry. How did this happen?"

"The Archon. . ." he whispered, but could not go on.

"Yes. Well, sleep now." He resisted, but I recalled the girl in the cothold, and I spoke the same word of power that had come to me then. He fell back like a puppet whose strings have been dropped. I covered him with a blanket and looked across the fire to meet Nina's eyes. There was nothing worth saying that we didn't already know. She had heard the damnable name. This boy, the god-gift blown into my path, was either a slave or a servant of the enemy. Better to have him sleep while I considered. Where would his loyalties lie? All the Archon's servants were slaves—some willing, some not. Some could be freed, some could be healed. Yet none could be trusted.

I withdrew into myself for a time then and cannot recall the paths I walked in my silence. When I returned, nothing had changed. Tad still slept, and I was no wiser, no closer to making a decision. I listened to the crackle of the fire and felt the wind's cold fingertips linger on my face. It all seemed very distant, like it was happening to someone else. I suppose I was not fully returned to my body yet, for I could still see, superimposed on the desert night, the path toward my goal. It led through the young man, and for that I could hate him a little and fear him more.

He slept like a child, knees drawn up to his chest. One hand hovered near his mouth as if he might begin to suck his thumb at any moment. His sleep was light, restless, his breathing quick and scant. Again, he reminded me of a wild animal. The fire was dying now. I sat with my back to it and pulled my cloak up around my shoulders. Nina was a dormant shadow beside me. Only Tad seemed real; only he seemed alive.

I watched him breathe. For all my time in this world, for all my travels, one feeling had never left me: the gnawing, aching wrench of loneliness in the pit of my stomach which would sometimes drop me trembling and sweating to the ground in a spasm of self-loathing and self-doubt. A private penance, for what sins I never knew. I had forgotten it briefly, with Brawley, and Nina assuaged the worse of it, but it was always there. A man should know his own name, and I did not. If there was a chance here, I must take it.

There was a sifting of shadows at my side. I turned in surprise to find Nina squatting beside me. *I had thought you gone*, I said with my mind and eyes. Not aloud, not ever aloud, not at a time like this.

Don't torture yourself, she replied, in the same sort of silence.

There are times when a sense of doom rises up around me, come to claim its own and drag me down into the abyss. "Don't torture yourself," is what she said. "Don't sacrifice yourself," is what I heard. And a memory surfaced, an old one, from the desert before Brawley, and I knew something in that instant that Nina did not. Destiny is a liar. This gift is mine, that I can refuse it. This gift also is mine, that I may choose my battles and their times. Names are shackles; I had none, and was therefore free to accept or reject the risk. In that moment, I chose acceptance.

She must have seen the determination in my eyes, for she lurched up, changed shape, and stamped a hoof in anger. I stood and held out my hand, begging for absolution, and she came to me and nuzzled my chest. I cast my cloak over our heads, and we stood that way for a measureless time. Then she pushed away from me and snorted a question. "You know I must try," I said gently. Something horn-shaped flickered into and out of visibility at her forehead and then the woman stood before me, long black hair covering her face.

"You are not ready for this effort," she said.

"Nevertheless."

"You do not know the danger."

I shrugged. I knew the potential gain.

"One small taste of power—you don't even know what to do."

"I have a general idea. I must try," I said, my voice firm. "He is helpless, wounded in body and spirit. He poses little danger. I *must* have access to the mind of someone who knows the Archon. My name depends on it. Should I try to waylay a healthy soldier instead?"

She snorted, halfway between a woman's laugh of derision and a unicorn's bray of challenge. "You are no fighter. You would die in the attempt."

"Therefore I choose Tad. What other chance will I ever have?"

"You have no chance here, either. He will not hold your name. And proving it will cost you dearly."

"I doubt he holds my name," I said slowly. "But he may hold a clue. And he is wounded deeply. Do I not owe him the effort?"

"You have only just woken to power," she argued, "and you have only touched the edges of it, stumbling like a blind man. You cannot see the whole of it, and therefore do not understand the costs. You owe him nothing."

"A god-gift is a double-edged sword," I said. "Grasping it always cuts. But honor demands I at least try."

"Honor?" She snorted again. "You think to earn honor by helping him, but instead you spend the little you have. I tell you again, as plainly as I can: You are not ready."

I wanted to believe her. I wanted to walk away from Tad and all he represented. I wanted him to die, secrets be damned. Yet at the same time, a niggling sense of purpose arose within me, a glimmer of destiny—or not precisely destiny, but a kind of compulsion, like submitting to a punishment I believed I deserved. I had not been able to save Brawley or my family. If Nina had suggested I meant to heal Tad to make up for that, I would have rejected the idea. Yet it was in the back of my mind as I made my decision.

"I have to try," I whispered.

"I will not stay with you if you do," she said flatly. "He is not worth it."

There was a roaring in my ears, and my vision narrowed down to a point. Her words sliced like coldness into my brain; I stumbled against her, buried my face in her fragrant hair, put my arms around her shoulders. *Ah, Nina! Don't force me to choose between you!* My voice, when I spoke, came from a distance, wrapped in velvet like the night itself, and I did not meet her eyes. "Is anyone worth it?" I asked, and the unfairness of the question made her shudder.

I could not trust myself to address her threat directly. I refused to reply, believing that to give it recognition would also give it power, make it come to pass. I concentrated instead on her objection. "What do you think he was to the Archon?"

She gestured dismissively. "A careless potboy, a disgraced squire, the unwanted son of a camp follower . . . who can say? Even nothing, nothing at all. Let be. He is not yours."

Now she was lying to me. "Yet you carried him," I challenged, daring her to continue.

Her eyes flashed. "I have already paid for that! But you, you are creating a debt you will never be able to pay."

"I intend for Gaheris to pay it. Your path and mine lie together, Nina, but our goals are not the same. I seek knowledge. This is mine to choose."

"This boy does not have what you want. And the price to prove it is too high. If you succeed, you will have hurt yourself for no reason, and saved an enemy to stalk at our backs."

"The scars. . . . Yes, I saw them."

"They are on his soul first. His *soul*, Grey. And if you fail—"

I raised an eyebrow and waited. Surely, that was my risk, my choice, my burden.

"—I will have lost you." Her voice wailed, bleeding away into the wind as her shape frayed. Shadows raced together and covered her. I winced at the pain it had cost her to hold human shape so long, to utter human speech, to admit her true fear. I waited patiently, then laid my hand on the wide softness between her eyes, and kissed her there.

"You need not stay with me," I offered gently, acknowledging her threat at last, giving her permission to hurt me beyond bearing. I was only beginning to suspect how much she meant to me, but the thought of separation brought our relationship to the fore, made me tremble with dread.

Her hooves danced lightly against the ground in agitation. Then she was gone, racing away across the ground at a hand gallop, blacker than night, swallowed up in shadow, until only the sound of her hoofbeats were left, and then not even that.

I turned back to Tad. The noise had awakened him, and he crouched, ready to flee, his eyes wide and staring. "Go back to sleep," I told him curtly, and folded myself back down beside the fire, facing the other way. After a time, his breathing told me he had complied, and I risked looking at him again.

He lay on his back, arms and legs spread, hair spilling on the ground. I settled myself cross-legged beside his head and studied him. My legs ached, but I ignored the pain. Tonight was his night, not mine. I dared not expect anything. Nina was right: I was a fool for hoping. His face in repose was not noble or strong, yet I found myself oddly attracted to him, to something which lay hidden. Or perhaps it was only the travesty of beauty which provided the allure, and there was nothing hidden, only something destroyed. It was the fascination of the charnel house, where a man may feel pity for the beasts and yet feel the rumble of hunger in his stomach at the same moment.

The darkness may be a cheat, but it is all we know. Is a man ever given to fathom his own soul that deeply? Some motives are best left unexplored. How did this young man's tragedy, the warping and twisting of his inner spirit, come to haunt me so? What did I owe him?

Nothing.

And yet, and yet.

Is anyone worth it? I had asked Nina. She had not answered— how could she? I massaged my neck. The physical trauma of what I proposed frightened me more than a little, but I knew and accepted those consequences. The risk was more than physical. If I became lost in him, the sacrifice would be for nothing.

A dozen times, I stretched forth my hand and drew it back again, lacking courage. What did I hope to gain? This young man, all unknowing, might hold the key to my search. The promise of that made me tremble with eagerness. If I did this thing, it would be as much for me as for him; any other thought would be a lie. Yet if the Archon's hold over him were stronger than my ability to break, this night would end with two slaves. Moreover, even if I did unbind the ties on his soul, the moral poison could overwhelm and drown me. Death would be cleaner, simpler.

Hesitation did me no credit. The night was waning, and with it my strength and my resolve. I reached out and ran my hand lightly up and down his body, never quite touching, but hovering like a hesitant moth, feeling the flows of energy which were so clear to the eyes of my mind that I fancied the eyes of my body saw them, too. I felt his patterns, his longings, his needs, his hurts. I remembered the desert before Brawley, and before that—not much, just a glimpse—but I knew the gift was mine, that I may look, and in looking know. I did not touch, not yet, but rather floated over and around him, peering from every angle into the fortress of his mind. I saw the name stamped on every stone of his mental edifice; I saw the signature of Gaheris in every deed, every motivation. I verged too close, and it became too late to pull back. The only way out was forward.

I entered his mind like a knife slicing flesh. There was no gentle way. His pain at the invasion was transmitted instantly to me, but I had no time to gasp, no thought of withdrawal. I forced my way brutally, all savage strength and heedless of the cost, to the core, the nexus. This, then, was the pattern wrenched awry. The limbs were meant to be thus: long, strong, straight, limber, capable. I laid the pattern across him like a mask, and filled it with life from myself until the material thing matched the pattern point for point. But the mangling of his arm was nothing compared to the serpentine labyrinth of his twisted mind. I made of myself a sink, into which his secret dreads flowed. Here, a look that scorned; there, a touch that burned; behind a wall, a memory of shame; in a bedroom, lust uncontrolled and guilty pleasure; in a courtyard, a remembrance of hot blood spilled in anger; on a grassy hillside, the hurt of rejection. Sad eyes, violent eyes, eyes that burned and eyes that stabbed. A brother dead. A lover lost. Memory upon memory and reaction upon reaction. Faces approaching and receding, hands reaching, mouths opening to scorn or curse or reject. And everywhere, behind each moment, watching each step, the Archon's glee and delight in anguish. I took them in, these memories, and absorbed them, made them part of myself.

Sweat poured from me, and pain lanced my chest with every breath. From a far distance I heard a shriek, a howl of agony and distress, and I retained just enough of myself to recognize the scream as my own. My strength began to wane, so I pressed him without mercy. Faster now—locked doors burst open, long-hidden passages revealed themselves. No corridor was left untouched, no hallway unexplored. And as I passed, I searched for a particular face, a certain memory, a gesture, a word . . . anything which would illumine my own quest. But there was nothing for me, as always; my name was not recorded here; the only name was the Archon's. The flow of strength was one-way, from me into Tad, as the flow of poison was the other, and it was almost more than I could bear. Where I passed, the memory of the Archon was erased, expunged, as though it had never been. I could not leave my own name in its place, but I left the young man's, an image of him whole and hardy, belonging solely to himself. It was the only thing I could give him in that place, the only thing he could accept. I found that he was in my arms and I was rocking him, tears streaking down my face, for the beauty and the pain, for the price I was paying. This also was my gift, that I may touch, and in touching, feel; in feeling, love; and in loving, heal. He clung to me, unconscious still, but with a hunger like unto starvation in his soul. I emptied myself into him like pouring wine into a bowl until there was nothing left. Then the darkness took me, cool and sweet, and it smelled of death, and I welcomed it.

The morning sun woke me. Tad was gone, and with him all of my supplies; he had not even left me water. I had not expected gratitude from him, and I shouldn't have been surprised by the robbery. Still, it stung. He had come to me out of the night, and gone back into it, blown by the same fickle chance that had brought him.

I gave myself a moment, then gathered my feet under me and stood unsteadily to scan the horizon. Something told me that Nina had gone ahead, toward Luvar or perhaps Landing, continuing the quest on her own. With my right hand, awkwardly, I drew my cloak up to shield me from the wind; my left hung useless and limp at my side.

Nina had been right. In the pride of my newfound power, I had attempted something I could not do, and my left arm bore witness to my failure. Tad had been a true god-gift after all—an opportunity that appears free and fortuitous, but carries a heavy, unforeseen price revealed only after the gift had been accepted.

My shadow stretched out behind me as I tottered toward the ridgeline, hoping to catch a glimpse of Nina on the Colonial Plain. As I reached the edge, my toe caught on a stone, and it turned under my foot. I stumbled, trying to recover my balance, but failed.

I fell, cloak flapping, toward the rocks far below.

4. Henna

I CRASHED into the side of the cliff only a few feet below the top, and rolled toward a shelf of rock. I had only a moment to hope that the ledge would stop me, then I was over it, rolling and flailing another ten or fifteen feet, only to strike another shelf and do it all again.

If I hadn't fallen near the trail, where the ridge reared up and leaned back from the plain like a man reclining against a tree, I would have plunged straight down to my death. But this was where the trail I had spotted wound its way up to the ridge, and there were ledges and shelves widely spaced all the way to the bottom—probably the same trail Tad had taken last night, and, for all I knew, again this morning. Despite the shelves, the cliff face was steep, and I earned no credit for stopping my descent. Careening as I was, with only one working arm, it was a tree that saved me, the same one that snapped my right shin like a twig as it caught me.

The snow started in earnest as I lay there howling, staring at the bone that protruded through my trouser leg. It was the big bone, the tibia, and my leg was twisted, the foot caught in a tree branch. The break was clean, and there wasn't much blood, but I knew that I would likely die without help. I tried to move and immediately fainted from the pain.

When I woke, I had no idea how long I'd been unconscious. The snow was several inches deep. I cupped some in my right hand until a little melted, then tried to clean off the raw edge of my shin. The pain was searing, but I peeled back the skin and muscle, washing off the raw flesh as well as I could. I clenched my teeth, took a deep breath, and jerked backward on my buttocks to pop the tibia back inside, trusting the trapped foot to hold the far end.

The next time I woke, the snow was even deeper, the sky was darkening, and I knew that even if I survived the leg, I was likely to freeze to death. Still, the ends of the bone grated together, and I knew I had—at least roughly—aligned the break. I sat up, leaning far forward, and worked at the forked branch that trapped my foot. The strength of desperation let me wrench the branch free from its anchor beneath the snow drifts. I had to stop, breath whistling through my throat almost in a scream, waiting for the pain to subside before I could strip off the twigs and smaller branches, leaving me a fairly long straight stick.

I broke off two pieces, each about two feet long, and shoved the ends into the top of my boot, one on each side of the broken shin. Then I tore strips from my cloak to bind the splints, trying to move the bone as little as possible. I lay back, utterly unable to do anything more.

It would have been far kinder for Tad to have knifed me as I slept.

The fever set in the next afternoon, and although most of the snow had melted, my choices seemed to be starvation, infection, or freezing to death—possibly all three at once.

Much of the next several weeks survives in my memory only as a nightmare. Agony, delirium, chill, hunger, and thirst warred for dominance over my body. I wandered among them, lost to myself and my surroundings. I remember trying to eat bark from the tree, and I know I shoveled mouthfuls of snow to get water before it all melted. I know I tried, foolishly, to walk using the rest of the stick as a cane, only to fall at once and break my splints. I remember making new ones, but not putting them on. I must have crawled the rest of the way down the slope, on one elbow and one knee. I remember seeing a sign for Luvar and thinking I should know the name. I remember seeing a man hunting with a bow and arrow, and I remember that he pointed it at me. At some later time, I had raw squirrel to eat, but whether he shot it and gave it to me, or I managed to snare it with my bare hands, I have no idea.

Time became a blur of sensations that happened in no particular order.

At some point, I woke to find myself in the back of a wagon, nestled down into the straw for warmth. I had no memory of climbing in. I judged it late afternoon by the sun. My right leg throbbed with each jolt, but my head was finally clear. I found cabbage in the straw beside me, and some root I didn't recognize. I ate as much as I could hold down. The donkey pulling the cart brayed occasionally as it plodded along, and I wondered if the driver knew I was in back. Had I somehow slipped aboard, or had someone taken pity on me and given me a ride?

When the road changed to cobbles beneath the cart's wheels, I carefully raised my head to look about. Stone buildings rose on both sides, some of them two or three stories, gloomy and silent in the slanted light. No one moved on the street.

The wagon had a plank seat, upon which sat a girl. From her size, I thought her maybe fourteen or fifteen years old. She drew the donkey up, turned her head, and told me to get off. She didn't seem surprised to see me, so she must have known I was there all along.

"Henna's in there," she said, pointing. I saw a rotting sign that read "Luvar Inn" hanging over the entrance to a stone courtyard.

"Henna?" I asked.

"She's a doctor. Well, not really, but she has medicine."

I had a vague memory that she had told me this at least once before, perhaps many times in my delirium. I nodded, but didn't move.

"Quick," she said, glancing nervously around.

"I can't get up," I told her.

She dropped the rein and hopped down. Coming around to the back of the wagon, she lowered the gate and pulled on my foot. I screamed.

"Quiet!" she breathed, looking panicked. "Get out."

I gave her my hand, and she pulled while I pushed with my good leg. I tumbled to the cobbles, knocking my head. I tried to get up, but fell back. She shoved my stick at me, and stood, hovering anxiously for a moment. Then, with yet another nervous look over her shoulders, she leaned down and hauled me to my feet. It was a sign of my starvation that a slight girl could lift me from the ground; it was a sign of her humanity that she bothered. I wanted to thank her, but she was already back aboard the wagon, urging the donkey to move. Without a backward glance, she drove off.

I never did learn her name.

Somehow I reeled across the courtyard and banged on the inn's door with my last strength. After an age, it seemed, the door opened and the innkeeper confronted me. I could hardly have seemed threatening in my condition. I held out my good hand in supplication. "Water. Food. Please."

He surveyed me with distaste. "The Archon's brother is loose and raising an army, so there's press gangs and soldiers everywhere. Not that you'll have to worry much," he added with a glance at my withered arm and another at my splints. "But we've almost no business because of it, and therefore no largess to spare for beggars. Anyway, we're closed until dinner. Be off."

He slammed the sturdy door in my face. I swayed there for a moment, staring stupidly at the iron straps and rivets which held the door together. I felt a moment of dizziness, then nothing. Blackness took me again, clawing me to the ground.

When I woke, I didn't open my eyes. It was essential for me to orient myself first, to recollect as much as I could, to place myself in relation to the larger world outside of my head. I sensed I was in an enclosed space, warm, resting on something soft, covered with a blanket. Safe, then, for the moment. I had no strength to wonder why or how, for I suddenly remembered that in all my pain, I had not only lost my direction, but I had driven Nina away with my foolishness. I felt a stab of pure loneliness and regret that overwhelmed my pitiful reserves of strength, and it was with something approaching relief that I relinquished consciousness and floated down into the depths. My dreams were filled with the sound of hooves thudding away into the distance.

When I woke again, it was with the sense that time had passed. But time was measurable again, and I knew I had slept normally, no longer in delirium. No more than a night had gone by while I lay senseless. Hunger gnawed at my stomach, and my leg still throbbed, but the lesser aches and pains had subsided. Something cool and wet lay across my brow, and I smelled wildflowers and heard the rustle of skirts.

I lay still for a moment, then opened my eyes. Framed against an open window in the clear light of day, a large woman with grey hair was fussing over something on a small table. Either I made a sound or she felt my eyes on her back, for she turned to look at me.

"Ah, you're awake then," she said. "I thought it would be soon. I've brought you broth and other light fare; you're starved." She waddled toward me, and I saw that she was old and gone to fat. Her hair was a thick iron grey, and her face was a map of wrinkles and contours. "Na," she said as I tried to sit up. "You lie there. Let Henna tend you."

She removed the cloth from my forehead and set it to one side. After feeling my cheeks with her papery hands, she clucked with satisfaction. "Ah, the fever's gone at last. Lucky for you I had my Jack, him that you met at the door, bring you up to the attic room. He has a good head for business, my Jack, but none of the wisdom. Never listens to his old mam. 'Bring him in,' I says to him, 'and never mind the stink.' He whined and would have drummed up a thousand reasons to leave you there, but I shut him up right quick with a threat he didn't rightly want to face. And so here you are, back almost from the dead and free of the flush. One good turn deserves another, and I've done you a fair good one by anyone's reckoning."

She said this last with a strange emphasis and paused for my response. Courtesy, if nothing else, demanded that I acknowledge her help. "Madam, I—"

"Call me Henna or Mam. I don't hold much with formalities."

"Henna, then. You must know I have no money to repay you. But what I can do, I will."

She still had many of her teeth, and she showed them to me in what I could only assume was meant to be a smile. "We don't want no money. If you had a purse and we was after it, Jack'd've had that off you and left you on the doorstep like carrion. It was a rare bit of luck that brought you to us, and rarer still that old Henna was there to see you and know what she saw. You'd have died within the day."

I agreed that I was most fortunate.

"Well, we could all use a bit of luck, don't you think?" she said. Again, there was an odd intensity to her words, and I felt my answer was somehow very important to her.

"Luck," I said slowly, "comes mainly to those with the foresight to pursue favorable circumstances."

"Hah! Exactly what I said to my Jack. Aye, you understand well enough. Let me fetch your broth. Na, lie you there. I've somewhat here to soothe the growl in your belly."

I was so weak that she had to spoon the broth into my mouth, but she fed me and gave me to drink as though seeing a grown man helpless as a child were no new thing to her. She continued to talk as I ate, but her words were lost to me. I found myself unable to listen. My world consisted of the soup and her hand as she brought it to me, and for higher thoughts I had no energy. There must have been medicine mixed in with the broth, I thought. At some point I fell asleep, and I woke alone in a darkened room.

The sound of hooves on cobbles awakened me. For a moment I thought it was my dream lingering on into my waking life, or Nina come to find me—but no, there were real horses in the courtyard below my window, several of them. I heard the rough and irritable cursing of the riders, the tired chuff of exhausted mounts, the slap of leather against stone as the riders stamped up to the inn. The pounding on the door seemed to last forever, but at length came Jack's indignant protest as he fumbled with the latch. His complaint suddenly chopped off as he admitted them, and then wooden chairs banged as they took seats in the common room. The men were loud and fearless; Jack's replies were apologetic, subservient. I could not make out individual words, but it was plain that these men were accustomed to having their way, and that Jack was frightened of them.

Soldiers, then, either outriders or couriers for the Archon, and I too weak to run.

A coughing spasm shook me as I tried to laugh. Run? Why bother? These men would not know me, would not be looking for me. Even if they were to discover me, they would see only a half-dead man with a game leg and a useless arm. They could not possibly connect me with . . . with. . . . A name hovered on the edge of my awareness, and a picture. I reached out instantly, but the knowledge slipped from my grasp, faded already, lost; from an unfathomed distance I could swear I heard a cavernous chuckle. *No!* It had been so close, so close! Almost I had held the key to something that had eluded me since the high desert. It was gone now, like the memory of a memory of a dream, leaving despair and anguish in its wake. A vast and ancient sorrow closed over me, a hungry black shadow to gnaw on my soul.

I fled the only direction I could, into myself.

The retreat I discovered was not precisely sleep, nor wakefulness, nor yet a trance. It was the kind of journey whose steps may not be retraced or remembered by the waking mind, but which always leads to a place within me that cannot be described. It is neither light nor dark, warm nor cold, good nor bad. Visions often come to me when I walk those paths—of the future, of the past, of those around me, and those most distant. The visions bring me many things: yearning always, knowledge sometimes, wisdom infrequently, and never peace or hope. I do not believe most of these visions to be anything but my imagination. I am nameless and unclothed within, and of my pain the visions do not speak. It is not a place I go to transcend, but to endure.

I spent the night thus, and the sorrow, if not healed, was at least abeyed, and of the world beyond my skull I knew nothing.

In the morning, I detected Henna's approach and began to order my mind to deal with a new day. But she erupted into the attic room almost as soon as I sensed her, and she startled me back into my body.

"Gold!" she cried ecstatically. "Gold!" In her cupped hands lay a small heap of coins, and the dull glint of gold was among the silver and copper. It was nothing compared to the excited gleam in her eyes. "Henna knew you would bring the northern luck!" She leaned over me, all elation and smiles, to show me the coins. I caught just a hint of the terrible hunger in her and drew away to the far side of the bed.

"What are you talking about?"

"Oh, he knows," she said slyly, winking at me. "He knows. 'Luck comes to those with foresight,' you told me. Well, foresight I had, and the luck's here, just like we had our very own saint chamber. Jack and me will be rich now, and the inn famous."

"Saint chamber? What are you talking about? Where did you get the money?"

"The money? Hah! This is just my firsters, as long as you're here. Them soldiers last night, the Archon's men, they fell to quarreling, don't say you didn't hear it! And two of them, why, they up and killed the third right in the commons, and this is our be-hush purse. Why, it's more than my Jack sees in a month! And it's just firsters."

"I heard nothing."

"Aye, pretend innocence if you must, poor babe. But old Henna knows where the luck's from, hey? She has the wisdom, the foresight: you said it yourself. And she knows your kind."

"My kind?"

She smiled at me fondly, possessively. "Oh, yes, old Henna has the wisdom. I saw it in you right off, the mark of the northern kind, with that white hair of yours and no beard. You're no man born. You've walked with the fair ones in the forests of Avermorn, and more, you're one of them. How came you here, never mind. You're ours now."

Elves, she meant, and not anything like what they were, but how the old stories dressed them up.

"Henna," I said patiently, "I'm no elf, and I have no luck." I lifted my left arm for emphasis, held it there until she was forced to recognize the damage. "I was lost, starving, wounded. Almost dead. I'm maimed. I barely have the strength to get out of this bed.

My companion and I were separated. As soon as I am well, I shall thank you and take my leave."

She was silent for a moment, appraising me. "Never one of the fair folk, you say. But your eyes give you the lie. Aye, Henna saw the way you flinched when she mentioned Avermorn—and you can't be denying the white hair and skin." She paused, and her gaze left me to fasten on the coins in her hand. "As for the luck, I dare say you've had precious little for yourself. But that's not required. Henna has the wisdom, from her own mam and grandmam before her. The holy ones all suffered, they was great sufferers, hey? And just by being in a room they made the whole building lucky. I ain't never had me a holy man here, but one of your soulless kind should do the same. You'll bring the luck, all right, like you have already."

I pushed my way up to a sitting position. "Henna, you are mistaken. I can't turn this room into a 'saint chamber' for you, and I had nothing to do with that money." I reached over and folded her fingers around the coins. "And were I you, I would think twice about the 'luck' of taking pay for silence over murder. Blood money stains your soul, not just your hands. Please get me clothing. I need to go. I need to find my companion."

She pulled away from me and waddled over to stand by the window. "You're a fine one, to be talking of souls! Coins is coins, and it don't matter where they come from long as they can get themselves spent. Na, you'll be staying here a fair bit yet." She looked suddenly wary. "Who's this companion of yours, anyway? Another na-souled creature?" She swallowed nervously. "It's not a demon, hey?"

I felt my vision narrowing down to a point. If I described Nina the way most people perceived her, Henna would just laugh. Yet if I told the truth, she would not understand. "You would call her a unicorn," I said at last, defeated by the frailty of spoken words, and apologizing silently to Nina, to whom terminology was so vital and yet so inadequate. I don't know what reaction I expected from Henna—awe, perhaps, or maybe fear.

A slow smile worked its way through her many chins and wrinkles. "And you say you're no elf! A unicorn, hey? That would fetch a lovely price!"

I had nothing to say to this; I did not trust myself to speak. And it was past time for words. Although I was still weak, I threw back the blanket and struggled to my feet. There was dizziness, yes; but it would pass, and my leg would bear my weight for now. She backed away from me. I found my clothes on a stool beside the wall and began to dress.

"I've the wisdom, I tell you! I've ringed you about with charms. You can't be leaving this room. And you can't be touching me, neither! Henna's not scared of you."

I still said nothing. Pulling on my boots one-handed was nightmarish. Several times I almost fell. But at length I was completely dressed, and I limped toward her. My intention was not to harm her, but to walk straight past, out into the hall, down the stair, out the front door.

She stood between me and the room's door, backing away one step for each of mine. Her voice grew shrill. "If you try to leave your flesh will burn!" she wailed. "I've set my charms, and you're mine now, do you hear me, hey? Mine."

"I am my own," I said grimly, and took another step.

She stayed a moment longer, then shrieked and fled the room. The door slammed shut behind her. I rattled the handle and heaved against it with all my might, but she had barred it from the other side and it would not budge.

Sometimes, there is no magic quite so strong as a door locked. Her "charms" and petty spells I feared not at all, for I did not believe she had any magic in her. Yet with the simple swing of an iron bar, the foolish old woman had defeated me.

I went to the window and peered out. It was perhaps twenty-five feet to the cobbles, too far for me to risk jumping. And with one arm useless, and one leg barely able to hold me up, climbing was out of the question. If I'd had the powers she imputed to me, I could have whistled up a steed of the air, vaulted lightly to its back and wafted away. Or opened a pathway through the mists and simply walked into an otherwhere far from my prison.

Instead, I began tearing the blanket into strips. It was hard work, one-handed. I stood on one edge, gripped the other with my teeth, and ripped with my right hand, using teeth and nails to start each strip. My jaw ached with the strain, and the blanket did not tear cleanly. I ended up with a dozen small pieces, roughly triangular in shape, and five good long strips. When tied together and twisted, they made a passable, if awkward, rope. It was too short, but it would have to do.

I tied one end of the rope to the bedpost, then shoved the bed itself over to the window. I bunched up the remainder of the rope and tossed it out, letting the far end dangle free down the side of the inn. It would be clumsy, trying to lower myself with one hand, but I had no other choice. I wrapped a length of the rope around my waist to act as a bight, and settled myself on the windowsill. The cobbles seemed very far away. They would be hard and unforgiving if I slipped. I took a deep breath, wishing I were more recovered, then gripped the rope firmly with my right hand and leaned out. I teetered on the edge for a moment, then the rope blanket was burning through my hand and I was falling.

I suppose it only lasted a moment, but my memory of the stones rushing toward me as I twirled wildly toward the ground seemed a thing of ages rather than seconds. My one-handed grip was too weak, and the turn of rope about my middle unwound itself as I dangled. I tried to grasp the rope with my thighs, and managed to slow my plunge somewhat, but I still fell like a rock. At the last moment I shoved away from the building, let go of the rope, and tried to land on my good leg. I smacked into the cobbles with a suddenness that knocked the breath from me, and landed halfway on my side, half on my back. I lay there for a moment, stunned, then groaned to my feet, gasping, raking in air with bruised ribs. The courtyard gate was only fifty paces off, and freedom lay beyond it like the promise of life itself.

I believe I made it almost halfway before Jack's beefy hand closed on my arm like a manacle, and he dragged me back inside.

There is no point in describing the vengeance Henna took on me for trying to escape. It was intended to be painful and humiliating, but she was careful not to kill me, and she left me my manhood. I could almost forgive her the torture, for she was clearly irrational. But Jack held me while she used the knives, and for him I felt nothing but hatred. When it was over, I found myself back in the attic room, bloody, chained to the bed with a shackle about my neck. The chain was perhaps a dozen feet long, giving me the freedom of the room, but even if I were to try to escape through the window again, I would only succeed in hanging myself on the fetter.

She fed me at regular intervals, but rarely spoke to me after that day: I never answered. Business at the inn picked up, no doubt reinforcing her belief that I brought luck to them. I lay on the bed, watching the days come and go while my body slowly healed and my mind slowly disintegrated. Henna was practical enough to keep out of my reach, but soon enough seemed to relax all other wariness in my presence, believing no doubt that I had come to accept my fate. After a fashion she was correct, for I could no longer discern the difference between waking and dreaming. The sound of hooves haunted me. The occasional burst of laughter or conversation from the commons seemed to be coming from another world, so distant was it, and so unconnected with my durance. And when Henna came in to leave food or empty the chamber pot, I did not so much as turn my head. Although I stirred myself to eat and care for other necessities, after a time these became mechanical functions, dissociated and unreal. I was caught up in my visions.

I suppose that by any definition one cares to use, I had become mad.

In my madness, I could not find my retreat, my mental fastness. That solace was denied me. The paths I walked were mortal and bespoke my own heart. I talked to Nina often, speaking aloud as if she were in the room with me, or as if I walked the green pastures and dappled forests with her. Her horn, the symbol of her power, glimmered in and out of visibility as we walked together, so that sometimes she appeared as a normal black mare, sometimes as an eldritch, dainty unicorn. Yet she was both and neither, and the horn was also the symbol of her defiance, her way of refusing fate and defining herself only under her own terms.

Though it was cold at night, the attic grew stifling at noon, creating a hazy unreality in my prison, and my walks with Nina were far more real to me than my surroundings. As we walked, we searched for something—something unnamed, yet dear. I had the feeling that, if found, all would be set right.

And in the night, when her power was strongest and my resistance weakest, she sometimes appeared to me as a woman with long black hair and a confident smile. In my madness I was able to do that for which I lacked courage or permission in real life: take her in my arms and murmur the words of love to her, and more than words. And those times, too, were far more real to me than the attic room, and I would sometimes startle awake, my arms still reaching, only to clasp the clammy darkness.

When I was not with her, my consciousness floated free, like a hawk riding a warm updraft, the land laid out below me like a map. I could see from far northern Avermorn, where the muria walked in gentle dreams of beauty among their beloved trees, to the Archon's citadel in far south Jappa, where drums beat and the acrid smoke of war hung in the air. And between, on the broad swath of torn land, armies marched day and night. From the mountains and fertile valleys to the forests and wide grassy plains, unease and the rumor of war stalked the land. Across and beyond the Abuttals, where no man had gone since the landing, the barren sand deserts curved to the horizon, stretching like a sea, and they marked the limits of my vision.

All this I saw without stirring from the attic room, Henna's saint chamber, my prison. The winds of the world gusted through my spirit and left me dry, effectless. I felt little or no emotion as I viewed the world from my aerie. I could watch but not interfere, and nowhere in all that land could I find one person whose mind held my name, save the Archon, and his spirit I dared not touch. I dreamed always of Nina, whom I believed loved me even as I was: mad, nameless, chained, and dreaming. No matter what I saw, I kept coming back to her. There were many I could hate, a few whom I could endure, but only one I could love. I treasured my illusory times with Nina then, and my world was once again imbued with the passions and longings which define us. No godling, I, in detachment lounging, but a mortal man in subsistence tenured, and that was enough.

I came gradually to believe that my images of the external world were authentic, just as my other visions were sometimes true. Nothing came to me on demand, but I found that, while riding the god-winds, I could focus my second sight on events and places with an accuracy which surpassed the boundaries of my imagination. It was not madness, but a power I had not understood, brought forth by circumstance to serve my need. It was like the seeing I had experienced on the ridge, but my range now seemed nearly unlimited. My proof that it was real, and the end of my madness, came when I located the inn where I was held captive. Nina, looking through my eyes, was oriented at last, and I felt the triumph and elation in her mind. It was this for which we had been searching together these many weeks. Her strength, purpose and resolve flowed across the land toward me like an onrushing wave, and her hooves were the thunder of a distant storm.

I stirred on the bed and gave thought again to escape. My arsenal was small if it came to a physical fight. But Henna had known more than she knew she knew: I had weapons of another kind. I pushed myself up and sat against the headboard to think, the chain dangling from my neck and looping in my lap like an overlong scarf.

Against Jack, I could do little. If it came to exchanging blows with him, the chain was my only weapon. I might possibly twist it about his neck and strangle him, but Henna carried the key to the lock, and killing Jack would serve me not at all. And he was not susceptible to my other weapons. His thick head had never entertained an idea long enough for it to grow comfortable and take up residence, much less frighten or teach.

Henna was a different matter. I could reach her surface thoughts from where I sat on the bed. I tried using the same type of control that had caused the young cothold girl to stick out her tongue. *Release me!* I demanded, but my order, unaccompanied by a word of command, just echoed like a random thought in Henna's mind, easily dismissed. I abandoned the attempt, suspecting that words of command were matters of impulse and inspiration, not things I could call forth by premeditation. I considered everything I knew about Henna, trying to conceive of different tactics. Frontal assault had failed, but perhaps deception and harassment would suffice.

Despite Henna's shortcomings and foolish notions, she looked beyond herself for something greater. She believed that the world was wide and mysterious, that power lurked in incantations and potions, that magic stalked the land—true enough, even if the ways of it were beyond her. She imagined that power meant coercion, the ability to force others to one's will. And she believed that good and evil existed not as extremes of judgment on a moral spectrum, but as opposites incarnate, icons to which she could point, forces she could invoke.

My world was more indefinite. Most power is a chicane, and at its best cannot coerce or enslave, but only frighten or kill. Knowing this, and knowing her, I had jurisdiction without pretense, power without delusion. Just as my body had allowed my spirit to roam freely, now my spirit created an image of my body, and I sent it forth to harrow her soul.

I spoke no words to her. My apparition was enough for now. It existed only in her mind, and her own fears gave it power and substance. I appeared to her in her own room, melting through the wall, looming like a nightmare. She shrieked and made the sign against evil, and I allowed my illusion to fade.

Within minutes, I heard her huffing on the stairs. She burst into the attic room. I sat without moving, eyes unfocused, as she had seen me a hundred times before when I was blind in my madness, and paid no attention. She stared at me, panting, but did not come within reach. I could smell her fear, the stench of doubt whirling in her mind, and I did nothing to relieve it. At length she left me, but in her face I saw the beginnings of my victory.

Immediately I appeared to her in the hallway. This time I re-created the wounds she had inflicted and allowed the illusory blood to splatter her face. I lifted the chain around my neck and moaned.

She clattered down the stairs in a panicked rush and slammed and bolted the door to her room, only to find my image reclining in her chair, drooling blood and spittle with an idiot's grin. "Begone!" she shouted, and the noise brought Jack running. I leaned forward and kissed her obscenely on her fat lips, then I faded from view, so that Jack found Henna gibbering and pointing at nothing behind her locked door.

I left her alone then, for I wanted her mind to have time to work on what she had seen, to invent reasons and explanations that I could later subvert or shatter. I gave her time to gather her wits between assaults, but struck repeatedly throughout the afternoon and evening, dredging nightmares from her own head to bedevil her. Here, a large green venomous spider; there, a gaping maw with ragged teeth . . . rats that scurried through the walls but were never seen . . . all the horrors of her mind I sent against her, one by one or in groups, the images forming as quickly as she became aware of new fears. She had many fears, and I used them all.

She came to me that night with a grim determination in her eyes. "Henna knows what you're doing," she said flatly. She moved across the room, carefully out of my reach. She shielded her oil lamp with one hand, and set it on the table beside the door. She closed the window against the draft and stood at the foot of the bed, between the lamp and me. The flame from the lamp cast an uneven yellow glow over the room, and shadows loomed large against the walls.

I sat in the same position she had seen earlier, and said nothing.

"You have no real power," she challenged. "You don't scare Henna no more, hey? The wisdom knows about specters and trickery. You can't make real things, just illusions and ghosts. Your tricks can only frighten Henna for so long, but she's on to you and your na-souled ways. Willing or not, you'll bring the luck to us. It won't get you free."

I gave her only silence in reply.

She leaned forward and spat at me. "If I have Jack hold you down again, the knives will make you talk!"

I kept my peace.

"What do you want me to do?" She was almost screaming now. "Why are you haunting me?"

I looked at her directly for the first time. "It is your conscience that haunts you," I said distinctly. "Even if you kill me, the ghosts will abide."

She sidled around to the side of the bed so that her bulk no longer shielded me from the light. She looked me in the eye, almost within reach. "Henna has the wisdom, she knows a lie. Your magics will die with you."

"If I have no power, then keeping me here serves no purpose," I told her. "If I do have power, then keeping me here means your death. Either way, you lose, old woman. Release me, and I shall depart without harming you." It was truth, and she recognized it. Fear and greed fought with each other in her. She still believed that I brought luck to the inn. Her heavy jowls worked up and down as she swallowed her responses unvoiced.

"You are clever with words, but Henna is clever, too," she said at last. "You have enough power to bring the luck here, but you cannot harm me. I can hurt you, hey, or kill you, or just keep you here forever." But she did not believe her own words. She leaned forward still further, and my hands ached where I clenched the chain.

She needed a demonstration. It was a small thing, but it nearly broke me: a wind arose at my desiring in the closed room and blew out the lamp. In the darkness, I intoned, like the voice of death itself, "Then kill me and be done with it."

It was enough to goad her into action. I smelled her breath then, and heard the whisper of her skirts. A knife whistled past my ear and sank into my left shoulder. The pain was a shock, but only served to propel me into action. I whirled on the instant and flung a loop of the chain in the direction I guessed her neck to be. It missed and clanked heavily to the floor, and I wasted precious moments retrieving it while she tried to stab me again in the darkness. This time I swung the doubled-up length of the chain like a mace, and it connected with either her head or her shoulder, for she fell across me on the bed and bellowed in pain.

From below, I heard Jack's answering roar, and I knew that I had only moments left. I cursed the idiocy of my inspiration to blow out the lamp, for with all her bulk and flailing limbs I could not find Henna's neck in the dark. I wielded the chain like a lash now, trying to keep her from slicing me again. She fought with desperation, stabbing at me blindly, repeatedly, in the dark, and more than one attempt slid home. I used my deadened left arm as a shield, and managed to twist around behind her, using my weight to keep her from getting off the bed. When I got the chain looped around her neck at last, it was like riding a wildcat. She bucked and twisted under me and tried to roll me off. We struggled in silence now, her breath rasping in her throat, and I could hear Jack clumping up the stairs. I hung on grimly, pulling with all my might, knowing that if she did not lose consciousness soon, I would have to fight both of them at once.

With a suddenness I suspected of being a feint, she stopped struggling and collapsed. I winched the chain tighter and held it there as long as I dared. She did not move. Jack was shouting now, and a part of me wondered why he was taking so long. But I couldn't spare the time to worry about it. If I weren't free by the time he got here, I would be dead. I searched Henna's body for the key, found it on a thong at her bosom, and frantically fit it to the manacle at my neck.

I rolled away from her and struggled to my feet beside the bed just as Jack, torch in hand, barreled through the door. He saw Henna lying on the bed first, then his eyes flicked to me and widened as he realized I was free. A look of fury twisted his face and he started toward me, torch held high like a club.

I took a deep breath and realized for the first time that at least one of Henna's stabs had cut open my belly, for raw air played across my intestines when I breathed, and blood spilled down my front. Death stared at me from that wound, and suddenly I had no more fear of Jack. "Come, then," I called, and crouched. I used my weak left arm to hold in my guts, and held out my right one to guard against the torch. He lumbered toward me and I saw something behind him that made me laugh outright in sheer delight.

That gave him pause. For all that he had no imagination, he was not stupid. In his practical, predictable world, men did not crouch to fight as their guts spilled over their hands, did not laugh, carefree, in the midst of a battle they cannot win. He did not understand my determination, and he did not know what stood behind him in the doorway. He paused, and I laughed again and straightened up. His eyes locked on mine warily, but he slowly turned his head. From the corner of his eye, he must have seen what I saw, for he gasped and whirled. In that instant, I leaped forward and pushed him forward with all my strength.

Nina gracefully lowered her neck, caught him on the tip of her horn, then threw her head back and tossed him over her shoulders to crash against the wall. Something that was not anger, not rage, flashed across his face, and I thought for a moment that he was somehow unharmed. Then I recognized his expression as one of disbelief, and I saw the gaping hole in his chest and the dark blood pumping freely.

He slumped forward, still surprised but no longer alive, and the torch dropped from his nerveless fingers to sputter on the floor.

"Nina!" I cried, and she looked at me then, fire in her eyes, her horn shining with eldritch power unbound at last. We had both of us passed some kind of boundary, some kind of test. The only word I knew to describe her was "glorious."

She trotted lightly around Jack's body and stood before me, the warm and living breath of a unicorn frosting in the too-fragile mortal air. I stared at her in wonder for a moment, then she blurred and I held her woman-form in my arms and stroked her hair, kissed her lips and throat, while flames crowded at our heels and licked hungrily at the walls. There were no words, and I felt no need for them.

She pulled away from me, and I stumbled in pain, fiercely aware of my wounds again. I watched as Nina crossed to the bed and felt the old woman's neck for a pulse. Nina's eyes met mine in question, and I knew then that Henna was unconscious, but still alive.

"She called this room a saint chamber," I told Nina. "She thought it would bring her luck." I paused, considering all that had transpired since I first knocked on the Luvar Inn's door.

We who are driven by necessity have little room for virtue, and a man must be his own judge in the final reckoning. For all that I may pretend to integrity, in the end there is only this honesty in me, that I do not deny my sins. My decision at that moment was made in cold blood. I do not flinch when I look in a mirror, but neither do I smile.

"Today is not her lucky day," I said harshly, and we left her to the flames.

In the fresh air outside, I stood watching the inn burn while Nina wrapped a bandage around my abdomen. No wisdom or comfort came to me. I felt the shadows shift at my side, and I turned to look at Nina's horn, glowing vibrantly and freely in the night, but asked no questions. If she had come to terms with herself while we were apart, she would tell me of it in her own time. Only one thing mattered to me now. "Stay with me," I said, and the look in her eyes was answer enough.

The god-winds blew cold at our backs as we left that place together.

5. Pia

Nina's change only lasted a day before she was back to being moody and argumentative. Whatever apotheosis she had experienced faded like a dream. Her speech became short, and she seldom took human shape.

During that day, my fever returned. I was fairly sure my bowel and internal organs were intact, but the deep gash from Henna's knife left me open to infection. I feared sepsis would make short work of me. My rate of respiration shot up, and again I looked delirium and death in the face. I was coherent enough at first to tell Nina how dangerous the wound could be, but then I ceased caring.

She said nothing about my leg or my arm, nothing about my stomach. She didn't acknowledge my pain or my fever. "I know a place," she said, and that was all.

I followed her, weaving, wondering if she would carry me when I could no longer walk, and if so, how I could possibly climb up onto her back. She led me through the woods to a small mound in a clearing. Stones ringed it, and a depression like a sunken grave lay on its north face. It was a dolmen, a tomb, and not a place humans would willingly go. Even through my fever, I felt the hairs on my neck rise, and a sense of preternatural coldness permeated my bones.

She pawed at the moss and dirt of the declivity with her hooves, digging out a rectangle, revealing stone beneath. It was like a door, buried almost horizontal in the ground. It even had a notch like a handle. She pulled the shadows around herself, took human shape to tug open the groaning, scraping door. I followed her inside, and the earth swallowed me.

Faerie mounds are not comfortable places for mortals, and the severity of my wounds gave me no room to doubt my own mortality. I slumped to the floor, sure that climbing through that doorway had torn my abdomen open again.

At first, everything was dark, but as my eyes adjusted, I saw the walls were pearly, faintly luminescent, as if studded with soft-glowing gems. The air inside the dolmen, redolent of moldy leaves, old bones, and rotted cloth, was cloying, thick. And it was cold, chillingly cold. My fingers and ears went numb.

"Wait," she said, and I obligingly sagged, laid my head on the stones, and let the coldness seep through me. Save for the fire in my belly, the cold seemed to turn me gradually into stone myself.

An unfathomable amount of time later, I became aware of music thrumming faintly. The beat of drums, skirl of pipes, and blend of voices in harmony was the most beautiful thing I had ever heard. I did not know the language of the singers, but I felt close to understanding the song. If only I could listen long enough, concentrate well enough, give it my full attention, the substance of the song would become clear. It seemed a meaning most worth knowing.

"Don't listen," said a voice I once had thought melodious, but now seemed like the screech of an old woman's harangue. "Wake up," the voice insisted, and the music faded, diminished, until the drums were just my own heartbeat, and any harmony evaporated like mist. I hated Nina for calling me back, and told her so.

"Drink this," she said, unperturbed.

She had brought herbs mixed in water, a bitter brew that had the indefinable but unmistakable taste of medicine. I choked half of it down, and she pulled apart my bandage to pour the remainder over my exposed intestines. The excruciating pain brought me fully alert. She ignored my cry of agony and pressed some leaves against the open wound before rebinding my bandage tightly.

When she was done and I could control my voice again, I asked, "What was that music?"

"Memories," she said shortly. "Don't listen."

"Muria?"

She sniffed and tossed her hair. "Elves never touched this place."

"Yours, then? Your people?"

"It was the Sleeper. Don't listen. Rest, Grey. Rest and heal."

I never heard the music again.

Months went by in that place, the tomb's temperature never varying. At some level, I knew that time was passing outside, but it felt distant, unconnected to me. Inside, it was just sleep, waking to find Nina had brought food, cleaned my face, or changed my bandages, then sleep again. During the waking periods, I was myself, but my sleep was torturous.

When I could no longer keep myself awake, I fell into evil dreams. I dreamed that I watched the Archon, sometimes even *was* the Archon. He strode along the parapet in the citadel, arguing with a cloaked man whose voice I could never hear, but who both frightened and infuriated him. He dallied with half a dozen women, loving none of them, and was blind to their loathing. He berated his captains and their lieutenants, lecturing them on things they knew better than he, unable to see how they hated his bullying and condescension. I sat with him while he received courtiers, read dispatches, judged quarrels, and was bored by entertainers. Sometimes I watched with clinical detachment, unmoved by his feelings, like a judge reviewing evidence. At other times, I was inside his head looking out, and his emotions became mine. I was dirtied by the delight he took in petty cruelties or even outright torture. Gaheris was filled with anger in my dreams. He became furious with his servants at the slightest infractions, and made them all watch if one of them was flogged or hanged. He himself branded his sigil on the women he took to his bed, deriving pleasure from their screams. The cloaked man on the parapet frustrated him most of all, but Gaheris never took out his rage on him. Instead, with icy control, he would wait for nighttime and take his special knives to visit the prisoners in the dungeon. Those times, I started awake, my heart pounding, my body drenched in sweat.

For an endless period, I couldn't be sure if I was starting to regain lucidity, or continuing in delirium. Nina constantly came and went, renewing the poultice with fresh herbs, bringing me water or food, and checking my fever. She seemed to hold her woman shape for hours at a time, her hand on my forehead. When I asked her how that could be, she said only, "You need me this way," which was typically uninformative. I decided those times were fever dreams, a product of my desire for companionship rather than reality. Moreover, I had other reasons to doubt my sanity. Sometimes Nina was neither unicorn nor woman: She appeared as an old man dressed in hierophant's robes; a tiny hovering dragon that blew flames to warm the chamber; a young girl who curled up to sleep with her head on my shoulder; a waterfall emerging from midair and disappearing before it touched the ground; a wheel of spinning colored lights that provided no illumination; and, once, Brawley, picking at his thumbnail and asking if it made sense to trust dreams. These visions, even the impossible ones, didn't frighten me, for I could tell they were all Nina underneath, a comforting presence, utterly unlike my nightmarish glimpses of the Archon and his activities.

I didn't talk much. I saw no reason to share my fever dreams with Nina. They were something tossed up by the confusion of my delirium. While awake, I could shake off the memories and recognize them for the sick imaginings of a desperately ill man. And indeed, they eased after a time. Either I learned to sleep through them, or they simply became less vivid as my fever faded.

Eventually, I healed—not the kind of rejuvenation I had performed on Tad, but a more normal, slow, natural healing. My gut knit together, my strength came back, and the dreams eased, but Nina's herbs could not touch my withered arm nor erase the pain in my leg. I hobbled in circles for exercise, and it became clear my tibia would never stop hurting, although it would bear my weight.

Winter came and went, and we emerged from the dolmen in the spring, finding the world had changed.

A farm girl told us that Ashe had lost all this land, from Luvar to Landing, keeping only Halmar-by-the-Sea and the coastal lands surrounding it. The first soldier we encountered sickened me. The body had frozen where it fell during the winter fighting and, now thawed, was bloated and putrefying. I could tell he had been young, but little else. Before long, we encountered the second fallen soldier, and then a group, and another, and at some point, I stopped counting. Some of them bore the Archon's sigil, but most were Ashe's men.

The forest thinned gradually, and we had to choose taking the roads or crossing fields. The thaw had brought out farmers, but I reckoned them less dangerous than armed men on the roads. Perforce, we must cross the roads from time to time, for this area was the most ancient of human settlements on Leonais. Well-kept highways and viaducts branched like arteries and veins in every direction. We found little traffic; it was an occupied country, and the military controlled the roads. The conquered traveled only when they must. When we came upon a lane or byway, we scurried across.

I argued for asking a farmwife for supplies, but Nina would have none of it. So I helped myself to food stealthily, climbing through windows when necessary, finding the farmers had not starved under Gaheris. Fruit and salt and meat and greens awakened my palate to mortal food, and I lusted for potatoes. Nina, as always, neither ate nor drank. Something sustained her, something she obtained only when we were apart. She would come back, radiant in appearance, but foul in mood. I began to have dark suspicions, and my heart was heavy, but I wisely kept my thoughts to myself.

I also needed clothes, for my own had rotted to tatters during the long winter underground, and the stink of the grave never left them. I would gladly have gone naked in the warm spring air, but we were not strolling through a carefully manicured glade; we trudged through ditches, skirting easy paths, pushed among the trees, and slept on the ground. My body needed protection. I found trousers and shirts that fit hanging on a line behind a bright yellow farmhouse, and boots tucked under a porch at the more modestly colored subsequent home. Undergarments and a cloak were next, the former because the trousers and boots chafed, and the latter because I thought it wise to cover my hair.

I wondered what the poor farmwives would think, when they came out to the lines to find their husbands' things missing. Would they search the fields for windblown clothes, or blame the faeries? Where once I would have laughed at their superstitions, I now realized the ignorance had been mine. A man who walks with unicorns has little room to cast aspersions on unlikely beliefs.

Of an evening, when we kept walking after dark, looking for a good campsite, we came upon a major crossroads and stood in indecision. Southeast was Landing, which I wanted to see, if for no other reason than its historical value. Northeast lay Halmar-by-the-Sea, Ashe's seaport and fortress. Near Halmar, we might hope to slip in behind Ashe's men and use them as shields for the southward journey toward Jappa. We had seen few soldiers that day, and I was of a mind to risk the southeast road for a while.

As I mused, Nina saw the little girl in the ditch and stamped a foreleg to draw my attention. I scrambled down into the trench beside the road, favoring my bad leg as much as possible, and crouched beside the waif. Something there was of life in her, but not much. I touched her and froze with shock.

"Is she alive?" Nina asked.

I neither moved nor answered. I was not able to do either.

"Are you remembering something?"

It was not a question I welcomed; it drew me back from a vast distance, drew me back into myself so that I could only see with the eyes of the body. "No," I said, and that was a lie, but agreeing would be deceit, too. I looked up at Nina and shrugged helplessly; words do not come readily to me at such moments.

The shadows around Nina shifted as the wind blew her knee-length hair into a cloud of fine black strands. "Will you tell me?" She held the form long enough to ask the question, then shadows covered her again, and she stood on all fours. Patient, waiting, remote.

"I know this child," I said slowly. "From dreams. Not mine. The Archon's. Her name is Pia."

It takes a lot to surprise Nina. While we were separated during my captivity at the Luvar Inn, she seemed to become more comfortable with her nature, and had come into power of her own. I thought I knew the source of that power and the price she had paid for it, but I said nothing, just as I had not spoken of the nightmares that plagued me underground. I had not thought words necessary. She was a faerie creature in her own right, with ways of knowing that surpass mortal wisdom. Yet my words clearly bothered her, and she seemed startled to learn that I had touched the Archon's mind. The look in her eyes was not compassionate. A hardness surfaced there, a look I would call greed if I saw it in anyone else. From Nina, the look simply demanded an explanation, whether for good or ill.

"I am beginning to dream his dreams," I told her. A swirl of shadows answered me; Nina almost, but not quite, shifted to human form. It seemed easier for her now, but still not something she endured without reluctance. Nevertheless, her meaning came through: acquiescence, permission to discuss something difficult.

"He is haunted," I began, then stopped, realizing even as I started that I was indicating a kind of empathy for him. There are no excuses; there can be none. Moral poison has an affinity for weakness, and I dared not show that, lest I become infected, too. "He is not wholly evil, not consumed by it. His sin is not in excess power, but in the smallness of his conscience. I did not know the dreams were real until now. I had thought them only nightmares."

She whickered softly and pointed her head at the girl. It was a question.

"Yes, she is my proof," I answered. "Pia is the first thing I have encountered in the waking world which matches my dreams of the Archon." A decision was required. "I will carry her," I said, and wondered as I said it if I was able. I guessed the girl's age to be between eight and ten; she wouldn't be very heavy, but I only had one working arm.

But Nina knelt on the roadway, forelegs bent in invitation, and I had only to struggle up out of the ditch with Pia, drape her across Nina's back, and my task was done. This was the second time Nina had borne a burden of my choosing, and it was a measure of her love for me that she did not protest.

Later, when all was quiet and we had made camp, I examined the girl carefully. There was nothing to be done for her other than providing warmth and time. Her mind, as far as I could reach, was deeply withdrawn into itself, whether from shock or injury I couldn't determine. There were no obvious wounds, but she would not rouse from her sleep, no matter what I did. I wanted to heal her, or at least ease her pain, but gave up in frustration after several minutes of trying. She was too far inside herself for me to reach. Nina came to me in woman-form, watched until I had finished with the girl, then said, "Tell me about the dreams."

I held out my hand; she took it briefly but refused to hold it. She sat beside me, though, which was comforting.

"It is all out of focus, like looking at something under the water," I began. "But not like that at all. It's also very clear. I think that I am remembering his life, in little snatches and fragments."

"You are linked to him." It was an accusation.

"It is like dreaming about myself, but from a distance, as if I were standing on a hilltop watching. I feel his feelings—" I stopped, shuddered, felt my breath beginning to come quickly. "Not . . . pleasant things." I looked at her, searched her eyes for understanding. "If these dreams are real, then he has done even more terrible things than I knew."

She almost smiled, but it was all coldness. "Thus do I pursue him," she said, echoing my own words.

"For vengeance?" I asked.

"Aye, but he is only the immediate goal. I seek more."

"Will you tell me what wrong he has done you? I know what he has done to humans, to the land. But how could Gaheris harm you?"

She ignored the question, and there was nothing I could say to that. I sat wrapped in thought for a long time, with her close beside me, and, though we did not touch, we were joined more closely than lovers. From inside, from the secret place only I could go, the place I had thought lost forever in Henna's attic prison, I brought forth a little bit of peace, and I spread it over us like a blanket, and we were silent for a long time.

"Tell me about the girl," she said at last.

"Pia. I know her name because the Archon knew it. She was nothing to him, though—the child of a courtier who was dismissed for suggesting peace with Ashe. They fled north, and Gaheris sent assassins after them. I don't know how Pia made it this far. She must have crawled off during the attack."

"You know all this from your dreams? If they were real, and the Archon holds your name, you should have gotten *that*, too."

"I didn't know the dreams were real until I recognized Pia. I thought they were only nightmares, products of my raging fever. It's not as if I could interrogate Gaheris. I saw what he saw, heard his thoughts, felt his emotions. He looked at this girl once and spoke her name. He never thought or spoke of me, except for a vague sense of unease."

"Why is she still unconscious?"

"Because I don't know how to wake her. With time, she may recover by herself. We'll have to wait."

Nina shifted uncomfortably. "You cannot heal her." I wasn't sure if it was a question or a command, but I answered as if it had been a question.

"No. She is too deep inside herself. There's nothing for me to touch. We might leave her at a farmhouse door, I suppose."

"And the Archon himself? What do your dreams tell you of him?"

I had to think about that for a minute. "He fears me," I ventured at last. "He knows I am coming. I am a grey cloud on the horizon; he dreams of me and fears my arrival, but he never calls out my name or even thinks of me clearly as a person. I'm just a nameless threat that troubles him. I'm not even sure he knows *how* I threaten him. But his fear doesn't waver."

There is truth in dreams, twisted sometimes, and distorted always, but truth nonetheless. I often speculate that waking life is the illusion, for while we wake, we delude ourselves that there are answers, solutions to problems, justice in the world. When we sleep, we know better; there are only terrors.

"Why should he fear you?"

It was an honest question, and a valid one. I was no warrior, had no army at my back. The few magics I held were no threat to him; he was mage-born, a sorcerer. I was a cripple, with one game leg, one withered arm, and barely enough strength to walk on my own. And yet, and yet. . . . "I don't know why he thinks I'm dangerous to him. I don't think he has the faintest idea, either. He only knows that I am coming, and he fears the unknown. The only thing I want is my name."

"You are still sure he holds it?"

"Yes, but I cannot pull it from him at a distance." As the words left my mouth, I felt sure; a moment later, I doubted. "He recognizes me," I said. "That may not be the same as knowing my name."

"Then what good, these dreams?"

"I cannot know." At some level, I did know, but it was not something I could express with words. "The more I learn, the more I understand. . . ." I broke off, suddenly uneasy. "It's not like recovering a lost memory," I said at last. "It's like talking to someone who knows you very well, and hearing in your own words little truths about yourself or others that you only knew subconsciously, but once said aloud, cannot be denied or refuted."

"What truths?"

I hesitated. "I know about your power," I said. "The source of it."

She suddenly froze at my side, not even breathing.

"I know about the blood," I said at last, and there was a long moment's silence. I felt the heat rise in my cheeks and ears. She just stared at me. Then she tossed her head and howled. It was an animal's noise, full of pain and denial, and my heart lurched to hear it. Shadows raced from all directions to cover her, and she leaned forward, dropped to all fours, and galloped off.

It was thus that I was undefended when the soldiers came later and found me there.

They were not rough, but not gentle, either. They left Pia, who still lay unconscious beside the fire, from either kindness or simple oversight. Perhaps, in the larger scheme of things, one little child does not even exist for such men. They were humorless, grim, and quietly efficient.

They brought me before Ashe at a makeshift camp. He must have been preparing for a major offensive to join the ranks himself and bring this many men into the field.

They didn't bind me; it was obvious that I was a cripple and posed no personal threat. Yet Ashe had a touch of the second sight —something I had not known until then—and he regarded me with more than the eyes of the body. Like Gaheris, Ashe was mage-born and commanded some sorcery. As I gazed back, he sensed my probe. I caught his curiosity, and his quick flash of fear, rapidly suppressed when he realized that I was aware of his mind.

He was a deep one, was Ashe. His mind moved carefully and relentlessly through the possibilities as he surveyed me, and I sensed he had restraint equal to his authority—a sure sign of a good leader. Yet as they brought me forward into the firelight, their hands digging painfully into my shoulders, I could also feel Ashe's disquiet. He was not one to take chances. His men pulled off my hood, and the firelight showed my face to them; I heard gasps of surprise and dismay as my beardless cheeks and white hair were revealed. But Ashe's soldiers were well-trained. Their hold on me did not waver for an instant.

I did not speak, but I met the prince's eyes with my face composed, expressionless. After that first involuntary exchange of thoughts, both of us guarded our minds. He stood with his hands on his hips for a moment, then stroked his jaw thoughtfully, and moved closer, letting the light reveal his own features. He had straight auburn hair, and his skin was a deep mahogany-red. Captain's Blood, they called it: the outward sign of those claiming lineal descent from the first captain at Landing. In appearance, he could have been the Archon's twin, though his face showed only guarded curiosity.

"You are no elf," he said at last. "Though you have the look of one. A hauflin, perhaps? By what name are you called?"

I did not answer him.

"Your name, sir," he persisted. "On the eve of battle, my kingdom at risk, spies lurking in all directions, I *will* have your name."

"People call me Grey," I said at length.

Something of my internal agony about namelessness must have surfaced in my eyes, for he blinked suddenly and backed off a pace, as though I had swung at him with my fist. I caught his reflexive thought then, for just an instant before he resumed his guard, and I realized for the first time that a good man may contemplate murder as easily as does an evil man. I was unknown, unvouched-for, without a reason to be there, and therefore a threat. One does not become a leader by leaving danger at his back. Whatever else Ashe might be, he was no fool. I knew my life lay in convincing him that I was no threat to him or his cause.

Despair struck through my heart, for I could not explain either my presence or my purpose. How could I satisfy this man's desire for knowledge when I myself could not even remember my name, my youth, my past? Yet before I could gather my thoughts to make the attempt, a dark figure from across the fire stood suddenly and paced forward to meet us. As he walked, soldiers quickly and wordlessly stepped aside, making an aisle. A silence advanced with him, a quietness of spirit. I suddenly felt no desire to speak. When he was only a step or two away, he stopped, threw back his cloak, regarded me. He was pale, white-haired, beardless, taller than most men, dressed in silver armor under his wine-dark cloak, a prince's laurel in his hair. He was full-blooded muria, no hauflin: dispassionate, insular, commanding. I wondered, seeing him, that anyone could have ever mistaken me for an elf.

"Release him," he said quietly, and they freed my arms.

"Qol," said Ashe, complaint and weariness in his voice. "Is he one of yours?"

The muria didn't answer Ashe. His eyes locked on mine and I started to kneel. It was an instinctive motion, struck at some level deeper than consciousness. I didn't realize I had moved until he said, "Don't," and I froze, halfway down.

For just a moment, his eyes held mine. Then everything changed. We were no longer staring at each other through the darkness of a cold mortal night, but walking side by side through the forests of Avermorn, green-dappled sunlight spattering through the golden leaves overhead, drenching us with warmth. A cool wind, insouciant, playful, caressed my neck, lifted my hair. His appearance had changed, too. He was younger now—not as though he had lived fewer years, but as if he had lived endless years without being touched by them. I thought of him as a youth, but his eyes were the ageless eyes of knowledge too full.

We paused in a small clearing with a fountain at its heart. I had been hearing the music of the water for some time without being conscious of it. Now it struck me that this fountain was the goal of our journey. It was a holy place, but the kind of holiness that brings healing rather than dread. I did not feel that I belonged there.

He knelt on the marble rim, filled his sturdy hands with water, and held them to my lips, a living cup.

His face was as still as a lake in summer, only small ripples betraying the thoughts behind his eyes. He was a pixie, a waif, a boy, a woman, an old man; none of these things and all. "Drink," he commanded in a complex harmony of all those voices, and I was suddenly powerless to disobey. The water was strong, heady like wine, almost stronger than I could endure. Yet drinking it made me strong enough, for it gave the very thing it demanded, and one who had drunk of it would always thereafter have something he could point to in his memory when he searched for the meaning of the word "pure."

"Remember this place," he told me, "when you are assailed." His voice whistled up and down the scale, and it seemed that hundreds or thousands of muria were speaking through his mouth simultaneously. My head ached from the intensity of his gaze. "Do not be deceived," he continued. "Though this is a vision, you are more awake now than you have ever been. You have seen the heart of Avermorn, and drunk of its life."

"You are not telling me anything," I protested.

He looked at me kindly, even compassionately. "I am telling you what you need to know for now. Remember this place. Both hope and despair are laid up for you beyond your imagining. When the time comes, choose hope."

I could not help myself. I touched him, and felt the swell and ebb of his blood and spirit like a living current. My bones ached and my fingers fluttered—mad butterflies, they—and there was a tearing in my soul, for I finally saw something in him which made me catch my breath in disbelief: Recognition. He knew me! But I could not probe him, could not look beyond the surface. It was almost as if Qol lacked underlying thoughts, but as soon as I conceived the notion, I discarded it as insufficient. He offered a purity of communication that was daunting in its intensity, frightening in its depth. All of him was involved in the current moment, and it was too much for a mortal to accept. Thus, while he offered all, I could take nothing.

My lips moved themselves in question. "Who. . . ?"

"We should not have met," he said at last, "at least not yet. You are not ready." He looked away. With the breaking of eye contact, I felt the deep, wordless bond between us snap. In the next moment, he and I stood in the mortal night again, his arms helping me rise, and I knew that no time had passed for the others. Even Ashe, the mage-born prince, could have no inkling of what had transpired.

"Let him go," Qol told Ashe. His easy tone assumed obedience. "He is nothing to you, not part of your efforts. He serves a different purpose."

Ashe licked his lips, looked back and forth between us for a moment as if he were about to ask. I wondered if he were mage enough to have caught at the fringes of my experience, but discarded the notion. What Qol and I had shared was private. Ashe's indecision was entirely human. "But Qol—" he began.

Qol glanced sharply at Ashe. "He can neither hinder you nor help you. Heed my advice, or lose your advisor. Let him go."

Ashe pondered the threat for a moment, then abruptly nodded. With a curt gesture, he dismissed me, and the soldiers half-carried, half-dragged me to the edge of camp, then tumbled me into a ditch where, mercifully, darkness hid my trembling. As I lay gathering my breath, one of the soldiers came back and tossed a bag at me. I caught it with my good hand.

"A gift from the prince," the soldier said and then left me in the dirt.

I crawled back to my own fire, made sure Pia was all right, and then examined the bag. Inside I found fresh bread, cured meats, and a flask of wine. I ate and drank my fill, then slept. My dreams were all of Avermorn—its purity, my insufficiency.

In the morning, Pia awoke. She saw me and screamed, and tried to crawl away. I grabbed her and held her, but she bit and clawed at me. Nothing I could do would reassure her. The wounds in her mind went very deep, and I saw now what I should have seen the night before: she was wounded in more than the mind; she was bleeding inside, and tearing herself open further by struggling against me. In the end, I spoke a word of power and made her sleep again. Weariness settled around my heart. While she slept, I entered her mind the way a rat scuttles through the slats in an old barn. The memories now lay unfolded before me.

The Archon's soldiers had come upon her party without warning as they camped beside the road. The men, including her father, had been slain immediately. For the women, however, the soldiers had had other plans. The screams echoed in our minds as I stood beside Pia while she relived, over and over, her mother's rape and beheading. But there was worse yet to come, for soon enough it was Pia's turn. She was spared rape, but little else. The soldiers threw her to the ground and took turns kicking her, losing interest only after she stopped moving.

The memories dissolved then into a confusion of terror and pain. There was a tearing, a ripping, a sudden gush of blood and fire. The laughter of the soldiers was like a sadistic descant in the background. They were like their master, and that was the sign of the Archon, that his men knew neither restraint nor pity.

Pia awoke then, despite my best efforts, and she wept. She did not try to escape me this time, but clung to my arms, sobbing. I think that she believed I was her father in those last moments, for she called out to him amidst her tears, and then the loss of blood took her finally, and she was a limp weight in my arms. I closed her eyes with my fingertips, scraped a shallow grave as best I could with just one arm, and laid the small body in the ground. I had no way to cover her save with branches. I felt I should say something, but no words came to me, and I stood in silence for a long time.

"Which way now?" Nina asked from behind me.

I did not look up from Pia's grave. "How long have you been here?"

"All night. I was never more than a breath away."

"Why didn't you try to stop the soldiers last night?"

"You were in no danger from Ashe."

I whirled, suddenly furious. "How can you know that? How can you be so sure?"

The color drained from my face when I saw her. She glimmered with power and shame, but I think that only I could have seen the contempt she had for herself. To other eyes, she was an eidolon of beauty, an iconic form cloaked in flesh. But she had blooded again during the night, to pay the price of her power, and I perceived her inner torture.

She knew that I saw and could not bear my gaze, could not bear that I knew. She bent her head to look away from me.

"How could you know I would be safe?" I demanded, thrusting away her pain for the moment.

"Because the elf was there."

"Then why didn't you come with me?"

"I prepared myself to rescue you, but then I sensed the elf," she whispered. "You didn't need me, and I didn't want *him* to see me."

"Why not?"

She shook her head, refusing to answer. "Which way now?" she asked again, her voice still the barest whisper.

"South, toward Landing," I said, and she nodded, melted, misted, reformed on all fours. I was weary, crippled, ill-used and heartbroken, but there was no question of our staying where we were. I looked a wordless request and did not have to ask. Something fundamental had changed in our relationship; she was not my servant, never that, but she had abrogated the right to hold herself aloof, given up playing at purity, finally acknowledged that I both fathomed her and accepted her. Her shame I could not remove; angst was now her right. My recognition of her vulnerability did not diminish her; it merely removed the cloak, the barrier. It did not lessen her pride, although perhaps it informed it, for she could set conceit aside now. And so, in response to my look, she knelt before me, lowered her noble head in invitation, and I slid across her back without a word.

South would lead us along the main road. Before he blocked me, I had gleaned from Ashe's mind the location of the troops in this area, both his own and his brother's, and I knew, therefore, that this road would be safe for a time. We must perforce pass through several towns along the way. I would have preferred traveling at night through the fields, as we had done so often, but nothing could induce me to stay so near Pia's grave any longer than necessary. I wanted to put distance behind us.

It was early enough in the morning that we passed like ghosts through the first town. Perhaps they sensed us, perhaps not; perhaps they dreamed of us. We were the substance of dreams, and, if we were not also nightmares, it was only in comparison to the ones we fought.

At the second town, we were not so fortunate. People were up and about, with the wary look and hostility toward strangers that told me they had already seen fighting. But we were no ordinary strangers. I saw the pinched, suspicious expressions turn to wonder and joy as they realized Nina's nature.

Such is the impression that Nina makes when her power is uncloaked that the villagers didn't even notice me at first. She pranced down the street, tail high, hooves light and nimble, looking neither right nor left, spiraled horn like a beacon before her. I heard the murmurs of awe: "A unicorn! Look, do you see? A unicorn!"

A small boy ran out from under his mother's arm, reached up one hand, then stopped, confused by conflicting impulses. I think humans know, somehow, in their bones rather than their brains, that unicorns are for looking at, not for touching. He drew back his hand and stood frozen as Nina passed him. Although he did not touch the faerie creature, Nina must have touched him at a deep and unnamed place within his soul. I saw the change come over him, as though he had taken a breath of some far country's air that was sweet beyond bearing, and he became drunk with her beauty. A poet was born in that moment. An ordinary child touched by the numinous is ordinary no longer, save he chooses to forget. Looking at him in that moment, I did not think he would soon forget. And that was the sign of Nina, that she gave a gift and knew it not, just by existing.

I began to hope that her glamour would carry me unmarked through the entire town, but there was a growing silence as they became aware of me. The adults knew from legend and tradition what the children only felt: No one should ride a unicorn. My position on her back was an offense; it reduced her rather than enlarging me. I did not appear to them as some powerful or mythic figure because of my place on Nina's back; rather, I was an interloper in their magic, perhaps the only magic their town would ever know, and I was an affront to their sense of propriety.

If my words had had any power, I would have used them. But I was weak and effectless, nameless among the named. Their surety frightened me more than their violence: I huddled on Nina's back, a sad lump of dirty rags, and begged her to hurry.

Hands reached to pull me down; voices shouted with anger. Nina reared and drove them off; then we were galloping smoothly, quickly, into the south, and the town was a memory behind us.

At length she slowed, stopped, and I slid gingerly to the ground, tried my legs, found them able to bear me once more. I draped my good arm around Nina's neck, and we walked side by side. The noon sun burned overhead, and the god-winds gusted fretfully around my heart.

I looked up into the sky and wondered why the gods, if they exist, are always silent. Is it that they do not speak, or that I do not know how to hear them?

Who can blame me for cursing to myself as I shouldered the

god-winds? It was the wind that tricked tears from my eyes, not rage or sorrow, for they were cold tears, and they might have belonged to someone else for all I felt them.

And it was surely a trick of the wind that I could still hear Pia's cry long after we left that place behind.

6. MARAN

LADY MARAN CAME upon us in the late afternoon as we rested by the road. The point of her fencing sword touched the side of my neck before either of us knew she was there.

"Your names," she demanded. At her nod, I rose, careful to make no sudden moves. She backed off a pace and circled around to the front of us.

"Call me Grey," I told her. "And this is Nina."

The lady lifted an eyebrow and looked at my companion. "She is not what she appears to be."

"No."

"She wears human form. What manner of creature is she underneath?"

Nina stood still, arms folded across her breasts, so I answered for her. "She is Nina." *Leave it at that*, I pleaded silently.

"Why is she naked?"

"It is the way of things."

"A bit unusual, nonetheless." The lady paused to contemplate me. She was middle-aged, I guessed, but carried her years well. Her skin looked like dark wild honey, well worn but still smooth. Her hair was a pale sandy brown, framing a heart-shaped face with a straight nose, wide lips, and bright green eyes that showed both caution and intelligence. She took life seriously, this one, and death easily. *True hauflin?* I wondered. *Is this what a half-elf looks like?* Her coloration and confidence supported the notion. And, with sudden curiosity, I suspected that her eyes had looked upon both joy and sorrow surpassing my own. She was not one to underestimate. Those eyes looked at me now, measuring, gauging, probing. Her sword arm did not waver.

"Your name is not Grey," she said at length.

"I didn't say it was." I paused, then added, "You see deeply, my lady."

One hand raised, fluttered briefly, a vague gesture of dismissal. The other remained rock-steady. "I see what I see, and I usually say it, which gets me in more trouble than not."

"What do you see?"

She glanced sharply at me, measuring, and then looked away again, focusing on Nina. "Does she talk?"

"When she wants to. When she has something to say."

"Fascinating."

I risked a small motion; instantly her attention was on me again—sharp, penetrating.

"Your blade is also fascinating, my lady. Especially from this vantage."

She blinked, dropped the point of her épée from my throat and slid it home through a small leather loop at her waist. "Damned if I know why, but I don't think you're a threat. I am the Lady Maran. Will you accompany me?"

"Where are you going?"

She gestured over her shoulder with her chin. I heard a tiny sound, like distant bells chiming. "Just behind that hill. I have a place there where we can talk."

"We have things to do," said Nina suddenly.

Maran smiled at her. "I'm sure you do, but my invitation was not really a request."

"You surprised us before," Nina said in her softest, most dangerous tone, "and you got your toy sword at his throat. That threat no longer holds. What if I killed you now?"

The lady laughed, a surprisingly gentle and beautiful sound. It started low in her chest and bubbled up through her lips, honest humor, not bravado. I heard the faint ringing sound again and noticed that Maran wore tiny earrings, worked of silver, that tinkled when she moved her head sharply. "I am in no danger from you. And you should not call the épée a toy sword."

Shadows raced to cover Nina's form, mingling with her knee-length hair. She blurred, shifted, stood on all fours with her head lowered, the tip of her long, dangerous horn pointed at the lady's heart.

"Wait!" I cried, but Nina danced forward. The lady stood calmly before Nina's charge, one hand upraised. Nina skidded to a halt, the point of her horn not quite touching Maran's palm.

"Well, will you have my blood?" Maran asked.

Nina made no answer, but trembled where she stood. A low, soft sound, like a moan, came from somewhere deep within her. I watched, transfixed by wonder. No one should have the power to dominate Nina so.

"I thought not," said the lady. She pushed forward with her palm and Nina collapsed, shifting form as she fell, so that a moment later the lady stood with her palm against Nina's forehead, and Nina knelt at the lady's feet.

"Nina?" I said. "Nina?"

The lady looked at me, smiling. "Come now. My house is just beyond that hill."

She turned and walked away, and Nina, again on all four feet, trotted beside her, nudging her elbow with her nose. Nina whickered from time to time, and the lady patted her occasionally as they walked.

What could I do but follow?

"Who are you?" I asked as we topped the hill and looked down on the small, hidden dale behind it. The valley was green, thick with life, unlike the dusty road behind us. A spring gurgled from the side of the hill and fed a small pond. A stone manor house stood beside the water, the faint curl of smoke rising from a chimney. Several sheep, a goat, and a small herd of horses grazed contentedly on the lush grass. I noted several outbuildings scattered throughout the valley and realized this was a small fiefdom. How was she protected? The horses alone spoke of great wealth, but I saw no guards, no defenses, not even ranch hands.

She tossed her head and smiled at me with the corner of her eye. The little clappers in her earrings chimed. "I told you. I am the Lady Maran."

"That's not what I meant. Why are you—" I gestured at the valley— "here, with no fortifications? Do you not fear molestation by travelers, bandits? And you are a lady, yet you walk alone beside the road dressed in hunting gear, wearing a fencing sword, and attacking harmless strangers. I do not understand."

She touched her leather leggings. "I wear other clothing on other occasions. I have no fortifications because this place is not easy to find unless I am with you. And I am not completely powerless."

I looked at her then with mind and heart, and saw that she was not lying. I did not trust her, not yet, not completely, for I could not see below the surface of her thoughts. She was like a clear glass filled with a smoky grey liquid, constantly shifting patterns. I could not read her at all—not without touching her, and for some reason I did not want to do that.

She slapped Nina's flank as if Nina were a horse, and I wasn't sure which surprised me more—that the lady would dare, or that

Nina would accept it. "Go on," Maran said, chuckling, and Nina picked her way delicately down the slope before us.

"Come," Maran told me. She led the way down a narrow path into the valley. I limped after her, and the moisture-rich valley air rose around us like a curtain. I did not need to look back to know that the path was disappearing behind us. I felt the enchantment of the lady's valley surround me, and it smelled of roses, honeysuckle, and sensuality.

"What is your power over Nina?" I inquired politely.

She laughed. "Magic."

"I know something of that art, my lady."

"And you don't see it. Does that concern you?"

"On the contrary. I see it all around us, but none such as would affect Nina. She is faerie. The glamour you have laid on this place would not beguile her."

Maran loosened the coif binding her hair and let it spill down her back. "This is my world, Grey. There are things you don't understand here. Don't try."

I was surprised to see the difference in the lady now that her hair was free. She was no younger than I had estimated, but she was more beautiful than I had first realized. That beauty, and her easy bearing as she walked, juxtaposed with the warning of her words, made me feel uneasy. I watched Nina picking her way ahead of us like an obedient pack animal, and my discomfort grew more profound. There was a power here, one I didn't understand, and while I had no presentiment of danger, I did not feel safe.

"I am walking into a trap," I said as the patterns clicked into place.

"That's an odd way of looking at it."

"I'm an odd man. What do you mean to do with me?"

She winked at me over her shoulder, and I caught the quick gleam of her small, even teeth as she laughed. Again, the bells on her earlobes jingled. "Bathe you and feed you."

"To. . . ?"

I matched her laughter with my own, but did not release her gaze until she answered.

"I am lonely, Grey. I saw you passing on the road and was intrigued. A unicorn and a man in rags traveling toward the Archon's citadel, the unicorn sometimes wearing the guise of a woman, the man looking to be albino, but not. Such things do not happen every day. I thought you might be entertaining."

"That's a lie," I pointed out.

"Well, yes, it is. But it will have to do for now."

We walked in silence for a few more minutes. Nina was far ahead of us now, almost to the floor of the valley. I could sense the enchantment settling more deeply around me, and I wondered idly if I would be able to escape. I didn't really care; the enchantment was already too strong. The only unsettling feeling to survive was that I no longer found the experience disquieting. I breathed deeply and felt a sense of peace, of security.

My game leg betrayed me on a loose rock a moment later, and I stumbled to my knees. Maran knelt beside me, touched my shin and withered arm in curiosity, then helped me back to my feet. Her eyes were pensive. "Does she know?" she asked.

"Who? Know what?"

Her gaze slid from me to Nina and back. More patterns clicked into place, and I realized how much of my secret thought she had read with that one touch. I fought down a sense of awe. What she had done was no more remarkable than similar things I had done, but always before I was the percipient one—the reader, not the one being read. I wondered how much more she had seen.

"Does she know?" Maran asked again.

"More than I do," I admitted warily. "She won't tell me—not completely—why she shares my road. We have similar objectives, but I suspect we have different ultimate goals."

"That's all very well, but I was asking if she knew of your power."

"I don't know much about it myself. Magic doesn't seem to follow the same rules as science. I'm figuring things out as I go."

"Don't evade the question. I'm talking about your power over *her*."

"She is my companion, if that's what you mean," I said stiffly. "It's not something we talk about much."

"Interesting. It will have to come out someday, you know. A devil's bargain like that—"

"—is my own business," I said firmly.

"As you like. Are you ready to go on now? It will be dark soon."

I nodded as if I had a choice.

Her manor house was more than a cottage, less than a palace, but had elements of each. It was small and comfortable, yet well furnished, with exquisite taste. A majordomo waited for us politely, and I smelled food being prepared. Nina, shifted now to woman form, stood quietly inside the entrance hall, looking out of place. I realized suddenly that I had never seen her indoors before, unless I counted the faerie mound or Henna's attic. I wondered if that was coincidence, or something to do with her nature.

The majordomo was unruffled by her nakedness. He snapped his fingers and a maid appeared from the other room. The maid took one look at Nina, clucked her tongue in sympathy, and scurried off. In moments, she was back with a large woolen gown, which she wrapped around Nina's shoulders.

"Dinner in an hour, Hasq," Maran said. The majordomo nodded. "Show our guests the hospitality of the house. The man is the Lord Grey. He will join me for dinner. The woman is the Lady Nina. The lady will no doubt be more comfortable in the stable."

"In the stable, ma'am?"

"See to it, Hasq. Give her plenty of fresh hay."

"Yes, ma'am. Hay. In the stable. Of course." The majordomo nodded to the maid, who led Nina off toward the rear of the house. "This way, sir," he said to me. I thought of telling him that Nina required no hay, but I kept my peace. How could Maran not know?

"You'll be wanting fresh clothes, and a chance to bathe," said Hasq. "I'll have water drawn immediately." He gestured, and I followed him through hallways and rooms paneled in dark wood to a small bathhouse, where another servant prepared a tub and helped me undress. I removed the grime while Hasq went to find clothing for me. The serving woman didn't touch me, but insisted that I wash again, giving me a stronger soap to use. When I had finished, she dashed me with some woody-scented powder, and offered a large towel. I felt refreshed, as if I had bathed my soul as well as my body. As my hair dried, it fluffed out into an unruly cloud of curls, obscuring my sight. Hasq returned, his arms full of clothing, but stopped dead when he saw me.

"Shall I call the barber, Lord Grey?" he asked diffidently.

To my knowledge, my hair had never been cut. It had been long when Brawley first found me, and had only grown longer since. Normally, tucking it behind my ears and under my collar at the back was enough to keep it controlled, but now, cleaner than it had ever been, it floated away as quickly as I patted it down. Still, I was used to having it long, and didn't want it cut. Hasq read my expression and signaled to the serving woman. She sat me on a stool and began the elaborate process of brushing and braiding my hair. Hasq waited patiently until she had finished, then dismissed her.

I felt my head with my good hand, finding the tight braids oddly comforting to the touch, as if some wild beast had been tamed. The woman had done an artful job, leaving the main mass arranged so it fell halfway down my back, held in place by its own weight.

"Much better, sir," said Hasq. He offered me the clothing at last. "These may not fit exactly, sir, but I can have measurements taken tonight, and new garments ready by morning."

I dressed quickly, marveling at the soft fabrics and rich embroidery. Hasq might not have been satisfied, but I was. The colors—soft grey and tan—suited me. Even the leather boots seemed exactly the right size. The cloak fastened at my neck with a jeweled broach.

"Thank you," I said and clapped his shoulder. The instant I touched him, my feeling of security evaporated. Under my fingers I sensed old bones, leaves, mold, clods of dirt. "You're not human," I said.

"Ah, no, sir, not quite."

"You're a construct, a golem."

"Homunculus, sir. Does that displease you?"

"Does Lady Maran know?"

"I should hope so, sir. She made me."

"I see."

"Will you join the lady for dinner now, sir?"

"First I must see to Nina."

"By all means, sir. This way, please."

He led me through the house again, this time taking me through a drawing room and into a library containing more books than I had ever seen. I stopped to look at a few, but couldn't read them. I put them back and tried several more. Finally, I found one in the common tongue of Leonais, the only language I knew. The book was a beautifully bound and illustrated novel, some kind of romantic mystery story. I replaced it on the shelf thoughtfully. Maran's house was as intriguing as Maran herself; without doubt one reflected the other. Hasq waited patiently until I satisfied my curiosity, and then led me out a rear entrance. The afternoon had waned while I bathed, and the sky burned a deep purple-red, fading to black while I stood for several minutes, gathering my thoughts. Hasq again waited without comment, guiding me on when I nodded readiness. Only two hundred paces across the courtyard, he showed me into a comfortable, warm stable, lit by torches anchored to the walls. Several of the horses were inside, one being groomed by a man who only nodded us and continued his work. As I expected, Nina was not inside. I closed my eyes and listened to the god-winds, heard them whisper from behind me, off in the dark to the left.

"I can find my own way back, Hasq."

The majordomo bowed and left me there. I waited until he was gone, then limped into the night. "Nina?" I called softly.

She came to me then, all warm and eager, and nuzzled my good hand. I rested my palm on the wide space between her eyes and said, "Will you come into the house with me?"

I felt her form begin to fray, then gather back together, as if she could not decide. *No,* she told me, not using words, but in that way the two of us can communicate sometimes, with a look, or gesture, or twitch of muscle.

"Then shall I stay with you?" I asked gently.

Her reaction this time was more direct. She whinnied, pushed against my chest with her nose, and shoved me toward the house. Then she whirled and was gone. The thick grass muffled the sound of her hooves. I stood looking after her into the gloom for several minutes, listening to my heart beat in rhythm to the emerging stars, then shrugged and made my way back into the house.

Lady Maran was waiting for me in the dining hall, torches, candles, and fireplace lit. She had changed into a long blue gown, swept back at the shoulders, laced at the bodice. Her hair, glimmering softly in the firelight, was bound loosely, left to drape

over one shoulder. She inclined her head regally and gestured for
me to sit.

Hasq, the maid, and another servant stood quietly alongside
the walls, moving only to fill our wineglasses or remove our plates.
A low window across from the fireplace was open to the night,
and the fresh scent of the valley breathed gently upon us as we ate.

I do not recall what we were served or what small talk we made
at first. But as we ate, chatted, and became more comfortable with
one another, I realized that once again I was being managed by
powers I didn't understand. It irked me, all the more so because I
was enjoying myself and was more relaxed than I could ever
remember feeling before. I fought that sense of contentment as if
it were an enemy.

"What troubles, you, Grey?" she inquired when a silence
developed between us. The meal was done; only the wine bottle
and glasses remained on the table.

"I am tired of being moved, controlled, by everyone else," I
told her. "Even now, you are manipulating me. I do not make my
own decisions often enough. Things happen, and I react to them."

"Your passivity is a function of circumstance," she replied, as if
she'd been waiting for precisely that lament from me. "You were
made to make certain kinds of decisions, to exercise power in
certain domains. Those things haven't come up yet, or, if they
have, you haven't recognized them. The comings and goings of
humans do not affect you. Your heroism hasn't been tested yet."

"Heroism? I am a pawn, a wisp, blown by the god-winds."

"I think not," she said simply. Her smile was warm, reassuring,
vaguely possessive.

"I am powerless," I protested, but even as the words left my
mouth, I knew them for false modesty. I tried to explain. "You talk
of power as if it's a weapon I can swing. I'm more often the sword
than the soldier. I admit to wielding small magics, some of which I
can control, some that come upon me whether I will or no. But I

am far from being a hero. In the greater game, I am a victim, like everyone else."

"You?" She laughed at my assertion. "Restraint is a kind of power, too, Grey. A greater one than is often recognized. Your power is like mine. We are very much alike."

A look of doubt must have crossed my face, for she suddenly cocked her head to one side. "You think we are not alike at all," she said, "but I will prove you wrong. You say you seek power over your fate, but I claim you already have it. Watch."

She turned to Hasq. "Climb into the fire," she told him calmly. "And take the others with you."

Hasq nodded, and the three servants turned toward the fireplace, removed the waist-high grate.

"Wait!" I demanded. "What insanity is this?"

"Not insanity—power. Watch!"

Without a word, Hasq picked up the little maid, held her lengthwise, and laid her across the logs. She gave a little gasp, but held still as the flames curled around her. I shoved back my chair in horror, stood for a moment rooted in shock. Hasq picked up the other woman and laid her across the maid. Then, as I sprang across the room to stop him, he calmly climbed into the fireplace himself, lay down, folded his arms across his chest, and gave himself to the flames.

The fireplace roared like a blacksmith's furnace, and the three of them lay quietly, stacked like cordwood, their clothes burning away, their skin crisping and turning black. Still they were silent. The stench was overpowering.

"It is too late," Maran said from behind me.

I scrambled to enter the servants' minds, to command them to save themselves. But I only sensed dirt, twigs, mold, straw, and something that seemed to flutter deep inside. There was nothing here for me to command, and the flames grew higher by the second.

The heat forced me to turn my head. I searched the room wildly for a tool I could use. Finally, I saw a poker leaning against the wall, and, shielding my face with the shoulder of my cloak, forced open the mouths of the burning servants. From each of their throats came a blue butterfly. They fluttered weakly up from the heat and perched in a row on my forearm. I carried them gently to the open window and the clean, fresh air. "Be free," I told them, and released them into the night.

I looked back at the fire, saw the clumps of dirt, muddy straw and string where the servants' bodies had been, and watched while the last traces of them were consumed.

I turned back to the table, reseated myself, and poured another glass of wine. Maran watched me speculatively, and for some reason I did not want to let her know how shaken I was.

"You knew, of course, that they were homunculi and could feel no pain," she said. "Yet in a moment of crisis, you acted to save them anyway. Do you see what I mean about power now?"

"Your lesson escapes me."

"Power is a function of self. What did you feel as you were rescuing them?"

"At first, horror. Then sadness."

"Their bodies were nothing. I can make them anew. If I feel sadness—" her lips quirked— "it is because there is now no one to wash the dishes. But the servants themselves, their spirits, were never at risk. You are a healer; that is your function. I knew that you would try to save them."

"How is that power? And how is it like yours?"

She waved her hand. "I am a maker of things. Deep within me I can see a thing before it exists and shape its coming. Deep within yourself, you can see the twistings and turnings a thing has taken, how it has departed from what it was made to be, and bring it back to itself. We see the same things—I from before, you from after. And we each shape the world around us according to our inner rectitude."

A thought came to me then, and I was surprised that it had taken so long to surface. I swirled the wine slowly in my glass before taking a sip. "What you say may be true," I told her. "But I am still intrigued by your power over Nina. How do you do it?"

"If I told you, Grey, you wouldn't believe me."

"How do you know?"

"Because you already know the answer and won't admit it. This knowledge is something you must find for yourself. My words will not convince you."

"Words would help. Are you trying to confuse me?"

"What is your own power over her?" asked Maran.

I was surprised by the tangential slash of the question. I started to protest, to say, "I have no power over her," but then I realized that it was just as inconceivable that Nina should travel with me, let me ride her back, as it was that she should do this lady's bidding so docilely. My mind turned over on itself, shocked to a sudden higher awareness.

"She loves me," I said, amazed that I hadn't realized it before now.

Maran nodded, lifted her glass in a mock toast. "That is one aspect, Grey. She would do anything for you, for what she consideres to be your good, although you may not always agree with her judgment." She took a sip, completing the toast. "Now answer your own question."

Maran's power over Nina could not be the same as mine, but it had to be related. Those things that are so obvious to others are often the most inscrutable to ourselves. Was I really surprised to know that Nina loved me? No, I had known that. Then why the feeling of elation, as if I had discovered some long-hidden truth? Was I so callous, so prideful, that I found pleasure in this additional bit of control over those around me? Was she but another tool to my hand? I retreated into that place within me, seeking the truth of the matter. As I let myself sink down, I let the surface thoughts slough away, until only knowledge and understanding remained. I rested in the timeless awareness of my inner being, and something else I had long known was suddenly obvious.

"I love her, too," I said, coming back to the world as if breasting a tide.

Maran lifted her glass again. "Just so. That is the second half of the bond between you. But 'love' is a slippery word. What kind of love do you share with her? Honor, devotion, friendship, companionship, romance, sex?"

I had to laugh. "Do you know, Lady Maran, how unicorns make love? It would tear a man in two." It was sheer bluff on my part, for I had no idea how unicorns reproduced.

But Maran saw through me and was not distracted. "She is also a woman at times."

I nodded to myself, thinking I suddenly understood Maran's point. "She is always . . . Nina. Her form may change, but her essence does not. The kind of love we share is based on respect, not cuddling in the dark. You needn't be jealous."

"No, I have no need of that." Her tone was self-assured, nearly impish.

She was smiling, and I was abruptly infuriated. "Why do you grin like that? Don't you believe me?"

She did not lose her smile, but her eyes fastened onto mine, and she rose from her chair, came around the table, sat beside me. "Grey, you have not yet answered your question."

True, I had not. What did my love for Nina, or hers for me, have to do with Maran's strange control over her? "I am tired of riddles," I said at last.

"As you will. I showed her a thing."

"What? Do you mean a vision?"

"I thought you were tired of riddles," she said, chuckling, teasing.

I stood up, grabbed her forearm with my good hand, drew her to her feet. "Tell me. What vision did you show her?"

She seemed unperturbed by my grasp. She leaned forward, her head only inches from mine, and I smelled the perfume of her hair. "I showed her *this*," she said and leaned up to kiss me, her mouth hungry on mine. My anger dissipated, my head whirled, and I was suddenly more confused than ever. I broke the embrace, thrust her away from me, and stood panting like a trapped animal. "*That. . . ?* That is not what I seek."

Maran reseated herself demurely, gave me time to recover my breath. I sat down, poured myself another glass of wine, and, after a moment's thought, poured for her, too. We sipped in a silence broken only by the crackling of the fire behind us.

When she saw that I had myself under control again, she continued the conversation as though there had been no pause. "Tell me then, Grey," she asked pensively, "what you truly seek."

"A name for myself."

"Are you a simple adventurer, then?" Her tone chided me.

"Not by choice. I seek the Archon."

"Why do you go against him?"

"I feel my name is there."

"Not for justice, or for revenge, or because he deserves to be overthrown? You walk the land like a ghost, half-crippled, accompanied by a black unicorn, setting yourself against the most powerful mage alive, meddling in things you don't understand— all because you're looking for your *name?* Nothing else?"

"What else is there? A man's name is not just a label, it is his focus. All that I do or think, I must measure against who I am. And I am a nothing now, just a thing without a name. I have no past, no childhood. It is as if I sprang full grown from the air."

"What has your name to do with that? Choose one for

yourself. End this charade. A name is just a word, a sound, something to be called. The name does not change the thing. Is it the identity you seek, or the word?"

"They are the same."

"Grey. . . ." She paused, as if searching for words, her green eyes flicking rapidly back and forth, studying me. Then, with a tone of incredulity, she asked, "Do you not know that you are a made thing?"

"By the gods we are each made," I said reflexively.

"No, that's not what I meant. You were not born. No womb held you. You have no memories because you are not old enough to have them. You were made, constructed, put together for a purpose, the way a carpenter shapes a house, or the way I shaped Hasq."

Something cold struck me in the pit of my stomach; my vision narrowed until the only thing I could see was Maran's face. From a far distance, I heard my own voice. "What. . . ? What do you mean? What are you saying?"

She leaned forward, put her hands on my cheeks, cradled me there. "Did you really not know? Poor Grey. I thought you would have guessed by now."

"I am . . . real. I am alive."

She looked surprised. "Of course you are! Those from Avermorn are good craftsmen. The muria are cold, but their hands are steady and their vision pure. When they turned their minds to the making of you, they made you as best they could, and that is no small thing."

"How. . . ? How do you know this?"

She smiled. "Because I am like you, one of the children of twilight. Neither human nor hauflin nor muria, but something in between, made for a purpose."

"I am not like Hasq; neither are you."

Her hands caressed my cheeks and temples, fingertips drawing slow spirals. "No," she said. "Not like Hasq. Qol is not so kind. Where I give the semblance of life, he gives the real thing. Which burden is harder to bear, do you think? And do you have any doubt which burden is yours?"

"How do you know Qol? Who *are* you?"

"Ask Qol, should you ever meet him. He might even answer, though I doubt it. Nevertheless, I recognize his tool marks on your soul. They match my own."

The fragrance of the valley permeated the room, honeysuckle and roses, and I realized all at once that it was she who gave the valley its enchantment. The life it had was hers, imbued by her long presence in this place. I struggled with dizziness, fought to keep my head clear. "You are lying," I accused softly, but my words had no force.

She shook her head slowly. "Do you know why humans hate the elves?" When I said nothing, she went on: "For the same reason they hate mirrors. Neither can lie."

How nauseatingly simple, how trite. I tried to rally, to shake off her enchantment, but her hand was on my cheek, and I nuzzled it. "You," I said, kissing her palm, "do not have that limitation."

Her hand moved from my face to my neck, and she drew me close. I did not resist this time, and as our lips came together, I put my good arm around her and we stood, locked in an embrace, swaying back and forth gently as if the god-winds swirled in that room. Her earrings tinkled softly, like the far-off laughter of children playing, and the opacity of her mind suddenly cleared. I saw clean desire written there, a desire that I matched with my own. I had a sudden need to prove that I was alive, that I was real.

"This way," she said simply, and showed me to her bedroom.

My gimp leg was awkward between us, and my left arm hung from my shoulder like a dead stick, but none of that mattered. I ran my fingers through her hair, stroked her face, kissed her throat.

"Wait," she said, and pulled away from me for a moment. She loosened the ties at her breast, slid back the shoulder straps, and stepped out of her dress. She was naked underneath, wearing only her earrings, and her nipples were crinkled with excitement. My gaze wandered down to the dark triangle of hair between her legs, and I felt the stirrings of my manhood. I stood still, breathing heavily, just looking at her for a moment, memorizing every feature. She came to me then and undressed me as if I were a child, but slowly, teasingly. Then she took my hand and led me to her bed.

Always before, no matter what I did or saw, I was apart from myself, off in a corner, watching, evaluating, thinking about what I was feeling rather than feeling it. And always before, there was a private place in my mind where only I could go. But that night with Maran, I found I could not retreat, did not want to. There was no room in either of us for past or future; the now consumed us, and we consumed it. There was no thought of hers I did not know, no experience hidden from me. I took her mind as easily, and with as much pleasure, as I took her body. And no matter where I looked within myself, there she was already, drinking as deeply of my soul as I drank of hers. I nuzzled her breasts like a hungry babe, mounted her like a man, and made the bells in her earrings peal until dawn.

After, though I was tired, there was no sleep in me. I listened to the birds stirring and marveled again at the full summer Maran maintained in this valley. Outside, I knew it was still only spring. Was it ever winter here? Did she allow autumn? I put my hand flat on her stomach and regarded her in her sleep. Her eyes were heavy-lidded, and her face had a full, sated look.

I had a waking dream then, the kind that humans call prescient without understanding what that means. There are things we can change about the future and things we cannot. Absolute knowledge is deadly; it paralyzes the mind, freezes the soul. The future is like the present: There are things that are true whether we will them or not, and some things, like love, charity, honor, that are true only if we believe in them.

What did I believe in?

Not yet myself, no, but perhaps in what I could make of me. And I looked at Maran again, thinking of her words about making and made things, and I perceived not the toys like Hasq, but the real thing we had made.

Out of blood and pain and long travail, I saw her raise a boy child in triumph from the darkness between her legs, and bring him forth naked into the sun. Thus do we refute our mortality, by the creation of new life. The power to destroy a thing is a cheat, a chicane, like the darkness itself. The power to create is truth.

Between us that night, we had made a child.

I caught many glimpses of him, from his birth through his early childhood. Glimpses, I say, for they came and went—a moment here, a scene there, as the fickle second sight, tattered like rags in the wind, flapped across my inner eyes. A chubby hand clutching a toy. A young mind discovering the joy of learning, of knowledge. A pair of narrow feet dancing through the grass, laughter trailing back behind like smoke. A woman chasing him, calling, "Aiden! Aiden!" A rose-blushed cheek angled against the wind, eyes like sentinels. Soft breath in untroubled sleep. All ages and none; growing and grown, revealed in flashes that were always too brief.

Yet one glimpse stayed with me, burned into my memory like a wound, seared across my soul like a brand. He was very young, with golden-white curls and his mother's green eyes. A sturdy child, wind-burned and tanned, he perceived my hungry eyes upon him all at once, and turned from his play to regard me.

From the future the child looked at me, saw across the mists of time, recognized me. In the instant our eyes met, I saw that the god-winds ran shrieking through his body like a hurricane, as if he were the fulcrum around which the worlds swung in their heavy, distant orbits, but he was unaware of them. "Aiden," I called, as the woman had done, thinking him well named.

"Father!" he cried joyfully and held out his hand to me across the years. I reached out to him, but the vision closed in upon itself, shut me out, and I was left alone in my body, huddled and suddenly cold, my hand empty.

Maran stirred and woke, her eyes blurred, sleep-softened, her face gradually taking up tension as though putting on a cloak. Her hands moved, clasped mine on the pale softness of her belly, and she looked at me without recognition for a moment. Then the dullness cleared, and I saw that she knew me, and knew of the child within her.

A look of joy, quickly masked, suffused her face. The expression was replaced by a blank, studied indifference. As she disentangled herself from the bedclothes and moved away from me, she also closed off her mind. It was like watching a homesteader shutter up his house before a storm, or before moving away from it forever. First clean everything up, put it in order. Then board the windows, inside and out, lest anything break through. Then repair the roof, hammer down any loose shingles and fill the chinks in the foundation with mortar and chips of stone. Finally, lock the doors with stout bars and chains.

It took her but a moment to complete her work; the space of time it took for her to stand and take a deep breath was enough. "Maran—" I said, but it was already too late. We were as separate as if we had never joined. I could still read her—the little movements of her hands, the angle of her head, the way she blinked her eyes and held her shoulders—all these things spoke to me, perhaps more deeply than to most other men, but it was shallow and cold compared to what we had shared the night before. I felt suddenly blind.

"Maran—" I said again, unwilling to believe, hoping that the sound of my voice, a word, a gesture from me, would open her up again.

"Get dressed, Grey," she told me. "It's time for you to leave." There was nothing but aloofness in her tone, nothing but impatience in her eyes.

I opened my mouth, almost spoke again, but then realized that whatever the two of us had shared was gone. I understood then that the past cannot be fixed in place: The meaning of events gone by exists only in the mind and will of those who remember them. She and I chose to recall the last night differently—who was I to say she was wrong? For surely, whatever import the night had had for me was something I had brought to the event, and whatever loss I suffered at its conclusion was also my invention.

She waited for my response, and I wondered if she was uneasy. Nothing showed in her face or posture to indicate it. She stood naked before me, still beautiful to my eyes, but I felt no longing to touch her.

I understood something else, then, from my brief vision of the future: Nowhere in my child's life had I seen myself. "You never intended for me to stay," I said at last, and I felt the certainty of truth in my words. Yet I also knew that the future was fluid, and that I could, by deliberate exercise of will, deny her control, or even wrest it from her entirely. Her enchantments, like her blandishments, could exist only so far as I allowed them to sway me. I took up the mantle of self-determination and shook off her power, suddenly wide awake and sure of myself.

A small wind of my desiring arose, fluttered the curtains, blew her hair across her face. Always before, the god-winds had blown me about; now they were mine to control. It had always been thus, I suddenly realized. There was no difference between what I thought of as fate and my own desires. I wasted several seconds pondering cause and effect, self-determination and predestination. Who was I to have such power, that I could choose which was which? Was this the power that Maran saw latent in me? If so, she had erred in assuming I wouldn't use it.

I bound the wind's name with a word of summoning, laid the pattern of my desire over it, and sent it forth again with a flick of my fingers. A few moments later I heard Nina's answering bray from far off, and the distant thunder of pounding hooves floated through the room.

"No," said Maran, seeming oblivious to the change in me. "I never intended for you to stay. I got what I wanted from you, and our business is through. You have been a pleasant guest, but the child is mine." She glanced at the window. "I see you have called Nina. Do you summon her so you can run away, or to have her spill my blood?"

I shook my head. She knew better. "Neither. I do not need Nina's power, should I wish dominion in this place. If I wanted you, I could have you now."

She laughed. "Brave words!" But there was fear in her eyes now, for now she perceived the god-winds twining through my hands as I arose and faced her. I reached within myself, to that secret place in my soul, and brought forth a hint, just the barest touch, of the anger and betrayal I felt. That tiny bit was enough to jerk her forward, bring desperation to her face. I bound her with a word, bound her lightly, yes, but enough for her to recognize my power. She stood frozen, helpless before me. My will lashed her like ropes.

"Did you not know?" I asked. "Did you truly not know what you brought under your roof?" I shook my head. "You knew, for you wanted the seed of power from me for our child, but you thought to control it, control me, control him. You shall do none of these things." My anger grew cold. "With a word, I could stop your heart."

"You wouldn't!" she gasped.

I regarded her sadly. "No," I said, releasing her, releasing my anger. "I wouldn't." She fell, as though freed from restraining hands, and stumbled to the bed. Some of her aloofness returned as she realized that she had judged me aright. I bridled my hurt, folded it inside myself, dismissed the god-winds, and became only a cripple again. My voice, when I spoke, sounded weak, mortal. "You knew I would not hurt you, else you would not have dared hurt me so. I have no desire to dominate. I wish you the joy of your life, Maran. The path you have chosen is a strange and twisted one."

"You make a good victim, Grey," she told me. "If you want to see me as just the latest in a series of thieves who have stolen from you, that is your privilege. I am more than that, and less—I took nothing that was not freely given. Don't blame me because I won't let you take more than I offered. And the future is not yet written."

"I know that much," I said.

She shouldered her way into a gown, belted it across her stomach, padded quietly to the door. She paused, head down, facing away from me. "Whether you believe me or not, I wish you the joy of your life, too."

"I forgive you," I said, and that last kindness was too much for her. She fled the room. Only in my imagination did she ever weep at our parting.

I dressed myself and went outside. Nina came to me, kneeled on her forelegs, bowed her head, waited. I contemplated her for a moment, wondering what obscure motives had led her to abandon me to Maran's graces, yield to Maran's desire. How much had Nina known? How much had she suspected? Yet no shadows raced to cover her; she remained before me in unicorn shape, distant, faerie, inscrutable. I briefly considered asking her to explain why she had succumbed so meekly to Maran's suasion, and then dismissed the impulse. I already knew the answer: Nina *approved* of Maran.

One thing I had learned from Maran, surely: A man may take only what is offered and yet not be sinless. Therefore I did not mount Nina's back as she so clearly desired, but laid my hand on her neck and walked side by side with her up the valley slope. Perhaps Maran had been right—perhaps restraint is a kind of power all its own. The power to take a thing, and yet withhold one's hand. . . . What is the morality of governance, if not the balance between ability and action, and what is the purpose of choice, if sometimes we do not refuse?

As we topped the ridge separating Maran's valley from the road and emerged from the mist, I felt the valley's influence chopped off behind me like the shutting of a door. I did not need to look back to know that I would see only hills and trees. There was no path backward for me.

And that was the sign of Lady Maran, that she kept what she took. And in privacy, to the chiming tune of tiny bells, she was a creator as surely as she was a thief. As I carved meanings from patterns to serve my own purpose, I knew she crafted life from chaos to serve her own.

I also knew that I would see her again, and I wondered if our purposes would conflict. I shook my head free from the riddle of Maran's enchantments and continued south with Nina, toward our inevitable meeting with the Archon.

7. TORREY

ASHE MAY HAVE GIVEN up the interior of Leonais, but he still held the coastal lands and roads firmly. Once past the trenches and skirmish lines, we traveled with more speed. The small hills between Luvar and Landing were gentle, and the walking was easy, even with only starlight for illumination. Farther south, where the great Leonais River emptied into Lyonmouth, there would be more hills, even mountains, but here the wide flatlands, nursed by gentle sea breezes, were fertile, rich, and well populated.

We still moved mostly by night, trusting the darkness to give cover, avoiding the towns and cities as best we could. My plan was still to get behind Ashe's men, following their line south as he advanced. But now I knew doubt, because his forces had been so depleted trying to hold the land west of here. Would he advance at all, or build up his defenses and let Gaheris come to him?

Either way, I had no intention of going near Halmar-by-the-Sea. Even if Ashe were afield with his troops, Halmar was a fortress in the midst of war, and strangers would not be given free pass. Those who hold compassion a luxury are known for stinting lesser decencies as well, and I saw no reason to test their good will. We would come close enough to find and follow his troops, but no closer.

Besides, my other reason for venturing this far east was to see Landing itself. I could not resist the lure. We first saw the starships, three of them, rising like needles against the dawn, from over five miles away. It was impossible to judge the scale, but the stories said each ship was six hundred feet from base to tip, and I was willing to believe it.

I avoided the monastery and pilgrimage gathering centers. I had no desire to encounter high-ranking monks, and didn't need the risk. Visitors could go right up to the base of the ships, touch the strange metal that had withstood three thousand years of wind and storm without markings or deterioration. Time and tradition did not allow weapons near the ships, and I thought even the Archon would not dare violate the taboo. Every person on Leonais would revolt, from the oldest woman to the youngest child, if anyone harmed a monk or brought fighting to that place.

Sunderlings didn't hold much sacred, but the starships and monks were inviolable. It started, I think, because the ships were the only way of retreat if the colony faltered. Eventually, they became symbols of what humans had once achieved, spanning and mastering the stars themselves, a source of pride. And finally, the ships became a testament to human arrogance, a mute promise that they had learned better and would never attempt such things again.

Reliance on tradition was perhaps unwise, but I dared the ships in daylight. Nina refused to accompany me, offering only disinterest as a reason, but I suspected it was more distaste than disinterest. She had no reason to love humanity, no desire to be reminded of how her world had been invaded, and I could grant her that. But for me, interest burned hot, and I eagerly limped the last few miles.

The monks I encountered beside the ships were scholars and docents, caretakers. If hierophants or other initiates lived at Landing, they kept to the monastery and didn't show themselves. The ships needed no maintenance, and indeed the hatches had been welded shut long ago, using machinery the art of which was now lost. No smith could fashion tools to scratch, let alone melt, that metal. I asked the docent assigned to me if anything could still be functional within.

"Everything of value was removed," she told me. "The Book of the Ship says—"

"Do you mean actual records, or just the stories?"

"The Book of the Ship was written by the captain's own hand, and by the hands of his lieutenants. The original was lost, but many copies survived. It tells of the long voyage, carrying the seeds of life suspended in time, where Captain Leonais was merely the grandchild of the grandchild of the grandchild of the original captain, praise his Unspoken Name. Captain Leonais, for whom this continent is named, called the planet Sundering, to mark that humanity was now divided yet again, in the Great Expansion, from which there could be no—"

I let her ramble, but stopped paying attention. It was clearly a memorized speech, probably unchanged for generations, and devoid of real content while featuring plenty of capital letters. She was a nice enough woman, quite earnest if somewhat vacuous, so I nodded politely from time to time.

A bell rang softly in the distance. My guide excused herself for devotions. I imagined the group of them, white-robed and barefoot, bowing to the ships, reciting lineages, and perhaps worshiping a stray bolt or screw. It was mean-spirited of me, but I didn't see any point in their existence. I thought the loss of technology a staggering blow to humanity, an irreparable harm. Celebrating the loss and glorifying their current ignorance was an insult to the men and women who had built these ships and piloted them across the void.

I laid my right palm on the cold metal, feeling the slight thrum as the wind, six hundred feet above, teased the nose. Something like a spiritual salute rose within me, and I neither moved nor spoke for a long time. It was overwhelming to contemplate how ships like these had carried the "seeds of life" through such unimaginable distances. Of the First Colony's contribution, no trace remained, save the fact of Earth-type life and the ecosystem to support it. Every Earth animal and plant on Sundering, from microbe to cattle, could trace its ancestry to frozen embryos, spores, seeds, or cultures borne on the cargo ships of the First Colony. Humans had forgotten it, reckoning time only from the founding of the Second Colony, whose ships I now touched. The scale of the vision and planning was inconceivable. And within the lifetime of the Second Colonists, humans had finished seeding the continent. They had tamed it, built cities, and remade Leonais into a land fit for a technological civilization. And yet, only three thousand years later, their descendants herded sheep, lived in stone huts, believed in saints, and made the sign against evil to ward off bad luck or demons. It was enough to make me cry, and I was still standing there, tears on my face, when the docent returned.

She could see the wetness of my cheeks, for I had thrown my head back to stare straight up the side of the ship, and my hood had fallen partway off. She touched my shoulder gently. "The holiness here is very strong. It moves everyone strangely."

I looked at her askance. "And the muria? How were they moved when these ships came down from heaven? Did they think them holy?"

"The Book of the Ship does not speak of the evil muria, save to note they fled in shame before the face of the captain."

Evil? Shame? These were lies. I wanted to hit the docent.

Instead, I threw back my hood and let my shock of white hair spring free. "I am not ashamed!"

She was unperturbed. "Neither are you muria. They are demons of the air, who walk without feet. You think to shock me, but we are not simple folk of cot and farm. We know that wheaten hair, even pure white, is one of the racial variations the captain brought to Sundering. The captain himself had red skin, like mahogany, and hair of russet, and his descendants still rule this world."

"So nothing discomfits you?" I asked. I wondered how she would react if she knew Ashe traveled with one of the muria, but I didn't think it worth my time.

"Only blasphemy. The Book of the Ship says that he who—"

I walked away and left her talking to herself. It was that or strangle her, and she wasn't the proper object of my anger. The entire human race infuriated me. I headed south, ideas spinning in my mind. I didn't understand why I had such an overwhelming reaction to the loss of technology, save that humanity had thereby been reduced. And what of magic, or faerie beings like Nina? Perhaps the Second Colony had traded science for magic. How could they be beguiled, or persuaded, to make such a sacrifice?

What *was* magic, anyway, and by what principles did it operate? Even I, a mage myself by anyone's estimation, had no answers. Half the time, I couldn't tell if magic controlled me, or I controlled it. Consumed by my thoughts, I walked aimlessly, only paying enough attention to keep heading south and to avoid other people.

Outside the town of Landing, far from the starships, Nina found me, and we waited for nightfall together. She didn't ask any questions, and I volunteered nothing. It was hard for me to find the quiet place within my mind. Scattered clouds dotted the sky, growing thicker as the day wore on. By evening, it was gloomy and raining lightly, but Nina had no trouble picking her way through the fields. I followed her, stumbling in the dark, cursing the rain and wishing I hadn't stopped to see the starships.

We saw signs of Ashe's outriders before dawn and decided to stop before they spotted us. I found an abandoned shed near a stand of trees on the outskirts of a tiny hamlet. The wood had once been painted red, but was now grey and brown, and half-fallen in on itself. I curled up under the leaking roof to sleep off the day.

Voices woke me in the late afternoon. It was foggy, but no longer raining. I sat up to get my bearings. I didn't see anyone around, and nothing seemed out of place. Nina had wandered off, as she often did, and I didn't blame her; watching me sleep must have been indescribably boring. The voices were coming from the other side of the shed's wall, and the speakers were very young, just children. I held still, listening.

"It has to be him."

"Shush."

"You shush. I found him."

"What's the knife for?"

"Defense."

"It's a butter knife. You going to butter him?"

"Shut up, pee face."

"You shut up. It's not him."

"Is."

"Can't be. Where's the horse?"

I cleared my throat loudly, and the voices stopped, chopped off in mid-squeak. After a long moment, two small faces peeked around the wall, eyes wide. I figured them for brothers, the older one maybe eleven, the younger no more than eight.

"It is him!" said the older one. "Are you him?"

"I don't know," I answered, smiling. "Him who?"

"The one the soldiers asked about."

My smile disappeared. "Soldiers? Whose? When? Be quick, boys!"

My tone frightened them, and they disappeared behind the shed. I heard furious whispering, but couldn't make out the words.

"I'm crippled," I called out. "I can't chase you or hurt you. Come tell me about the soldiers."

They peeked back around the corner, and I pulled up the sleeve of the cloak so they could see my withered arm clearly. Braver now, they stumbled over each other trying to explain. The older boy, Owen, did most of the talking.

Ashe's men had gone town to town, farm to farm, house to house, earlier in the day, asking about a white-haired man with a black horse. They offered reward money. The younger boy—Torrey—had spotted me in the shed and immediately gone to fetch his brother. Now they had "caught" me and had no idea what to do next.

Torrey reminded me achingly of Drust. He had the same trusting face, insatiable curiosity, rapid speech, and air of utter innocence. A small lizard rode his shoulder, and he petted it with a forefinger from time to time. I noticed his left ear was missing, but couldn't tell if it was a birth defect or an injury.

Owen was like a wary, more worldly version of his little brother. Yet for all his caution, it was surprisingly easy to get him to talk. In only a few minutes, I knew this was their shed, and they lived with their grandmother Tessa in the house just across the field on the other side of the trees. Their father—Lane—had been drafted by Ashe's army, and their mother had died giving birth to Torrey.

"Where's your horse?" Torrey asked, suddenly remembering.

"Around somewhere," I answered vaguely. "She always comes back."

"Why does Prince Ashe want you?" asked Owen, with narrowed eyes. "Are you a thief?"

"Not by choice," I said, which confused them both. "I'm just sleeping here, on my way by. Perhaps Ashe is looking for some other white-haired man."

Torrey got excited by that idea. "That's right, I bet that's right! It's like that time Solon stole the candy, but everyone thought it was Bell because they're twins, and—"

Owen put a hand over his brother's mouth. "Why don't you use hair dye?" he asked.

"What?"

"Your hair. Dye it. Grandma's hair turned grey, so she rubs juice from a root in it. They're looking for a man with white hair, not brown."

I started to say, "I never thought of it," but then felt so embarrassed that I shut my mouth instead. How had I managed to stay alive this long without having an eleven-year-old around to think for me? It was a very good idea. Of course, it wouldn't help hide Nina, but at least I could get that damnable hood off my head. My skin would pass, as long I kept my face dirty and my hair didn't draw attention. If Nina stayed in woman form and wore clothing. . . .

"I'd like to meet your grandmother," I said, pulling myself to my feet.

"You can come for dinner," said Torrey excitedly. "I bet Grandma won't mind. She makes really good lamb stew."

Owen answered more slowly. "I think it's okay. You won't hurt her, will you?"

I held out my hand to him, and he touched my palm gingerly. "I promise I won't hurt anyone," I said. "Call me Grey."

They led me to their house, and I asked to see Torrey's lizard while we walked. The boy chattered happily, telling me how special and rare it was, how to feed it, what insects it preferred, and how he had found it. The creature was green, about the size of my little finger, with a red stripe down its back. It looked like an ordinary lizard to me; it blinked a lot, but otherwise sat motionless on my hand, gripping the skin with tiny, sharp nails. I carefully handed it back.

"What do you call him?" I asked.

"*Her*," he said scornfully. "Don't you know *anything*?" He tossed his head, flipping his curls away from the missing ear for a moment. I looked away quickly. I didn't know if he was shy about it.

"Her, then," I said. "Does she have a name?"

"Zoxo."

I agreed it was the perfect name for a lizard, and he seemed mollified. I marveled that neither of them seemed disconcerted that I was a stranger, or that I looked hauflin. Living so close to Landing and the monks, they must have heard poisonous stories about elves and half-breeds. Perhaps it was the mark of children everywhere that by nature they found new things fascinating rather than threatening. Drust had certainly not cared.

The old woman, Tessa, was less accepting at first, but gracious once she saw I meant no harm and that her grandsons hung on my every word. Country folk everywhere are eager for news from afar. I told her plainly that I had no money, but she waved that off.

The lamb stew was thick and hearty, and there was warm fresh-baked bread to go with it. Between mouthfuls, I regaled them with tales of my travels—leaving out, of course, any of the real story. They were happy enough to hear about the monks, the valleys, the industry in Sallas, the windswept plateau, and my farm life in Wyland. In turn, Tessa told me of growing up in Halmar-by-the-Sea, her few travels on the Colonial Plain in her youth, her marriage and life here near Landing. Her knuckles were large and rough, her voice was coarse, and her face was lined with years of care and worry, but she seemed happy enough.

It was full dark when we pushed away from the table, and Torrey was worried about Nina. Thinking her an ordinary horse, he fretted that she might have gotten lost, or tangled in branches, or stolen, or lamed. He got down a lantern and demanded we go search for her. Tessa gave me a look, waiting for me to say something, and I met her eyes while shaking my head ever so slightly. She told Torrey to put up the lantern and let me worry about the horse. When he complained, she sent him to bed in a back room. Owen busied himself in the tiny kitchen without being told, hoping, no doubt, to escape Tessa's notice.

I thanked her for the dinner, and asked about dyeing my hair, being sure to give the lurking Owen credit for the idea.

She explained about the root she used and promised to give me some of the extract. Then, "Tired of being hauflin?" she asked. A clatter came from the kitchen as Owen dropped a handful of spoons. A tiny smile graced the corner of Tessa's lips, and I decided I liked her.

"I am not hauflin," I said. "I'm not sure they exist."

She grunted. "Then what of your unicorn?"

The jangle from the kitchen was deafening. Owen had knocked over an entire shelf of pans. Tessa called out, "Tea would be nice. Then take your ears to bed with you."

"Yes, ma'am," came the tiny, embarrassed reply.

Tessa and I smiled at each other. "Unicorn?" I asked casually.

"Aye, there's been talk all up and down of a black unicorn. The children love such stories. And this one has the beast traveling with a hauflin cripple. And the soldiers came around, asking for a hauflin and a black horse, only they didn't mean a horse."

I offered that children's stories were often instructive, even if not wholly accurate.

"I think so, too," she said knowingly. We made small talk until Owen brought the tea. Tessa swatted him lightly on the rear and sent him off. He had barely left the room when she called him back.

"You," she said sharply to me. "Don't move."

I held my position, teacup half raised, eyebrows fully raised.

"Get Zoxo," she said to Owen. "On his shoulder."

The boy came quickly to my side and pulled the little lizard away. I had not known it was there. "Sorry, Grandma," he said. "I know Torrey put her away." He looked apologetically to me. "Sometimes she gets out. Ow!" He pulled his right hand away from the lizard quickly and sucked at his thumb. "Sometimes she bites, too."

Tessa insisted on examining the wound. A fairly large chunk of skin was missing from the fleshy part of his thumb, and it bled freely. It was deep enough to scar, I thought, but Tessa clucked her tongue and dismissed it. She washed his thumb thoroughly, and bound it tightly with a rag, then sent him—with Zoxo—off to bed.

The house became quiet. We sat, looking at the table and stirring our tea for a bit. Then Tessa sighed. "They're awake and listening, no doubt," she said. "The walls are thin."

"They seem like good boys," I said.

"They are. Fearless. You'd never know the little one cries for his father at night."

"All boys do that," I offered.

She paused, then said, "Would you like to take some air on the front porch?"

I agreed, and we stepped outside, taking the lantern with us. The fog hadn't lifted; if anything, it was thicker. The lantern shed no light at all. Small breezes sent tatters of fog this way and that. Tessa led me to a little bench set against the wall, and we sat staring at the white air for a while in silence.

"Damp," she said, at last.

"Quite," I agreed.

"Does the bones no good."

I allowed as how my arm and leg pained me when it was humid.

"Good for the flowers, though," she said.

"It will probably burn off in the morning," I replied, wondering how long she would keep this up.

"Damp now, though. Would you like your tea?" she asked.

My patience ran out. "Tessa, ask me."

"Ask you what?"

"Whatever you've been holding back. What do you want?"

"I want my tea," she said and excused herself. When she came back, she settled next to me on the bench and sighed. "Just as I thought, they were both awake. I put the fear in them."

"Children are like that," I said. "Don't be hard on them."

"Oh, I never am, though that's not what they'd say. Shame about the little one, though. I go too easy on him. I shouldn't, but pity makes bad decisions."

"Torrey? You mean his ear? How did it happen?"

"Born that way," she said, and sighed again.

"He seems to hear well enough."

"Oh, aye, one ear is better than none. Notice he always keeps his right ear pointed at you?"

I hadn't noticed, so I just nodded.

She seemed content to say nothing more, and sipped at her tea, which was certainly cold by now. I decided to wait her out. Some things cannot be rushed.

While we sat, a whinny came from the fog. "Here," I called, and Nina trotted into view, suddenly looming close. Her horn was visible. I stood and reached over the porch's railing to pat her nose. She permitted it, but looked inquiringly at the old woman. I shrugged. "I have business with her," I said softly. "Will you bide?"

Nina tossed her head and snorted, but trotted back into the fog.

"So it's true," said Tessa after a long moment.

"I'm sorry you saw that."

"A body should be touched by wonder every now and then. I didn't really believe until just now. But I'm sorry, too. The make-believe was better."

I cocked my head to the side. "How so?"

"Unicorn horns can cure anything," she said, then hastily added, "or so they say. I was hoping for the boy. I wouldn't have asked. And I won't now. I didn't really believe, you see. If I had, I'd have known the stories weren't true."

"I know nothing of unicorn horns healing or curing," I said kindly. "But I don't understand you."

"It's you," she said, setting her cup aside. "If that beast of yours was real and could cure anything, you'd hardly be going around with your own injuries. So I thought it couldn't be real, and I comforted myself with daydreams of healing the boy."

I had no answer to that, but at least I understood Tessa better.

"May I have the dye for my hair?" I asked. "And a cloak—or a dress, if you have one to spare." When she looked at me oddly, I added, "The dress is for a friend."

She nodded and stood up. "You may have all three. Will you say good-bye to the boys? I'm sure they're still awake. Like as not, you want to fade into the fog, but it would be a kindness if you said good-bye, and maybe let them see your unicorn."

"She is not mine, and don't call her that," I said absently. A thought had been forming in my mind, and I had little attention to spare. I shook my head to clear it, and said, "I cannot command her."

"As you will," she said, a little stiffly. "I'll fetch the things you wanted."

I was acutely conscious that Nina was not far off, and that she had been listening to the old woman. I hoped she wouldn't interfere. I followed Tessa into the house, leaving the door open, the god-winds already starting to roil the fog behind me as I gathered my will.

Tessa found the supplies and wrapped them up with some food for the road, neatly bundled in a pack. The boys came out, dressed in thin white linen nightgowns that reached their knees. They stared at me, eyes solemn, no words forthcoming. I suspected they sensed the power thrumming like a low harp string in the night; children are often more sensitive to such things than adults. Tessa let them look their fill, then sent them back to bed and seated herself at the table.

The wind of my desiring knifed across the door, filled the house. I twirled a strand about my fingers, took hold, tugged, and cast the home into sleep as easily as blowing out a candle. Tessa's head fell to the table, knocking over my teacup. The shards tinkled and rattled in the wind, skittering across the floor. Nina whinnied outside.

My will regnant in that place, I crossed into the back room calmly, deliberately, as if following an ineluctable path laid out by destiny. My body began to glow softly, wavering like the lick of flame atop a guttering lantern. Nina whinnied again, and I knew she was rearing, pawing the air, either in protest or exultation.

Torrey and Owen lay sprawled across each other where they had crumpled, nightgowns and limbs askew, brown skin and brown hair stark against the white linen, eyes closed, breathing softly. Fog swirled outside the window, and the only light in the room came from me. I stood contemplating for a moment, then stooped over Torrey and unleashed the power.

This thing is mine, that I can sometimes grant a wish. When I left that room, Torrey had two ears, and I had only one.

The healing was not as hard as with Tad, for this boy's soul was already clean. I did not have any names to erase, nor memories to soothe. His patterns were clear and uncomplicated, and it did not take long to set him aright. Yet the effort was exhausting, and I staggered at the house's doorway, suddenly blind as my uncanny light extinguished itself. I had thought to heal Owen's thumb, too, but I had no strength left for it. I released my hold of the god-winds and instantly fell to my knees.

There was no pain; a nubbin protruded under my hair on the left side where an ear had been. I touched it wonderingly. I could still hear well enough on the right. The diminution of my body was minimal, the augmentation of my spirit supreme. I thought it a fair trade.

I wearily levered myself to my feet and called to Nina. Even carrying Tessa's package was an effort. It was far too heavy, and I dropped it on the ground while waiting. The fog was gone, at least from the immediate vicinity, and stars burned like torches overhead, bright enough to cast sharp shadows.

One of those shadows swirled, condensed, and became Nina. She pulled back my hair and examined my ear critically. "Expensive dinner," she observed.

I pulled away from her in annoyance and fatigue. "I bought you a dress," I said. "Just don't ask for shoes. I can't afford them."

She had of course known what I was doing. Though my use of power was gentle that night, it must have reverberated like a shout to those who were able to hear it. She touched my cheek gently, perhaps in apology, then moved away and changed form without a word. I shouldered the pack, cast my cloak over my head, and stared at the ground while we walked.

She was right, I supposed, to chide me. I couldn't bring Pia back, nor lessen the grief of her death, by helping random strangers. Brawley, Lyne, Sylva, and Drust were also beyond help. Henna and Jack I had killed myself. Tad I had healed, but as much to seek knowledge as to bring health.

At some point, it becomes needful to examine the implications of power, and Torrey had been my test. Despite the death that trailed behind me, and the death that lay ahead, I was not wholly without virtue. I had done this thing tonight with unmixed motives, and though weary, I also felt refreshed.

My shadow stretched before me as I walked. I did not recognize its shape, yet it walked with me, matching me step for step as though it belonged to me, as perhaps it did. Sorrow and hope, like brothers clasping hands, walked not far behind.

8. Sleeper

Heavy clouds came back before dawn, moving swiftly inland, bringing rain again. Water swelled the small streams. Although the downpour wasn't torrential, it was steady and persistent, and the ground quickly became saturated. Rivulets and freshets overflowed. Slippery mud covered the roads, making it difficult to walk without my feet sliding out from under me, and it was so dark I would have been completely lost had Nina not guided me.

As always, she seemed unaffected by the weather. She walked beside me, surely as wet and cold and splashed by mud as I, but not letting it change her pace. I envied her the extra two legs, especially since one of mine ached and dragged. I stubbornly refused to ride, because that would be surrendering too much. In the darkness, I had to give up my sense of direction; if I also yielded my sense of control, it would be like descending into delirium again.

Nina either understood or didn't care, but when we came to a small river, she said the current was too strong. I must either ride or find a bridge. Clinging to the last shards of my pride, I asked her to go upstream in hopes of finding a crossing I could manage. We turned to the left, my good hand on her withers for balance and guidance. With her sure-footed and sturdy body between me and the rush of water, I felt I could keep going, even though I couldn't see anything but vague shapes in the almost-black air.

We came to a plank bridge where the embankment rose a bit. From the sound, the channel narrowed, and the splashing and gurgling of the river became a foamy roar. The water washed the bottoms of the boards, but the structure felt solid when I knelt to explore it with my hands. It wasn't wide enough for me to walk by Nina's side. I told her to go first, and I grasped her tail as she went by.

My bad leg betrayed me on the slick wood of the bridge. One moment I was carefully feeling my way forward; the next I was on my face, splinters in my hand, my nose poking through the gap between planks with the water racing only an inch below. Nina stopped immediately, and I carefully got back to my feet, but it was too late—the pack from Tessa had slipped over my shoulder and disappeared.

I cursed and felt about for a minute before acknowledging that I had lost my food, Nina's dress, and the hair dye. I clutched her tail, shivered, and yelled for her to get me off this damned bridge. She obligingly edged ahead, and I followed, muttering and cursing until we reached the other side.

She shifted momentarily, checking me for injuries, asking why I had fallen. I pushed her away angrily. She stood a pace off for a moment, then whipped her head violently. Her long hair cut me stingingly on the face, I suppose as a kind of rebuke. But her voice, when she spoke, was mild. "Will you ride now?"

"Is there any shelter? Can we stop?"

"Not here," she said.

I rubbed my face wearily. "I'll walk. I lost the pack."

"We can get more food," she said, "and I wouldn't have worn the dress anyway." I couldn't see her expression in the dark, but I suspected she was grinning. I felt, rather than saw, the shadows gather. Her horn glimmered softly in the dark, illuminating nothing but Nina herself. She knelt, her head lowered, but her eyes still on me. *Will you ride now?* she asked again, this time without words. The flick of her ears, the slight change in the depths of her eyes, were as clear as speech.

It would be graceless of me to decline again. I slid across her back and she lurched upright. No bridle, bit, reins, or saddle had ever touched her, nor ever would. To stay on, I needed to lean forward, wrapping my legs tightly around the barrel of her chest, twining my good hand in her mane.

She turned, trotting at first, then moving to a swift, smooth gallop. The miles flew by under her unerring hooves. I didn't understand how she could pick her way through the rain and darkness until, after hours of straining against her, I stopped resisting the motion, stopped trying to see with the eyes of the body, and began to trust. The eyes of my mind needed no external light to show me fields and roads. By abnegating independence, I gained some of it back, and gained another thing, too: the freedom to relinquish control without feeling guilt.

She sensed my relaxation, my accommodation, and increased her pace yet again. The rain slacked off, becoming a mere blatting nuisance sometime long after the sun came up. Weak light finally shouldered its way through the clouds, changing the world around us from pitch black to a dank, enervated grey spread of shapes and shadows. Nina crossed the land, weaving, dodging, leaping, and prancing, flowing like a shadow herself. I floated above her, anticipating every flex of muscle, every change in attitude, no longer leaning over or hanging on. We moved together as if we were one creature. Even after there was enough light to see, I rode with the eyes of my body closed.

Near mid-morning, I saw ahead of us, as if limned by strokes of glowing paint, another of the faerie mounds. Each standing or hanging stone around the perimeter pulsed in a slow hypnotic rhythm. The door, set nearly horizontal like the last, blazed like a beacon with a constant blue-green light. I opened my eyes and scanned ahead, but saw nothing other than the hill itself, even the standing stones being too far off to make out under the overcast skies. But with my eyes closed, I not only saw the stones and the door, but also a spiral path winding between them, snaking around the mound in concentric loops. I wondered if all such mounds shone to those who knew how to see them, or if this one was somehow different from the last.

Nina made straight for it, the great muscles in her hindquarters bunching as she climbed toward the outermost menhir. As soon as we passed it, the air changed. Nina stopped, and I slid from her back. Outside the circle of standing stones, the sky was blustery, heavy with moisture, raindrops still splattering and blowing. Inside, the air was crisp like the touch of autumn, and the ground radiated a bone-chilling cold. Spring hadn't penetrated the circle yet; fallen leaves of gold, red, and brown crunched beneath my feet. I felt shadows shifting at my side, and I glanced over to see Nina pushing her hair back behind her ears. We walked hand in hand, following the path that led widdershins—counterclockwise—toward the door. As we passed each monolith, a sound grew, like the chiming of a glass bell that never faded. The ringing was immeasurably deep, as if the bell were the size of the planet itself.

The last time I had entered a faerie mound, I had been half-dead from a stab wound; I had spared no attention for the standing stones or exterior of the mound. And I had not yet learned to perceive unseen things by conscious choice. This time, I saw bands of light, like iron straps at chest height, connecting each menhir to the next. The path on the ground, etched in light, led us to cross the bands instead of avoiding them. As we passed through each band in turn, a tingling sensation ran down my back, and the cold deepened. I saw that the bands were really one long strip, a single band, spiraling from the lowest standing stone to the highest, winding around the surface of the mound. It would be possible to reach the top without crossing any band, but somehow I knew that following the spiral that way would lead to a different kind of door than the one our path showed; perhaps that door would open on just a hole in the ground. It was the band that imbued power, or perhaps expressed it. The feeling was ancient and obscure, not a kind of power I recognized. When we came to the king stone, the largest by far, in whose shadow lay the door in the ground, I saw it was covered in hoar frost, an intricate network of ice crystals etched over the surface.

Nina tried to lead me past it, going to the door in the ground, but I pulled away from her and laid my fingertips on the king stone. Instantly, the bell tone stopped, and my hand became numb. My awareness expanded to encompass the entire dolmen. Pulsing strands of power, invisible to the eyes of the body, arose from the top of the king stone, springing thousands of feet into the air and arching away into the distance like the threads of some continent-spanning spider web. I realized that all the faerie mounds in Leonais were linked, connecting and interconnecting dolmen to dolmen, forming a vast, humming network of power. But the dolmen network was dormant—or had been, until I touched the king stone—and no currents flowed along the strands. I felt that all I had to do was tune my mind, turn my thoughts a certain way, and I could make the net spring to life, ride those currents, control the immense store of energy it represented. A voice, deeper than the bell tone, rumbled from beneath the stone, from even deeper than the hidden chamber below our feet.

Just a single word, over and over, that I couldn't quite make out. I felt a sudden irrational desire to know what it was saying.

Nina nudged me. "Don't wake it," she said urgently.

I stared at her in wonder. Every hair sparkled and lifted away from her body, as though charged by lightning. The ground trembled slightly with every breath I drew. I felt the rumble of air in my lungs and the breath of the earth locked in step with each other. Palpable power still fountained from the king stone. I felt I could spring from my body, race along those traceries of invisible light, and reform a moment later at any point.

"Why not?" I asked, my fingertips still touching the rough, cold stone. "What is it?"

"Something old. We call it the Sleeper. Leave it, Grey."

The Sleeper was nothing like the god-winds. No tinge of fate or inevitability ringed the power here. It was raw potential, strength to be tapped, with no ancient myths to account for it or to guide my understanding. It was a power older than humans, older than muria—something that arose from Sundering itself, from deep in the planet's core. The ring of standing stones was a lens, bringing that power to a sharp focus at this spot. I began to sense other abilities inherent in the network. I flicked my nail against the stone, and the vast web sprang into a higher state of tension, luminescent green and gold to my inner sight. The sky began to roil and churn. Lightning flared. The voice from beneath the ground spoke again, and this time I understood the word.

"Who?" said the voice, a rumble of rocks grinding against each other at an unimaginable depth and pressure. "Who?"

I froze, unable to answer. I had the sensitivity to detect the slumbering power, to wake it, perhaps even to use it, but not to control it. No one could command this kind of power while yet nameless. Nina yelled frantically and tugged on my arm, but my fingers were wedded to the cold stone, and her sounds and efforts might as well have been miles away.

And mine was not the only hand touching the web of power. I felt a questing mind from Jappa, aware of my touch, arrowing toward me with murderous haste. At the same time, another mind, cooler but no less deadly, cast itself across the network toward me from the northeast. A third mind stirred in sleepy surprise and retreated into a corner of the web to watch. Far away, southwest beyond the Abuttals, a group of old men in Amrhyn chanted in time with the pulsations of light. They wore blue robes and were ancient, wizened men, bent and twisted from the proximity to the stones where they lived. And all the while, the pressure of the slumbering power rose toward wakefulness, the voice booming, "Who?" over and over. The bell-like chime began anew, deafening, insistent.

The tip of Nina's horn, burning like a blue-white star, wedged itself between my fingers and the king stone, pried me loose, threw me back away from the menhir. The two searching minds, suddenly blind, groped past me, faded into the distance like scudding clouds, one of them shrieking in fury, the other bitterly disappointed and afraid. The quiet mind that had held itself apart flicked like a caress across my consciousness before disappearing, and I seemed to hear the ringing of tiny bells. *Maran?* I wondered, but the connection was broken, and I got no reply. The chant of the blue-robed Amrhyn sorcerers became a soothing murmur as they urged the power back to sleep, and then they, too, were gone.

Nina stood regarding me curiously, as if I were a child who had just completed a puzzle far beyond his years, but she was not pleased. "You," she said severely, "should not have done that."

I was shaking. The mind from Jappa, the one filled with hate, had been the Archon's. I knew Gaheris from my dreams in the last faerie mound; the touch of his mind was intimately familiar, infinitely abhorrent. The other mind I felt sure had been Ashe's. Had they found me here, would they have worked together to destroy me before turning on each other, or ignored me as irrelevant to their conflict? Either way, I knew my brief contact with the dolmen was enough to set something irreversible into motion. Even now, though the direct link to the Archon was broken, I could hear his commands echoing over Leonais, setting long-prepared plans in motion. Gaheris was no longer willing to wait passively for me to come to him. I imagined his captains everywhere raising their heads, lifting their swords, calling their troops. Tall ships, standing off the coast in readiness, would be hoisting sails. Agents and spies would be whetting their knives. And on the other side, Ashe's soldiers suffered a wave of fear. As if my touching the king stone had been a signal, the fighting escalated to a fever pitch.

"I didn't know," I whispered.

"And yet," Nina went on, "discovering a power you knew nothing about, ignoring a warning from your only friend, sensing that you had no control, you went ahead anyway. You are not a mage, Grey, not yet. You should not dabble in sorcery."

"I thought—"

"No," she said, shaking her head, "you didn't. This was supposed to be a *safe* place, a place for you to rest. We could have lain hidden here in the chamber for as long as you wanted, had you only remained quiet. But you saw power, and like a little boy you reached out to grab it. And then you are dismayed that it burns."

It was a very long speech from her. The tone hurt more than the words themselves, though I recognized she had every right to scold me. I tried to explain, to tell her I was only curious, that no harm had been done, but she cut me off angrily.

"They know where you *are*. I may have cut the strings of power for now, but you have announced yourself as a player, and they know where to find you. I can't protect you from armies. Sorcerers work through human agents only when they cannot work any other way. And every soldier the Archon controls is now hurrying this way. Ashe's, too. They will collide, with you caught in the middle. And if you die. . . ."

She stopped and caught her breath, her eyes flashing with an emotion I couldn't identify. "We must leave," she said shortly. Shadows tore themselves from the air, enveloped her like a shroud, then fell away in tatters, leaving the unicorn shape pawing the ground, horn dimmed but still flickering with anger.

I heaved myself to my feet and across her back. We left the faerie mound behind, and for a long time I shut both the eyes of my body and my mind, and rode in blindness, untroubled by conscious thought.

When Nina shrugged me from her back at last, it was evening. I had not eaten since the meal with Tessa, and I was tired in a way that had nothing to do with bodily fatigue. Still, there would be little rest now. I sat on a rock and used the eyes of my mind to survey the entire seaboard. Soldiers from both sides boiled angrily along the coast, from Halmar-by-the-Sea to the Justian Bridge. In one long day, the Archon's men had swept across the bridge and overrun Draycott, the main city north of Lyonmouth. Somehow, I had precipitated a showdown. Gaheris had finally tired of sparring with Ashe and decided to end it—because I had waked the dolmen? No, I sensed that was less than half of it. In most ways that humans could account, the war had nothing to do with me. The Archon had long been ready for this push, building up his supplies and forces, but only fielding enough power to keep Ashe bottled in, waiting for the proper moment to unleash his full array of offenses. Yet everywhere I looked, I found the minds of the Archon's captains and officers filled with images of my face. I had been more than just the trigger; I was somehow also one of the goals.

Battles and skirmishes still sputtered in every little hamlet, but the war itself was almost over. Small bands of Ashe's soldiers struggled to hold each bit of ground, but were being beaten relentlessly back toward Halmar and Landing. Most cities had fallen. The Archon's men controlled all the southern roads and had insuperable numbers. Each enemy Ashe's forces killed was replaced by five more. Just as Ashe had lost the interior, he was now losing the coast. Only his stronghold at Halmar remained untouched. At this pace, Gaheris would drive Ashe into the sea within another handful of days.

Ashe supposedly had Qol for advice, and I fervently hoped this was some brilliant elvish plan I was too thick to understand. It was hard for me to believe that, drawing on muria knowledge, Ashe couldn't have put up a better defense. But then, was Qol truly a *military* advisor, or was he something else? He wore the clothing of a prince and had commanded within Ashe's camp, but perhaps his advice was of a different order altogether—or maybe Qol had no better idea how to stop Gaheris than anyone else. Qol was an elf, not a god.

My plans for following Ashe's army south evaporated like the foolish dreams of a child. Ashe would not be going south. I had not understood the Archon's numerical advantage, nor how ruthlessly his armies fought. The captains fired the lands and slaughtered the animals behind them, not only out of cruelty to the conquered, but to give the foot soldiers no option but to continue the attack. Food lay only ahead for them. And the horses! Gaheris must have emptied the Amrhyn grasslands to find so many. Soldiers thundered in mounted herds, with spares for relays or carrying packs.

Nina had found a spot removed from most fighting, but we had come a good way south, almost to Draycott and the bridge. The Archon's main skirmish line was already north of us. There would be no going back to find Ashe. Only a few of his soldiers survived on this side, mostly riding in hard retreat, or holing up to hide in whatever shelter they could find. My only way now was forward, through already conquered land, into the heart of the Archon's power.

At some point, I found myself laughing at the absurdity. I had no idea why the Archon knew me or what he thought of me. In my very first true dream, he had recognized me and then turned away in contempt, as if I were neither challenge nor gadfly worth acknowledging. Yet now I had felt his murderous rage, and I knew that for some reason, he also feared me. The thought that I could creep like a dog to his table, hoping to be fed instead of whipped, was ludicrous. That I could do it undetected was even more laughable. Yet I had no choice, not unless I abandoned my quest. He and Qol, perhaps alone in the world, knew my name. The elf would never tell, and I had no power over him. But Gaheris, perhaps, I could trick or force. And at that thought, I laughed again. Had he found me today, he would have flensed the skin from my bones.

Nina sat beside me in woman shape and asked why I was laughing to myself.

"Because I don't know what else to do," I said. I tried explaining my thoughts, and she nodded, listening, until I had done.

"Your quest has always been absurd," she said, untroubled.

If she believed that, why did she stay with me? Why had she joined me in the first place? It wasn't something she ever deigned to discuss, and after a time, I had stopped asking. But there was a mystery here, living and breathing beside me, at least as deep as the question of the muria, or my insane drive to confront Gaheris. She had information, or at least understanding, that I lacked. And if I were to have any hope at all, I needed to understand everything. I needed a weapon.

"The power under the mounds," I said slowly. "Could it—?"

"You cannot control it," she said.

"But the muria," I said. "Qol. Couldn't he—?"

"They are the ones who put the power to sleep. They will not gladly awaken it. And the elf has withdrawn from this conflict. Can you not feel it?"

The moment she asked the question, I knew. Somehow, I had already known. In my search of the coast, in my perception of the battle, in my questioning of why Qol's advice had failed, I had known Qol's touch was gone. It was not the advice that failed, nor the advisor: Ashe had turned away from Qol and lost the war all on his own. Perhaps Ashe had never been a good commander. Perhaps, without Qol's help, Ashe would have fallen long ago.

My second sight was too limited to show me the past or the complex thoughts of people far away. Yet I could see the present. Just as I knew that Gaheris was still in his citadel in Jappa, and just as I knew that Ashe was now besieged in Halmar, I knew that Qol was absent from the field. The quality of resistance, the ability to see past the moment and believe a conflict had a higher purpose, was missing from Ashe's men. Their resolve had collapsed, and their fear ruled. No wonder Gaheris could advance so quickly. He could not take victory so easily did his enemy not grant it.

Ashe's men were only human. I could understand their despair. But Qol puzzled me. Surely his purpose had not failed, even if I didn't fathom it. "Where is he?" I asked. "Why did he abandon Ashe?"

"Ask the wind," she said, gesturing helplessly.

She meant the question was futile, that mortals had no hope of understanding muria motives, but I chose to take her answer literally. I started to gather the god-winds, pulling in my will. Dust rose in spirals around us as I concentrated. A single fork of pale white lightning flickered overhead, then the meager winds I had stirred guttered and dissipated. With a groan, I released my will. My vision reeled. Inanition and fatigue defeated me for now. I had neither eaten nor slept, and the encounter with the dolmen network had drained me, too, in a way I could not identify.

I slumped over sideways, and don't recall hitting the ground.

When I woke, Nina was standing guard. She had raided a farm while I slept, and she had bread and cheese waiting. There were plenty of small streams for water, and I guessed she didn't dare do any more. "No fire," she said. "Too many people."

I thanked her, stuffed myself, and promptly lay back down. The countryside was teeming with soldiers, she informed me. Every house was shuttered, every inn was barred, every road had checkpoints. Only the military moved freely. We would have to avoid the roads and move only at night again. So I slept the rest of that night and most of the following day.

The next time I woke, my head was clear. We skirted Draycott and headed for Justian Bridge. The ground climbed steadily ahead of us toward the ridge that separated the northern half of the continent from the Leonais River basin and Lyonmouth estuary. It was hard to find paths which did not dead-end. Only the road was sure, but it was dangerous. As the land grew more rugged, it was harder to see what was ahead—a band of fighters might lie around the next corner in a hollow, or come riding over the next rise four abreast on lathered horses—and there were fewer places to dodge aside.

Just after dawn, Nina and I heard a horse's whinny from ahead of us, the soft jingle and slap of leather harnesses, and a curt, low-voiced command. Either a checkpoint or an ambush lay ahead, and only a trick of the wind had let the sounds warn us. We melted silently to the edge of the road and picked our way through the yellow gorse and thickets, up and to the west, until we reached the top of a small tor, crested it, and were hidden from the road. It was mostly bare rock on the far side of the outcropping—rock and dust and pebbles, covered here and there with thin patches of pale green wild grass. Farther down the slope to the south and west, the land rolled and bucked, as if some god had pinched it the way a baker pinches wrinkles into a crust. Somewhere to the north, lost in the distance behind us, Maran lay nursing her secrets, our child growing in her belly. There, too, lay Luvar, where Henna had imprisoned me, not far from the crossroads where I had dug Pia's grave. Nearer, but still over a hundred miles behind, the Monks of Landing would be up already, worshipping the Book of the Ship. Somehow, I didn't think even the Archon's soldiers would touch the relics of Landing. I assumed that Maran was safe in her hidden valley, but Tessa, Owen, Torrey—all the other villagers and farmers in the surrounding area—would not be so safe. I touched the nub of my left ear, remembering, and hoped they would survive.

The wind knifed out of the north, and I turned my head almost as much to avoid the dust as to avoid the past. Ahead of us, the outcropping curved smoothly to the left for perhaps a half-morning's walk, then suddenly broke on the foothills into a jumble of impassable crevasses. Only the main road, buttressed by struts and pillars of ship's metal laid down three thousand years ago, promised passage.

Nina's nose nudged me gently from behind, and we made our way along the ridge for several hundred paces, then eased back over the top and down toward the road again, angling carefully to make sure we regained level ground far beyond the sounds we had heard.

The slope was hard to navigate downhill; my bad leg kept slipping on the scree, and my left arm was useless for catching myself when I fell. Each time it happened we froze, listening to the rocks slither and tumble down the hill ahead of us, wondering if this time we would be heard, if this time we would be discovered. But we were fortunate, and as the light grew stronger, it became easier to pick my way across the rubble. By the time we reached the bottom, I was sweating and trembling. I had to rest for several minutes before continuing.

Nina, for all she outweighed me, skipped as nimbly as a goat across the rocks, with never a misstep, and did not seem wearied at all. She, the faerie creature, must forever wait on the cripple to catch up. Yet if she was impatient, she did not show it. Nina had her own reasons for traveling with me, reasons she had not shared in full, and perhaps her goal was not best served by speed.

The second time we encountered men was more costly. In mid-afternoon we heard horses behind us on the road, coming up at full gallop, a dozen or more by the sound. It was at the worst possible place. The road was winding through a cutting, and the sides were too steep to climb. The ravine itself extended, with only a few slight turns, for perhaps a mile, and we were near dead center. There wasn't time to traverse the length of it ahead of them, and trying to run backward would just get us caught all the sooner. I had some faint hope that perhaps they would be Ashe's men, but a moment's reflection told me that we would fare no better with them.

I turned to Nina. "We'll have to try running for the end of the canyon," I said. The rumble of the riders' hooves echoed and thundered off the rock walls on either side. I put my good hand on her mane, and prepared to swing up. But a moment later, I was holding only a handful of hair, and she turned, in woman form, to face me.

"I cannot outrun them with you on my back," she said.

"Then what? Wait here?"

"No. I require a gift from you. Do you give it?"

"What gift? What are you talking about? I don't—"

"There is no time," she interrupted. "Do you say yes or no?"

The horses were almost upon us. I saw that she had a plan of some sort, and I had none, so I nodded mutely.

"I will draw them off. You must promise not to look," she said. "When they are gone, follow the cutting to the end, then climb the hills to the left and wait. I will find you by nightfall. Do you understand?"

I nodded again. "How will you. . . ?" I stopped, for she had taken my good hand and placed it on her forehead. Suddenly, I understood the gift she required. "Yes," I said.

Shadows leapt to cover her, and under my gaze where a black-haired woman had been, a black unicorn now stood. My palm, which a moment before had rested on a woman's forehead, was now pierced through by the slender tip of the unicorn's horn.

9. Glamour

THE PAIN WAS A SURPRISE, for I had thought she would scratch, not puncture. I could see the tip sticking through the back of my hand, the color of ivory or old bone. So quickly had she lanced me that there was no blood on the tip. She tried to pull back, but the muscles in my palm contracted in a spasm, resisting her motion. The tip of her horn was razor sharp and thin, perhaps as big around as a child's little finger, but spiraled, like a sea shell. I wrenched my hand away violently, feeling the small bones grate against the scrolled ridges of her horn. The blood started flowing immediately, more than I would have guessed, and I held my hand still, palm cupped, letting the blood spill onto her horn.

The transformation was almost immediate. She seemed to grow in stature, though her size did not change. Her coat took on a luster, a sheen, and her hooves danced against the ground with barely suppressed energy. For just a moment, the doorways to our souls were held open, and a path was laid between them. Something of me, of my spirit perhaps, for I know it was not physical, nor anything as mundane as strength or vitality, went into her, filled her, completed her. Then the tip of her horn, glistening wetly with my living blood, reentered the wound; when it withdrew this time, there was no trace of the injury or the blood.

All this transpired in a few seconds, from when I said "Yes" until she withdrew her horn from my flesh the second time. Then she was gone, dancing away to the north around a bend in the cutting, toward the horsemen. I was left clenching my hand around a wound that no longer existed, wondering what I had given her, and if it matched what she had taken.

I limped quickly to the side of the canyon, found a largish rock, and curled myself into its scant shadow. I flung my cloak over myself and hoped that Nina's diversion would be sufficient to keep them from looking my way. Even though my cloak was black, and I was in a boulder's shadow, it was hardly a good enough disguise to hide me from someone passing a few feet away, unless that person's eyes were drawn elsewhere.

Echoes can seem to amplify sound or cast it strange directions. After a minute or two, when I still heard the horses, but they had not arrived, I realized that they must have been farther away than we thought. I risked peering out from under the edge of the cloak when the sounds became softer rather than louder. Had Nina somehow passed through their midst and led them back the other direction?

But no—a moment later, Nina came prancing around the bend toward me, her hooves barely seeming to touch the ground, her tail and head held high. Behind her, seated but walking their horses, eyes entranced, followed the group of soldiers, perhaps twenty of them. I didn't see the Archon's sigil; these were Ashe's men.

They didn't talk amongst themselves or look from side to side. Every eye was fastened on Nina's glossy black form and the shimmering of her ivory horn. Her entire body seemed to gleam, a pearly luminescence surrounding her like an aura. Her glamour had captured them, and she led them, faerie-wise, bound by the nets of her beauty, through a timeless dream. When they awoke, I knew, they would have no memory of passing through the cutting, or of Nina. Yet each would be changed somehow, in the marrow, for having seen a wonder and for having lost it. In the future, when they saw something beautiful, or felt a pang of loss at a parting or a death, their feelings would be sharper, deeper. They would feel a keen sense of sorrow, an inconsolable longing, and perhaps find themselves crying unexpectedly, not for what they saw before them at the moment, but for something they had seen today and forgotten.

Too late, I remembered that she had warned me not to look. Her glamour ensorcelled me as cleanly, as easily, as it had snared these men. I rose from my hiding spot, even as the thick of the company was passing me, my head empty of thoughts but full of visions, to catch a clearer glimpse of her, to follow wherever she led.

My unexpected motion was enough to break the delicate spell she had woven. As if we had been looking through a silvered glass that suddenly shattered to let in honest light, our sight cleared, and we remembered ourselves. The company muttered to themselves, stirred as if from sleep, and rubbed their eyes. I saw that they were mostly young, with hard-bitten faces, dented armor, chipped blades. They were survivors of yesterday's battles, perhaps the only ones of their company left alive.

The one nearest to me didn't hesitate. He swung his leather-mailed fist into the side of my head. The next thing I knew, I was lying on my back with my ears ringing, my jaw aching. The young soldier swung down off his mount, drew his sword, and raised it above me, point-down.

At that moment Nina screamed and reared. Such was the power of her call that I looked, forgetting the sword above me, forgetting the pain in my jaw, forgetting the ringing in my ears. I saw her fore hooves flash in the sunlight as she pawed the air, and her horn glittered and beckoned. Something in her eyes spoke of hidden secrets, power, mystery, desire. I felt my heart yearn toward her, and my feet moved of their own volition, trying to make me stand, let me follow her.

Everyone looked when she reared; everyone was recaptured by her glamour. Even the soldier above me turned and was caught, the sword falling from his suddenly nerveless hands. He reached blindly for his horse, not taking his eyes off Nina, and I continued trying to stand up.

She did not lead them on a stately march this time. She reared again, neighed her challenge, whirled, and flashed down the road to the south. A mighty roar came from the throats of the company, and they lashed their horses to follow.

If I weren't a cripple, with a bad leg and a withered arm, I would have been caught by her, too. I would have followed however I could, no matter the cost, until at last she disappeared over some final horizon, and I woke from the dream among enemies without knowing how I got there.

But because I was crippled, I stumbled as I rose, crashing into the young soldier who, now far behind his company because he had dismounted, was still trying to get on his horse to follow. Suddenly I felt the pain of my jaw again, and knew myself to be free of the glamour.

"You filthy old man, let me go!" he cried, still half-caught in the dream, not even looking at me. But when I tried to catch myself against him, my leg slipped again, and I tripped us both. I landed beneath him, and the clatter we made spooked his horse. It took off after its fellows, and the soldier cursed, now fully awake.

He levered himself up with both arms, pushed away from me, and rose. I did not try to move. I had landed on my left arm, the withered one, and the dry, brittle bones snapped like twigs when he fell on top of me.

He picked up his sword, and I saw that he was younger than I had thought. Little more than a boy, really—nearly beardless, perhaps twenty years old. Yet there was death in his eyes and in his hand when he came back to me.

It is said that some men meet death with laughter, others with tears. Some men are brave at the end, some die in cowardice and shame. Kings and lords are allowed the dignity to choose the manner of their passing; commoners are stuck like toads by beardless boys on the side of the road. Still, all men die eventually, and in the end, no matter the lord's brave words, the warrior's screams of challenge, or the coward's blubbering for mercy, there is only silence and, finally, peace.

The young man's face loomed over me, and I saw he was puzzled by something, perhaps by my continued silence. But then he leaned away again, and I closed my eyes, unwilling at the last to watch the blade fall. I heard the leather of his armor creak, and imagined his sword arm rising high. Still the sword did not fall, and I opened my eyes again. He was unslinging his pack, his sword already resheathed at his side. From the pack, he pulled a flask and a bag, which he threw on the ground beside me.

I turned my head, looked at the leather bag, recognized it. It was my own, from long ago, the one Claude had given to me. Then I looked back at the young soldier in wonder, realizing suddenly who he must be. My jaw screamed in pain when I moved it, but I managed to mumble, "Thaddeus," I said, "called Tad."

"There's food in the bag, water in the flask. Stay off the road," he told me.

I lifted my good hand toward him. "Tad. . . ."

He didn't meet my eyes. "I have to go," he said, and then he did that thing, leaving me alone in the dust without a backward glance. I suppose I should have been grateful that he hadn't killed me. In a sense, I suppose I was. But at the moment, my mind only had room for pain and bitter disappointment.

After a long time, I managed to work myself to a sitting position and, awkwardly, fashion a sling for my left arm from my cloak. I didn't have the strength or the tools to tear the cloak, so I just wrapped it around my chest, binding the arm immobile within it. I groaned to my feet. For my jaw, I could do nothing at the moment, and the pain would not let me eat, but I drank a little from the flask, hung it and the bag on my belt, and started stumbling south along the cutting.

Near nightfall, I reached the end of the ravine and made my way off the road into the jumble of rocks and trees on the east side, as Nina had instructed. I climbed for a while, then found a narrow gorge by tripping over an upthrust tree root and falling into it. It was as good a place as any, out of sight from the road, sheltered from the wind, and I decided to wait for Nina there.

It was cold. My jaw ached, my arm throbbed. I woke without realizing I had slept. There was a hand on my shoulder, fragrant hair hanging in my eyes. I looked up to see Nina's face inches from my own in the dim light.

"I told you not to look," she said. "I led them on a merry chase, left them exhausted many miles from here." Her eyes were dark orbs, for she blocked most of the light, but her breath was sweet in my face, warm, and spoke of life. She herself was like a breath, I thought; she is here, then she is gone, and one breath is much like any other, but each is unique, never to be repeated.

I felt my jaw gingerly with my good hand. It had swollen during the afternoon, and even more while I slept. I did not even try to speak, although I could have. Instead I groped for the wordless bond I shared with her, tried to communicate with my eyes and my mind. I tapped the channel we had opened back on the road, when she had drawn my blood. It took a moment to orient myself, to recapture the feeling. I built a mental doorway, stepped through it, and suddenly I could speak directly to her mind. I sent a picture, a memory, of her with the glamour revealed, leading Ashe's men. *I didn't know you could do that.*

She didn't seem surprised to hear me talking inside her mind. It did not differ substantially from the communication we had always shared, except in clarity. Perhaps she had always heard me this well, and I just didn't know it. But no, I saw that this was new for her, too. Or rather, not new for her, but new for us. She had always spoken this way and been chary with words, but I had not been able to hear. I suspected this kind of speech was natural for her, for her kind, and words were hard.

"You saw me for a moment the way I appear to others," she said. She didn't use those words; I hardly think she used words at all. What she conveyed was a feeling, an impression, that resolved in my brain to words, since that is what I was able to understand.

"No," she added aloud. "You do not understand. That is only half of it, maybe less."

And then, blindingly, I did understand her. "This is not the first time you have led soldiers away from me."

Her face was guarded, and her mind snapped shut.

"Wyland," I said, forcing speech through the pain in my jaw. "That night. When you warned me. Now I know why the soldiers didn't keep searching. Why they didn't attack other farms. Why they didn't go back to their garrison."

"Yes."

"You led them somewhere and left them, then came back to look for me."

"Yes."

"*Why?*" The word was torn from me. "Why didn't you do it *before* they killed Brawley?" *And Lyne, and Sylva, and little Drust. Why let them die?*

She would not meet my eyes. "Because I didn't know. I hoped if they didn't find you, if you ran away, they would go themselves.

So I stayed to warn you. I had to choose without knowing. And you must not die."

"It's not your fault," I whispered, "that you don't know the future."

"Sometimes," she said sadly, "I wish that I didn't."

"Meaning you know some things, but not everything. How does that work?"

"Grey," she said, her voice still sad, "I don't know the future, but I know that if you throw a stone into a pond, ripples occur. The difficulty with prescience comes from not knowing if one is the stone or the ripple."

I started to sit up, to question her further, but her hand on my shoulder tightened, and she pushed me back down, suddenly all business. "You are wounded. We stay here tonight and tomorrow. Sleep now, if you can." She leaned closer, kissed me on the forehead, then stood up. "Sleep now," she said again. She shimmered, blurred, and re-formed in unicorn shape, black as the night itself. I knew she would stand guard over me until sunrise.

The next day I did not move save to ease myself, eat and drink a little. My jaw still ached and would for some time, but it was not broken, and the healing process had begun. My arm was another matter. The break was clean, and Nina set it for me at first light, but I feared infection. The skin was hot, tender, and the arm itself swollen nearly double.

Nina spent most of the day scouting the area, returning every few hours to check on me before disappearing again. She brought me herbs to ease the pain and arrest the disease, and she made sure I had plenty of water, but otherwise left me to rest alone. I lay in the gully, half-asleep most of the time, dulled by pain and fever, hearing in my dreams and wakeful moments the thunder of horses on the road as company after company went past to the north.

That night I still was not well enough to move, nor the next, but by the end of the third day after the incident on the road, her febrifuge had done its work, and my mind was functional again.

"The Archon owns all but Halmar," she told me, sending a mental picture of his army spread out like a blanket from Justian Bridge to Landing. I felt despair rising. The past few days had eliminated my hope. The quest felt impossible, and in some ways, I no longer even cared about my name. But something, perhaps merely stubbornness, drew me to my feet.

I swayed unsteadily for a moment before I caught my balance. Instantly, Nina was beside me in unicorn shape, kneeling, urging me to mount. My debt to her could not be made higher by another gift: I already owed her my life itself. If we were to continue onward, there was no other way. So, at length, in weakness and surrender, I learned a lesson to balance Maran's, that we cannot help but use one another, that there is no more shame in accepting a gift than in offering one. Perhaps the art of friendship is little more than learning how to do each with equal grace.

Whether it was some power of hers, or the god-winds bringing us good fortune, we slid like shadows through the darkness, avoiding encampments. We hid during the days and made good progress at night.

On the second evening since leaving the gully, we came upon a ruined and apparently deserted building in a slight hollow. It was very old, made of stone dressed in a style I did not recognize. Nina wanted to give it a wide berth, but something drew me toward it, and I slipped from her back while she was still arguing with me. I limped down into the hollow where the building stood. The night was dark, but in the faint starlight I could see that the roof had long since fallen in, and the walls themselves, while still standing, were canted over, leaning on one another. The closer I got, the more curious I became. My skin tingled strangely, and I felt a heightened sense of awareness. I turned to beckon to Nina, but stopped with my hand upraised when I saw her.

She was limned by the stars against the rim of the hollow—human, long hair cascading down to her knees, facing away from the building, from me. I shot a mental query her direction, but got nothing back except anger and a desire to leave. "Nina," I called aloud, and at that she turned. "Do you not feel it?" I said. "There is something here . . . something of power."

"It is an elvish place," she answered. "I cannot enter." She spoke aloud, and the words she used were "I cannot," but what I heard in my mind was, "I will not." I saw it then, a barrier of some sort, surrounding the hollow, and I realized that I was seeing the building briefly through her eyes. The nature of the warding was unclear to me—certainly I had not perceived anything when I passed through it only moments before. Yet I saw that to her it was all but impenetrable. She regarded the barrier not so much with fear as with loathing and shame.

"Yes," she answered my thoughts, "that is how it is." She sent an image then, a collection of thoughts bundled one atop the other, of muria gathering in places like this on star-studded nights in ages past, to practice their strange rites. I saw Nina herself, other unicorns, and many of the poor half-folk I had thought only legends, drawn to this place, or other places like it, year after year, drawn but denied admittance for some lack I didn't comprehend. This had been a holy place for the muria; something of their essence still lingered after all this time, and their wards against the impure were still in place, after millennia of abandonment. The muria had withdrawn to Avermorn, and with very few exceptions were no more to be found in mortal lands. Millennia? I understood something then that perhaps I had always known, but hadn't thought about—or hadn't been willing to think about.

There are blind spots for every man, places where he is either unwilling or unable to look. I had been so wrapped up in my own mortality that I had not truly considered Nina's nature, or rather the implications of it. She herself had watched the muria celebrate their obscure rites in places like this one, millennia ago, at a time when the world was younger and the Second Colonists had not yet arrived. Unchanged, unchanging, still in the flush of youth, she had stood still while the ages rolled slowly past, watching, measuring, waiting, judging. . . .

"We do not judge," she said in answer to my thoughts. But then, before I could object, she added, "As a race, we do not judge. As individuals, we are as free to hate—or to love—as any other."

"The Archon," I whispered. "Why do you hate him so? Will you tell me, Nina?"

"Come out of that place," she told me, and I did, and she put her human arms around me. "I hate," she said into my shoulder, "because I also love."

"I don't understand."

She pulled back, pushed her hair behind her ears, regarded me with eyes like open wounds. "Not only the muria have withdrawn from the world," she told me. "Of my kind, I am the only one. . . ." A welter of images and feelings poured from her—shame mixed with pride, sorrow with joy, longing with fulfillment—and over and above and through it all, winding like a thread, a sense of loss too deep for words, and bittersweet hope for something she dared not name even to herself.

I felt the tears on my cheeks. *Ah, Nina! Keep your secrets!* "I'm sorry," I breathed, thinking only of the pain she felt.

"I don't want your pity!" she snapped.

I lifted my good hand to her. "What do you want from me?"

"Everything. Nothing." Shadows leaned on her from crazy, impossible angles. She tossed her head, swirled her hair, and stood on all fours to regard me. "I want you to see me as I am," she said without words, "not as you imagine me. I am both more and less than what you think."

I didn't know how to answer that. "I don't even know who *I* am," I said at last, and something in my tone must have touched her, for the fire died from her eyes and we stood in silence for several minutes.

My thoughts there, under the cold stars, led me to wonder if perhaps men are defined by what they seek, and women by what they have found. "I do not know my name," I ventured finally, "and I have no past like yours. I am not immortal. But when I find my name, surely I will find that part of it is yours, and that you have known and held it for me all along."

"Neither am I immortal, not in the way you imagine," she told me, still without words. In my mind I saw a vision of her stepping away from the herd, crossing an invisible boundary, returning to mortal lands, knowing that the way back was sealed forever behind her.

I groped for understanding, for reasons, but her thoughts eluded me. That one glimpse I was granted, but no more. I retreated into my inner self, the place where patterns sometimes take on meaning, where questions are often their own answers. Something she had told me was vitally important; I sensed that she had not meant to say so much. My mind rested in a web of meanings, and I strove to stop analyzing, stop reasoning . . . to let myself acknowledge something I already, somehow, knew. This conversation had started when we found the old elvish building; everything depended from that. The key was already in my hand, and I had only to fit it to the lock, turn it, and let awareness come.

"The muria found you impure, unworthy," I said aloud, feeling the rightness of my words, the inevitability of my conclusions. I gestured at the ruins behind us. "That's why you cannot cross the wards. They rejected you, all your kind, long ago. But you do not hate them for that rejection—if you hate them at all, it is because you believe their judgment was condign." She waited, saying nothing, perhaps thinking nothing I would recognize as thought. I could not follow the eldritch pathways her mind trod as I spoke. "But you are not here because of the muria, or because of something that happened thousands of years ago, before humans even reached this world. You are here because you hate, and you hate because you love." Suddenly I was unsure of myself. It made no sense—or perhaps it made a kind of sense that I was not yet able to understand. "What was your impurity?" I asked. "Why did they reject you?"

She blurred, twisted, yearned into human form for a moment. Her hand touched my cheek, slid down to cover my heart. "Because we were not elves," she whispered, and the shadows frayed the edges of her form, tore it from her like a cloak, leaving her again a faerie creature, a unicorn, a smudge of darker black against the night.

The pattern was finally complete, at least in this respect: She, and the ones like her, had rejected themselves far more harshly than the muria had rejected them. I felt the nature of the warding keenly then, felt it push outward against her while it simultaneously drew me. "No," I told her. "Not because you weren't elvish, but because you were not yourselves. You longed to be something you were not. I can pass this barrier because I want, more than anything else, to be me, to become myself. Inside this place, there are no illusions. That is the nature of the power that lingers here, to strip away pretense."

She quivered, metamorphosed into human form, held up her hands as if to push me and my words away. "You do not understand," she said.

"I *do* understand. You wanted me to see you as you are. I do. Look at yourself through my eyes, Nina, and see what I see." The god-winds stirred at my back, and I spoke with the echo and authority of the winds in my words. This was prophecy, I suddenly knew—not the foretelling of the future, but the true telling of the present. My words carried a physical force with them, and the winds howled and moaned around us. From far off, I felt the attention of an elf suddenly focused on me, drawn to my use of power in this ancient place. I ignored it, concentrating on Nina, on the picture of her that I built in my mind.

This gift was mine, that I can sometimes see truly, sometimes see past the appearance, past the mannerisms, past the habits and deeds, to the person underneath, to the hopes, fears, desires, and loves that define each of us. In that moment, my sight was clear. I saw her as a bright circle, glorious, but with a darkened heart. The circle was her outward shape, the glamour and allure, the faerie creature all men long to follow. The darkness was her self-doubt, her loathing, her fear, her sense of loss at what could never be recovered. In that moment, too, I saw the shame she felt at the dark rites she performed in lieu of her abandoned birthright: I saw the heat of living blood pulsing in her veins, her dark thirst for power, her hatred of the Archon and all he stood for.

All this she accepted from me as if it were her due. She accepted my judgment the way she and her kind had accepted the judgment of the muria for those long ages. But then I showed her something the muria had not, perhaps could not, show her: the bright spark at the center of the darkness which she habitually overlooked or discounted. Though she had spoken truly when she said that she hated because she also loved, she had not come to terms with the love at the center of her being. I showed her the things she did not see when she looked at herself: the honor, the self-sacrifice, the essential goodness of who she was. *This is what it means to be alive*, I showed her: to accept the good and the bad, to judge oneself no more and no less harshly than any other.

This is what it means to be alive: to treasure each moment, whether of pain or of joy, knowing that the moment will never come again, and whatever feelings one has are right because they are one's own.

This is what it means to be alive: to see yourself in someone else, to see someone else in yourself, to build bridges between persons, to forge something between oneself and another that is both part of each, yet something more.

I felt the barrier begin to falter as she started to believe me, started to see the parts of her that I saw, started to see the whole of who and what she was. I raised my hand to her, beckoning, entreating. "Come."

But it was too much for her, too strong, too intense. She was not ready, not yet, not now. I perceived suddenly that it was within my power to force her, to so whelm her mind with my own that no thought but mine would exist there, no idea that I did not plant could take root. The link between us was open; I had only to place my patterns over her own, rechannel the energies. It would be much like a healing, I realized, when I overlaid the pattern of injury with the pattern of health, and forced the one to conform to the other.

Almost, I persuaded myself that it would be for her own good. I had no doubt that I was seeing truly, that my vision of her was clearer than her own in that moment, that I had the power to make our visions identical.

That folly lasted only a moment—the dream that I was master, not victim—and then sanity came on me again. I released the god-winds, felt the power drain from me into the air, the ground, the very rocks. The doorway between our souls was still open. Nina had seen both what I could have done, and what I did not do, and the freedom I had given her to choose for herself.

She flickered into human form, started to speak, then stopped, a look of surprised concentration on her face. "He comes," she said, and I saw in her mind what she felt. In the dark, an elf, unseen but known, drawn to this place, drawn to me and my use of power, spinning through the night toward us like the wind itself. "This is between the two of you," she added, and then the shadows covered her, took her, and I was alone in that place.

10. QOL

HE CAME to me as the sky first turned pale, at that time of morning when everything is still grey but has a promise of color yet to come. He came out of the west, blown by the god-winds, but he was no leaf, no stray wisp. I felt him long before I saw him, and now that I knew the way of it, was surprised that I had not always known when he was near. That night on the crossroads he had surprised me. Never again.

I chose our meeting place quite deliberately. I sat waiting for him on a low block of fallen stone inside the old building. The mossy walls leaned over me, and the strongest of the stars still shone bravely through the opening where the roof had been. A lone thrush trilled somewhere nearby, then was silent.

He came with three others, but they were not muria, and I hardly noticed them at the time. They rode down into the hollow, and the three remained with the horses while he dismounted and strode softly toward me.

I could see his breath in the morning's cold, and that surprised me, as nothing else had this past night. It was unreasonable, I knew, to think that he would be exempt from this smallest of physical laws. And, had I thought about it beforehand, I would have known that mortal or no, he was still flesh, and the warmth of life was in his lungs and heart.

He threw back the hood of his thick cloak and stood looking down at me for a moment. He was taller than I remembered, but no less fair. Indeed, like Nina's, his was the sort of beauty that can never be remembered correctly. It was not so much that humans cannot perceive elves truly, but that we have no way to understand what we see, no hook on which to hang the memories. And so, unless they stand directly before us to correct and guide our perceptions, our remembrance becomes frayed, entwined with our dreams and our imaginations, and what we recall is not what we have seen, but what we desire to have seen.

His white hair and beardless, dispassionate face were unchanged, but I saw him afresh, and I saw not only what he presented to me, but what I knew by other means, and it was as if we had never met before.

"Qol," I said, and inclined my head fractionally.

Whether he had intended anger, or reproof, or only questions, he changed his mind when he saw the challenge in my face. "I felt your power in this place," he said by way of greeting. "A place where power has slept untroubled for many ages. I did not know it could be reawakened. You have grown."

I nodded toward the three who stood outside with the horses. "Your men do not seem to feel that power. They walk here unafraid."

He shrugged. "They are human," he said, as if that explained everything. "Like most humans, they fear the things that can harm them least and ignore true peril until it has overwhelmed them. You ask too much of them. For them to be affected by your workings here would require a delicacy of spirit they do not possess. If your path leads you to contend with humans, I recommend you use less subtle weapons."

I stared at him. Was he offering advice, or warning me? "Why have you come?" I asked.

His mouth quirked. "To answer a question."

"One of mine?"

"Perhaps—or perhaps one of my own. Do you have a question for me?"

My pain surfaced in my eyes. Qol knew what I wanted from him; he could not help but know. I flung the question at him like an accusation, by my look, by the way I held my head, by the shame I felt.

"I cannot tell you your name," he said, unmoved.

"But you know me! I saw it in your mind at the crossroads."

"Peace," he commanded, and held up his hand. "I cannot tell you your name because I do not know it. Human children have a conceit as they grow, thinking they know their names, for they are always called by one, and they learn to differentiate themselves from others by that token. But it is conceit, for they do not earn their names, do not make them for themselves. What you saw in my mind was not a naming, but a recognition. I know you, but I do not know your name. You have not given yourself one yet."

I understood only a fragment of what he was saying, but there was an admission in his words, something I had not thought to hear him say. "What does 'Qol' mean?" I asked.

He nodded. It was the right question. "Once I was Ketlan, which means 'beloved' in the human tongue. Now I am only Qol. It is a word with no direct translation, but it carries the meanings of 'outcast' and 'abandoned.' Thus every time humans greet me, they remind me that I am alone among strangers."

His words were accompanied by no outpouring of feelings; I could not read him the way I read Nina. Only if he chose to let me into his mind could I venture there. Outwardly, he showed no emotion at all. He stood with his arms crossed, his cloak thrown back, his face calm, yet I knew, if only by his choice of words, both what he said and what he did not say, that there was an unguessable penalty associated with his name, and that the price he had paid for it was terribly high.

I looked at the ground. "When you *made* me," I said in a low voice, "did you know that I would someday greet you with that name?"

He did not answer, and at length I looked up. There was expression on his face at last, but not one I could read. He met my eyes, and it was all the confirmation I needed.

"It's true then," I said bitterly. "Everything Maran said is true. I am a made thing, not a person at all. I'm not real. Did I spring like a thought full-grown from your head one day, or did you fashion me from mud and twigs and spider webs?" I stood, walked near him, my good hand outstretched. "Why did you make me? What task did you have in mind for me?"

"All children are made," he said, without any sign of discomfiture. "Some more deliberately than others. Why should the method I chose make you any less real?"

He handled me then, the way a father handles a child, gently but possessively. He lifted my hair to examine my ear, ran his long, sensitive fingers across the withered ruin of my left arm. His touch was intimate and arrogant, but not offensive. I submitted to his examination with trembling, as though fearing his judgment.

"You make strange choices," he said at last. He touched my hand with his own, then dropped it. "But they are yours to make, just as I make my own. I will not tell you why you were made. If I were to give you a purpose, it would become yours, but it would still be mine. That is insufficient. You must delve your own purpose, just as you must forge your own name."

He paused, as if considering, then continued: "I have not been watching you closely enough; I knew you would call me to you one day, when you were ready. I did not know you had met the one who calls herself Maran."

"Do you disapprove?"

His eyes narrowed. "What is that to you? Do you need my approval? Does she? You are what you are, each of you, and, like persons born of man and woman, must come to terms with yourselves. You are of my making, yes, but you are not mine. I will not own you."

Yes, well, wonderful. Very noble, in a self-righteous and smug sort of way. I could not hate him; whether he demanded it or not, I owed him a kind of filial duty. But I could be angry. Duty didn't include accepting whatever he said without questions. If he would not tell me my purpose, perhaps he would reveal his own.

"Why did you abandon Ashe?" I asked sharply.

"I did not abandon him," he said.

"I don't understand."

He said nothing, made no gesture. I hadn't expected him to explain, but I had hoped he would acknowledge the question. He could at least challenge me, or say he was under no obligation to answer. But he did nothing other than meet my gaze. After a while, I dropped my eyes. Telling him I did not understand was like a child telling its parent that the sky was blue, or that water was wet. Of *course* I didn't understand; I didn't even know the proper questions to ask.

"Will you tell me? About Ashe?" I asked.

Qol shrugged. "He let fear rule him instead of reason. In the end, he failed of his purpose, and I could no longer help him. I am therefore forced to use other means."

Purpose again. Ashe's purpose, or Qol's? I didn't care right then. "And the people who died?" I persisted. "The towns, the cities, the villages, the farms, the ships—the livestock, the grain? What of them? Could you have prevented those deaths, prevented that destruction? Why do you not oppose Gaheris?"

"Human wars," he said, "do not greatly concern me. Humans are isolates, each trapped in a single body. They think they communicate, but they only wave flags at each other from opposing hilltops. The level of discourse is insufficient to address the underlying problems."

"So you let them die, because they aren't like you. Is that it? I can't tell your kind of evil from the Archon's."

"Perhaps because you understand neither of us," he suggested. "You are very young yet, Grey, and outrage is a young man's disease. Evil is not an absolute kind of thing. The wife eating mutton believes her husband kind, but the sheep who died for that meal would surely disagree. You must see all the actors, and all their actions, before making judgments. In the end, most motives are mixed. Black and white values are for children. I am concerned with war, and with suffering, but the war I fight is not the war you see."

Perhaps. But I had already made some judgments. "What of Nina?"

"What?" For the first time, he looked startled, even guarded. "Say that again."

"Nina," I repeated, and his eyes narrowed further.

"What do you mean?" he asked. I cocked my head, wondering if he truly didn't know. He said he hadn't known about Maran. I wasn't sure I believed him. But I could refuse him nothing, so I answered.

"The unicorn," I answered. "Not really a unicorn. She hates being called that. She's also a woman." I tried to describe the essential contradictions that lay at the heart of Nina, knowing I was failing miserably. It is true, I know, that we cannot explain things we do not fully understand; it is equally true that we cannot understand things we cannot explain. The ineffable may be experienced, but remains intrinsic. Sharing it renders it meaningless, for language is effectless in the end. I could say what she looked like —to me, at least—and relate what she had said, but that was all.

After I'd babbled for a minute, he waved me to silence and bent to look me steadily in the eye. I froze, unable to move or think, while he riffled my memories, hunting out each image of her, each conversation. I felt violated, helpless. He only held me for a few seconds, but in that brief inspection he had seen every moment I had shared with Nina, since she first appeared to me in Wyland until she had left me to meet Qol by myself.

He looked away, to the door of the temple and beyond. For a long time, he said nothing, and I waited, not having any idea if he was upset or pleased.

At length, he sighed and turned back. "I cannot offer guidance about your companion," he said. "Another player has entered the contest and changed the rules. Your companion will make her own purpose clear when it suits her. But I can say this much: Do not always believe what others tell you. Misinformation comes from many sources, among which are misperception and unfounded enmity. Nina is not who you think. And having said that, I ask you to trust me, even if she cannot. I am glad she is with you on your search."

"You didn't plan it?" I asked. "You didn't make her my companion?" I had always thought she was part of some grand scheme I was too ignorant to grasp. But his reaction to her name gave lie to that idea. Without her, I would have been dead many times over. And Qol seemed to be the only one to know what was going on. If he hadn't planned it, who had?

"*Plan* for her? *Make* her? I would not, even had the thought come to me. There is danger in planning too much. Actors tend to interpret parts on their own, leaving the playwright behind. The greater the actor, the more improvisation. I am neither foolish enough nor wise enough to plan for someone like her. And I doubt I could make her do anything useful. She would refuse my bidding on principle. Her hostility is not wholly unjustified. She is not on my side. I hope someday she can come to believe I am on hers."

He turned from me, glanced again out of the doorway of the temple. The sun had finished rising, and the light frost was melting from the grass. "Walk with me," he said, "and I will tell you a story."

I limped after him, out of the building and into the early morning sun. It felt, somehow, like rising from a grave. The three men who had accompanied him still waited patiently with the horses, and I realized that although it seemed like hours to me, not much time had passed since Qol had arrived. He turned right, away from the men, and paced quietly ahead of me around the corner of the building. He waited then until I had caught him up, and we walked side by side through the wet grass.

"There was a boy once," he began, "a human child, the son of a hard-working, honest, but unimaginative man. The boy was dreamy eyed, with a mind full of fancy and adventure. One day, as he was hiding from his chores and playing by himself in the woods, he used his knife to whittle toy soldiers for himself from bark. He waged a mighty war there, but near dark he heard his father calling him, so he left his soldiers on the ground and went home for supper.

"When he came back the next day, the soldiers had all moved. He thought at first that some animal had come in the night and scattered them, but when he got down on his knees to look, he saw they were ordered neatly, but that the side that had lost yesterday was in a winning position today. 'That's all wrong,' he told them, and put them back the way he had left them. But he was troubled, for the arrangement of the soldiers had been strategic and thoughtful, perhaps even brilliant. Then he held another battle, and trounced the opposing side. Again his father called him away, and he left the soldiers on the ground overnight.

"The next day, they had moved again, and his general, which

he had left in what he thought was a position of clear superiority, was surrounded by enemies. 'No, no!' he said, and moved them back again to their proper places. 'Now *stay* there,' he told them severely. Again he held a great battle, and this time the other side won, but it wasn't much fun anymore, and the next day he didn't come back.

"As boys grow, he grew quickly enough and became like his father. Chores occupied him, and he had no more time for games of make-believe. But one day, years later, he chanced upon that very spot while collecting firewood. The soldiers were exactly where he had left them, and he suddenly remembered the game he had played with them. But though he begged and hoped and threatened, the soldiers never moved by themselves again."

He fell silent then, and I realized after several minutes that he intended to say no more. "Why do you tell me a children's story?" I asked. "Am I the boy, or one of the wooden soldiers?"

"I don't know," he answered. "You still move by yourself."

I pondered that for a moment, then let it drop. The meaning of his story was either too simple or far too complicated for me to appreciate. "You said you came to answer a question," I told him. "Have you found the answer yet?"

"No. It has been asked, but not answered. Does the hand complain that the arm swings it, or the foot resent the knee for dragging it forward?"

"I don't understand."

"By asking me to name you, or give you a purpose, you are asking to be my servant. I refuse this thing; it is self-abdication on your part. I will not make your decisions for you. Your power is awakening. Most people are hands on the end of a powerful person's arm because they have no choice. You have a choice, and I require you to make it."

He stopped walking, turned to face me fully. "Some would say that the arm is master, for it moves the hand where it wills. Others would say that the arm is just the hand's servant, for it does nothing but move the hand to where it wants to be. Both views are wrong, for sometimes the hand serves, and sometimes the arm serves, but neither is master, for if they do not work together, nothing is accomplished."

"What are you asking? I am not your equal."

"What has *equal* to do with it? The eye is not equal with the ear, nor should it be. They are different things."

"Then what do you want me to say?"

His eyes held a challenge. "Tell me about yourself."

I shrugged. "The first thing I remember is the desert and being cold."

"No, not that. I could take your memories if I wanted a diary. It is your thoughts I want. Tell me what it means to be an individual, to be you. What makes you different from that rock over there? What is your self?"

Humans have created many myths about muria—they are kind, they are cruel, they are powerful, they are vain, they are foolish, they are wise. In truth, they are all these things and none —they are *different*. Just how different, I was only then coming to understand. The cut of his question fit me, and I found to my surprise that I was able to answer it as if I had been rehearsing for it all my life. It wasn't until much later that I began to suspect that I had. At the time, however, I focused only on my words.

"The first belief is that self is the body, but even very young children soon realize that there is something more—that self is both the body and the one owning the body, the one knowing that he owns the body. Separate, certainly; but not always divisible."

"A beginning," he agreed. "In service of the body, humans understand 'yours' and 'mine,' and the concepts of ownership and desire. Thus it becomes possible to steal, to rape, to covet, to murder. Also to give gifts, to know rapture, to experience love.

But what would make someone care for more than essential needs and wants?"

I answered immediately. "The choice is between 'I' and 'you,' and if circumstances dictate that only one may live, or only one may possess a desired thing, then there is really no choice at all. 'I' triumphs, because others have selfdom only by logical extension."

"Yes," he said. "Does the wolf stop to think of the sheep's feelings before he kills it? But you have not answered my question yet."

His eyes held a curious intensity. This was not idle conversation. It was vitally important for me to answer correctly, though I couldn't fathom why. I spoke slowly, thinking through my answer with care. "At the animal level, there is only 'I' and 'you,' 'mine' and 'yours,' and if someone else has what we want or need, then the stronger, or faster, or more clever wins. The morality is clear. It is also insufficient for anything but children, fools, and animals."

"Good. Why?"

I paused, leaned against one of the stones fallen from the roof. "The idea of self does not stop at the physical level. In adulthood, humans come to include their community, their nation, their religion, in their concept of self."

He nodded. "Thus is born the social self, and thus is also born war. Continue."

"'I' becomes 'we,' and 'he' or 'she' becomes 'they.' But the social self feeds on the same drives as the body self. If 'they' have what 'we' covet, or if the social self is threatened by others, then humans band together and make war on one another. The body self is not submerged in the social self, but rather it is broadened: It includes one's own body and spirit undiminished, and also includes 'those like me.'"

"No," he said, interrupting. "The characteristics chosen for this bonding, this identification, are almost arbitrary—a locality, a common tongue, a religion, a philosophy."

"That's what I meant. Humans love to make those distinctions, love to place boundaries around things, around people. 'This person, this group, is one of us; that person, that group, is not,' they say, and think they have said something meaningful. They do not realize that what they share in common with strangers is of a far greater magnitude than what separates them. Do they not each rise in the morning, have dreams and hopes and fears about the day, speak to their loved ones, labor at their work, put food in their mouths, put clothes on their backs, put wisdom and knowledge and learning in their minds? Surely these things outweigh differences in appearance or custom."

He smiled at me then, and I wondered if I had ever seen him smile before. But the expression was gone almost before I saw it, and he nodded for me to go on. I took a deep breath. "Some understand this, either intuitively or from disciplined analysis. They see the common threads and form a species self. 'I am human,' they say, 'and what is human is me.' They understand that harm done to any member of humanity is harm done to themselves, just as one with only a body self realizes that he has been hurt when his arm is bruised, or the social self realizes he has been hurt when his wife or son or cousin or friend is brutalized."

"You have given this some thought," he said.

"I'm not done yet." I was beginning to see the point to his questions. "They do not go far enough, these wise humans. The true concept of self is one that recognizes its place as a member of the community of all intelligent life—that regardless of race or breed or shape or nature, we are all part of the same whole." Thus my common ground with Qol was greater than our differences— we were both alive, both wakeful, both standing in the full light of day, looking upon the world with eyes that watched and minds that thought, both with power in our hands. That he was immortal muria, and I a made thing . . . what of it?

"Who is master, who is slave?" he asked softly.

"I am both," I said, "and neither. I serve myself, and that is every living thing."

"And your name?"

"When I know it, I'll tell you."

He laughed. "You still move by yourself." He straightened his cloak, drew up the hood. "I am answered," he told me. "And now I must go back."

"Will I see you again?" I asked.

"That depends on a number of factors, some of which are still hidden. A person I had not considered has decided to interfere. My options are thereby altered—perhaps reduced."

"You mean Nina?"

"Only indirectly. Your companion's presence reveals the hand of someone else, a far subtler power. Remember always that you and I are not fighting the same war. When you decide who and what you are, the entire planet will shudder in recognition."

I had no idea what he meant, but his words terrified me. *How could finding my name shake the planet?* I forced the feelings down, and concentrated on the rest of his comment.

"If not Nina, then who is interfering? And interfering with what?"

He eyed me calmly, but I could see the calculations roiling behind his bland facade. "I told you there was a new player in this contest," he said. "Leave my battles to me. Nothing has changed for you." He turned and took a few steps away, as if the conversation had ended.

I called out, "Qol!" and my word stopped him from leaving. He faced me once more; patient, dispassionate, remote, waiting.

"Good-bye, Ketlan," I said softly.

"That is no longer my name." He raised his hand in a curious gesture. It took me a moment to recognize it as denial. "Do you grasp the nature of the test you endured this morning?"

I nodded curtly. "You let me live."

He smiled for the second time. "Yes, I did. Now you may ponder the difference between cruelty and mercy."

"You are not my judge."

He nodded. "No longer. You have assumed that mantle for yourself, as is proper." He started to turn again.

"Qol—one last question."

He looked back over his shoulder. "Yes?"

"What of Gaheris, the Archon? Am I right to pursue him?"

Qol paused a long time, as if considering how to phrase his response. "Gaheris is not what you think," he said at last. "When you encounter a puppet, look for the puppeteer. This one is Vastil. Your companion will know the name. Ask her."

Then he turned and left me, and I waited until the sound of the horses was lost in the distance before I buried my face in my arm and wept from sheer emotional exhaustion.

It is not often given to a man to meet his maker and survive. I counted myself fortunate, but my bitter tears would not stop.

11. JUSTIAN

NINA REJOINED me as I stumbled my way south, striving to get my emotions under control. Neither one of us spoke of Qol. We traveled together in silence for several miles, then cut east up a steep hill to scout the land ahead.

I crouched in the lee of some rocks and studied the vast expanse of the Justian Bridge dwindling south away into the mist. Lyonmouth, where the Leonais River started spreading to meet the sea, was twelve miles wide even this far inland, not including the surrounding floodplain. The bridge, a single span made of ship's metal, was the largest human artifact on Sundering. It stretched nearly twenty miles from end to end and reached two hundred feet above the river at its apex, forming a slender grey aerial thread that tied the north and south halves of the continent together. Like the starships themselves, the bridge had stood unscathed by the passage of three thousand years, a testimony to the lost technology and vision of the ancient engineers.

I had no problem setting aside my awe and cursing the bridge. For me, right now, it wasn't so much a wonder as a challenge. Unless I could fly or swim, the only way across the river was the bridge. Farther east, where the river opened into the estuary proper, a hundred miles across, the river looked calmer, but was rife with underwater currents that fought the tidal bore at all times, and the spring melt runoff, gathering power all the way from the Abuttals, was ferocious. Some ships dared it, but most would not. Even here, where the water was swift but more predictable, boats rarely braved the central currents. Too many sister ships had been lost over the centuries. Fishermen hugged the banks, looking for fish in the more sluggish waters of the coves and innumerable inlets.

The problem, of course, was getting across it without being spotted. It was rather hard to sneak across a narrow span only a hundred feet wide, but that ran, unbroken, for twenty miles. The massive economy of Leonais depended on that bridge. Now that Gaheris had secured the north, wains and wagons and foot traffic had resumed. At each end, where the gigantic support pylons anchored in bedrock, gates controlled access. On the bridge itself, soldiers on horseback patrolled regularly, thrusting roughly through the civilian crowd.

The soldiers all wore grey uniforms with a red patch on the left breast, sporting the sigil of the Archon. Even the wagons had the sigil scratched on their sides. The lines approaching the bridge were very long, stretching miles back up the road toward Draycott. Shops and inns clustered around the gate, catering to weary travelers coming off the bridge or preparing to cross it. For a person afoot, twenty miles was a long day's walk, especially when food and water must be carried. I presumed the same huddle of boarding houses and shops littered the southern end of the bridge.

I ran some risk of being spotted, here in my perch on the cliff off to one side, for nothing announces a man as well as his outline against the sky. I forced myself to remain crouching, with my hood drawn up, and discarded plan after plan for gaining the bridge. Hiding in the back of a wagon, my first thought, would clearly not work. Guards at the gate were inspecting each vehicle before letting it onto the bridge. And even if I could manage, somehow, to evade the search, where would Nina hide?

The only horses on the bridge were ridden by soldiers, leading to my next idea. If Nina could keep her horn invisible and could make herself walk ploddingly, like a horse, perhaps I could steal a uniform and pretend to be one of the guards. But as the day wore on and I observed the patterns, I realized the patrols on the bridge were special detachments. They obviously knew each other, and each group stopped to talk with riders coming from the other direction. They probably quartered in lodgings near the ends of the bridge. Still, perhaps I could pretend to be a courier or an officer—someone with a valid reason to cross the bridge but whom the others weren't likely to know. It would mean waylaying someone to get the uniform, for both couriers and officers wore fancier clothing than plain soldiers did. Nina could overpower a lone soldier easily enough, assuming we found one. The more I thought about riding across disguised as an officer, the more I liked the idea . . . until I remembered the effect Nina had on ordinary people.

In the dark or from a distance, with her horn hidden, she might appear to be a horse, but only at first glance. Her carriage was wrong—she could never manage to tread heavily like a horse. Her hooves danced as she walked. Worse, she exuded mystery and an otherworldly lure even when she was trying to be inconspicuous. Heads would turn even before she came into sight. In the villages where I had ridden her openly, children had run out and crowds had formed. She was a faerie creature, and though she walked in the mortal world, she brought a piece of faerie with her. Even the dullest guard wouldn't hesitate more than a moment.

Ashe had known I traveled with her, probably from the villagers where I had been forced to ride openly. His soldiers back in Landing had asked for a man with white hair and a black horse, but according to Tessa, everyone had known they were asking about a unicorn. I had to assume that if Ashe knew about Nina, then Gaheris probably did, too. Therefore, the soldiers were even less likely to be fooled, even if I coated her with mud and draped an old blanket over her hide.

I cursed quietly to myself and looked underneath the bridge. For as far as I could see in the mist, pylons drove up out of the river to support the bridge at regular intervals. The water raced past them, foaming and spraying, revealing the strength of the current. If I stole a skiff or rowboat and went at night, could I possibly row against that pull? I didn't think so, even without considering how big the boat would have to be to hold Nina, or the fact that I had only one working arm. I didn't even consider the tall ships that plied the East Ocean, even though the nearest deep harbor was probably only twenty miles downriver. I couldn't pay for passage, and the Archon had either sunk or commandeered all of them anyway.

I slithered around the rock face and made my way down to where Nina waited for me in a thicket at the bottom. She whickered softly, tilting her ears forward in question. I touched her nose gently, and shook my head. Before I even set foot on it, Justian Bridge had defeated me.

Nina inhaled shadows and transformed under my hand. "There are other roads," she said.

"Over the river? This is the only bridge for—"

"No," she said. "Not human roads. The dolmens."

The dolmens? The last time I had touched the sleeping power under the faerie mounds, I had nearly put myself directly into the Archon's hands. It was true I had sensed the dolmen network enabled travel, letting me step from place to place physically, as if stepping through a doorway. The wakeful power of the dolmens would carry me, make the places adjacent. I scarcely understood the mechanics, but I knew the risk was enormous, for I would first have to rouse the Sleeper. Even if I could control those energies, surely Gaheris would sense me. I had no confidence that I could do it quickly at all, let alone quickly enough to escape detection.

"No," she said again, seeing the surprise on my face. "Not you. Not like that. I can use the web of energy without waking the Sleeper."

"Tell me."

She shook her head, tossing her hair, and didn't answer directly. She exhaled the shadows again, transforming, and her equine nose tickled my human one. She sent me a mental picture; words were insufficient for this. As if from a distance, I saw myself on her back, her horn energized with my blood, her hooves pawing the stones of a faerie mound's floor. Within the ambit of the dolmen, she could superpose one mound over another. For an infinitely short period of time, we would be in *both* places simultaneously. Then, as she let awareness of one fade and the other strengthen, we would dissolve in one spot and reassemble in the other. It was all Nina's power, her strength of will. Her method did not use the dolmens directly at all; rather it used the mounds only to locate the points in space, which could be done without stirring the dormant power.

I grunted a query, and she obligingly fired another picture to me, this one a confusing welter of ideas and images. I could not grasp it all, but I understood enough to know this ability was similar to the way she made her horn invisible, or the way she changed her own shape.

"Okay," I said. "Let's try it."

She neighed, head low, ears back. There was more. She sent me a final image, showing the cost. For her, it was only an exhausting expenditure of energy. For me, it would be terrifying. Superposition was not something humans could tolerate easily. Her final image showed me screaming in pain as my body was torn to bits at the source and reconstituted at the destination. The image and accompanying feeling were so clear in my mind that I could feel my flesh shredding and exploding away, my bones bursting into ash beneath.

I recoiled, literally pushing her away. "No," I gasped, shuddering.

Relentless, she sent an image of us retreating, going back to the upper plateau and abandoning the quest.

"Not that, either," I said.

The shadows came gently, tremulously, to transform her. "It is the only way I know to go forward," she said. "But the choice is yours."

Then she changed back, the small white star on her forehead glimmering where her horn could appear. I shook my head again, rejecting the idea. Maybe, if all else failed, I would consider it. But it felt too much like death. I was not faerie, at ease in multiple worlds. Places had reality for me; I could not superpose them, even in imagination, not without risking madness. And the searing pain . . . even if it lasted for only a breath, it could undo me. I would have to *be* mad already, or so desperate that no other choice sufficed. There had to be a better way.

I stared gloomily into the distance, riffling my memories, hoping for inspiration. When I had sensed that the interconnectedness of the dolmens allowed transportation, I had not perceived a cost like the one Nina described. Could my power differ from Nina's? To use it, I would have to risk waking the Sleeper—and that hinted at other forces, too, far more potent and deadly, although I barely understood them. I had to weigh each option against the agony of superposition. Going a hundred miles upstream suddenly didn't seem so bad. I opened my mouth to tell Nina, but a sudden rush of the god-winds arose, accompanied by cold dread in the pit of my stomach, demanding my attention.

Grey! came the call, like a scream, but soundless.

Distance constricted; my sight narrowed, focused, engrossed

me to the exclusion of all other senses. Abruptly, I was *seeing* Maran being wrested from the lip of her valley by two blue-robed sorcerers. I beheld the coruscating field of their power, running like the bars of a cage going up around her, surrounding her with compulsion. She lifted one hand toward me across the miles, the other curved protectively around her womb. She cried an entreaty I could not make out, and tears streamed down her face.

"Maran!" I bellowed.

Nina changed back to woman form. "Grey, what's wrong?"

"Can't you see it? It's Maran!" But even as I spoke, the vision started to fade. "Two men—Amrhyn sorcerers—they're taking her. I have to help her—"

"Grey!" Nina took my head between her hands, gripping my hair painfully. Her look was urgent, but I could barely concentrate on her. "Is it the future? Are you seeing the future?"

I pushed Nina's hands away, and strove to hang onto the vision. It was like trying to clutch water with my fist. The vision split into a thousand running rivulets, dripping through my fingers and slipping away, evaporating even as I watched.

"Grey! Is it happening now? Could it be a lie? An illusion? A warning?"

I shook my head to clear it. The vision was gone. "It could be the future," I said slowly. "It could be the past. It could be now. I can't tell. I saw her, reaching out for me. But it was real. As real as you are. I think it's now, something happening now. A true vision."

"Can you reach her?"

Helplessly, I stared at Nina. "How?"

"Try!"

Try how? Too many miles separated us. I didn't know where to look, how to begin. The god-winds stirred fretfully at my distress, but I had nothing to focus on, nowhere to send my inner sight. The vision had come by itself and now was gone. I cast my mind out, the way I had on the upper plateau long ago, but I found only darkness. Tears rolled down my cheeks from frustration and impotence. I wiped them away roughly with the back of my good hand. "I can't, I can't," I said.

"You must try. Think of your son."

Aiden, my unborn child. It hadn't been all that long. He would only be a clump of cells now, less than an ounce in weight. Unformed. Vulnerable. But I had seen his future, there on the night he was conceived. I had seen him, stared into his eyes, heard his voice, and had almost been able to touch him. That once, Aiden had breached the walls of time to speak with me from the future, though I didn't know whether that power had been his or mine. I tried reaching for him now, but as with Maran, I didn't know where to look. Nothing came to me. But I was sure, unshakably, that Aiden would be born. That meant Maran was free from harm, too, didn't it? I felt relief wash over me.

"She's safe," I said. "She has to be."

Nina was watching me intently, doubting. "You reached her?"

"No, but I know my son will be born. I saw it. I saw him—Aiden. His name will be Aiden." For a moment, I saw his golden-white curls again, as if he stood before me. His eyes, bright green like Maran's, laughed with life and happiness. "I saw it, that night in Maran's valley. So she must be safe. It was a true vision."

"Like today's?"

My heart dropped. "What?"

"Inaction *is* action," she said. "To make your vision of Aiden true, you must make this one false."

I stared at her wordlessly. Did she expect me to leap on her back and gallop to the rescue, madly waiving a sword and shouting a challenge? It was ridiculous. I was a cripple, not a warrior. But was she right? Could the future be at risk if I didn't do something to make it happen? Was reality itself fragile enough that it needed my hand to steer it? I should just trust what I had seen. But if I trusted the one, I must also trust the other. And Maran was at risk *now*. Nina was right: I suffered from conflicting prophecies. I couldn't be sure Aiden would be born if I didn't save Maran first.

"How?" I whispered. "I don't even know where Maran *is*." I had a duty to her and to my son, but no way to fulfill it. "They are sorcerers, the ones who took her. Blue robes, from Amrhyn. What has Amrhyn to do with us?"

"When you are ridden down, do you blame the horse or the rider? Amrhyn is in the Archon's pocket. They will take her to Gaheris."

"But why *her*? What will he do?"

"You know him. You've dreamed his dreams. He will kill her, slowly, painfully, negligently, for sport." Nina's tone had no room for compassion or pity; she left me nothing to argue against. She stated a fact and didn't bother daring me to deny it.

Yet it made no sense. There were hundreds of thousands of women, perhaps millions, on Leonais. Why pick this one, one who could contact me? Asking the question provided the answer. He had sent sorcerers to collect Maran *because* she could contact me. To get at me. And now that they held her, he would go to her, work his will, knowing that she would relay it all to me, that it would hurt me, too. It was either blatant enmity or a trap; perhaps it was both.

Nevertheless. "I can't let him do this," I said.

"He has raised the stakes," said Nina, speaking distinctly, each word hitting me like a blow. "You must defeat him before he hurts her."

Defeat? I focused on Nina carefully, as if she, too, could turn to water and run between my fingers. My balance was suddenly precarious; motion in any direction could topple me. Defeat the Archon? That wasn't my plan; it hadn't ever been my plan. I didn't even think it was possible. I wanted my name from him, and I was foolish enough to try to get it, hazarding my life in the attempt . . . but I had never considered battling him or trying to change the course of history. That was for other people—Ashe, if he still lived; or Qol, if he cared; or the nobles of Leonais, if they could.

Defeat him?

Me?

A spasm of understanding made my stomach lurch. Fighting Gaheris had never been my goal, but it had always been Nina's. *That* was why she stayed with me. *That* was why she helped me. For some reason, she thought I could accomplish something even she could not. Defeating the Archon was *her* goal, and she thought the way to reach it was through me. Was I just a tool for her use? And what power did she see nestling unborn in me the way Aiden grew in Maran?

A coldness came over me, and I looked fixedly at her, trying to see myself through her eyes. I measured her thoroughly, finally seeing her help and encouragement for what it really had been. No wonder she was chary with speech. It only took one slip, one incautious word, to betray her true intent. Her face became guarded as I continued staring silently, judging her and not liking what I saw. After a bit, she looked away, her body sagging, as if she were granting me a counter in a complex game.

"Grey," she whispered, "listen to me. You shouldn't be surprised. Fighting Gaheris is what you were made for."

I bit back my first retort and tried to keep my voice level. "How do you know?" I asked. "You said— You said you didn't know *what* I was. And Qol said—" I broke off, realizing suddenly that she hadn't asked what had passed between me and the elf. Was it because she didn't want to know, or because somehow she already knew? "He said . . . he said to ask you about someone named Vastil."

She froze, gaping at me for a moment, as if I had slapped her.

Then she cried out, a wounded animal's bleat, and shadows sprang from all angles to subsume her. She fell forward, hands outstretched, landing on all fours. Clods of dirt sprayed my face as she raced away.

She had a unique way of ending conversations—or at least interrupting them. But I knew her pattern now. When she came back, she would tell me more. Perhaps not immediately, and perhaps not in a way I could understand, but eventually, up to the limit of her peculiar self-imposed strictures, she would tell me. And I meant to have the truth this time.

I limped deeper into the thicket, grateful for the overcast sky and the mist from the river, even though the dampness made my leg ache. The mist gave me a feeling of privacy, reduced the world to manageable proportions. I found a tree stump to sit on and pulled my cloak up. Things were happening too fast. None of it made sense. Fragments of thoughts and impressions struck me as if they came uncontrolled from the outside. The plea from Maran . . . the slumbering power under an ancient network of stone circles . . . chanting, blue-robed sorcerers . . . Ashe defeated . . . Gaheris gloating . . . Nina saving my life, over and over . . . Aiden threatened . . . Nina wanting to tear my body apart to step from one place to the next . . . Qol himself, inscrutable, cold, remote, fashioning me to fight the Archon. *Making me* for it, the way Maran made Hasq—to do a job, then be casually discarded when the task was done.

I tried to fit the shards of my thoughts together. Qol had denied imbuing me with an innate purpose; moreover, he had refused to give one even when I asked. He said I needed to make my own purpose, forge my own name. It felt more like the nattering of a philosopher than the advice of a parent. An incredibly ancient phrase came unbidden to the surface of my mind, rising from what hidden memory store I didn't know: "Know thyself." The language came from before the Landing, before the ships had even left Earth. I suspected it had been ancient even then, before humans knew of other worlds. That was the sum of Qol's advice to me: "Figure it out on your own."

I decided elves were sanctimonious, stuck-up snobs. Nina didn't trust them, and that was probably a good indication of their worth. On the other hand, I had felt nothing but clean compassion from Qol, with no tinge of manipulation. Was that because I wasn't perceptive enough, or because he truly granted me freedom of choice? I didn't understand either one of them, elf or unicorn. *Na-souled*, Henna had said, speaking of me—but she meant them: devils, faeries, elves, gods, creatures distant and disdainful, insolent in their superiority. No human walks easily in their shadow. Even their disregard was dangerous. I was beginning to understand there were things worse than malice.

Did they see power in me, potential? I saw none. Some small magics, yes; and a sensitivity that let me reach behind reality at times, see things normally hidden. But power to change destiny, to control others, to *fight*, to impress my will on the world? No, or at least, not yet, not really. My actions had only affected myself and those beside me, like any other human's. Perhaps I had unusual ways, and sometimes the god-winds filled me, but I didn't see myself commanding armies or engaging in sorcerous duels. Weary, I closed my eyes and leaned over with my good elbow on my knee. If I had power, surely I could use it to reach Maran, to rescue her from her captors.

Well, what power did I have at my disposal? My body was useless—a scholar's build, with one arm withered. I had long since come to think of my body as a shell, a container. I fed it, gave it water, let it sleep, and expected it to bear my weight. I might as well be a detached head. But in my head were resources human bodies seldom commanded.

The strongest force I knew of was the dolmen network, but I didn't dare touch it, not even for Maran and Aiden. I didn't know how to use it without waking the Sleeper, and Gaheris would perceive me in an instant. But Nina's option could accomplish the same thing. What if I endured the agony and let her carry me to a dolmen near Maran? Yes, that would get me closer, but no, it wouldn't help: I would be just as ineffective there as I was here. Changing location was not the answer.

That left the power of my mind. I had never really explored its limits. I knew I could heal, at ruinous self-cost, and I had touched upon other abilities. I had sent ghostly visions to Henna, and I had led Nina to me. I had broken Maran's spells. I had made Tessa and the boys sleep. Words of command hovered behind my lips, just out of reach. Could I ride the god-winds on purpose, be an eagle instead of a blown wisp?

A small whirlwind of my desiring sprang up in my right palm. It wasn't raw power I wanted, nor skill to coerce, but the freedom of the wind itself, something that could blow without let or hindrance wherever it chose. I lifted the tiny, tightly controlled gyre and batted it away toward the north. It hummed, spun, and sped off into the distance faster than the bolt of a crossbow. I followed with my mind, reaching out for Maran, trying not for a specific location, but to locate her essence, wherever it might be. I probed to re-create the vision I had seen.

That place within myself where I retreat does not know time or location. It might have only been moments, or it might have been hours, before I felt her. She was not near her valley to the north, but south, already inside the Archon's citadel in Jappa, across the bridge from me. And *this* vision was happening now—I was sure of it. My tiny whirlwind hovered near her forehead. Its eye became mine, and I could see her. She stirred restlessly at my mental touch, but did not rouse.

"Lady Maran," I said aloud, not knowing whether my words would carry across the fragile link I had forged.

"Maran!" I called again, willing more strength into the link. I let the god-winds take me on this side, rising into a roar. Leaves and branches flew into the air around me, but I held very still, all my concentration focused on contacting Maran. The vision took on a new clarity, and it encompassed her surroundings. She was in a prison of some kind, a dungeon—the walls were stone, set with iron rings and chains. She was slumped against the wall, shackles on her arms. Others were chained beside her, and the two blue-robed sorcerers lounged indolently nearby.

One of them looked up, saw my miniature whirlwind and recognized it for what it was. He laughed, and his face loomed as he bent near. He was small, gnarled with age, but his eyes glinted with mixed contempt and animus. "I hardly think so," he said dryly. "If you want her, you'll have to come here." He closed his palms on my gyre, snuffing it out like a candle, banishing me from the room, a ghost dismissed. I was thrown back into myself, god-winds in disarray, my heart pounding, and the tendril of my power severed.

I tried to reestablish the link, but the dungeon was now impenetrable, as if he had somehow blocked me from further attempts. I would need greater power than I now possessed to break through his spell. But I had seen enough. Chained to the wall on Maran's right were Ashe and Tad. To her left lay Owen, Torrey, and Tessa. How had Gaheris collected them so quickly? Was this really in response to my touching of the dolmen's power? If so, the Archon baited his trap with desperation and used his captives ruthlessly. I knew that to bring them all together in such a short time, Gaheris or his Amrhyn helpers must have used the dolmen network themselves. Weren't they afraid I would sense their touch, as I was afraid they would sense mine?

Was there anything for them to fear?

I lurched to my feet and found Nina squatting only a few paces away, her silky hair spread around her in a cloud. Impatiently, roughly, without permission, I forged the mental link between us and thrust the picture at her all in a breath: Ashe slumped sideways with blood streaming from his face; Tad staring sullenly at the floor, unmoving; Maran unconscious, murmuring in her dreams; Owen and Torrey sitting miserably with their hands in their laps; Tessa standing, her hands gripping the chains, fingers working back and forth, back and forth, her hollow eyes staring. They were all of them nearly naked, with only bloody rags and straw to cover them. Filthy. Bruised. Beaten. Despondent.

Nina looked away. "He means for you to try to rescue them," she said.

I agreed it was a trap, a lure. But why them? I had no love for Ashe, nor did I owe him fealty. Tad wore my good left arm as though it were his own, but I would hardly go screaming into battle for him. Maran was a good choice of hostage, for despite our differences, she carried my child beneath her heart. Torrey, Owen, Tessa—I had affection for them, but like so many others, they were pawns in this game.

"Why them?" I asked again, this time aloud.

She shrugged and gathered herself to her feet. "Because each of them either helped you or let you go. Perhaps the Archon believes you care for them." She paused and looked directly at me. "Do you?"

"Yes," I said, and immediately, "no. I don't even know them, not really. They're just people I've met. Why would he think I would risk my life for them?"

"Perhaps Gaheris believes you afflicted with nobility." Again, she treated me to a meaningful pause. "Are you?"

No, it was a luxury I never indulged. She knew that. Why wouldn't Gaheris? My head hurt. I didn't want to think about it any longer. I shook my head, refusing to answer her.

"Grey," she said firmly. "Either you try to rescue them or you don't. The world won't be destroyed if you don't. Only your self-respect."

"You are trying to goad me."

"Yes."

"Because you think I can win. That's insane. I couldn't even *spy* on them without being discovered. When that sorcerer spotted me, I was overmatched instantly. He was *amused*. And that wasn't even Gaheris." I flung my good arm in her direction. "You and Qol. You're alike. You both think I'm something I'm not. I'm not a hero. I'm not a fighter. I don't have the *ability* to do what you want."

"A hero is someone who acts like a hero. A coward is someone—"

I cut her off angrily. "Don't *dare* offer platitudes. You run away all the time. You never answer questions. You have some grand plan you don't bother sharing. You want to use me. You don't care what it costs, as long as you get what you want. But you won't even answer a question. Tell me about Vastil, or just shut up."

Chest heaving, I forced myself to stop. I stared at her, daring her to answer me. *Just once, Nina. Just once, tell the whole truth. Please.*

She pushed her hair back behind her ears. "Vastil is muria," she said quietly, without any special emphasis. "He and Qol are playing a deadly game. Vastil made Gaheris; Qol made you. You are their instruments. They do not contend directly, but they can shatter the world between them."

Oh, gods. It was true. I knew it instantly. That story Qol had told me—it wasn't metaphor or lesson, it was bald fact. Pieces on a board. Toys. *You still move by yourself.* Would he poke me with a stick if I stopped? My legs wobbled and I fell to my knees. Even Maran had known: *You have no memories because you are not old enough to have them.* I had thought she was lying. I had thought Qol benevolent.

"Grey, listen," Nina said urgently. "This is an ancient game.

Vastil destroyed civilization on Leonais once before. It's why there's nothing left of the Second Colony but the useless starships and a few artifacts. Now he means to do it again. Humans have upset the balance among the muria. He means to put you down."

"What—? What did we do? How do you know?"

"Because he did it to us."

The link between us was still open. She placed in my mind what I had seen before: Nina stepping away from the herd. But this time, she corrected my interpretation. She was not abandoning them, she was escaping a prison. An island, far west of Leonais, in the middle of the West Ocean. *Alfheimr*, she named it. She showed me the muria raising a barrier, speaking words of binding, trapping all of her kind in that one place. Ten thousand muria, working as one—no, they *were* one. Different faces, different bodies, but only one consciousness. A single mind had wrought that prison, a single will dominated. Vastil. The *same* Vastil. Three thousand years ago. Unchanged, unchanging, unflinching after all this time.

Tears blinded me. "How? How can he be the same?"

"Muria means 'many-bodied.' They are the children of the First Colony. We were here first. We tried to help them, but the effort went awry. That is our great failing, the reason for our impurity. We changed them more than we knew, and they surpassed us. There are only five muria. Qol you know. He has always been neutral, even in our betrayal. But Ulat commanded it, and Vastil did it, and Qol did not stop them. Tamil and Bastion stood aside and let it happen."

Five! But—

"Tamil, Bastion, Vastil, Ulat, and Qol," she recited. "Only those five persons, those five minds. Each mind exists in thousands of bodies simultaneously. What one knows, each knows. Losing a body to them is no more than losing a fingernail to you, and is as easily replaced. They are effectively immortal.

The same Qol who met you watched my people imprisoned. He is not your friend."

"Ketlan," I whispered. "He said he used to be called Ketlan. It means 'beloved.'"

"He misled you by telling only part of the truth," she said flatly. "Ketlan is what they call their children before they affiliate with one of the five."

Lies. Lies and half-truths. Games. He played with words the same way he played with my life. And I had believed him! "Stop," I begged. "I can't—" *I can't handle any more.* "I don't want—" *I don't want to know it.*

"You asked, you *demanded*. Therefore, I answered. What will you do now?"

"Do?" I echoed numbly.

She stood over me, dauntless, stark in her anger. I peered up at her, appalled that she could say such things without weeping. But she had known all this time. Known about Gaheris, about me, about Qol and Vastil. And she expected me to do something about it.

"Now you know the stakes," she said. "Some of them."

"There's *more*?"

"Vastil will imprison me, and can unmake you. Isn't that enough?"

No. No, it wasn't. My search for my name seemed a puerile quest now. But it was so much a part of me that I couldn't give it up. And Nina was entwined with it. I still didn't understand how. I wanted to ask why she stayed with me, but I didn't dare—she might answer. Instead, I asked, "How did humans 'upset the balance'?" After all this time. Three thousand years since the Landing. An ancient game. And Vastil had done it before. It was nothing I had set in motion, had nothing to do with my identity. But it was connected somehow, all happening at the same time. "Why now? Why would he—?" Then suddenly, blindingly, I blurted out: "How did you escape?"

She was silent.

I got to my feet and stood there, shaking. "Nina—"

"Trust me," she whispered.

"That's what Qol said. 'Misperception and unfounded enmity.'" *She is not on my side.* "He said he was glad you were with me, but he was startled, even shaken." What could rattle the confidence of an immortal elf? *You have a choice, and I require you to make it.* "Whose misperception did he mean? Whose enmity? Which one of you is lying to me?"

"Both. Neither. It doesn't matter. It won't help Maran, or Torrey, or Aiden, or—"

I laid my forefinger across her lips to stop her. I had to ask, had to know. And now, finally, *finally*, the god-winds stirred again, rose up about us, started to howl. Lightning forked across the sky. Thunder rumbled. I was calm, as calm as I ever remembered being. This wasn't about rage, or fear, or control. It was about truth.

Her form started to bleed shadows as she backed away. I pushed the shadows off with a thought, but held her with nothing more than my bald desire. *No running away. Not this time.* I knew I could compel her, but I did not. I knew I could force her into any shape or none, but I did not. This was what she had seen in me, the hope she held out. That I *could* do a thing, but *would* not. Maran had told me that restraint was a kind of power, too, and she was right. How can we trust someone who gives no choices? Compulsion was the liar here. I refused the temptation, growing stronger by it, and the god-winds rose into a tornado. I thought the ground would crack apart at my feet, it trembled so. Instead, the sky opened up. Torrents of rain slashed from all directions. I heard the distant crash of waves against rocks. The ship's metal of the Justian Bridge shrieked in protest. Nearby trees uprooted themselves and flew high overhead, whirled away by the strength of the wind. But around us, in the eye of the storm, it was utterly still.

Qol had given me a choice after all. And not just one. Each choice I made led to another, either constraining or empowering all choices thereafter. And so I gave Nina the right to refuse me when I said, "Tell me what you really want from me." Though I spoke quietly, my words sounded like a shout in that stillness.

"Free my people," she said simply.

"Yes," I said, just as simply. No promise, no vow, no oath. Just my intention, my choice. "How did you escape?"

"The door I used closed behind me. A much stronger power is needed to breach the wards surrounding Alfheimr."

"That's not an answer."

"The war among humans is a simple thing, orchestrated by Vastil to keep humans ignorant and impoverished, too busy scrabbling in the dirt to rediscover the principles of industry and technology."

"All to keep humans from reaching your island prison?"

"Yes," she said, "and no. It's far more complex. The struggle among the muria is of a different nature. The five have lost consensus. They work against each other in subtle ways."

I wanted to ask how, but it didn't matter. She still hadn't answered my question, but what she had said was enough for me to make decisions. Many things had changed here today, the most important of which was my resolve. The rest could wait. I released the god-winds, and instantly we were drenched as the storm crashed in.

She sensed my refusal to remain passive, my determination to stop being a toy soldier and begin waging battle on my own behalf. I imposed duty upon myself and took up the burden.

"Maran first, or Gaheris?" she asked, as if she had always known this moment was coming and had been patiently waiting for it.

"Maran," I said without hesitation. "I don't know what the Amrhyns will do if Gaheris suddenly stops controlling them."

"Will you fight them?"

"If I must," I said.

"And then the Archon?"

"If I can."

"And then Vastil?"

"If need be," I said.

"And Qol?"

I didn't answer that.

"Will you let me take you to Maran?" she asked. "Will you endure the anguish of superposition?"

"No," I said instantly, "there is another way." I took a deep breath before committing myself. Yes, it felt right. I was finally ready. Qol had told me to choose hope over despair, and I finally understood the choice he demanded.

"Tell me," said Nina.

I took another deep breath, steeling myself to continue. I felt my face tighten. There could be no turning back from my next words.

"I'm going to wake the Sleeper."

She shouted, a wordless cry of fierce exultation, as if I'd finally justified her every hope for me. Her eyes burned like coals through the shadows that suddenly thronged her. She dropped to her hooves, quivering, her horn brighter than I had ever seen it.

We galloped down out of the hills overlooking the bridge, the rain falling in grey sheets. Thunder boomed off the cliffs. It was the mother of all storms, but it was mine, and I did not fear it.

I reserved my fear for what lay ahead.

12. JAPPA

NINA THUNDERED down toward Justian Bridge, leaping stones and bushes, skirting the edges of the cliff recklessly, sending chunks of mud and gravel flying on the corners. Her horn blazed a path through the rain. I clung to her in terror, sure that at any moment we would skid over the edge. I had no thoughts other than survival.

Abruptly, we were off the rocks and pounding down an unpaved road. The deluge had turned the dirt to a sluggish river of mud, but Nina ran lightly over the top, her hooves neither sinking nor catching. We skirted a small shack and surprised an old man bent over a wagon wheel. He couldn't possibly get out of the way in time. He screamed, and I just had a moment to see his rounded eyes before the great muscles in Nina's hindquarters bunched, pushed, and launched us over him and the wagon both.

With a jarring thump, she landed again, just in time to swerve around another mired wagon. Behind this one stood a pair of soldiers, battered by the storm but standing bravely to guard the road with drawn swords. They were quick, but had no chance of stopping us. Nina dipped her horn and took the one on the left through the heart. She twisted her head to the side and he slipped off her horn, just now falling but already dead. I used my good arm to push the other one aside, ducking low over Nina's back to avoid the sword. In moments, he was lost in the rain and muck behind us.

I shouted, and Nina brayed. She skidded through another turn, and our path joined the main road to the bridge. As we neared the collection of stores and inns at the foot of the bridge, I caught fleeting glimpses of men and women huddled on the porches, watching us open-mouthed as we raced past. The checkpoint gate was closed, and a double row of bedraggled but grim soldiers blocked our path.

Nina reared, hooves flashing, and I held on with just my knees, gathering the god-winds. A sudden gust came off the river, pushing the driving rain aside for a moment, letting me see the gate clearly. I willed my percipience, my ability to see things with my mind, into the storm, feeling through tremendous tensions for the point of greatest strength. *There!* I clenched my fist and brought it down. Lightning drove from the sky like a lash and exploded against the heavy gate. Soldiers sprawled in every direction. The ones not killed instantly scrambled to their feet and fled. The heavy timbers of the gate splintered and caught fire, but they held. Again I pulled lightning from the sky, and again, until I thought I would be deafened. The coruscations left blinding afterimages on my eyeballs.

Nina screamed her challenge and charged. She smashed through the last of the timbers and we gained the base of the bridge. Her hooves clanged against the ship's metal as she pawed her way up the wedge at the foot. The god-winds shrieked and twisted around us, barely under my control. The storm raged and spun, growing more savage by the moment. I rotated my wrist, splayed my fingers and *pushed*, sending a tornado ahead of us to clear the path.

Only then did I remember that civilians made up the majority of the traffic.

Men and women flattened themselves on the metal plates of the bridge, holding onto their children and possessions. In the first few moments, several walkers slid over the edge, or were whirled up into the sky. Wagons groaned and collapsed, boards and wheels splintering, metal straps torn loose and winging through the air like crossbow bolts. The few horses near the end of the bridge were immediately swept over the rail. Mules further away planted their feet and bellowed, but would not stay standing long.

With a savage, violent thrust of my will, I sent the tornado spinning up and away from the bridge. Cold air from the sea rushed in to fill the sudden vacuum, but I lifted my arm and held it back by main force of will. The effort nearly unseated me. I held my concentration until the wind gentled and no one else was in danger.

We barreled down the center of the span. Nina nimbly leaped obstacles or ran them down. Even in their fear at the sudden violence of the weather, crouching and clutching each other, people watched Nina with wonder. We passed a blur of open mouths and reaching hands on either side. Ahead of us, as far as I could see, merchants, wagon drivers, and pedestrians scattered from the center of the bridge, crowding the edges, leaving us a wide lane. A few soldiers thought to stand against us, wrenching their horses' reins to keep them still, but Nina didn't slow down. The poor beasts either panicked, carrying their riders over the edge, or reared to acknowledge Nina's suzerainty and let her pass.

Rain still pelted down, although I had thrown the main body of the storm into the East Ocean. The sky began to brighten, and more and more people stood, recovering from their fear enough to see what was happening. I became aware of a roar mounting over the sounds of the wind and rain. For twenty miles, as we crossed the gigantic bridge, the people clapped and shouted, pounding each other on the back, pointing, laughing, and yelling encouragement. Children stared, mouths agape, some of them crying from the overload of emotions wringing the crowd.

The few soldiers still ahorse, captains mainly, raced ahead of us, trying to reach the safety of the far end. But no horse could outrun Nina. Her horn shone like mage-fire, and I clung to her neck, participating in her glory. One of the foot soldiers threw me a sword, a long glittering arc turning end over end through the rain. I snatched it from the air by the hilt even as he tore off his sigil and merged with the cheering throng.

One by one, we overtook the fleeing horsemen. Those who slowed down were pulled from their saddles by the crowd. Those who turned to fight were betrayed by their mounts or thrust aside by Nina. I swung the sword, and once even hit something. I don't know what I struck, but it grabbed at the blade and almost pulled it from my hand. After that, I simply held the weapon in the air like a firebrand, trusting Nina to get us across.

The bridge started curving back down toward the ground, and the south end hove into view at last. Nina was breathing hard, but still moving at the same clip, seemingly tireless. The gates at the checkpoint were closed, and at least two hundred men stood behind them, swords, pikes, crossbows, and longbows at the ready. They had been watching us approach for twenty miles, and had had plenty of time to prepare.

On the near side, civilians tried to crowd out of the way, but they were too many. Gone now, the shouts of encouragement that had followed us for twenty miles. Screams of fear replaced them. The milling civilians compacted themselves, pushed as far to the sides as possible, but still they were too many, and the gate was blocked by noncombatants. The terror of Nina's coming was on them, and they had no escape. A few dozen tried to scale the gate, but the soldiers on the other side simply speared them with their long pikes and let the bodies fall back into the crowd. Others dove or jumped off the sides, but we were still eighty feet or more in the air. Whether they landed in the racing water or the rocky shore, their chances were very poor.

I could not summon the lightning again without more murder. It had been bad enough on the north end; I would not repeat the mistake. But I still had hold of the god-winds, and I was determined to use them to better effect this time.

"Slow down!" I yelled to Nina.

She immediately reduced her pace to a trot, trusting I had a reason. She pranced forward, ears and tail up, feet light, her horn still radiating brilliance. When the first hail of arrows from the longbows arced toward us out of the sky, I simply batted them aside with a thought, and they were swept harmlessly over the side. The bowmen obligingly fired in volleys, so it only took a small amount of my attention to defend us. But soon we would be in crossbow range, and I would not be able to see the deadly bolts as easily. It would only take one, streaking horizontally, to end the quest. And by now, we were within the crowd by the gate. Even if I could see the bolts, I could not release enough power to deflect them without blowing innocent people off the bridge.

I tucked the sword under my dead left arm, hoping not to lose it. Then I leaned far forward, reaching with my good hand for Nina's forehead. "Glamour!" I called.

She whinnied in response, and made her horn disappear. I slapped my palm on the star marking, and the horn reappeared through my palm. I wrenched my hand away, blood spilling freely. She could not pause to heal the wound this time, nor did I ask her to. Instead, I clenched my fist over the pain, and watched as her glamour grew, moment by moment.

She was transformed. Even though I had seen the effect before, I was amazed. People quieted, their faces going blank. The soldiers on the other side of the gate let their arms, suddenly nerveless, fall to their sides, their weapons forgotten. Nina slowed to a walk and wound her way through the crowd. A few hands reached out toward her, but no one actually touched. They sighed, yearning, and some sobbed. They all swiveled their bodies to follow our progress. At the gate, she stopped, and I dismounted.

I carefully kept my eyes from straying back toward her and walked right up to the huge timbers, heedless of the army just yards away on the other side. Even when my bad leg made me stumble and cry out, no one even glanced at me; all eyes remained fastened on Nina.

A log and iron chain secured the two huge wings of the gate. I could not possibly lift the log, even if I climbed over and managed to release the chain. But this close, I could focus the god-winds tightly, without risk to others. I laid my bleeding hand on the wood, and let the power roar into me, focused only inward, until I vibrated with suppressed energy. It felt like being shot with a thousand burning arrows, but instead of sapping my strength, each jolt renewed me. The energy built and built until I knew I had to release it or explode.

I curled my fingers and crumpled the log the way one crumples paper. Ashes and sawdust flaked down, then the log sagged, broken in half. The heavy iron chain twisted like string in my grip, and I cast it aside. I threw down the gate with a touch. I shuddered from the power it took, feeling not just the god-winds but my own vitality draining away. I stood, numb and dazed, until Nina's warm breath over my shoulder brought me back to myself. Careful to avert my gaze, I felt my way along her back until I could slide on and lie, panting and exhausted, across her spine. The god-winds guttered, flickered, and failed.

Nina pranced lightly forward, pushing her way through the remnants of the gate, and then among the entranced soldiers, who moved quietly aside to let her pass before turning to follow her.

The entire mass of people at the gate, civilians and soldiers alike, followed us up the road from the bridge, murmuring under their breath, walking stiff-legged, eyes blank. More streamed in, coming from the city and the countryside. Nina kicked up her heels and cantered ahead, breaking into a gallop only after she sensed I'd recovered enough to stay seated. The crowd broke into a run behind us, chasing her the way children chase balloons. I didn't have the force left in me to brush away flies, let alone let alone sweep arrows from the air; only Nina's glamour protected us.

The storm had done its work. The clouds lifted, letting shafts of bright yellow noonday sun bring color back to the world. Steam rose from the ground in tiny wisps as the rain-soaked vegetation dried.

Jappa lay directly ahead, a warren of streets and alleys, snarled and jumbled. The Archon's citadel rested on the crown of a cliff commanding the harbor. A gigantic flag bearing the Archon's sigil flapped from atop a turret. The white stone of the fortress gleamed proud and stern in the sunlight; the surrounding bastions of mixed tan and brown outlined its ponderous might. Gaheris had taken the citadel for his own, but his touch hadn't ruined the majesty and stark beauty of the ancient fortress rising above the capital of Leonais.

The city spread out beneath the towers, wealthy homes with orange tile roofs hugging the coast, while warehouses, factories, and poorer homes clustered haphazardly as far inland as I could see. Garrisons, forts, and stockades, easily identifiable by the cleared land around them, sprinkled the city. Troops here were for maintaining order, not repelling invaders. Everywhere I looked, I saw people. Young, old, pushing carts, cleaning up storm debris, selling food, selling clothing, going about their lives under the watchful eyes of the grey-clad soldiers.

I rode as high on Nina's back as I could, trying to see all around. Her glamour was fading, and the crowd behind was slowing down, shaking their heads, rubbing their eyes. Fewer and fewer joined them, and those on the edges were starting to wander away, dazed but free of the spell. Ahead of us, the road was still clear. We were too far from the city to have attracted much attention. I wondered what the mounted soldiers behind us would do when they woke to themselves—would they, too, slink away, or would they whip their horses into a lather and give chase? They could so easily crush us between themselves and an advancing army from the city.

Nina came to the same conclusion, and struck off cross-country, heading toward the hills north of the city. She increased her pace, the uneven ground not troubling her, and the following soldiers soon fell out of sight.

One particular hill caught my eye. It was a tor, a single upthrust rising abruptly from the smooth side of a gentle green hill. The tor itself was natural rock, but menhirs surrounded it— an artificial ring of standing stones. A dark hollow in the hillside made me think of tunnels and tombs beneath the stone. I leaned forward to get my mouth close to her ear, and pointed. "There. A dolmen. We can rest."

She whinnied and changed direction slightly.

The stones in the ring were chalk-white, like the citadel, and didn't match any of the surrounding stone. How the builders had dragged them up to the top of the hill beggared my imagination. But even if I didn't know how, I knew why. I could feel it before we were halfway to the first menhir—a rising static that pulled at the hair on my arms and made my face tingle. But unlike the last dolmen, this one had no king stone guarding the entrance into the hill. There was a hole in the ground with rounded edges where the chief menhir had once stood, as if it had been dragged away long ago, like a tooth uprooted from a jaw.

The dark hollow I had seen from below was a short tunnel into the side of the hill, below where the king stone had once rested. The tunnel was a smooth bore into the living rock and came to an end at a door only a dozen feet inside. The door was a massive slab of the same white rock as the menhirs, but long broken to chunks and rubble. I had to climb over pieces the size of my torso and push aside smaller rocks, to gain entrance. From the way the shards lay, it looked as if the door had been shattered, exploded outward by some great pressure. Nina transformed to woman shape and picked her way beside me.

My breath frosted the air of the chamber within the dolmen. Cold seeped up from the stone floor, chilling my bones and heart. Once my eyes adjusted, the familiar faint pearly luminescence from the walls was just enough to see by. I sneezed in the dust we stirred up.

I turned around slowly, taking in the arched ceiling, the perfectly flat floor, and the rounded walls that leaned inward smoothly to meet the ceiling's arch. I couldn't tell where the wall ended and the ceiling began. I sensed the Sleeper, far below, stirring restlessly at my mere presence in this place. With a word or a gesture, I could reach out and waken that imponderable might, rouse it to a crescendo of puissance sufficient to topple the Archon's citadel and throw down Justian Bridge. No crude winds would be needed. I could make the rocks beneath any point on the planet rise up, overtop the puny human construction on the skin of the world, and come crashing back down to bury a castle, a town, a whole city—bury them so deeply that the heat and pressure would transform them to a layer of magma. But the Sleeper, once fully awake, would not be so easy to put to rest. That was why, I suddenly understood, the group of old sorcerers in Amrhyn had been monitoring the Sleeper. They weren't interested in me, or not interested in me the way Gaheris and Ashe had been. They were interested in anything that touched the Sleeper, anyone who might wake it. They wanted to keep it stable, quiescent, just barely awake so they could siphon the surface of its power without rousing it fully. Too much power unleashed at once could unmake the world.

I could perceive their touch even now, although I wasn't linked well enough to see them or communicate. Their murmurs rose through the stone, as I supposed they did through every dolmen's floor, soothing, quieting, hushing. Who had assigned them this task? How long had they been doing it? And how in the world does someone discover a task like that needs to be done, let alone how to do it?

Nina became a column of slowly spinning shadows beside me, with a pale white thread, like a single flame, at the core. She was neither woman nor unicorn, yet her essence remained unchanged, still recognizably Nina. My head spun and my vision blurred when I gazed directly at her; I had to look away. I knew without asking that this pillar of smoke-shrouded fire was her true shape, or rather the best representation my brain could interpret. I had only glimpsed it before, during her transformations. The unicorn and the woman were only bodies she wore, the way humans put on clothing. In this place, with me, she had no need.

Her thoughts came cleanly, directly, into my mind, speaking from the flame at her center. "The Sleeper lies at the heart of the world," she told me. "It hasn't been truly awake for three thousand years. The muria wrestled it into uneasy sleep."

Three thousand years. Since Nina's people had been imprisoned, in other words.

"Did you control it before the Amrhyn?" I asked.

"No one *controls* it," she replied instantly, sounding almost scornful. "The Amrhyn sorcerers serve it. They think to share its power, but they do not know the peril."

"They are working to keep it asleep," I said. "I can feel that much."

"Their only wisdom."

"Yet you want me to wake it."

From the corner of my eye, I saw the shadows swirl violently in their orbits about her flame. Answer enough.

I extended my good hand, palm down and flat, hovering, feeling the flow of energy that pulsed in gentle somnolence through the air. Immediately, the bands of light I had seen before sprang into visibility, arching like iron ribbons in all directions, flooding the chamber with a nonphysical brilliance. They had always been there, connecting and interconnecting the dolmens in a vast, world-spanning network, but it took my will to make them evident. I did not touch, not yet. My hand hovered, fluttering gently, sampling the currents, like wetting a finger to sample the wind. I knew the way of it now, at least partly; I could ride the currents without disturbing them.

The sorcerers in Amrhyn immediately came into focus. Ten old men, deep in meditation, stood about a king stone in the heart of the horse lands far to the west, chanting, almost singing, their heads hidden in the cowls of their blue robes. They were unaware of me, and I let them be. They were not the ones who had taken Maran, though for all I knew they were part of the same plot.

I reached south—not far—following a thick yellow strap of light. The Archon's citadel lay only a handful of miles away, and it only took a moment to locate it. The band of energy connected this dolmen to the citadel directly. The missing king stone was buried under the citadel's foundations. Not the Archon's doing, although its presence there perhaps explained why Jappa was his seat of power. Humans of old, sensing the potency of the dolmen, had dragged the king stone down the hill, then laboriously lifted it up to the top of the cliffs, only to bury it beneath the fortress.

I kept my touch light, concentrating on sight rather than confrontation. If I could explore fully before Gaheris was even aware of me. . . . My percipience wheeled like a hawk across the battlements and courtyards, dove through a window, and scurried like a rat through the corridors. I followed the path of memory.

Remembering Gaheris and his nighttime forays to the dungeon with his special set of knives, I wound my way down stairwells, past cisterns and garderobes, under flickering torches, down until the stones wept with moisture and the air stank from fear, sweat, and pain.

No human could have sensed my passage, but I didn't know if any Amrhyns still watched the prisoners. I went cautiously, my mind wary, expending no power other than for my senses. I came to the dungeon door, barred and guarded. I passed through it like a ghost, disturbing neither the door nor the armed soldier stationed there.

And there, finally, I found Maran, just as I had seen her before, with Ashe and Tad on one side, Torrey, Owen, and Tessa on the other.

"Can you see what I'm seeing?" I murmured to Nina.

"No. Can you open a door, or do I need to take you?"

I thought about it, feeling for the pathways I would need. Yes, they were there. I could step through from here to there in a heartbeat, crossing the distance as if it didn't exist. But I had no idea if I could keep the door open behind me, or if I could take anyone alongside. I still had the sword, but I had no skill with it. Should I step through, hack at the chains, and hope to get away again?

"I'm not going anywhere yet," I said. "I want to keep looking."

I swiveled my gaze, not seeing the dolmen at all anymore. Only the dungeon was real to my senses. There was no sign of the sorcerers, but there were other prisoners, and a human guard. A table and a brazier occupied the center of the room, and the guard huddled near it, drowsing, not paying any attention to those who were chained to the walls around him. I counted fifty-two prisoners besides my six, and I didn't recognize any of them. I didn't think they had anything to do with me, for my six were drawn apart a little, a space on either side of their sad line.

I saw no evidence of torture among my friends—at least nothing too terrible. Bruises, yes; rough treatment, yes; hunger and cold, certainly. But no knife wounds, no missing limbs. Unlike many of the other prisoners, my six had yet to feel the edges of the Archon's blades, but the stench of old blood lay heavy in that place. Only a few of the prisoners had clothing beyond rags left, and some not even that much. They sat or sprawled or stood despondently, some shivering and clutching at the filthy straw for warmth, some moaning softly, all staring woodenly into the middle distance, none of them daring to talk. Having no choices left to them, they waited for whatever fate lay in store. Many of them, I thought, would welcome death. It was likely the only door that would ever open for them.

Maran raised her eyes and glanced about when I stared directly at her. There was only a thin barrier between us, like clear glass for me, but opaque for her. With a thought, I could break the glass and let her see me. But not yet; not until I had a plan. The dungeon had no windows. The guard's brazier and a few guttering torches provided the only illumination. Beside the table, a foul-smelling pit drove down deep beneath the floor. I supposed they threw the offal there, and perhaps the bodies of those who failed to survive being tortured. It also seemed to be the garderobe for the soldiers. The only other opening to the room was the massive door through which I had floated to reach this place. I remembered the soldier guarding the bar on the other side of the door. Even if I could free the prisoners and we could overcome the inner guard, the door would still be closed to us, and the outside guard would be free to yell for reinforcements. A real swordsman would be needed, not some thin, crippled bumbler like me. I'd be more likely to chop off my own leg than attack an enemy successfully. But I had Tad. He looked wounded in spirit but hale in body. If I could free him first, give him the sword, would he use it to help the rest of us? I had to know.

Crouching so my lips touched his ear, I let myself become just a little more real in that place. "Thaddeus," I whispered, "Tad. Don't move, don't talk, just listen."

His deadened eyes didn't move, not even a flicker, but his shoulders tensed, and I saw one fist clench tighter. "I healed you once, and I travel with a unicorn. Blink if you know me." For a long time, he did nothing, then slowly and deliberately he blinked once. "Good," I said, continuing to barely breathe the words. "I have a sword for you. I'm going to try to prop it up behind you, against the wall."

"I can't see you," he said, using only the corners of his lips.

"I'm not really here. But I can bring the sword to you, and it will be real."

"Cut me free now," he whispered.

"I'm not strong enough. You know me. I have not the strength. But when the time comes, I will free you somehow, or create a distraction, and then you must take up the sword and fight for freedom. Will you do that, Tad?"

He blinked again, very purposefully.

I reached backward with my good hand, found the sword, and pulled it through the doorway I had made. Had the guard been alert and watching in our direction, he would have seen just the sword floating in mid-air, for my physical hand was on the dolmen side of the door and therefore hidden from him. I moved it swiftly against the wall, taking great care that it not clank or ring as I balanced it on its tip against the stone wall. Tad, feeling the cold steel suddenly appear, settled to hold it upright with his back.

"I have to go now," I whispered. "There's more to do. Which one of you is most injured?"

Tad gestured slightly with his chin, indicating Ashe. The prince hadn't moved since my first sight of him. He was crumpled over himself, hands to his face. I hadn't thought him injured at all, but now that I looked closely, I saw the blood trickling down between his fingers.

I moved to his side and spoke in his ear as I had spoken to Tad. "Prince," I said as softly as my breath would allow. "Prince Ashe. You probably don't remember me. I came upon your camp one night, and you thought me hauflin, but Qol bade you let me go. I owe you for that night, and am here to repay the debt. Will you let me help you, lord?"

Ashe made no response at all. I risked putting my good hand through the door for just a moment, so I could touch his shoulder. "Please, lord, look at me. Don't alert the guard, but look. You will remember when you see me."

Slowly, with dignity and intransigent purpose, he dropped his hands and turned his ruined face just enough for me to see that Gaheris had taken his eyes. Then he covered the awful empty eye sockets with his hands again, and let himself sink back into despondency.

"I'm sorry," I whispered over and over. "I didn't know. Maybe something can be done. I don't— I don't know."

Miserably, I left him and went to Maran. She was awake and alert, her eyes darting around the dungeon. Had she heard my infinitesimal whispering, or was her second sight helping? Did she almost see me? Qol had all but admitted he had made Maran, too, and I knew she was full of magics—but did that include seeing things that weren't physically present? Before talking to her, I scanned her belly, checking on Aiden. He still nestled in her womb, unaware, unharmed, floating in a kind of soft red velvet bag. Then I let my attention travel up to Maran's face, and I saw her eyes were fixed on mine, looks of hope and incredulity warring for possession of her mien. I smiled gently, holding one finger in front of my lips in the age-old sign for silence. "Patience," I mouthed. She nodded suddenly, understanding the message.

To Torrey and Owen I did not speak. They were young

enough that they might start, or even cry out, drawing the guard's attention. Instead I went to old Tessa, still standing with the chains in her gnarled fingers, eyes staring blankly at the horror she had been unable to prevent her grandsons from knowing. I moved behind her, breathed warm human breath on her neck, touched her hair softly. She jumped only a little, then held herself rock-still. "You were kind to me once," I whispered. "And to my unicorn. We do not forget. This durance is but a dream. You will wake back in your house, all three of you, if I can manage it."

"Yes," she mouthed. "How?"

"Wait for the signal, then protect the boys. I will do the rest."

Then I faded back into the dolmen, chasing the same thick yellow band that had taken me to the citadel, until I found my own body and took up residence again.

Nina's flame regarded me dispassionately. She had brought me to this place, but the choice of action was mine. No doubt she expected me to wake the Sleeper now, rouse its fury to rain destruction on the city while somehow sparing my friends and all the innocent people of Jappa. The potential she saw in me . . . it was unjustified. Yes, I could wake the Sleeper. I might even be able to direct the resultant destruction toward the citadel. But once woken, might not the Sleeper have ideas of its own? And while Gaheris was mortal, what of the muria, the many-bodied Vastil? I didn't think I could defeat his world-spanning consciousness by dropping hot rocks on one of his avatars. Any single body of his could be destroyed—at least, I had no reason to think otherwise— but doing so would not stop Vastil himself. At best, it would be a temporary inconvenience while a new avatar hustled from Avermorn to Leonais.

I agonized over my choices in silence, always aware that Nina still waited. That I had been able to investigate the citadel without being discovered was important, but I thought it likely more luck than skill. The Amrhyns had certainly caught me easily enough the first time. But that time, I had not been using the dolmen as my power source. Could the dolmen network allow me to spy with impunity? I knew I could transfer myself from this place to any other, and I had seen—without planning for it in advance—that I could move an object from here to there without going myself. Tad now had the sword, after all. But I didn't see any paths among the bands of light that would allow me to move things or people from there to here. I would have to be there myself to open the door between places, but the very act of going there would cut me off from the dolmen's power. How could I get back? How could I bring the others? I let my thoughts run over the surface of my mind like quicksilver, and turned to Nina, the question foremost in my brain.

The cloud-wrapped flame shimmered, and I heard her voice clearly: "I can go by superposition from anywhere to a dolmen, and, once inside a dolmen, I can go to any other. But I cannot make or hold a door like yours."

Accompanying her words came a sense of shame, of insufficiency, as if it were somehow her fault that she could not do what I needed.

I reached out to the shadows and startled her into shape beside me, choosing the unicorn. This power had always been mine, I suddenly understood. Left to herself, she might take any shape, or none at all. But my will could seduce her, tease her into a shape of my desiring. It was a sign of her trust—perhaps also her desperation—that she allowed it without protest. I patted her flank, rubbed the indescribably soft fur between her eyes, and buried my face in her neck.

And then she was suddenly the woman, her arms around me, her hair a floating cloud around us both, as if we were both part of the shadows surrounding the flame of her spirit.

She kissed me tenderly, then drew back and with a familiar gesture, pushed her hair behind her ears. "For this you were made," she said, whispering, her eyes searching mine, "and for this I escaped to join you." Unspoken, but clear as daylight, came the corollary: *Qol never promised you would live through it.*

So. It came to that. I was disposable, Qol's tool in his age-old struggle against the other muria. My quest for my name, turned by circumstance into a mission to rescue my friends, transformed by necessity into a conflict with the Archon, and by extension, contending with Vastil, the many-bodied puppeteer behind Gaheris—all was just a tactic in Qol's war. I was expendable, as was Nina, as were my friends.

I took one of her hands, and we stood side by side facing the stone wall of the dolmen. Behind us, through the dolmen's open door, the last of the day's sunlight eased weakly into the room, and the sweet scent of clover from the hillside trailed behind. Far off, a small stream, swollen from the rains, chuckled quietly as it made its way downhill. Peace wrapped me like another cloak. Only this morning, I had climbed the rocks on the other side of the river, defeated by the mere sight of the Justian Bridge. We had come perhaps thirty or thirty-five miles since then, through storms and armies. And now I stood at the nexus, bands of energy fountaining in all directions, each spangle humming and thrilling softly, quiescent, awaiting only my touch to spring to life. The song of the distant Amrhyn sorcerers lay like a lullaby over the rumble of the Sleeper far below. Perchance I would not survive this night's work, but it would not be for want of trying. I was not yet ready to surrender my friends or myself without a fight.

Before I loosed the cataclysm on the world, I had to try.

The god-winds arose at my bidding, and I held them tightly coiled, poised like a sword to strike in any direction. They would not serve me for transportation, but I had the dolmen network in the air all about me. I was not the master of those powers, nor yet the master of the Sleeper below. But now I knew how to use them both.

I closed my eyes and laid my mind to the task. Concentrating on the strands of light, I plucked at them the way a harpist might trill over the strings of his instrument, evoking a ripple of harmonic reactions. Each band flickered, vibrated, grew brighter. In a breath, the chime began, softly at first, but growing in power with each moment's passing. Far off, the Amrhyns sensed the disturbance and redoubled their song, but all was dissonance, effectless against the clarity and purity of the chime's single bell-like note.

Outside the chamber, and outside all the dolmens in Leonais, the standing stones—the great menhirs so carefully placed to capture and channel this energy—vibrated and knelled, shaking off centuries of dirt and lichen to blaze forth, clean and indomitable. The bands of energy connecting each dolmen to the rest of the network sprang into visibility—and not just for me. No longer limited or held in abeyance, the lines of force lit the sky like lightning that stands and endures, bringing harsh brilliance to the entire continent. Every color of the rainbow sparked and twisted like streamers from horizon to horizon. And, as if it had been actual lightning, there came the tingle of tightening skin and the scent of energized air. Every head on Leonais suddenly jerked upright to stare at the sky. Around me, the chime rang like overstressed steel bent in anguish, and my mind leaped out onto the network, instantaneously enlarging so that my awareness spanned the continent, too. The Amrhyn sorcerers fell back, blasted from their feet by the awakening power of the Sleeper. No song would soothe it now.

"Who?" demanded the Sleeper.

I used my newfound awareness to align the energies, opening a doorway between places, but I did not step through. I realized that Gaheris had been right to fear me. I no longer hoped to get my name from him. My name came from my choices, both the ones I had made before and the ones I was making now. I was not just the sum of my experiences, waiting for a noun to be bestowed upon me by a greater or wiser person. There was nothing the Archon could offer me, no secret knowledge I could wrest from him, no name he could offer that I would accept. Nor was I Qol's tool, acting out a predefined part in his script. I was writing the role as I went along—defined, constrained, illuminated solely by my own ethics. In the end, what human is ever anything more?

"Who?" demanded the Sleeper.

The ground shook, and boulders tumbled. In far off Landing, the ships trembled and rocked, threatened for the first time in three thousand years. Across the valley, stones toppled from the uppermost turrets of the Archon's citadel. The floor beneath our feet lurched and juddered. The ship's metal of the Justian Bridge belled in protest as the bedrock shifted beneath it. Still I did not answer the Sleeper, and still the lightning endured and endured. I rode the god-winds and the dolmen energy over the land like a hawk effortlessly soaring on an updraft, motionless yet embodying motion, seeing the entire world laid out below me like a map. I was not muria, nor hauflin, nor faerie, nor human. I had become all of these things, a marriage of the disparate, a unity of selves, an alloy, more than the sum of my parts. I was something new.

"*Who?*" demanded the Sleeper a third time.

Drust floated before me in memory, laughing in delight at my appearance, at the dust that had covered me from head to foot. "It's a grey man," he had said, with all the cheerful bluntness of a child, and 'Grey' had been my name from that day forth, but it was never me.

It was the day of the giant. The day Qol's plans came to fruition. The day I sloughed off all pretenses and became what Qol had crafted me to be, the day I chose to become myself. The realization was bittersweet, for the liberty to refuse was still mine. I could turn away even now; he had left me that freedom. I could retreat without ever knowing what might have been. Or I could take the final step, let cry the consequences, and become something more.

I was something new, but something ancient at the same time. Qol had given me a shape, but he had *not* created me. I was as old as the planet itself. The power that coursed through the air around me was not extrinsic. It was as much a part of me as my skin or my heart. It was my own passion that drove the Sleeper. It was my own self-imposed doom that I struggled against. And ultimately, with a sense of inevitability that I finally knew for a chicane, it was my own birth that I allowed to occur.

In a voice that shook the air, I announced my nativity.

"I was the Sleeper," I said. "But now I am awake."

I had finally taken a name, and I almost welcomed the cataclysm that followed.

13. VASTIL

WITH ONE PACE FORWARD, Nina and I stepped from the chamber of the dolmen into the Archon's citadel. Behind us, the doorway between places snapped shut, even as the chamber itself collapsed with a crash, a thousand tons of rock sealing it forever.

Power flowed into me, through me, out of me. I had become the pivot on which the world balanced. The part of me that was the Sleeper roared in protest as I wrestled it for control of the energies, fought to keep the earthquakes from leveling every structure on Leonais. Even Avermorn, isolated by deep ocean, riding across Sundering's mantle on a separate rocky plate, shuddered in sympathy with the unimaginable potency of the force I had become. And on Alfheimr, the island in the West Ocean where Nina's people were imprisoned, the volcano awoke and spewed ash and fire skyward.

Peripherally, I was aware of people screaming, stones falling, walls exploding, winds tearing through the corridors. My mind was still among the strands of energy fountaining from the dolmen network, and I could not focus on my surroundings. It was too much. The primal urges of the Sleeper were stronger than my determination. I was losing the fight. The conflagration underground grew by the second. The illusion of control slipped away, and I knew I would be torn apart if I did not release my hold on the power. But I could not. I could not even find myself amidst the destruction. The Sleeper's rage expanded exponentially, and I lost all concept of time. With each new earthquake, the Sleeper subsumed more of me, until only the chaos of destruction remained.

Nina suddenly shifted beside me, blurring through shadows from woman to unicorn. She dipped her head, and the tip of her horn penetrated my side, sliding between the ribs like a razor. Blood sheeted out as she withdrew, but this time she was not trying to take power from me. I was too full of the Sleeper's passion for disorder to help her that way. I vibrated in time with the earth's convulsions, and the blood that fell from my body was liquid flame.

The pain reached me as nothing else could have. From my vantage high above, seeing through stone as easily as through air, I watched my body slide sideways, fall over, curl in on itself, and spurt fire. I fluttered toward myself like a crow blown from the sky by a storm, and fell into my own body with a gasp as Nina bent her head again.

The tip of her horn was just withdrawing anew, healing the wound, when I finally opened my eyes. The tear in the muscle knitted, and the skin puckered and drew closed over it, but I was still awash with fire inside. Every vein and artery burned. Searing white light sprang up, leaking through my skin. My clothing burned away. The flames spilled from my mouth as I screamed. No mortal body was meant to contain this kind of power. It would kill me if I did not let go, but I could not, not yet. My obstinacy was the only restraint left on the Sleeper. If I released it without quieting it first, the ensuing upheaval would rive the world to the core.

In desperation, I called for Qol, like a little boy begging his father for help. The muria had put the Sleeper to rest once; surely, they could do so again, even if it meant killing me to do it. But no elf responded to my summons. I had the percipience with which I was made, and the god-winds to enforce my will, but even my puissance was not an imperative to their kind. They acted—or refrained—according to their nature, not according to anyone else's edict. Yet thinking of Qol brought a moment's respite, lifted me out of the Sleeper's dark appetency for devastation. Just for a breath. Just long enough for me to remember. His face swam clear in my memory. We stood in Avermorn beside the fountain he had shown me when we first met. *Remember this place when you are assailed.*

Something of the serenity from Avermorn surrounded me. I saw again the marble fountain, cool water plashing gently, thousands of muria speaking simultaneously in a complex harmony that nevertheless sang a single note of meaning. The water of that fountain had been like rich wine, heady and strong, and I had drunk from the living cup of his hands. The memory of that draught drew me to my senses, brought a higher order of clarity to my thoughts, gave me the space I needed to focus. I heard Qol again, his eyes boring into my own as he spoke, his face utterly still and dispassionate. Many throats, one voice. Many brains, one thought. Many bodies, one person. *You are more awake now than you have ever been.* Yes. And with the wakefulness came peace, timorous at first, then swelling in waves until I was overwhelmed with the sweetness of it. This was not the peace of surrender. It was not the peace of truce, or even amity. It was the peace brought by scrupulous honesty, brooking no deception. It was rectitude. It was acknowledging I was not finished, that nothing ever is, that the process of becoming is itself a virtue and a rede. *You have seen the heart of Avermorn, and drunk of its life.* Yes. I clung to that support like a lifeline at first, then discarded it, swimming to the surface, breaching, and staying afloat on my own.

Coolly, cleanly, I drew a free breath, and then another. Moment by moment, I grappled with the raw anarchy of the Sleeper, mastering it not by sovereignty but by substitution. I took the anger and gave back acceptance. I took the havoc and replaced it with order. I took the fear and turned it into courage. I laid my patterns over it, but did not coerce. Rather I soothed and persuaded, showing the Sleeper that fury was bootless, destruction pointless. Restraint is a kind of power, too, and slowly, ever so slowly, I exercised it, bringing the disparate parts of my being into alignment with my will. And gradually, quiescence came. The Sleeper portion did not truly sleep, but it waited and watched, dozing, unified in purpose with the rest of me, willing to forbear . . . for now.

Tottering, barely able to maintain my interior balance, I shambled forward, one hand resting on Nina's neck, sending my percipience questing ahead. Though I had quelled the majority of the violence, the citadel was still falling apart around us from the upheaval already inflicted. Huge blocks of masonry crashed from the ceiling, dust and grit billowed, and the ceaseless patter of small, grinding stones filled my hearing. Only a score of minutes had passed since Nina and I entered the fortress, but during that time, those who could escape had fled. We found no defenders in the corridors. There were plenty of bodies, most of them in the grey uniform of the Archon, but some were courtiers or petty officials in fancy dress. Those fortunate enough to have been killed immediately, crushed when ceilings collapsed or flagstones convulsed, lay scattered in all directions. Moaning and sobbing told me of those less fortunate.

I hadn't wanted to kill anyone. Not even Gaheris. I only wanted to free my friends and throw down the Archon's loathsome sigil. Grief and regret blinded me as I stumbled forward, searching for the stairwell leading down to the dungeon.

I felt as if one wrong motion, one unguarded gesture, could unleash the fury of the Sleeper again. But if I let it go completely, I might never have the strength or courage to waken it again. And so I balanced the strain of containing it against the possible need for defense, hoping secretly that Gaheris and the Amrhyn sorcerers had fled along with the troops. On bones that felt fragile as twigs, I limped beside Nina, trusting her to guide me through the rubble without falling. I cast my mind ahead, wary of traps or ambush, and sought ever for the path downward.

Finally, we reached a portion of the citadel that I recognized. A mosaic looked familiar, then a lintel with carvings I remembered, and I suddenly had my bearings. The main staircase lay just around the corner. Gaheris had gone this way many times, and this was the same path I, myself, had taken in spirit while seeking my friends.

It seemed incredible to me that the Archon had not responded to our invasion. The first time I had touched the dolmen network, Gaheris and Ashe had both sensed me almost immediately. They were adepts, mages. Only Nina's intervention had kept them from using the network themselves to attack me. And later, when the whirlwind of my desiring had finally located Maran, just one of blue-robed sorcerers from Amrhyn had easily banished me. The clamor of the awakened Sleeper certainly would have alerted them to my presence in this place. Even if they had been caught off-guard at first, they had had time to regroup. Logic indicated they were waiting to ambush me ahead.

We took the stairs together, Nina now in human form, one arm wrapped around my waist to keep me upright. My bad leg buckled over fallen stones and other detritus on the steps, and I would have tumbled to the bottom without Nina's support. We debouched into the short corridor outside the dungeon, where a lone soldier had once guarded the iron-strapped door. Now the post was deserted, and the door stood open.

"Wait," I whispered, as Nina transformed back to unicorn and made ready to charge through.

I sensed Gaheris and the Amrhyns were waiting inside the dungeon, but I did not understand their plan. Even if they had not perceived my approach with magery, surely the clattering on the stairs would have alerted them in the ordinary way. Their magics, and even their swords, should be poised for battle. I had not come gently, and they had no reason to think I would not unleash the Sleeper's rage again. Fire still ran through my veins, quieted for now, but quivering and eager for release.

But their minds were sluggish, unready, as if they were caught in dreams. Something, some potency, held them in abeyance. The other power had a flavor to it that I knew, a feeling of familiarity . . . something almost, but not quite, recognizable. I reached for it, not with the destructive power of the dolmens, but with a light inquisitive touch of god-winds, extending my perception to the other side of the door. It was a muria, but not Qol, and he was waiting for me.

"Vastil," I said aloud.

And then Nina screamed as a mind, powerful beyond anything I had ever imagined, wrenched her effortlessly from shape and drew her inside the dungeon. Her shadows were torn away, leaving only the pale white flame of her soul writhing in a grip of iron. I staggered back from the impact of that mighty mind, driven to my knees, dismayed as much by its casual cruelty as by its strength. But I was not cowed. From somewhere deep within me, rage boiled up to sustain me. I knew who my enemy must be. The Sleeper stirred, and the god-winds roared. I crawled forward, naked as the day when Qol made me, my knees bloodied, my left arm hanging like a useless branch, but resolute and indomitable. As I crossed the threshold, I climbed weakly to my feet and raised my head.

Nina hung suspended in midair, her white thread-like flame limp and guttering. A force like a translucent orange nimbus held her, and she spun slowly, hypnotically, within its globe. I could sense that she was alive, but I could not reach her mind. Gaheris and the two Amrhyn sorcerers hung beside her, each enclosed in a cage made of sparkling orange cloud. Their eyes were open, but they saw nothing.

Behind them, still chained and arrayed against the wall as I had last seen them, my friends watched, too terrified to speak. Only Ashe did not look up, and I remembered that his eyes had been taken. But neither my friends nor the fifty-some other prisoners were watching me. They were watching the elf who lounged beside the table in the center of the room, his cloak on a chair beside him, one hand idly toying with a pair of dice.

Vastil. One of Vastil's avatars, that is. Like Qol, he was white-haired and beardless, with icy blue eyes, but there the resemblance ended. His power was not veiled; no one could look upon him and not know he was muria. He didn't even bother shielding his mind from me. He was contemptuous, unworried by my rage that even now was scaling up to storm force. If he feared the Sleeper's raw violence, or the surgical precision of the god-winds, I saw no sign of it.

"Touch me," he said very softly, "and she dies." Without any gesture or mental effort I could perceive, he contracted the nimbus around Nina. She whirled faster, her flame flickering in the wind as no mortal wind had ever affected her. Even the god-winds did not touch her so. But Vastil's nimbus held her securely, and she was vulnerable to it. Faster and faster she rotated, her flame sinking lower and lower, almost lost in the orange glow.

I froze, watching. "Stop it!" I cried, and the echo of the Sleeper's might resounded in my voice. A mortal hearing it would obey without hesitation or volition, but Vastil merely raised an eyebrow and smiled.

Unperturbed, he tossed the dice from hand to hand. "Release your power," he said. "You are too reckless to be trusted with it. Let it go, or she dies."

The god-winds sputtered in my hand, suddenly reft of my will. They dwindled, lost force, and collapsed. I closed my palm on the last of the gyre, extinguishing it like a candle.

"Release her," I said when the last vestige was gone. I matched his softness of voice with my own.

"Put the Sleeper back to bed, too," he said. "Men of reason have no need for such conflicts. You only hurt yourself, your companions, and thousands of innocents."

I had no choice. Forcing down the Sleeper was harder than dismissing the god-winds. The Sleeper was part of me, the outraged part, the part that had power and desire to avenge wrongs. It knew neither sympathy nor compassion, and could not be quiesced with promises. Only action, rough-hewn and direct, would satisfy it. And I longed to unleash it again, give it full rein. Here at last was a perfect target, a focus deserving of all my unabashed fury. But if I let the unreasoning part gain ascendancy, it would have no constraints. Yes, I might kill this body of Vastil's, but I would assuredly kill Nina, my friends, and the rest of the prisoners, too. With an effort that I thought would tear me in two, I pushed my awareness of the Sleeper deep down, beyond my own reach. Subject to my will at the last, it acquiesced and was gone. The fire ran out of me, and I was suddenly mortal, and unutterably weary.

"It sleeps again," I said at last. "Now release her."

"Certainly," he said, and immediately Nina resumed the slow spin, her flame coming back to normal strength. I fancied for a brief moment I caught a fleeting thought from her, like a caress, and then the contact was gone. Still, it was enough for me to begin to hope. She was alive!

He gestured at the empty chair across the table. "Sit. Talk. I am curious." His tone was easy, even friendly, but when I hesitated, he became brusque: "Do as I say."

Grimly, I limped to the table and took the indicated place, resting the dead weight of my left arm on the wooden surface. "We have nothing to discuss," I told him.

"Perhaps not." He lounged back, eyeing me curiously. "Qol's folly," he said at last, and I knew he meant it for an insult. "What happened to your arm? Qol would not have made you so. And you're lame. You have been careless."

I shrugged. Diminution was a matter of perspective.

"What name do you go by?" he asked.

"Grey," I answered.

"Only that? No grand title? Just Grey?"

I shrugged again. My search for a better name was none of his business.

He leaned forward suddenly, pushed the hair back on the left side of my head before I could pull away and hide my missing ear. "Fascinating," he said, letting my hair fall back. Then he laughed. "You are running out of body parts. You will disappear altogether if you continue your course. Despite your tricks, Grey, you are not muria. You are limited to the one body. Even Qol could not make you otherwise."

Stiffly, I said, "If I were reduced to one eyeball, that eye would still see you for what you are." It felt both pompous and hollow, even as I said it.

I felt his mirth, echoed in all his many bodies simultaneously, ten thousand throats chuckling in synchronous laughter. It was the same quality of joy I had sensed in Qol, not cruel at all, but delighting in wonder, still fresh despite his vast age and experience. It was the laugh of a man watching a puppy roll in the grass. It was indulgent, even parental. But I was not a puppy, and I found it disturbing. This was the elf who, according to Nina, had wiped out human civilization once before, and he was trying to do it again. What right had he to laugh at me?

I was aware of my friends, their eyes swiveling back and forth between us as we spoke. I dared not glance at them, not even when Torrey whispered "Grey" like a prayer. We all knew they were hostages in this contest, their lives part of the winnings in a game I barely understood. Right now, the rules called for the pretense of civil discourse, no matter what tensions ran beneath.

"What of them?" I asked as casually as I could, gesturing at Nina, the Archon, and the sorcerers, who still revolved in their misty orange prisons of light above our heads. "They are no threat. They are nothing to you. So why not let them go?"

His levity faded, replaced by curiosity. "What would you do with Gaheris if I freed him?"

"Nothing," I said after a moment's thought, "unless he attacks me. He was your tool, a misdirection. He is nothing without you behind him."

"Just so," said Vastil, tossing the dice between hands again. "His purpose is accomplished, superseded by another. I have no more use for him."

"You did make him, then. The way Qol made me."

"Not the same way, but yes. He was twinned from Ashe, modified to become Ashe's foeman if the need should arise."

"Ashe and Gaheris are twins?" I asked.

"Near enough, but Ashe is the elder by almost ten years. I used his genetic material to fashion a sibling, one with true Captain's Blood and a legitimate claim to the throne. The old king and queen never knew they raised a changeling. Do the mechanics actually interest you?"

"No," I said, "not really. I'm more concerned with why you did it."

"I foresaw the potential need. Even as a child, Ashe had a mad devotion to ancient technology. I held Gaheris in reserve until it became clear Ashe would never become manageable. I can see a matching lust for technology in you, just from my mention of it. Qol should not have given you that particular passion. Left unchecked, such desires would eventually doom us all. I therefore unleashed Gaheris to oppose Ashe."

I recalled my reaction to seeing the starships, and mentally granted Vastil a point. At the same time, I did not believe it was Qol's doing. My desires and feelings were my own, driven by rational analysis rather than implanted passions. I felt Vastil following my thoughts with admixed delight and mirth. "You should leave epistemology to your betters," he said, breaking my train of thought. "You lack the discipline to distinguish justified belief from opinion."

I shook my head, unwilling to grant him another point. He was not my philosophy tutor, nor would I let him critique my reasoning. Hoping to put him on the defensive for once, I asked, "Why admit all this about Gaheris and Ashe?"

He chuckled. "Because you asked. Because I'm curious about you and your reactions. Qol's handiwork fascinates me."

Was he truly that arrogant, that detached? I decided to keep playing the game; I saw no other choice. "It would have been simpler to kill Ashe outright," I suggested. "Then there would be no contest over the throne, no continent-spanning war."

"The struggle served my purposes better," said Vastil.

"You wanted this war, then. Nina was right about you. You are trying to destroy human civilization."

"Destroy, no. Restrain and redirect, yes. The old king and queen, like the witless monks, did my bidding without even perceiving my hand. Gentle suasion from afar sufficed to channel their thoughts. Ashe was another matter, much more self-directed and stubborn. He would never have bent to my will. Therefore, I encouraged Gaheris to consider the throne. His choices thereafter were his own. He preferred war."

"Like father, like son," I murmured.

Vastil was unmoved by my jibe. "Has Qol taught you nothing? He and I differ in methods, not goals. All muria see value in preserving the human race, but we also know you must be restricted. Ruling you would be an onerous burden. Better to limit your reach, and let you govern yourselves. You have been an excellent help to me. I could almost wish you were mine, not Qol's."

"What do you mean?"

"You, Grey, *you*. All your actions have conduced to my ends. Do you realize that you brought down Justian Bridge? It withstood every storm for three thousand years, but your earthquakes just now twisted the foundations from underneath it. You wrought more destruction in one afternoon than Gaheris managed in years. And before that, you and that creature sowed discord behind enemy lines as if I had sent you myself. It was over you that Ashe and Qol fought. Ashe wanted to protect you."

"What?" I wasn't asking him for clarification; I was simply dumbfounded. Surely it was the other way around. . . ? But I knew the truth about my destructiveness. I had gone from being impotent to nearly omnipotent, and had handled it badly. And now, bereft of power, Nina captured, my friends in chains while I bantered with the elf who, with a casual flick of thought, could extinguish all our lives . . . it was too much. My head felt thick, wooden. I couldn't understand what he was saying, and I didn't want to. I wanted to despise him. Only love requires understanding; hatred can manage on much less. But despite all the reasons to distrust him, all the reasons to revile him, all the reasons to oppose him, I could not do it. He radiated no malice, didn't *feel* threatening. He was amicable. Except for his curiosity and mirth, I recognized no emotions in him at all. My percipience was useless with him. Like Qol, he was too far above me for comprehension. What can an infant know of abstract reasoning? Compared to the muria, I was less than a child. Their passions and their motivations were obscure and could not be otherwise. I was not old enough to understand. I was wrong to question them, let alone set myself against them.

"Yes," he whispered, seeing my thoughts as clearly and easily as I saw the dice in his hand.

I nodded miserably. It was hubris to challenge him. His eyes loomed large, glinting oddly in the orange glow from overhead. His expression was candid, even warm. *Let it go*, his eyes seemed to say. *Let it all go.* "Yes," he said again, speaking very softly. "Trust me."

Qol had said that, too. And I *had* trusted Qol, beyond reason, beyond hope. As Vastil's soft persuasion wrapped me, layered me in comfort and security, I wondered if it was *possible* for a man to distrust an elf, if the elf desired otherwise. I could as easily distrust my own hand as doubt him. Did the muria exude glamour like Nina's, but aimed directly at the human heart, consisting of complaisance rather than mystery? If so, it was working. I could not muster enough energy to resist. I knew he was manipulating me, but it was already too late. I sank into his eyes, and let him riffle my memories without protest.

Like Qol, he spent most of his time examining my interactions with Nina, seeming fascinated by her. But unlike Qol, he offered nothing back, neither analysis nor advice. And I had no questions for him. I sat dumbly, my head sinking lower and lower. Waves of tranquility and contentment emanated from him to roll over me. He moved on from Nina, looking at my control over the dolmen network, questing for every insight into it and my use of its power. He queried my comprehension of the god-winds, distantly skeptical of what he found. Under his examination, I felt like a schoolboy who didn't comprehend the point of his lessons, doomed to fail again and again, no matter how patiently the teacher explained. There was something blindingly obvious to him that I could not see. Here, finally, I bestirred myself to ask for clarification, but he shushed me, and went on.

At the memory of my time with Maran, he chuckled, but did not explain. I burned with embarrassment, mortified to have him laughing over my only love affair. But he did not laugh at my prescient vision of Aiden, though he only saw my memory of it, not the child himself.

"Qol let you *breed?*" Vastil asked, incredulous. He glanced at Maran, who, like the others, sat quietly alongside the wall, waiting for him to decide their fates. The other prisoners, like my friends, seemed spellbound, held immobile while Vastil and I talked. Torrey had stretched his chain and curled in Maran's lap, knees drawn up, head nestled between her breasts. One hand hovered uncertainly beside his mouth. His eyes were hollow wells, unseeing. Maran's arms circled his thin shoulders protectively, and I saw, just for a moment, the kind of tenderness she would have for Aiden when he was finally born. In that moment, I forgave her everything. Our eyes met briefly, and I spoke directly to her mind, saying so. Vastil chuckled again at that. Startled, Maran and I realized he could overhear our mind-speech.

Then Vastil demanded my attention once more, and continued exploring my memories. Oddly, he skipped over my percipience, that ability of my mind to see things at a distance. He never looked at the healings I had done. He didn't seem to know what these things were, and therefore didn't examine them. It was as if he literally couldn't see things he didn't already recognize. I would have explained to him, had he asked. I would have told him how my second sight and my healings were really the same thing at the core, how patterns were everything, how all of the non-Sleeper powers I possessed proceeded directly from compassion and rapport. I would have told him anything he wanted to know. But he didn't deign to ask.

And that was the sign of Vastil, that his arrogance was unbounded. How can either human or muria believe himself to be self-sufficient, when manifestly he is not?

He reviewed my meeting with Ashe, and I saw afresh how princely and proud the man had been back then. Now he lay chained on the cold stone floor, his kingdom, his eyesight, and his freedom all taken. *Ashe wanted to protect you.* And Qol had not? Was that really their disagreement? Had Ashe gambled everything on me?

Vastil sensed the direction of my thought and shook his head. "Words and meanings seldom coincide as you want them," he told me. "But for such as you, language is all there is."

"Tell me, then," I said, stung by his condescension.

"Ashe wanted to acquire and protect you so that he could guide your power against Gaheris. Qol thought it better to let you stumble into your heritage on your own."

"And now that I'm here?"

"Qol's folly, as I said before. We are not blameless in your predicament, but we are not responsible for your choices. You bear witness in your own flesh that actions have consequences. Qol left you free, and I shall not gainsay him now."

"So I could leave if I wanted to?"

He set the dice gently on the table between us. "I found these here," he said, as if in answer to my question. "The guards used them to gamble for the prisoners' possessions. They threw dice, told jokes, and spoke to each other about their families or careers, while prisoners bled to death in the straw at their feet. Gaheris encouraged it, but it would have happened anyway. They did not see themselves as evil, because they did not see the prisoners as people. There is something broken in humanity."

"I see," I said, and though my mind was still muddled by his influence, I thought I saw a chance in his musings. He had partially released me from his forced interrogation in order to correct me, and our dialogue gave me the opportunity to engage him further. I would not answer his bigoted assertion—he could keep his disdainful opinions. I had no interest in fighting casuistry, but perhaps I could use it against him. I pointed around the circumference of the dungeon, where chains held both my friends and the fifty-some other prisoners. "Qol would not keep captives so," I said slowly. "Even I understand that much. Muria do not seek cruelty for its own sake."

"Just so," he agreed equitably. "Gaheris brought them, not I. My only action here was to forestall the conflict so you and I could talk. What do you propose?"

"Gaheris is your own creature," I continued, as if still working through my reasoning while I spoke. "He is yours to deal with by right. And the Amrhyn sorcerers are proven traitors to humanity. They brought my friends here solely to entrap me. Nina—" I hesitated, giving every appearance of saying something against my own interest. "Nina has a history with you. I don't pretend to understand it. But these others, they are innocents. Some of them are just children." I gestured again at my friends and at the other prisoners. All of them watched intently, not daring to breathe. "Justice demands their release."

"You had only to ask," he said, shrugging. "They are yours now."

Suddenly chains clanked, slithering from the rings in the wall and coiling themselves in heaps on the stone floor. Shackles broke open and clattered down beside the chains. For a stunned moment, no one moved. Then I shouted, "Go! Now!" and there was a mad rush for the door. Men and women scrambled to their feet or scuttled sideways, ducking their heads. In moments, they reached the door and jostled to get through, kicking up the straw and dust.

Vastil and I locked eyes during the evacuation, neither one of us moving. He seemed unconcerned, as if the scattering and uproar of the prisoners was nothing more than a momentary interruption in our conversation. I wondered if he were truly that immoderate in his conceit, or if this was merely another test to see what I would do.

I surveyed the dungeon. My heart beat faster, and the skin on my neck tingled. *Not one of my friends had left*. Not one of them had chosen freedom over loyalty. Despite being cold and nearly naked, despite their fear for themselves, despite their long hunger and privation, they remained with me. Ashe I did not count as a friend, and I didn't think his apathy counted for allegiance. He clutched his rags and lay motionless on the floor. But Owen stood at rigid attention beside Tessa, his face shining. If I had asked him in that moment to launch himself at Vastil, his eleven-year-old heart would have burst with the effort to obey. Tears of relief crawled unnoticed down Tessa's cheeks as she smiled, her face wrinkled with a complex kind of joy. Tad crouched in a soldier's well-practiced stance, his back against the stone wall, his eyes telling me he was ready to fight, wanting only my word. Maran still cradled Torrey on her lap, her head bent over his, but her gaze was uplifted toward me, fierce with pride.

I looked back at Vastil, wondering what he thought of their choice. He still watched me curiously, revealing no sign of his thoughts. The clattering and shouts of the freed prisoners echoed down the corridor and stairwell, growing fainter as they gained distance. Amid the noise of their flight, I heard the soft jingle of tiny bells. A very soft voice whispered: "He doesn't understand."

My flesh crawled with recognition. I knew that voice; it was Maran's. The bells were her earrings, hidden under her hair, tinkling gently as she spoke. But she still sat across the room holding the little boy, and was too far away for her whisper or the sound of the bells to carry. Yet she was not speaking directly to my mind. Vastil would have overheard that, had she tried. This was something different, a power outside his reckoning. Until that moment, it had been outside mine, too. But I knew instantly what she had done, and what it meant. She was whispering in Torrey's left ear—*my* left ear, the one I had given him—and I could hear her as clearly as if it were still attached to my head.

I didn't dare react outwardly, but I felt hope flare inside me as the final pieces of Qol's plan clicked into place. How Maran had known, I didn't begin to guess, but I saw now that Qol had given me the tools I needed to take the next step. I wondered if I would survive it.

I picked up the dice and threw them into the pit behind the table. They made no sound as they tumbled through the air and disappeared. I suppose it was a gesture of some sort, though I could never have explained whether I meant it as defiance or acceptance.

"You are very like one of our Ketlan," said Vastil admiringly. "Full of fire and spit. We love our children, Grey. They belong to all of us when young. Some grow up to align with Qol and some join me."

Or the others. "Tamil, Bastion, Vastil, Ulat, and Qol," I recited, as Nina had taught me. "The five persons of the muria on Sundering. There are only five elves, no matter how many bodies each wears."

He lifted an eyebrow. "That creature told you too much."

"That *creature* has a name," I said hotly. "She is Nina, and I owe her my life."

Now he laughed, long and loud, and I heard again the echo of his ten thousand separate throats joining in. "Ah, Grey," he said at last, "forgive. I do not mock you. But she has not told you everything. 'Nina' is not her name. Nina is what she *is*. There are muria, humans, and nina on Sundering. Three sapient species. The nina are fey, the only original inhabitants of this world. They are unarticulated words from the beginning of time. Their true shape is the unending flame. The shadows are their cloaks, the flesh they assume. Your creature is not a unicorn, not a woman, not even alive the way you and I are. She is nothing but unbridled and unformed passion. She is a potential, waiting for any other mind to impose a shape on her."

A muria-like mask settled over my face, showing no expression at all. Now I knew why Qol had been surprised by my mention of her, and why he had forced me to explain. He had not known Nina at all; he had recognized the name for her species, and it was not a name he had ever expected me to know. I recalled my first meeting with her, the night Brawley had died. *Names don't matter*, she had said. *Call me Nina.* She had never pretended otherwise, and now I understood why my own quest for a name had bemused her so. But despite Qol's plans, or my own, I had come to love Nina. Whatever she was, whatever shape she wore, she was as surely a part of me as my own heart.

"Nevertheless," I said stoutly. "She is a friend. I owe her my life. Names don't matter."

"That *you* should say that," he marveled. "Of all persons. Listen! They owned this world when it was sterile, just oceans and bare rocks. They altered the First Colonists, subverting their offspring to create the muria. They are attracted to life, as insects are drawn to fire. But they cannot resist changing whatever they touch. Their nature is to corrupt, simply by existing. They tempt with power, seduce with illusion. Look at what she did to you. In the early days, before we understood the danger, there were worse monsters than you, crosses between muria and nina that could have unmade all life. We destroyed those monsters at great cost. We learned, finally, how to protect ourselves, how to control them. The price for that knowledge was our remaining humanity; we gave up every vestige of it to become fully muria. After that, we co-existed uneasily until the Second Colony landed. We locked the nina away on Alfheimr before they could corrupt the Second Colonists the way we had been corrupted. We have guarded the Second Colony against them ever since. *That* is the history between muria and nina. They are the only true evil we know. And now one of them is loose, and the worlds of both elves and humans are at peril."

"So you mean to kill her after all," I said.

He stood, dusting off his cloak. "No, but I will imprison her with the rest of them on Alfheimr. She is too dangerous to leave loose. I don't know how she got out, but I will find and seal the breach."

The four orange globes, hovering this entire time, floated down to our feet. Gaheris and the Amrhyns stared witlessly from their prisons. Nina's flame flickered weakly. I tried to reach her mind, but the nimbus surrounding her was as impenetrable as a stone wall.

I stood, too, leaning my good arm on the table for support.

"And what of me?" I asked.

He cocked his head. "What about you?"

"Am I to live?"

A small wind of my desiring found its way into the dungeon, stirring the dust, straw, and rags on the floor, sweeping them into a pile near my friends. Vastil either didn't notice or didn't care. He was clearly preparing to leave.

"Qol gave you life," he said with false camaraderie, "so I imagine the usual rules apply. It would be churlish of me to interfere. I only wanted to inspect his handiwork. But I should warn you—once the creature is gone, you will not be able to raise the Sleeper again. It was her influence that led you into that misstep, and her presence in this world that let you wake it."

A jingle of tiny bells, infinitesimally soft, and a whisper tickling my ear: "Now!" said Maran. "Don't let him leave with her."

He caught my motion the instant it began, and froze me in place. His mind, urbane and cordial, was nevertheless impossible to resist. I suddenly became a statue. He stopped me with my good hand only an inch from Nina's nimbus. I don't know what would have happened if he had let me touch it, but I saw a flicker of uncertainty in his eyes. He didn't know, either. I could feel him scanning all of us rapidly, watching for mental communication.

Good. Let him focus on that.

It took all my willpower to force my lips apart. "Watch," I said. I still could not move my body, but I had no need. The action I contemplated wasn't physical. I had never intended to free Nina that way. Instead, I caught Vastil's eye, and stared at him.

Curious rather than concerned, he met my stare.

I reached with my percipience, that power he had not condescended to study, and found Ashe on the floor near Tad, both of them behind Vastil. Healing him was ridiculously easy. I had, after all, mastered earthquakes that day, and this was a much simpler task. As Vastil stared, appalled, a film grew over my eyes. Then my eyeballs shrank, dwindled, lost their fluid and collapsed into dust, leaving only hollow, staring sockets.

"Mad," said Vastil, not realizing that I had lost nothing. "Qol has made you insane."

My perspective suddenly shifted. Just as I could hear through the ear I had given Torrey, I could now see through the eyes I had given Ashe. As he raised his head in wonder, I twitched Tad's arm —the one I had given him in my very first healing—bumping his hand against the sword still hidden behind him. He grasped the hilt, and in that moment, I linked the four of us together: Ashe, Tad, Torrey, and me. My person was split among them, and we functioned together as one.

It wasn't quite the same as being one of the many-bodied muria; I didn't have tens of thousands of trained elvish minds behind me to boost and focus my puissance. But I had four times the power of only a moment before, and there was only one avatar of Vastil in the room to resist me. It would be enough.

Despite your tricks, Grey, you are not muria. You are limited to the one body.

Oh?

I gave him the lie by breaking the paralysis he had laid on me. The god-winds rose to a pinpoint fury, with better control than I had ever managed on my own. I trained their might like a whirling set of chisels on the masonry above his head. Before he could think to leap aside, a multi-ton block of stone fell and crushed the life from him.

14. ARCHON

OWEN STARTED CHEERING AND CLAPPING, but I shouted, "It's not over."

And indeed it was not. Though the incarnation of Vastil was dead beyond all doubt, the rest of his vast mind was still active. Without an avatar in the room, I hoped his power to interfere would be limited. The loss to Vastil was like the loss of a fingernail to a human. It inconvenienced him, perhaps annoyed him.

The nearest avatar was undoubtedly hurrying this way even now, and Nina's orange nimbus prison hadn't burst the way I'd hoped. Even acting remotely, with no physical presence, Vastil was able to keep all four cages intact. We needed to hurry. Who knew how long it would be before he responded?

Tad, Ashe, and Torrey came to stand beside me. Their proximity wasn't necessary, but it was comforting. In Ashe, I saw renewed hope and vigor. The prince he had been was coming back, bit by bit, as he straightened his shoulders. I could see him begin to think like a military man again. Tad held the sword ready, still looking for an enemy to fight. Torrey shyly took hold of my good hand. He rooted in a torn pocket, and withdrew his pet lizard. He put Zoxo on his shoulder and stood proudly beside me.

I had cheated Vastil somewhat. The sacrifice that made our gestalt possible had not robbed me of my sight. I still had my percipience. As I had while riding with Nina through the utter dark at night, I could see the natural world without using the eyes of my body. Being able to use Ashe's eyes was just an additional perspective, letting me watch front and back at the same time. More importantly, I could use his mind. It was *our* mind now. Ransacking my new memory, I saw the plans for the citadel, mapped the surrounding roads, learning where checkpoints might stop us. I was the focal point for the gestalt, but only that. What one knew, we all knew. What one felt, we all felt. Our feelings and experiences replicated back and forth until it became an overwhelming cacophony of images and tastes and sounds and memories. Vastil had been right about one thing: We were *not* muria. I didn't think we could hold the gestalt together much longer without destroying ourselves.

Despite our fourfold strength and wealth of experience, we could not release Nina from the orange nimbus. We lacked the knowledge and didn't have enough raw power to break through without understanding how she was bound. The destructive might of the Sleeper would not avail us, not for this. It would be like using a cannon against a spider web. But there was one other person in the room who might be able to join our gestalt.

With only our desire, we drew Maran to us. I hadn't given her an organ or a limb, but I had given her my seed, and that seed now grew inside her: our son Aiden. Once before I had breached the barriers of time to speak with him in the future. I hadn't planned it and didn't know if I had reached forward or he had reached back, but I meant to try again.

When we spoke, all four voices sounded at once in that same queer harmonic unison the muria sometimes used—Torrey's soprano, my tenor, Tad and Ashe's baritones. "Golems, as many as you can make," we said to Maran, drawing on my own memories for this task. We pointed at the piles of rags and straw. Maran understood immediately and got busy, being careful to skirt the edge of the yawning pit.

Meanwhile, since Aiden was my son, the other three minds quiesced, granting me the executive position. I reached with my second sight for the boy I had once seen, recalling the white-gold curls and rose-blushed cheeks, the sturdy legs and laughing voice. At first, there was nothing, but then I felt a tug, as if someone had tied a rope about my waist and yanked me forward. "Aiden!" we called.

"Father?" came a startled voice, from a long way off, as if we had reached him on the other side of the planet.

But he came no closer, so I pushed harder. It was difficult, like rolling a stone as large as a horse uphill. I summoned the god-winds, not knowing how they could help, but needing something to break through the resistance. We all pushed, and the god-winds swirled the dust around us like Nina's shadows.

And then suddenly, as easily as reaching out a hand, I held him.

He squirmed damply against my chest, his hair plastered down and streaming, hugging me with all his strength. We had plucked him from a lake, I guessed. He was older than I had seen him before, perhaps ten or eleven now, a well-grown boy. He was breathless.

"This is so wicked," he said, his green eyes laughing. "Mother will be angry. But I *am* glad to see you."

"Mother will understand," said Maran from a few feet away, her eyes flowing with tears. She had not shared my vision of him the night he was conceived, so this was her first glimpse of the reality of her child.

He blinked at her in surprise, suddenly sober, and backed

away from all of us, his bare feet leaving splotches of wetness on the stones beside the pit.

He looked at our faces, and then looked at his surroundings as if just noticing them. I caught a startled look of recognition on his face when saw Torrey.

"This is the past," he said flatly. "I shouldn't be here. I'm not even born yet."

My breath caught in my throat. I nodded. "I know, but we need your help. Nina is still trapped."

"It's not allowed. I must go back." A sudden storm of god-winds flew up around him, not called up from the outside the way I did, but emanating naturally from within. He was as strong as Vastil had been, maybe even stronger, irresistible in his determination. I had been right about the kind of power he would wield. It was a blend of muria and human, with all of their strength tempered by our heart. He began to fade from sight.

"Wait!" I called desperately, stepping toward him. "Free Nina." I gestured at Nina's flame, still struggling feebly in its nimbus. "She is my friend. I never would have survived without her. She deserves our help."

"A nina from before the change? I'm sorry, Father. It's forbidden."

"Before *what* change?" I asked, taking one more step. "Can you at least explain?"

Before I finished asking the question, he was already gone. At that point, our gestalt, strained beyond its limits by the effort of summoning Aiden, fell apart completely. We were each of us alone in our own bodies.

Forbidden by whom? I wondered. I sensed this differed from the old "forgotten or forbidden" saying. A vast network of rules, as ineluctable as gravity, arising from nature itself, governed interactions between past and future. I might never understand its complexities or restrictions.

Torrey wailed and clung to me, frightened by his sudden isolation. Tessa came and took him away, and although she and Owen both spoke comfortingly to him, I could no longer hear through his ear.

Ashe said decisively, "The effort has failed. We cannot succor the trapped ones, and probably should not. It is time for us to see to our own safety."

It was a sound military decision, and I hated him for it.

Nevertheless, I held my peace. The effort of summoning Aiden had exhausted me, and my percipience had foundered. With the breakup of the gestalt, I was therefore doubly blind. I could no longer see through Ashe's eyes. I hardly had the strength to continue standing. I swayed, reaching out wildly for something to hold.

There was nothing to my right to grab. On the left, my dead hand brushed against Tad, who called out in concern and tried to hold onto me, but I slipped through his grasp and crumpled to the floor. I was desperately afraid I had stepped too near the pit and would roll over the edge. I thrashed with my legs and good arm, finally touching something.

My hand sizzled as if I had dipped it in fire, and the stench of burning flesh suddenly mingled with the other foul smells in the dungeon. I snatched my hand back at once, but the damage was done. My fingers had brushed one of the orange balls of light, and I suddenly understood why Vastil hadn't wanted me to touch them.

As if the potency of the nimbus had been a trigger, the Sleeper sprang to full wakefulness. The jolt of energy from that brought back my percipience in a rush. I rolled over and sat up, just in time to see all four of the nimbuses pop like balloons, spilling their prisoners to the floor.

Instantly, the room darkened as the lambency from the nimbuses flickered and went out. The only remaining light came from the few torches set in sconces on the walls. My empty sockets used percipience rather than light to see, so for a moment, I was the only one who could tell what was happening.

My first care was for Nina. She was weak, hard pressed by her confinement, but she struggled, her flame brightening and taking on color. I knew no way to help her, and could only watch. She gathered her shadows sluggishly, drawing them one by one from the corners of the room as if unreeling skeins of yarn, by pulling each string slowly toward herself.

Gaheris rolled out with his sword in his hand, gained his feet in a leap, and stood en-guard, his stance sure, magics crackling about his head. He paused, momentarily unnerved when he saw Vastil's legs poking out from under the block of masonry that had crushed him. But he shook himself free of that, and focused on the rest of us. He measured everyone in the room, seeing me last, for I still lay on the floor near the pit. His eyes widened.

"You!" he yelled, leaping in my direction.

I threw myself, rolling, to the side, narrowly avoiding his first thrust. His blade clanged on the stone floor and sparks flew as the edge grated. I tried to get to my feet, but my bad leg betrayed me, and I stumbled, falling at his feet. His next blow would surely spit me where I lay. But the Archon's descending sword was met and deflected by another. Tad, finally presented with an enemy he knew how to fight, sprang to my defense, and his fury was palpable. I rolled quickly out of their way.

There was neither chivalry nor quarter in their battle. Gaheris was easily the better swordsman, but Tad was younger and fighting for his life. They rained blows back and forth, dancing and thrusting. Gaheris seemed to move languidly, his blade always in the right place to meet Tad's without visible effort. Tad meanwhile flailed wildly, clearly outmatched. Gaheris was playing with him, savoring the growing fear in the young man's eyes.

In desperation, Tad tried to lunge as if the saber were an épée.

The Archon easily sidestepped, and crashed the hilt of his sword against Tad's forehead. Tad went down in a heap, but his very inexperience saved him. Instead of bringing up his own sword to ward off the inevitable killing stroke, he clutched at the Archon's arm for support and almost dragged him off his feet. Surprised and caught off balance, Gaheris jumped back, giving Tad time to regain his stance. But Gaheris was done playing. He beat back all of Tad's offenses, and step by step forced him toward the wall.

On the other side of me, the Amrhyn sorcerers were regaining their senses, coming to their feet and bringing their magics into focus. The air crackled with energy, and my hair rose. Nina was still recovering, only half swaddled in shadows, and could neither protect herself nor help me. I shouted a warning to her, but only succeeded in distracting Tad. In that unguarded moment, Gaheris landed a flurry of blows, and suddenly Tad's sword flew from his hand. It slid, grinding across the grit and dirt on the floor, coming to rest hilt-first at Ashe's feet like an invocation.

Ashe scooped it up, and in the same smooth motion leaped forward to engage the Archon before Gaheris could finish Tad off.

As they parried each other's first probing thrusts, Gaheris remarked teasingly, "I thought I'd blinded you, brother."

Ashe refused the temptation to spar with words. He was too experienced to fall for that kind of ploy, but he nodded once in acknowledgement before pressing his attack.

The swordfight began in earnest, and I was too busy ducking and rolling out of their way to make sense of what was happening. I knew nothing of proper technique, and couldn't even tell who had the better reach. But I could see it was a fight of an entirely different order than the previous one, much faster, and much more deadly. From my point of view, they were evenly matched. Ashe was as skilled as Gaheris, and neither man could risk flashy moves or gambits. They fought using the same style, and they even looked alike. They had the same height and build, even the same straight auburn hair and mahogany-red skin. They dripped with sweat, beating each other back and forth in attacks and parries too fast for me to follow. Neither one seemed able to get the advantage of the other. Their motion forced me toward the center of the room to avoid tangling in their battle. I scuttled sideways, not quite ever managing to keep my feet, relying more on my knees and the one good arm, my fingers scrabbling in the grit. I watched them over my shoulder lest I needed to leap suddenly a different direction, sharply aware of the yawning pit only a few feet away.

I was so focused on the swordplay that I didn't realize the Amrhyns had finished raising their power until the first bolt crackled past my head. It was sheer luck that they missed me. Tad had backed warily into a corner, also watching the fight, but had seen the blue lightning of the sorcerers rising behind me, and pointed frantically, even starting forward, trying to get my attention. I thought he was pointing at Nina or one of the others, and had just leaned over to see around Ashe when the bolt stung the air where my head had been. It detonated against the dungeon walls, knocking down one of the torches and tearing out a chunk of stone. I spun on my heels, not knowing if they were aiming at Ashe or me.

Nina was just coming back to herself, but she was not yet ready to fight. Shadows raced toward her now, careening at impossible angles, creating her essential contradiction of simultaneous light and darkness. Her flame grew solid, flashing intolerably bright for a moment before the shadows muted it. By then, the Amrhyns were already prepared with another bolt. Their fingertips sparkled as they extended their arms in concert, chanting, and the blue lightning arose, aimed squarely at Nina. There wasn't time for me to intervene, even if I had known how. Their minds were guarded against compulsion, much the same way they had blocked my percipience of the dungeon itself before. I couldn't even interpose my body to block the energy.

But Tad was close enough. He had continued forward after warning me, and now was only a step away from Nina. There wasn't time to plan. Without knowing what I was doing, I raised his left arm—*my* left arm, the one I had given him—and intercepted the lightning. The arm exploded in a sudden rain of blood and bone. Tad cried out and fell, blasted backward by the shock of impact. But incredibly, even as the Amrhyns readied their next blow, he staggered to his feet and purposely stood between them and Nina, his young face adamant. It was none of my doing this time. I had used him shamelessly in a moment of panic when Nina was threatened, but what he did now, he did in cool calculation and bravery, of his own accord.

As with his fight with Gaheris, he was overmatched. Twin bolts of blue energy flew from the Amrhyns' fingertips, and caught him full in the chest, roasting him where he stood. He swayed for a moment, his face registering more surprise than pain, and then toppled over, dead before he hit the floor.

His sacrifice gave Nina the grace of time she needed. Her shadows seemed to explode outward before rushing back to envelop and transform her. The unicorn reared in defiance, climbing the air with her mane streaming. She bellowed her challenge, the shrill neigh sounding like a hundred horses screaming at once, echoing and reechoing from the stone walls.

She lowered her head and raced toward the sorcerers, a shaft of white-hot light blazing forward from her horn, threatening to incinerate anything in its path. The Amrhyns scattered before her charge in terror, one of them tripping over me where I crouched beside the lip of the pit. I used my good arm to help him continue rolling, and he disappeared down the garderobe with a long trailing cry. I didn't know how deep the pit was, but it seemed a very long time until his fading wail chopped off with a sudden, sodden thump.

Nina caught the other sorcerer before he could get far, goring him just below the groin. A broiling blast of light from her horn lit him from the inside, briefly revealing his entire skeleton, and I smelled burning meat. He screamed in pain, but managed to twist aside and get around her before she could skewer him again.

He dashed to the corner where Torrey, Owen, and Tessa had been cowering. Getting behind them, his back to the wall, he clutched Tessa against his chest with one arm, using the old woman as a human shield. With his other arm, he lobbed searing balls of fire at Nina, one after another. She batted them aside easily with her horn, deflecting them right and left, but could not attack for fear of injuring Tessa. Owen and Torrey should have fled; it was the only sensible thing to do. But they would not desert their grandmother. They had no weapons, but from either side they grappled with the sorcerer, using nails and teeth and fists and knees, not doing any damage but distracting him from attacking Nina for the moment. Tessa struggled, too. She couldn't do more than shuffle with her feet and try to wriggle free of his grasp. And still Torrey and Owen attacked. Every time he threw off a boy, he had to loosen his grip on Tessa for an instant, and she somehow got a hold of his arm, biting the fleshy part of his inner wrist. She had good teeth, had Tessa, and the will to use them. With a howl of exasperation, the sorcerer tore his arm free, a long strip of flesh dangling in bloody ruin. With Nina approaching, and his shield turning against him, he had little choice. He drew a knife and held it at Tessa's throat to keep her still. With his free hand, he whipped the boys with flicks of blue lightning. They fell away immediately, but he lashed them again and again until they lay motionless and insensible on the cold stones.

I had started to run to Tessa's aid when a searing pain punched through my temples. I thought at first Gaheris had nicked me with his sword as he and Ashe pased me, but there was no wound. Another spike of pain drove me to my knees, and I suddenly understood what was happening. I was not being attacked, not in any normal sense. In my fear and anxiety during the fight, I had lost my fragile hold over the Sleeper.

The underground vibrations rocked the entire citadel. Bands of light sprang up again, showing me the pathways of power, if only I could decipher which one did what. But there was no time, and the bell tone of the chime rang so loudly that I couldn't think. I was lost among the spangles and streamers. The knelling and vibration grew until I screamed from the pain in my head. Fire poured from my throat instead of sound. The Sleeper had gained ascendancy, and would not be talked down or soothed this time. It wanted to overthrow the continents themselves, wipe all biological life from the planet, restore Sundering to its pristine and sterile condition.

Desperate to hold off the cataclysm, knowing I could not satisfy the Sleeper without violence, I tried to find a substitute target for its rage. I scrambled among the bands of light, clawing for sight. And suddenly, as clear to my percipience as if I were a bird flying over the water, I saw the volcanic peak of Alfheimr rising from the West Ocean. Smoke still spiraled from the cone I had awakened before, and small pebbles danced and skittered over the rocks, but the eruption was contained. Vastil, in a hundred avatars stationed around the island to keep the nina trapped, had calmed the tension belowground. Given time, they might even succeed in restoring the volcano to dormancy.

Free my people.

Yes.

I had only to suggest a direction, nudge the violence of the Sleeper toward my goal, and it was done. The volcano erupted, shooting flaming rock and smoke thousands of feet into the air. Magma bubbled up from below the rim and turned to lava. Liquid devastation flowed down the mountainside, consuming everything in its path. No elvish ward could possibly contain that fire. Vastil's avatars were instantly overwhelmed. They turned to flee, but it was already too late. Lava rolled over them, snuffing out their wards along with their lives. And as their ring of protection failed, the nina were released from their long durance.

The sky around Alfheimr became bright with thousands of arrow-like sparks shooting into the air. Each spark was a living flame, clad in shadows gathered from the volcano's penumbra of smoke. They spiraled and twisted, glorying in freedom. And as ash slowly blanketed the island, they flew effortlessly, joyously, across the West Ocean toward Leonais. They would touch down in Amrhyn, bringing faerie with them, and I suspected the sorcerers there would be soon become quite busy.

I could not spare the attention to watch the nina. Now that the Sleeper had vented its rage once, it wanted more. But something of the rapturous beauty and joy of the ninas' flight persisted in me. I held the memory of their freedom like a periapt against the Sleeper's urge toward destruction. It was not a sovereign remedy, and it could not last forever, but it was enough to lull the Sleeper into a temporary somnolence. It slumbered uneasily just below the edge of my consciousness, but it was not gone. Perhaps it would never truly sleep again. It merely waited, and its fire still burned in my veins like slow poison.

Nina somehow perceived what I had done, and whinnied in triumph and gratitude, but she could not break off her battle with the sorcerer. It was still a deadly standoff. She could not reach him to stab with her horn or slash with her hooves without injuring or killing Tessa in the process. She couldn't disengage, either. He kept hurling lightning and gobbets of blue fire as if he had an inexhaustible supply, and the knife was rock-steady at Tessa's throat. If Nina didn't intercept or deflect each blast, he would have reduced everyone in the room to cinders. She had to stay there, neither advancing nor retreating. She could not even reach the boys who still lay on the floor, either unconscious or dead.

Perhaps, with Nina occupying his attention, I could break the stalemate. I edged around the pit toward where Maran knelt, still working feverishly with her rags and straw to make golems. She had no blue butterflies to animate her creations this time, but I imagine she found cockroaches and rats aplenty, and perhaps they would be better for this job. I hoped to slide along the wall from there and approach the sorcerer from the side while Nina continued attacking from the front.

Ashe saw my motion from the corner of his eye and divined my intent. He stamped his foot and leaped backward, trying to draw Gaheris in the other direction so my path would be unhindered. But Ashe's boot came down on Tad's outstretched arm, and he had to hop to avoid falling. Gaheris drove in immediately, taking advantage of Ashe's imbalance. In strokes too rapid for me to see, even with percipience rather than eyes, he beat aside Ashe's blade and sliced him deeply across the abdomen.

The sword dropped from Ashe's nerveless fingers. He collapsed jarringly to his knees, waiting for the killing thrust, but it didn't come. Maran had finally finished her work. With a loud cry, she threw up arms, fingers spread, and the bundles of rags sprang to motion, a small army of golems. She collapsed, sagging from the expenditure of energy, but her task was complete. As she had done before with Hasq and her other servants, she bestowed life, or at least its semblance, and Gaheris stared at the golems with frank fear as they rushed toward him. Qol had not given his children equal gifts. Just as it was mine to heal, it was hers to create. And while Gaheris might scoff at my gift, he was terrified by hers.

The golems were unarmed, but persistent. Gaheris slashed at them wildly, his movements frantic and uncoordinated. And though he cut them, hacking away limbs, they shrugged off the injuries and kept coming. One disconnected hand even pulled itself by the fingers across the floor toward him. Gaheris stamped on it with his heel, and fell back. But the Archon had more weapons than his sword, and he finally thought to use them. His hands held magics similar to the Amrhyns. He fired strings of green and white lightning into the golems, setting them alight.

He'd have been better served keeping to the sword. Although the homunculi burned with a terrible stench and gave off roiling clouds of acrid black smoke, they didn't stop advancing. Slowly, inexorably, they surrounded him with arms that burned like tree trunks in a forest fire, and pulled him down. When they finally fell to the ground in a bonfire, Gaheris was consumed by the blaze.

Ashe still knelt, holding his intestines in with both hands, his life pouring in rivulets from the wound. I had frozen beside Maran, unable to look away from the Archon's pyre, but at Ashe's call I went to help him. I could not heal such great damage without more time, but I could stop the bleeding. The fire that still burned in my veins leaped forth through my right palm, rough and painful cautery. The bleeding slowed to an ooze. I stuffed his intestines back inside the wall of his abdomen, and pulled the lips of the cut closed over them, sealing the gash with more fire. Mercifully, he fainted before I finished. I could do nothing to ward him against infection. He would either live or not, as fortune willed. I knelt to feel his pulse, then, satisfied his heart was strong, lifted my head to survey the room.

Energy jittered through me. *Enough*, I thought. Tad was dead. Ashe was unconscious. Maran was exhausted. Tessa was in danger. Owen and Torrey lay like stones. Nina was slowing, her hooves dragging as she kept leaping left and right to intercept the sorcerer's fire. And for all I knew, Vastil's next avatar was even now speeding down the stairs toward us.

It had to end. I pushed myself shakily to my feet, and went to Nina's side.

The standoff had not changed. Tessa was the sorcerer's shield, from behind which he hurled fireballs. Nina doggedly deflected each one, but could not strike back without killing his hostage or trampling the children. I came up beside her, putting my good hand on her head. She quieted, stamped a hoof in exasperation, and asked what the hell I thought I was doing. Our mind-speech had never been clearer.

"Fulfilling my purpose," I said, and left her behind.

The Amrhyn lobbed a fireball at me, and I let it splatter on my chest. My clothing had long since burned away, back when I first roused the Sleeper. Now I let the fires within rise without constraint, and my flesh began to smolder. I was no longer afraid of death, or even pain. This was my task. His fireballs could not increase the agony; they actually cooled the furnace that wanted to consume me from the inside, by drawing some of the energy to the surface in defense. I tottered another step forward, stronger. Two more luminescent missiles struck me, one on the face, one on my thigh. I let the fires wash down my body, feeling my skin tingle and begin to heal. Unwittingly, the sorcerer had provided the answer, not just to counter his attack, but to resolve my deeper quandary. Resisting the internal fire was pointless. Letting it rampage outward was reckless. But meeting his magic, measure for measure, consumed the poison, balanced it. Balanced me. I felt equal to anything. Inside, the Sleeper had found immolation commensurate with its passion. The fire was no longer hot. The ground stopped trembling. The dire urge toward destruction was laid to rest. The Sleeper, its needs met, finally slept, yielding its vast power to my conscious control.

Strength like I had never known suffused me. I wrapped my flame in shadows as solid as stone, and sprang forward to bear the children away. Lifting them as easily as if they were hollow sacks, I shielded them from the Amrhyn's assault with my own back, his lightning splashing harmlessly around me. I laid them carefully beside Maran. Torrey was awake and breathing, but Owen was neither. Maran gathered Torrey in her arms, and I was startled to see Zoxo still clinging to the little boy's shoulder, apparently unharmed. I smiled involuntarily, but my amusement faded when

I knelt to examine the older boy. My fingertips trailed across Owen's thin chest, touching lightly where the sorcerer's lightning had blasted in his ribs. His heart was not beating.

It was one death too many. I would not permit it. I touched him with cold white flames, as cold as frost, and spoke in the language of fire itself, using the words of command to call him back. This was not a healing. He was too far gone for that. I did not speak to his flesh, but to his spirit. The chime belled, and the entire room flashed into momentary brilliance. All the might of the Sleeper, potent enough to tear down mountains, concentrated in this one action, this one moment. But the power was focused elsewhere, on a plane not visible, and there was no obvious detonation of energy. Anyone able to hear that call could not help but answer it.

Owen jackknifed forward at the waist, his head jerked back by the sudden motion. His arms flew up and his heels thumped. His back arched, and breath whistled into his lungs. Then he exhaled and fell back, brown eyes wide open and staring.

He was still dead.

Again, I jolted him. Again, his body thrashed lifelessly.

Maran stirred and put out a hand to restrain me, and Torrey wailed that I was hurting his brother.

I let neither of them distract me. I sent another bolt of energy through Owen's body, then another, and another, willing his heart to beat, his spirit to return.

Though his body flopped and his eyes rolled when I jolted him, he was beyond my reach. The boy I knew was gone. Liquid fire rolled down from my empty sockets, wetting my cheeks as I gently closed his eyelids and stood up. Some things cannot be changed. Some griefs cannot be annealed. Some decisions cannot be undone. If I had only mastered the Sleeper earlier, I could have kept the Amrhyn from killing him. If I hadn't rushed here without a plan, Tad and Owen might not dead, and Ashe would not be injured. If I hadn't sought my name at all, none of them would have been taken prisoner. They were all of them here because of me, and one by one I was letting them die. I might as well be killing them myself. All their suffering was my fault, and all my actions bootless.

Torrey cried helplessly, struggling to escape Maran's embrace, but she held him tightly, her own eyes brimming. Her look told me she shared my grief. I could do nothing to console either of them, nothing to console myself.

But the Amrhyn sorcerer? *Him* I could do something about.

I fairly flew across the room in rage to face him. He still held the knife at Tessa's throat, but his fireballs momentarily stopped so he could watch my advance. He was in desperate straits. Not only was the injury to his groin spilling his lifeblood onto the floor, but I had withstood everything he could throw at me. Nina pawed the ground at my side, and her glare for him held death. His eyes swiveled frantically between the two of us, as if he had never seen such things before. I don't suppose he had.

He should be terrified.

Tessa wasn't looking at us. I don't think she was even aware of the knife at her throat anymore. Her eyes were focused behind me, at where Owen lay dead. I wanted to comfort her, but it would have to wait. The sorcerer could see our deadly intent, and he was too far gone to consider retreat. Perhaps he was at that stage where surrender seemed worse than death. His arm convulsed, drawing the serrated edge of the blade across Tessa's neck in a swift juddering motion.

My mental connection with Nina was continuous now. We had no need for mind-speech or even shared pictures. In that moment, we surpassed language altogether. We moved as one person, guided by my eyeless sight, no missteps possible. My fingers clawed bright trails through the air as I raised my good hand. A green flame of my desiring burst from my upraised palm, acutely focused and irresistible. I spiked the sorcerer through the forehead with a bolt of hot, furious energy, and his skull exploded from his shoulders. Even as he started to collapse like an empty sack, Nina was already sailing forward to catch Tessa, transforming as she dodged under my blast, her arms outstretched. She came up in woman form, Tessa cradled in her arms, before the sorcerer's knife finished clattering to the floor.

It took only an instant, from when his arm twitched until I had my good hand on Tessa's wound, stanching the blood that was only just then beginning to jet out. I had lost Owen, but I would not lose her. I scrambled into Tessa with my percipience, searching out the severed ends of the artery. *There!* I pulled the ragged edges together and welded them with icy fire. Between one heartbeat and the next, the blood flow to her brain was restored. But he had also cut through her windpipe. Her larynx and supporting muscles flapped. I needed to work quickly before she choked and suffered from lack of oxygen. I used my fingertips to stroke the tissues back into place, and repaired them with stitches of fire. She took a deep gasping breath, free of blood, and felt her throat in wonder.

The effort exhausted me. The Sleeper's energy might be limitless, but my ability to tap it was not. My head wobbled, and the room suddenly spun. Nina quickly set Tessa down and moved to support me. I leaned gratefully on her shoulder for a moment, then waved her away. We had to get out.

Torrey and Maran came to my call. Together, we went to see about Ashe.

I had nothing left in me to use for healing him. As far as I could tell, he was unconscious but stable. Nina transformed without being asked, bent her forelegs, lowered her head, and waited. Maran and Tessa managed to heave the prince up without tearing open his wounds, and Nina surged easily to her feet. The two women carried Owen's body between them, but we had to leave Tad.

I gave Torrey one of the torches and told him to hold it high so the others could see. With my good hand, I guided him through the smoke and dust to the dungeon door, trusting the others would follow the beacon of his torchlight. I led us out of that place, up the stairs, through the deserted corridors and chambers, and into the clean night air.

We came to a halt in the courtyard, momentarily stymied. The topmost turret of the citadel had fallen inward, toppling onto the paving stones before the main gate, choking the doorway with tons of rubble.

We saw no crushed bodies, so I assumed the turret had fallen after everyone had fled. This was probably the reason no soldiers had reentered, and why a new Vastil had not shown up. I didn't know if the elf could transport himself using the dolmens, but I suspected he either could not or didn't dare—not with my touch now forever intimately associated with the Sleeper. And there was no point now, except revenge, which I suspected the elves didn't indulge.

I took a deep breath and summoned the energy to blast a path through the debris. The effort nearly undid me. My percipience turned dim, and I couldn't even tell if I'd succeeded. But Torrey tugged on my hand, leading me as if I were finally as blind as my empty eye sockets would suggest. In a few minutes, I recovered enough to walk on my own. I told Torrey to hang onto the torch, for it was not yet dawn, and dim light of the sun behind the horizon was insufficient for us to pick our way safely over the rubble. I found a soldier's cloak amongst the wreckage as we walked, and I worked it free from its former owner to cover myself.

As we passed below the gates, we noticed the flag—the Archon's sigil that had flown so proudly high above on the turret.

Now it fluttered weakly on the ground amidst the dust and scrap off to one side, stirred briefly to life by a surge of fresh air whistling through the archway. I thought it sufficient that we had overthrown the Archon, but Nina took a savage delight in trampling the sigil thoroughly before she would go on.

I didn't upbraid her, for just on the other side of the archway, soldiers and citizens of Jappa filled the hillside, holding torches and weapons. They had skittered back when I first blasted open the citadel and emerged, and I saw they were both frightened and dangerous, looking upward with serious, determined faces. The sun finally rose, letting the gathered crowd see us clearly. Cocked crossbows trained on me, and a thousand swords came up as one. I swept Torrey behind me with my good arm and stood to face them.

But then Nina came forth. Swords wavered, and shocked questions surged through the crowd. I had forgotten *again* how the sight of her affected ordinary humans. Mortal flesh has no choice but to salute the immortal. We may not be able to understand or even remember what we see, but we know in our bones what it is.

The citadel—what was left of it—perched atop the hill, so that the city spread out below us, the people nearby ranged as if we were on a stage and they were the audience. They could all see her. Even dusty and weary, Nina held her head high and pranced, her hooves barely seeming to touch the ground, her horn outshining the dim light from the rising sun. Maran and Tessa set Owen's body down gently. Torrey dropped the torch and raced to his brother's side, sobbing. Tessa tried to comfort him, but he pushed her away. Wearily, Maran and Tessa eased Ashe from Nina's back and tried to make him comfortable.

Freed from the burden of Ashe, Nina reared and neighed, shaking her mane, and let her horn blaze in a paean of glory. Then, like shooting stars, a thousand other nina streaked through the sky in response, taking shape from the shadows to stand beside her. I had expected them to form many different faerie creatures, but they were all unicorns.

In the crowd, hands extended forward from all sides, weapons and fear forgotten. Nina stayed with me, but the other unicorns wandered curiously through the human crowd, spreading glamour, fascination, glory, and mystery as they went. Sighs and murmurs filled the air.

Faerie was loosed on the world, and nothing would ever be the same.

15. ULAT

AT THE BACK of the crowd, a quiet circle grew around a shrouded figure. Nearby nina skittered suddenly away, and the humans drew back. I probed with my percipience and discovered a woman, white-haired and blue-eyed, and I didn't need second sight to know she was muria. Even at this distance, her preternatural emanations were like the blare of trumpets. The qualitative feel of her temperament told me she was neither Vastil nor Qol.

Some people in the crowd knelt, even before she threw back her hood. They must have felt the edges of mystery and enchantment flowing out from her. She paced slowly forward, bringing the circle of silence with her. She mounted the citadel steps in a stately and graceful fashion, like a queen assuming her throne. As she neared the top, she loosened her cloak to reveal a sweeping gown of forest green with embroidery made from threads of gold.

At length, she stood before me. Like all muria, she had that piercing beauty which defies description, a dispassionate face, and an unfathomable depth behind her eyes. Her power was now fully unveiled; her face seemed to shine with a burning light from within, making a mockery of the soft glow I had exuded at Tessa's house. Seeing her, I wondered why the Second Colonists had called the muria elves instead of angels. Yet I was under no illusion that she was benign. I edged back warily.

Nina quickly interposed herself between me and the elf, the brilliance of her horn giving an unambiguous warning. The elf paused, looking at Nina's defiance with something approaching compassion; but she remained remote, reserved, mostly unreadable.

"Step aside," she said to Nina. "I mean no harm to these people."

Nina stamped a hoof, but otherwise remained steady. *She is Ulat,* Nina told me in mind-speech. *The one who commanded our imprisonment.*

Should I kill her? I asked. I didn't know if I could summon the strength for another fight—but at Nina's word, I would try my best.

No, she is here by right. Do not contend for dominance with her.

Ulat laughed gently, listening to our mental communication. "Can you control her?" she asked me.

"Never," I said.

"Yet all the nina here are in the shape of unicorns. You know they have no inherent shapes of their own. They impinge on the human brain below the level of consciousness, tangential to normal perceptions. It is *your* mind that gives them this form." Ulat gestured gracefully at the onlookers in the city below us. "The people here are enraptured because of your choice. Had you perceived the nina as dragons or ogres, the crowd would be screaming and running, not standing spellbound, struck dumb by beauty and glamour."

I had sensed long ago that I could force Nina into any shape I chose, just by imposing my will. Respect had kept me from exercising that power. The thread-like tongue of fire, wrapped in shadows, came closest to representing her true nature, but even that was a trick of my brain. Vastil's description came back to me: *They are unarticulated words from the beginning of time.* I put my good hand on Nina's neck, stroked the fine strands of her mane, felt the reality of her. I marveled that my mere desire for familiarity could have chosen shapes for the nina, but my old intransigence asserted itself, refusing to let me be distracted.

"I misspoke," I said. "I meant to say that I *will* not control her."

"Yet you do. Yours is the strongest human mind present, and the nina respond to you. What will happen when you falter, sleep, or finally die? They will draw their shapes from the minds of the common folk, and the horrors will return. The nina were locked away for your protection. Should they be imprisoned again, or destroyed? Even as we speak, they terrorize across Leonais, just by existing. Nightmares walk in daylight across the land. Only these here in your presence are constrained."

"We'll figure something out," I said stiffly.

"You lack the power."

Maran came to stand beside me. She said, "I will help him."

"You lack the power, even acting in concert," said Ulat, "but a way has been prepared." She turned her attention to Nina. "You have played your part well. As foretold, Vastil and Qol are even now returning to Avermorn. Muria will no longer interfere with human progress. Your companion released your kin. The balance is restored, and all the provisions of our bargain are met. Now payment is required. After my final task, I, too, shall withdraw."

Shadows fled from Nina, spiraled in the air, and reformed into the woman I had come to know, her long black hair shrouding her face and body.

"Grey," said Nina. "You once asked how I escaped from prison to become your companion. I didn't answer you."

"Yes, I remember." My entire body tingled with apprehension, fearing her next words.

"I did not escape. Ulat freed me. There were conditions."

Neither am I immortal, Nina had said long ago, *not in the way you imagine.* Dread filled me, and I cast my cloak over our heads, so that Nina and I seemed to inhabit a private world. We stood forehead to forehead for a long moment, not exchanging thoughts, not embracing, but sharing ourselves nonetheless. The deep wordless connection between us became strong enough to encircle the world. Finally, Nina's complex contradictions resolved in my mind.

"Is there no other way?" I asked.

"No."

"Then let me pay the price," I begged.

"You cannot."

"I can."

A god-wind of my desiring arose, lifting the cloak from us, blowing back the crowds, riving the shapes from all the nina on Leonais, save one. By sheer determination, I held the pattern of wind against them and denied them bodies. I turned to Ulat, my hands full of power. "Take the others if you must, but this one is mine."

Nina laid her hand on my heart. "I am my own," she said softly, "as ever. You promised to free my people, not flense their flesh away. Even with the best intentions, you cannot maintain the winds. You are mortal. That is your curse and your blessing. You and Maran were quite literally made for each other. Qol, whatever his faults, saw to that. It is time to let me go, live your life with her, raise your child."

"No."

"This was my choice, my doom, set in motion ere we met."

"I never agreed."

Nina's form began to fray at the edges. Shadows slid away in all directions, leaving only the naked white flame at the core of her being. *You were never asked*, she said. The god-winds guttered and failed as tears trickled down my face. I could not hold her.

Ulat upheld her palm and drew Nina to her hand. Nina danced and flickered there, like a candle flame caught on a wick. Then Ulat closed her fist and extinguished Nina's fire. At the same instant, all across Leonais, the remaining nina were wrestled out of the air, startled into bodies, bound to one shape permanently . . . and they were all of them unicorns.

"How?" I breathed. "Why?"

"She is not lost," said Ulat kindly. "I have scattered her and reified her a thousand-fold. Your bond with her will endure to bind the others. The shape was your choice; their actions henceforth will be their own. Sundering was their world first, and they are sentient beings. We are not immune to compassion. I grant them as much freedom as I dare. Is this fate not better than eternal imprisonment? All nina are now, after a fashion, your own beloved Nina. She gambled everything on this outcome and emerged victorious. She chose this doom freely, knowing the stakes. Do not dishonor her sacrifice by weeping."

I paused, striving to encompass what Ulat had done. Then, my loss unblunted and my anger rising, I asked harshly, "May I still hate you?"

She patted my cheek. "No, but you are free to try." As with all muria, I could not help but trust her. Her touch was intimate, maternal, infinitely possessive and infinitely remote. In her many bodies, she was immortal, beyond my grasp, with plans and motives that spanned centuries, millennia, perhaps eons. She had skillfully maneuvered people and events to achieve her desired outcome.

Another player has entered the contest and changed the rules, Qol had told me. *A far subtler power*. Now I knew whose hand he had perceived. Ulat's fingertips still lingered on my cheek, feeling my very human tears. Before she disengaged, she graced me with a vision to combat my grief.

For just a moment, I could see all the unicorns across Leonais. They danced nimbly away, eluding all pursuit, slipping into wild forests and quiet glens far from human habitation, their glamour shrouded but not diminished. In those places, they could live their eldritch lives unfettered, keeping mystery and wonder alive for the lucky few who would encounter them in the untold years to come.

Before the vision faded, I shared it with Maran, and she helped me see joy amidst my sorrow, a path through the pangs of loss. I would miss my Nina, but she would never truly be gone. She had pricked my manufactured soul, and I treasured the bleeding, for it proved, in the end, that I had been worthy of her. The nina posed no threat beyond an occasional touch of the numinous, and that was a risk well worth taking. The world could do with more poets. We stood hand in hand, Maran and I, and regarded the elf in a new light. Perhaps the muria cared for others after all. Or perhaps it only pleased them to have us ponder their motivations.

"Will we meet again?" I asked Ulat.

She smiled enigmatically, turned, and walked away, disappearing from my life as abruptly as she had entered it. She shrouded her glory—or perhaps revealed another aspect of it—for no one saw how she departed.

Maran went down into the city to find medical help for Ashe and to rouse workers to ensure care for the dead and wounded. In the meantime, there were griefs other than mine. Tessa and Torrey still held their silent vigil over Owen's body. I hugged Tessa warmly, kissed her cheek, then knelt on the flagstones beside Torrey. He had finally stopped weeping, but had not moved from his brother's side since we emerged from the citadel. "I'm sorry I couldn't save him," I said. "I tried."

He rubbed the back of his hand against his face and sniffled. "I know."

"Owen can never be replaced or forgotten, and you are right to mourn him. But your grandmother will need your strength now. Can you be strong for her? She grieves with you, as do I."

He buried his face against my cloak. I expected him to break out into fresh tears, but he just hugged me for a moment, then got to his feet and took Tessa's hand. I leaned forward to kiss Owen's forehead and then pushed myself upright to stand with them.

"You may travel with us," I told Tessa. "Or if you prefer, I can find—"

"Where will you go?" Tessa interrupted.

"To Maran's valley. Your house is not far off our path."

"Will you stop for tea from time to time?"

I smiled. "Of course."

"And your unicorn. Is she truly gone now?"

My smiled faded. "Yes."

"Then we have each lost a beloved today. Please take us home."

Maran rejoined us, bringing four men with her. "Take care of Ashe," she instructed them, pointing to the unconscious prince. "Gaheris is dead. As you love your lives, treat Ashe gently. He is your king now."

The men looked confused. One of them jerked a thumb at me. "Not him?"

I blinked, unable to speak, but Maran laughed freely. "No," she managed after a moment, "not him."

"Gods, no!" I cried. "Find him a doctor and a crown, but leave me alone."

The men shrugged, lifted Ashe carefully, and bore him into the city. A long train of workers, bearing pry bars, ropes, picks, and stretchers, began to ascend toward the citadel.

I told Maran that Tessa and Torrey would accompany us, and then said to the entire group, "It's a very long trip. Many days.

Let's get started. I don't know how we can cross the bridge now, but there may be ships left. I'm sure—"

"Wait!" said Torrey urgently.

I looked at him. "Yes?"

"We can't leave Owen just lying here."

Maran answered for me. "While I was in the city, I made arrangements for him. You can see the workers coming now. He will be buried in the Tomb of Kings, with all the honors due a hero. No other commoner has ever been laid to rest there. He was very nearly the bravest boy in all Leonais."

Torrey's eyes widened, then suddenly narrowed. "Only very nearly?"

Maran nodded solemnly. "It takes more courage to go on after a great loss than to die in battle."

"You mean me," Torrey said, suddenly standing taller.

I shared a look with Tessa, for we both knew that Maran had been speaking to us as much as to the boy. I turned, thinking nothing else needed to be said, but again Torrey cried, "Wait!"

"What now?" I asked. "Do you want a medal?"

"Zoxo," he said apologetically. "Just there, on your sleeve. Hold still." He carefully pried the little lizard's claws free, and transferred it to his own shoulder. He gently stroked Zoxo with a forefinger. The lizard blinked at us.

"Okay now?" I asked.

"Yes," said Torrey, "we can go home."

As we left that place, I wondered what the word "home" meant to any of us now. A brief gust of god-winds propelled us gently northward, but if it carried a message, it was too obscure for me to grasp. The art of prophecy had deserted me, too. I could not see beyond my next footsteps, save for one fact: At some point, I would meet Qol again and be forced to account for my actions. Intuition told me it might not be a happy encounter, but also that it lay comfortably far in the future.

Perhaps between now and then I would learn to understand him. In the meantime, I would not be his toy soldier. If I could help it, I would never be anyone's plaything again. I still lacked a name, but I no longer cared.

Whoever I was, I still moved by myself.

About the Author

Jeffry Dwight is an author, editor, musician, pencil artist, poet, programmer, and father of two sons. He was born in Illinois, and currently lives in the suburbs of Dallas, Texas. In 2014, he received the *Kevin O'Donnell, Jr. Service to SFWA Award* from the Science Fiction & Fantasy Writers of America. Of himself, Dwight says, "I hate writing, but love having written."

Dwight's brief book of poetry, *Phantas*, and his immensely popular collection of short fiction, *Mortal Dreads*, are available from Amazon and most other retail outlets.

In addition, Dwight authored or co-authored multiple textbooks on programming and Internet technologies, as well as writing several articles for technical journals. Before that, he worked in social services among developmentally disabled and abused/neglected children and adults. All of these experiences inform his storytelling.

Dwight is a self-taught singer-songwriter who plays keyboards, guitars, drums, and several other instruments. His style covers ballads, jazz, and 70's soft rock. His songs are available on YouTube, Amazon, Spotify, Pandora, iTunes, Apple Music, and other services. You may listen for free on most platforms, or purchase the albums in MP3 format from Amazon.

Explore more creative works by Jeffry Dwight:

Short Fiction Collection:
  Mortal Dreads: https://books2read.com/u/bMYZwk

Amazon Author Website:
  https://www.amazon.com/Jeffry-Dwight/e/B000APBJWS

Music on Amazon:
  All Jeffry Dwight results: https://amzn.to/3rAeOYM
  All Jeffry Dwight Album results: https://amzn.to/3rxUI16

Albums:
  Changes: https://amzn.to/3iJuuov
  In My Right Brain: https://amzn.to/3rvRZp0
  Vintage: https://amzn.to/3kSBRMN

YouTube Channel:

YouTube Links:
Changes: https://bit.ly/2V7L8G3
In My Right Brain: https://bit.ly/3y6IkYl
Vintage: https://bit.ly/3kSEo9L

www.ingramcontent.com/pod-product-compliance
Lightning Source LLC
Chambersburg PA
CBHW030526120726
47904CB00005B/1636